Annie O'Neil spent most of her childhood with her leg draped over the family rocking chair and a book in her hand. Novels, baking and writing too much teenage angst poetry ate up most of her youth. Now Annie splits her time between corralling her husband into helping her with their cows, baking, reading, barrel racing (not really!) and spending some very happy hours at her computer, writing.

Three-times Golden Heart® finalist **Tina Beckett** learned to pack her suitcases almost before she learned to read. Born to a military family, she has lived in the United States, Puerto Rico, Portugal and Brazil. In addition to travelling, Tina loves to cuddle with her pug, Alex, spend time with her family and hit the trails on her horse. Learn more about Tina from her website, or 'friend' her on Facebook.

THE ARMY DOC'S CHRISTMAS ANGEL

ANNIE O'NEIL

THE BILLIONAIRE'S CHRISTMAS WISH

TINA BECKETT

MILLS & BOON

First Published in Great Britain 2018
by Mills & Boon, an imprint of HarperCollins*Publishers*
1 London Bridge Street, London, SE1 9GF

The Army Doc's Christmas Angel © 2018 Harlequin Books S.A.

The Billionaire's Christmas Wish © 2018 Harlequin Books S.A.

Special thanks and acknowledgement are given to
Annie O'Neil and Tina Beckett for their contributions
to the Hope Children's Hospital series.

ISBN: 978-0-263-93384-0

MIX
Paper from
responsible sources
FSC® C007454

This book is produced from independently certified FSC™ paper
to ensure responsible forest management.
For more information visit www.harpercollins.co.uk/green.

Printed and bound in Spain
by CPI, Barcelona

THE ARMY DOC'S CHRISTMAS ANGEL

ANNIE O'NEIL

MILLS & BOON

This one goes out to the service men and women
in our lives.

The sacrifices they make are unimaginable.

The things they see and the work they do
can often come at a high cost.

Family life, physical health,
even, in those awful cases, loss of life.

And they still go out there and I hope stories like this
one prove we all think their bravery and strength
are extraordinary.

CHAPTER ONE

"You planning on wearing a track into the floor?"

Finn looked across at his boss, startled to see him in the hospital given the hour, then gave a nonchalant shrug. "Maybe. What's it to you?"

Theo barked a good-natured laugh. "I paid for that floor. I was hoping we could keep it intact for a few more years before your lunking huge feet are embedded in it."

Finn looked down at the honey-colored floorboards then up at his boss as he scrubbed his hand through the tangles of his dark hair. About time he got a haircut. Or invested in a comb. It had only been...oh...about fourteen years since he'd given up the buzz cuts. Didn't stop him from thinking of himself as that fit, adrenaline-charged young man who'd stepped off the plane in Afghanistan all those years ago. Once an army man...

He took a step forward. The heat from his knee seared straight up his leg to his hip. An excruciating reminder that he was most definitely *not* an army man. Not ever again.

He gave Theo a sidelong look. "What are you doing here, anyway? It's late."

"Not that late." Theo looked at his watch as if that

confirmed it was still reasonable to be treading the hospital boards after most folk were at home having their tea. "I could ask you the same question."

It was Avoidance Technique for Beginners and both men knew it.

They stared at one another, without animosity but unwilling to be the first to break. Lone wolf to lone wolf…each laying claim to the silence as if it were an invisible shield of strength.

Heaven knew why. It was hardly a secret that Finn was treating one of the hospital's charity patients who was winging in from Africa today. He just…he was grateful to have a bit of quiet time before the boy arrived. His leg pain was off the charts today and once Adao arrived, he'd like to be in a place where he could assure the kid that life without a limb was worth living.

"Want to talk about it?" Theo looked about as excited to sit down and have a natter about feelings as Finn did.

"Ha! Good one." Finn flicked his thumb toward the staff kitchen tucked behind the floor's reception area. "I'll just run and fill up the kettle while you cast on for a new Christmas jumper, shall I?"

Theo smirked then quickly sobered. "I'm just saying, if you ever want to…" he made little talky mouths with his hands "…you know, I'm here."

"Thanks, mate." He hoped he sounded grateful. He was. Not that he'd ever take Theo up on the offer.

It wasn't just trusting Theo that was the issue. It was trusting himself. And he wasn't there yet. Not by a long shot. Days like today were reminders why he'd chosen to live a solitary existence. You got close to people. You disappointed them. And he was done disappointing people.

Christmas seemed to suck the cheer—what little he had—right out of him. All those reminders of family and friendship and "togetherness." Whatever the hell that was.

He didn't do any of those things. Not anymore.

All the jolly ward decorations, staffrooms already bursting with mince pies, and festive holiday lights glittering across the whole of Cambridge didn't seem to make a jot of difference.

He scanned the view offered by the floor-to-ceiling windows and rolled his eyes.

He was living in a ruddy 3D Christmas card and wasn't feeling the slightest tingle of hope and anticipation the holiday season seemed to infuse in everyone else.

Little wonder considering…

Considering nothing.

He had a job. He had to do it. And having his boss appear when he was trying to clear his head before Adao arrived wasn't helping.

He'd been hoping to walk the pain off. Sometimes it worked. Sometimes, like today, it escalated the physical and, whether he cared to admit it or not, emotional reminders of the day his life had changed forever.

Should've gone up to the rooftop helipad instead. No one ever really went there in the winter. Although this year the bookies were tipping the scales in favor of snow. Then it really would be like living in a Christmas card.

"Why are you here? Was there some memo about an all-staff welcoming committee?" Finn knew there wasn't. He was just giving his boss an out if he wanted it. Bloke talk came in handy for a lot of emotional bullet dodging.

Theo sighed. "Ivy."

Finn lifted his chin in acknowledgement. Her mystery illness had been the talk of all the doctors' lounges. "Gotta be tough, mate."

"'Tis." Theo flicked his eyes to the heavens, gave his stippled jaw a scrub and gave an exasperated sigh. "I hate seeing her go through this. She's five years old. You know?"

Oh, yeah. He knew. It was why he'd retrained as a pediatric surgeon after the IED had gone off during a standard patrol. The loss of life that day had been shameful.

All of them children.

Who on this planet targeted *children*?

At least he'd had an enemy to rail against. Theo was shooting in the dark at a mystery illness. No wonder the guy had rings under his eyes.

"Had anything good today?" Topic-changing was his specialty.

Theo nodded. "A few interesting cases actually." He rattled through a few of them. "Enough to keep me distracted."

Finn huffed out an "I hear you" laugh. Work was the only way he kept his mind off the mess he'd made of his personal life.

You're on your own now, mate. Paying your penance, day by day.

"The diagnostician. She managed to clear her schedule yet?"

Theo nodded. "Took a bit of juggling but she's here now."

Finn waited for some more information—something

to say what Theo thought of her—but received pure silence. Any topic related to Ivy was a highly charged one so it looked like his boss was going to reserve judgment on the highly touted globetrotter until she'd had a bit more time with his daughter.

"What's her name again?" Finn tried again when Theo obviously wasn't going to comment further. "I heard one of the nurse's call her Godzilla."

Theo gave a sharp tsk.

He didn't like gossip. Or anything that stood in the way of the staff acting as a team. "She's a bit of a loner. Might give off a cooler edge than some of the staff are used to. Particularly around the holidays. But she's not yet had a chance to get her feet on the ground, let alone establish a rapport with the entire staff." He gave Finn a quick curt nod, making it very clear that he let facts stand. Not rumor. "She's called Madison Archer. Doesn't get much more American than that, does it?"

"Short of being scented like apple pie, I guess not." Finn smiled at Theo, trying to add a bit of levity, but raised his hands in apology at Theo's swiftly narrowed eyes.

More proof, as if he needed it, that Finn was no star at chitchat. He called a spade a spade, and other than that his conversational skills were operating on low to subterranean.

Theo's expression shifted to something indecipherable. "It's at times like this I understand how the parents feel when they walk in the doors of our hospital. Makes it that much more important we treat each other with respect. Without that, how can we respect our patients? Ourselves?" He lifted up his hands as if seeking an answer from the universe then let them fall with a slap against his long legs.

They looked at one another a moment in silence. This time with that very same respect he'd just spoken of.

Theo was a class-A physician and this hospital—the hospital he'd *built*—was one of the finest in the world, and still not one of them could put a finger on what was behind Ivy's degenerating condition. Lethargy had become leg pain. Leg pain had escalated to difficulty walking. They were even considering admitting her full time, instead of dipping in and out, things were so bad.

How the hell Theo went about running the hospital day in, day out when his little girl was sick…it would've done his head in.

Precisely why being on his own suited Finn to a T. No one to worry about except his patients. No emotions holding him back…as long as he kept his thoughts on the future and his damn leg on the up and up.

He gave his head a sharp shake, silently willing Theo to move on. A wince of pain narrowed the furrows fanning out from his eyes as he shifted his weight fully onto his right leg.

The infinitesimal flick of Theo's eyes down then back up to Finn's face meant the boss man knew precisely what was going on. But he knew better than to ask. Over a decade of wearing the prosthetic leg and he still hadn't developed a good relationship with the thing. The number of times he'd wanted to rip it from his knee and hurl the blasted contraption off the roof…

And then where would he be? In a wheelchair like Ivy?

Nah. That wasn't for him.

Helping children just like her—and Adao, who'd

learned too much about war far too soon—were pre-cisely why he kept it on. Standing beside the operating table was his passion. And if that meant sucking up the building pressure and tolerating the sharp needles of pain on occasion? Then so be it.

"Well..." He tried to find something positive to say and came up with nothing so fell back on what he knew best. Silence.

After a few minutes of staring out into the inky dark-ness he asked Theo, "You heard anything about the boy's arrival time?"

Finn was chief surgeon on the case, but Theo had a way of knowing just that little bit more than his staff. Sign of a good leader if ever there was one.

"Adao?"

Finn nodded, unsurprised that out of a hospital full of children Theo knew exactly who he was referring to. Although they didn't have too many children flying in from Africa just a handful of weeks before Christmas.

Then again, war never took much time to consider the holidays.

"Did they get out of the local airport in Kambela all right?" Theo asked.

"Yeah." Finn had received an email from one of the charity workers who'd stayed behind at the war-torn country's small clinic. "Touch and go as to whether the ceasefire would hold, but they got off without a hitch. They say his condition's been stabilized, but the risk of infection—" He stopped himself. Infection meant more of the arm would have to come off. Maybe the shoulder. Flickers of rage crackled through him like electricity.

This was a kid. A little *kid*. As if growing up in a country ravaged by war wasn't bad enough.

There had been a fragile negotiated peace in the West African country for a few months now, but thousands of landmines remained. The poor kid had been caught in a blast when another little boy had stepped on one. That boy had died instantly. The second—Adao—suffice it to say his life would never be the same.

They'd been out playing. Celebrating another renewal of the ceasefire. The horror of it all didn't bear thinking about.

Not until he saw the injuries, assessed damage limitation, talked Adao through how he would always feel that missing arm of his, but—

Don't go there, man. You made it. The kid'll make it.

Hopefully he wouldn't actively push his family away the way Finn had. If he had any leanings toward giving advice, he'd put that top of the list.

Keep those you love close to you.

Pushing them away only made the aching hole of grief that much harder to fill.

He knew that now.

Theo pulled his phone out of his pocket and thumbed through the messages. "He was meant to have been choppered in from London a couple of hours ago, right? The charity texted a while back saying something about paperwork and customs, but you'd think a boy with catastrophic injuries would outweigh a bit of petty bureaucracy."

Finn brought his fist down on a nearby table. That sort of hold-up was unacceptable. Especially with a child's welfare at stake.

"Hey!" Theo nodded at the table, brow creased. "You'd better apologize."

"What?" Disbelief flashed across Finn's features

then a smile. "You want me to say sorry to the table? Sorry, table. I don't know what got into me." He held his hands out wide. *Happy now?* the gesture read.

Theo closed the handful of meters between them with a few long-legged strides, crossed his arms over his chest and looked Finn square in the eyes. "Are you all right to handle this?"

His hospital. His terms.

Fair enough.

"'Course." Finn said. "But if you think I'm not up to it? Take me off. Bear in mind you'll have to drag me out of here and nurse the black eyes of whoever you think can operate on Adao better than me."

No point in saying he'd have to deliver the punches from a wheelchair if his knee carried on mimicking a welding iron.

He ground his back teeth together and waited. Theo knew as well as he did that the last thing he'd do was punch someone. But it was Theo's hospital. Theo's call.

Theo feigned giving Finn a quick one-two set of boxing punches, making contact with his midsection as he did.

Finn didn't budge. He had a slight edge on Theo in height, weight and age. The Grand Poo-bah of Limb Specialists, they'd once joked.

"Look at that." Finn's tone was as dry as the Sahara. "I'm turning the other cheek."

Theo widened the space between them and whistled. "Have you been working out again?"

Finn smiled. Always had. Always would.

Pushing himself to the physical limit was one of the things that kept the demons at bay.

Theo gave Finn's shoulder a solid clap. "You're the

one I want on this. The only one." He didn't need to spell out to Finn how his time in the military had prepared him more than most for the injuries Adao had sustained. "Just want to make sure you're on top form when the little guy arrives."

"What? Nah." Finn waved away his concerns, gritting his teeth against the grinding of his knee against his prosthesis. "I just save this curmudgeon act for you. Someone's gotta be the grumpy old man around here."

"I thought that was Dr. Riley."

They both laughed. Dr. Riley had yet to be seen without an ear-to-ear grin on his face. The man had sunbeams and rainbows shooting out of his ears. The children adored him. Most people called him Dr Smiley.

Finn nodded toward the Christmas tree twinkling away in the dimly lit reception area where they stood. "A bit early, isn't it?"

"Not if you're Evie."

Finn grunted. Evie was the resident Mrs. Claus around Hope Children's Hospital. Especially now she was all loved up. Just being around her and Ryan made him…well…suffice it to say it brought up one too many memories he'd rather not confront. Love. Marriage. They'd never got as far as the baby carriage, he and Caroline. Now he supposed he never would.

Guess that made him the resident Scrooge. Not that he had anything against Christmas in particular, it was just…seeing these poor kids in hospital over the holidays always bugged him. He may not want to hang out with his own family, but he was damn sure these kids wanted nothing more than their mums and dads at the end of their beds on Christmas morning.

"Anyone else about for Adao's arrival?"

Finn shook his head. "Not that I know about. I've got the usual suspects lined up for tomorrow so we can give him a proper assessment." He listed a few names. "Right." He clapped his hands together. "I'm going to get on up to the roof, if you don't mind. Clear the cobwebs before Adao arrives." He stood his ground. Theo was smart enough to take the absence of movement as his cue to leave and turned toward the bank of elevators.

"Hey," Theo called over his shoulder as he was entering the elevator. "You know we have a team of experts who look after that sort of thing."

Theo didn't have to look at Finn's knee for Finn to know what he was talking about. He knew the offer was there. He just didn't want to take it. Pain equaled penance. And he had a helluva lot of making up to do. Parents. Brother. Ex-wife. Friends. And the list went on.

"Good to know." He waited until the elevator doors closed before he moved.

A string of silent expletives crossed his lips as he hobbled over to a sofa, pulled up his trouser leg and undid the straps to ease the ache in his knee, not even caring when the whole contraption clattered to the floor.

One breath in…one breath out…and a silent prayer of thanks that he had this moment alone. He didn't do weak.

Not in public anyway.

The handful of moments he'd let himself slide into self-pity over the years…those would remain buried in his chest as bitter reminders of the paths he shouldn't have taken. The lessons he should've learned.

He gave his prosthesis a bit of a kick.

"It's just you and me, mate. Guess we'd better start finding a way to make nice."

CHAPTER TWO

"ARE YOU HANGING about for a meet-and-greet with Adao?"

Naomi went wide-eyed at Evie's question. She hadn't said anything, but that had definitely been her plan. A volley of responses ricocheted round her chest and lodged in her throat because she didn't want Evie to hear any of them.

I know how he feels.

He's probably as scared as I was.

I wanted him to know there's someone here who understands what it's like to live in a world ruled by guns and fear.

But Evie knew nothing of Naomi's past. Having Adao here would be the biggest emotional challenge she'd faced since arriving in Britain at the ripe age of fifteen. Scared. Utterly alone.

Two things she never wanted Adao to feel.

At least he knew his family was waiting at home for him.

Naomi pinned on her bright smile—the one she ensured her patients and colleagues knew her by—and asked, "How'd you guess?"

Evie shrugged in her elfin way. She just did.

Naomi liked to think of Evie as the entire hospital's resident Christmas faerie. She had a canny knack for intuiting things. That and a heart the size of Britain. She smiled as Evie shifted Grace on her hip, the baby who'd been abandoned at the hospital a few months ago and who was to be adopted by Evie and her soon-to-be husband, Ryan.

"I have a really ridiculous question." Evie looked at her a bit bashfully.

"Shoot."

"I'm not exactly sure where Kambela is."

"Adao's home?" Naomi knew what Evie was really asking. *Is it anywhere near where you're from?* Her English, no matter how hard she tried, was still lightly accented. "It's on the coast of Africa. Near the Horn."

Right next door to her country. Zemara.

"Hey…is everything all right with you?"

Uh-oh. Evie's emotional intuition radar was beep-beep-beeping like a metal detector in her direction… not so good.

"Fine! Great." Naomi tipped her head toward the glass doors leading out of the front of the hospital and grinned. "Did you see that?"

"Violet being discharged early? Amazing. You did such good work with her." Evie grinned and shifted Grace from one arm to the other. "*Oof!* This little girl's putting on weight at a rate of knots! I'll have 'mom arms' soon."

Naomi smiled and gave the tip of the baby's nose a tickle. Hope Hospital had hit the headlines with this little girl and would again soon with Adao…if the surgery went well and the rehab was successful. So much of recovery had to do with a patient's will. The will to fight. The desire to survive. The stamina to confront what had happened to them head on.

She crossed her fingers behind her back for Adao, ignoring the tight twist of nerves constricting the oxygen in her lungs.

"Are you waiting for Ryan?"

Evie nodded, her smile hitting the ear-to-ear register. If a couple of red-breasted robins flew in the front door and began adorning her with mistletoe, she could easily be the poster girl for Cupid's arrow. "He's just come out of surgery. I'm swotting up for nursing college in the new term and he's promised to talk me through all the signs, symptoms and early treatment for scarlet fever if I make him an early Christmas dinner."

"Turkey and all the trimmings?" Naomi couldn't hide her shock. She knew they were in love, but Christmas dinner on a "school night"?

"Giant prawn cocktails and pavlova." Evie shrugged and shifted Grace in her arms again. Whatever her Australian-born fiancé wanted...

Naomi giggled. "You are well and truly loved up, aren't you?"

Evie blushed in response. Her whole world had changed. "It's not just me, is it? Have you seen Alice lately? Sunbeams. Everywhere she goes. And Marco can't stop humming opera during surgery these days." She drummed her free fingers on her chin and gave Naomi a mischievous sideways look. "I wonder who's next?"

Naomi put up her hands and laughed. "Not me!" That ship of possibility had sailed long ago.

"Why not? You're beautiful. Amazing at your job. You'd be a real catch."

If cowardice was something a man could ever love, sure. But it wasn't. Which was precisely why she kept herself just out of love's reach.

She was just about say "Finn Morgan" to be contrary, but stopped herself. The man had scowling down to a fine art. At least around her. But the season of good cheer was upon them so she stuck to what had served her best when her past pounded at that locked door at the back of her mind: a positive attitude. "I reckon Mr. Holkham down in the cafeteria could do with a bit of a love buzz."

Evie threw back her head and laughed. "A love buzz? I don't know if that's a bit too energetic for him. What is he? Around seventy?"

"I think so. I love that Theo hired retirees who wanted to keep active, but…if anyone needs a love buzz it's him." She made a silly face. "Anything to make him chirpier when he serves up the lasagna. Who wants garlic bread with a side of gloom?"

"Good point."

Naomi could almost see the wheels turning in Evie's mind…already trying to figure out who she could couple with the sweet, if not relatively forlorn, older gentleman. She'd tried to tease a smile from him every day since the hospital had opened, to no avail. Perhaps she should ask him for a coffee one day. Maybe he was just lonely. A widower.

She knew more than most that with love came loss and that's why being cheerful, efficient and professional was her chosen modus operandi.

"Ooh, Gracie, look. It's Daddy!" Evie took her daughter's teensy hand and made it do a little wave as Ryan approached with a broad smile and open arms.

Naomi gave Evie's arm a quick squeeze and smiled. "I'd better get up there."

"All right. I'll leave you to it, then," Evie said distractedly, her eyes firmly fixed on her future husband.

Naomi took the stairs two at a time all the way up to the fifth floor, as she usually did. She put on the "feel good" blinkers and refocused her thoughts. She was feeling genuinely buoyed by her last session. A cheer-worthy set of results for her patient followed by a discharge. What a way to end a work day!

Watching a little girl skip—*skip!*—hand in hand with her parents straight out of the hospital doors and away home, where she would be able to spend Christmas with her family. A Christmas miracle for sure. Four months ago, when Violet had been helicoptered in from a near-fatal car accident, Naomi had had her doubts.

It was on days like this her job was the perfect salve to her past. Little girl power at its finest. And knowing she was playing a role in it made it that much better.

If she could keep her thoughts trained on the future, she could hopefully harness some of that same drive and determination in Adao. This was definitely not the time to let her own fears and insecurities bubble to the surface.

Then again, when was it the time?

Never. That was when.

So! Eyes on the prize and all would be well.

She hit the landing for the fifth floor and did a little twirl before pushing the door open.

Happy, happy, happy— *Oh.*

Not so happy.

The doctor's hunched shoulders and pained expression spoke volumes.

And not just any doctor.

Finn Morgan.

Of all the doctors at Hope, he was the one she had yet to exchange a genuine smile with. Well…him and the cafeteria chap, but she had to work with Mr. Morgan and he made her feel edgy. The man didn't do cheery. Not with her anyway.

Some days she had half a mind to tell him to snap out of it. He was a top surgeon at an elite private hospital. He worked on cases only the most talented of surgeons could approach with any hope of success. And still… King of the Grumps.

It wasn't as if he wasn't surrounded by people doing their best to create a warm, loving environment at Hope Hospital, no matter what was going on in their personal lives.

Not that she'd ever admit it, but most days she woke up in a cold sweat, her heart racing and arms reaching out for a family she would never see again.

If she could endure that and show up to work with a smile on her face, then whatever was eating away at him could be left at home as well.

She pushed the door open wider, took a step forward then froze. Her breath caught in her throat at the sound of the low moan coming from his direction. As silently as she could, she let the door from the stairwell close in front of her so that all she could see of him through the small glass window was his rounded back moving back and forth as he kneaded at something. His knee? His foot? She'd noticed a slight limp just the once but the look he'd shot her when he'd realized she'd seen it had been enough to send her scuttling off in the other direction.

Even so…

He was sitting all alone in the top floor's central reception area, his back to her, the twinkling lights of the city beyond him outlining his broad-shouldered physique.

Her gut instinct was to go to Finn… *Mr. Morgan*, she silently corrected herself…but the powerful "back off" vibes emanating from him kept her frozen at the stairwell door.

She'd been flying so high after finishing with Violet she'd thought she'd put her extra energy to use helping Adao settle in. She'd already been assigned as his physiotherapist—work that wouldn't begin until after his surgery with Finn Morgan—but she thought meeting him today might help him know there was someone who understood his world. His fears.

She pressed her hand against the glass as another low moan traveled across from the sofa where Finn remained resolutely hunched over his leg.

Something about his body language pierced straight through to her heart. A fellow lost soul trying to navigate a complicated world the best he could?

Or just a grump?

From what she'd seen, the man wouldn't know a good mood if it bit him on the nose.

She pulled her gaze away from him and searched the skyline for Adao's helicopter. She'd come here to find her patient, not snoop on a doctor clearly having a private moment.

She had little doubt the little boy was experiencing so many things that she had all those years ago when she'd arrived in the UK from Zemara. The language barrier. The strange faces. No family.

She swallowed against the lump forming in her throat and squeezed her eyes tight.

It was a long time ago.

Eleven years, two months and a day, to be exact.

Long enough to have moved on.

At least that's what logic told her. But how did you ever forget the day you saw everyone you loved herded into a truck and driven away off to the mountains? Mountains rumored to be scarred with pre-dug mass graves for anyone the rebels deemed unfit for their indiscriminatingly cruel army.

Blinking back the inevitable sting of tears, she gave herself a sharp shake and forced herself to paste on a smile. Her life was a good one. She was doing her dream job. In one of the most beautiful cities in the world, no less. Every day she was able to help and nurture children who, against the odds, always found a way to see the good in things.

So that's what she did, too. Focusing on the future was the only way she had survived those early days. And the only way she could live with herself now.

She pressed her forehead to the small, cool window in the door. In the dimly lit reception area—the lights were always lowered after seven at night—Finn had turned his face so that she could clearly see his profile.

He was a handsome man. Not storybook English—blond and blue-eyed, the way she'd once imagined everyone looked before she'd arrived in the UK. More... rugged, as if he'd just stepped off a plane from a long, arduous trek across the Alps rather than a doctor who had taken the elevator up from the surgical ward where he could usually be found. Not that she'd been stalking him or anything. Far from it. He was an arm's-length kind of guy judging by the handful of terse encounters they'd had.

Come to think of it, every time their paths had crossed since the hospital had opened—either going into or coming out of a session—he'd bristled.

Physically bristled.

Not the usual effect she had on people but, hey…she didn't need to be his bestie, she just needed a quality working relationship. That…and a bit of professional respect would be nice. Having seen his work on a near enough daily basis, she knew he respected her work… it would just be nice if that respect included the occasional smile or "Thank you."

His hair was a rich, dark brown. A tangled mess of waves that could easily turn to curls if it grew out. He was a big man. Not fat. No. Tall and solidly built. A "proper" man, as her birth mother would have said. A real man.

She swallowed back the sting of tears that inevitably followed when she thought of her mother. Her beautiful mother, who had worked so hard to pay for her extra lessons from any of the aid workers who had been based out of her hometown for as long as she could remember.

And then, of course, there was also her foster mother. The one who had taught her that she still had it in her to be brave. Face the maze of applications she needed to complete to get into medical school one day and, eventually, fulfil her dream of working as a pediatric physiotherapist.

Touch, she'd come to realize, was one of the most curative things of all.

Finn shifted around on the sofa and— Oh!

Her fingers wove together and she pressed her hands

to her mouth to stem her own cry. He wore a prosthesis. She'd had no idea.

And from the looks of things, his leg was hurting. A man as strong and capably built as Finn would have to be in some serious pain to look the way he did now. Slightly ashen. Breath catching. Unaware of everything else around him.

Instinct took over.

Before she thought better of it, she was by his side.

"Please. Perhaps I can help massage…" The rest of her offer died on her lips as she saw equal hits of horror and anger flash across his gray eyes.

She stood, completely frozen, mesmerized by their near-mystical depths.

How had she never noticed them before? So… haunted. She wondered if her dark eyes looked the same.

"What are you doing here?" Finn hastily grabbed his prosthesis and strapped it back on, despite the redness she saw engulfing his knee.

"I was just— I…"

I wanted to help.

"Well?" Finn rose alongside her, the scent of cotton and forest hitting her senses as he did.

She was tall so it took a lot of height to make her feel small. If the irritation radiating from him wasn't making her feel as if she'd invaded an incredibly private moment, she could almost imagine herself feeling delicate in his presence.

Delicate?

What was that about?

Finn scanned her uniform for her employee badge, though she was sure he already knew her name. It was his signature on the forms requesting her as Adao's physio.

She sucked in a breath. This was about Adao, not about Finn. Although…

Not your business. You have your secrets. He has his.

"Sorry. Please. I didn't mean to interrupt."

"No." Finn stared at her for a moment then swiped at the air between them, causing her to flinch. "What do you need?"

"I-I was here to help with Adao," she stammered. "I thought perhaps I could help settle him in."

"What?" Finn bridled. "You think I'm not up to being my patient's welcoming committee?"

She tilted her head to the side and pinched her lower lip with her teeth. Was he hoping for an honest answer? Or was this the famous British sense of humor at play?

Her silence seemed to give him the "No" he was expecting. His swift change of expression told her he was already dismissing her.

So much for trying to go the extra mile! She was about to tell him Adao was her patient too when, mercifully, Finn's phone buzzed and those penetrating, moonstone-colored eyes of his relaxed their spotlight grip on her.

He was as chatty on the phone as he was with her. A few responses of "Yeah. Yeah. Got it…" later and he was beckoning her to join him.

Okay.

He swiftly crossed to the bank of elevators—so quickly it was difficult to see how he hid the pain—and punched the illuminated button as he pulled his key card out of his pocket. Only staff were allowed up onto the roof and the magnetic key cards were the only way of taking the elevator up there. "Adao's ten minutes out. You done any helicopter arrivals before?"

She shook her head. Not here anyway. She'd seen more than her fair share before she'd left Zemara, but usually those helicopters had been filled with rebels wielding machine guns. Not charity workers with patients about to undergo life-altering surgery.

"Right." Finn pulled a crumpled bit of notepaper out of his pocket. "Adao's seven years old, suffering from—"

"Multiple injuries as a result of a landmine explosion," Naomi cut in. She'd read the case. Memorized it. It had all but scored itself straight into her heart if the truth be told, but that wasn't what this showdown was about. She kept on talking as the elevator doors opened and the hit of wintry air all but took her breath away. "Adao's injuries include loss of his right arm. Efforts have been made to keep infection to a minimum, but our goal is to ensure he retains as much use of his shoulder as possible so that any use of a pros—' She stopped, her eyes clashing with Finn's—*Mr. Morgan's*—as he wheeled on her.

"Fine. Good. I see you're up on the case. How's about we have a bit of quiet time before the chaos begins, yeah?"

Naomi nodded and looked away, forcing herself to focus on the crisp, starlit sky above them.

No problem.

She'd obviously seen far more than Finn—*Mr. Morgan*—had wanted her to. An incredibly private moment for a man who clearly didn't do vulnerability.

Vulnerability and strength were two of the reasons she'd chosen to work at Hope. Most of the children here were going through something frightening. Loss of a limb. Surgery. Illnesses that meant they would be facing a future that would present hurdle after hurdle. And despite all the pain and all the suffering, the bulk of the children confronted their futures with a courage that amazed her on a daily basis. If she could be a part of making their future something to actually look forward to, then she was going to give it her all.

She tipped her head up and let the wind skid across her features as she sought out the Milky Way. The night was so clear she spotted it almost instantly. She was constantly amazed by the band of light made up of so many stars, so faraway, they were indistinguishable to the naked eye. In Zemara, they called the spiral galaxy they were such a small part of the Path of Spirits. This was where her family must be now…far above her… looking down…

A rippling of goose-pimples shot across her arms, but it wasn't the cold that had instigated them.

Guilt had a lot to answer for. Here she was at one end of the galaxy while her family were…only heaven knew where. It wasn't fair.

"Look." Finn's rich voice broke through the thick silence. "Over there."

She turned and followed the line of his arm and saw the helicopter emerging from the darkness.

CHAPTER THREE

NAOMI'S EYES WERE trained on the helicopter but all Finn could focus on was her.

Why had he snapped at her like he had?

It wasn't her fault she'd seen him in the lounge… without his leg…exposed as the embittered man he'd become ever since the future he'd thought he'd have had literally been torn away from him.

It also wasn't her fault that every time he saw her his senses shot to high alert. There was no way he was going to put a name to what he felt each time their paths crossed, but his body was miles ahead of him on that front.

A white-hot, solitary flame had lit that very first staff meeting when they'd all gathered together in the hospital's huge atrium and he'd first seen her. Even at—what had she been? Fifty meters from him? Twenty? Whatever. The impact had been sharp, forceful, and, if today was anything to go by, unabating.

From the response his body had had to her, she may as well have sashayed up to him in a curve-hugging negligee and wrapped him round one of her long, elegant fingers.

Not that he'd thought about her naked.

Okay, fine. Of course he had.

But it had just been the once, and the woman had all but floated out of the hospital's therapy pool in a scarlet swimsuit that had made him jealous of the droplets of water cascading down her body.

What else was he meant to do?

Treat her with respect, you numpty.

Everything about her commanded a civility he could tap into for the rest of his colleagues, but Naomi? Whatever it was he felt around her it meant he simply wasn't able to extend it to her. Not in the manners department anyway.

Naomi's entire essence sang of grace and an innate sensitivity to both her patients and her environment. Her movements were always smooth. Fluid. Her voice was carefully modulated, lightly accented, but he didn't know from where. He'd thought of asking once or twice, but that would've verged on curious and with half the hospital staff staggering around the hospital with love arrows embedded in their hearts…bah. Whatever. He should just stuff his hormones in the bin and have done with them.

And yet…even now, with her head tipped back as it was, the wind shifting along that exquisitely long neck of hers, there was something almost regal about Naomi's presence. Not haughty or standoffish, more…wise.

Where he shot from the hip, she always took a moment before responding to his sharp comments and brusque reactions to her.

She wasn't to know his brush-offs were the age-old battle of desire versus pragmatism.

Where he felt big and lunky, she was lithe and adroit. Long-limbed. Sure-footed. High, proud cheekbones.

Skin the shade of… He didn't know to describe it. A rich, warmly colored brown? Whatever shade it was, it was beautiful. The perfect complement to her full, plump mouth. Not that he was staring at it. Much.

There was something fiercely loyal shining in those dark eyes of hers. He saw it whenever she was with a patient. But he could also see it now as she trained her eyes on the sky above. For whom or what it shone, he would never know, because he didn't do personal. Didn't do intimate. Not anymore.

As if feeling his gaze on her, she turned and met his eyes.

"Is there anywhere we're meant to stand when they land, Mr. Morgan?"

Finn scowled. Why'd she have to catch him mooning over her? And what was with this *Mr. Morgan* business? Made him sound like a grumpy old man.

Humph.

Maybe that was the point she was making.

"It's Finn," he said. "Over there." He pointed toward the covered doorway where a porter was wheeling a gurney into place then turned his focus on to the approaching helicopter…willing the beats and syncopation of the blades cutting through the thin, wintry air to knock some sense back into him.

Bah.

He hadn't been mooning. It had simply been a while. Once he'd cut ties with his past, he'd thought that part of him had all but died.

He should be relieved his body was still capable of responding to a woman like a red-blooded male. So many of the soldiers he'd met during his stint in hospital… hell…he didn't wish their futures on his worst enemies.

All these thoughts and the raft of others that inevitably followed in their wake fell to the wayside as the helicopter hovered above them for a moment before executing a perfect landing.

And then they all fell to what they did best, caring for their patient.

There were too many people in Adao's room. It was easy enough to see from the growing panic in his wide, dark eyes as they darted from person to medical contraption to yet another person.

When they landed on her, all she could see was fear.

He was strapped to the gurney, completely surrounded by medical staff from the charity and the hospital all exchanging stats and information at a rate of knots that would have been impossible for him to comprehend.

Short, sharp counts dictated the swift shift from the gurney to the hospital bed and yet another stream of instructions flowed over him as they hooked him up to fresh IVs and peeled out another ream of information as they pressed monitors to his skinny, bare, little-boy chest. And when he called out for his parents it was all she could do not to tear her heart from her own chest.

"It's too much!"

The room fell silent as all eyes turned to Naomi.

"I beg your pardon?"

Finn hadn't moved a muscle, but his voice may as well have been a drill boring straight into her chest for the pain it caused.

She lifted her chin and met his steel-colored gaze. Yes, she was still smarting from his curt form of issuing orders.

"Not on that side."

"Not too close."

"Not too far."

There didn't seem to be a single thing she could do properly under his hawk-eyed gaze. But when it came to the child—*this child*—enough was enough.

"Please. Give the boy some peace. He's known nothing but chaos. This place—this hospital—must bring him peace. Comfort. Not fear."

Finn's eyebrows lifted a notch. It was written all over his face. She'd overstepped the mark.

Just as she was about to run out of the room, find a computer and start composing her letter of resignation, he spoke.

"You heard Naomi." He pointed at one nurse and one doctor, both of whom were on the overnight shift in Adao's ward. "You two stay. The rest of you…" He made a shooing motion with his hands. "Out you go. And you…' He pointed directly at Naomi. "You come with me."

Finn's eyes were glued to Naomi's throat. The tiny pulse point, alive with a blaze of passion he'd not seen in her before.

Their paths had never really crossed in this way. Neither had their temperaments.

Fighting for a patient.

It showed her high-energy, positive approach to work was more than skin deep.

But what he wanted to get to was the *why*. Why this little boy? Why the specifics? Her slight accent intrigued him. Maybe it was from a French-speaking country? He wasn't sure. Either way, there was something about Adao that had got under her skin and was making an emotional impact.

Problem Number One.

Finn flexed his fingers, hoping it would rid them of the urge to reach out and touch her throat, smooth his thumb across her pounding pulse point. From the meter or so he'd put between them, he could still tell her skin looked as soft as silk. But her spirit? Solid steel.

The combination pounded a double hit onto his senses. Primal. Cerebral.

Problem Number Two.

He bashed the primal response into submission and channeled his thoughts into figuring out what made her tick.

Work.

That much was obvious. Not that he kept tabs on the woman, but he'd only ever seen her in work clothes. Never did she shift to casual or night-out-on-the-town outfits as loads of other doctors did when they threw their scrubs in for washing. Then again…he wasn't exactly a social butterfly either.

She was top of her game. No one came more highly recommended in her field of pediatric physio than she did.

Snap. He was up there in the top-rated limb specialists.

She was opinionated.

Snap again.

Fair dos to the woman, she hadn't blinked once when he'd all but marched her to an empty room a few doors down from Adao's and wheeled on her.

He counted to ten in time with her heartbeat before he'd steadied his own enough to speak.

"So." He crossed his arms and tipped his head toward Adao's room. "What was that all about?"

She gave her head a quick shake as if she didn't understand.

He waited. His failsafe technique.

Far more effective than saying the myriad of things he could have:

"There's only one person in charge in that room and it's me."

Not his style.

"Since when is a physio a psychiatrist?"

Ditto. He wasn't into tearing people down, but he did like explanations for outbursts.

The seconds ticked past.

Naomi threw a quick look over her shoulder, stuffed her hands in the pockets of her Hope Hospital hoodie then said, "Okay. Fine. I just feel for the little man, you know?"

He loved the way she said "feel"—even if it was a verb he didn't include in his own vocabulary. She said it as if the word had heft. Gravitas, even. As if it *meant* something.

What a thing to have all that emotion churning round in your chest. Way too much extra baggage to haul around the hospital if he wanted to do his job properly. If he professed to know one solitary thing about himself it was this: Finn Morgan did not do baggage.

Ha!

He coughed into his hand to hide a self-deprecating smirk.

If his ex-wife could read his thoughts, she would've pounced on them like a mouse on cheese.

One of the last things she'd said to him before he'd

left his past where it belonged was that he was "*Made of baggage*." And one day? "One day," she'd said to him, "all of that baggage will tumble open and wreak havoc with the man you keep telling yourself you are."

How about that for a "let's keep it friendly" farewell.

On a good day he recalled her "prophesy" as tough love.

On bad days? On bad days he tried not to think of her at all.

He shifted his weight off his knee and brought his thoughts back to Adao and Naomi. "How do you 'feel' for him? Are you from Kambela?"

"No, I'm…" She started to say something then pressed her lips together and started again. "I know what it's like to arrive somewhere new and feel…overwhelmed. Not know who to trust."

"Oh, I see. So you're the only one he can trust here, is that what you're saying?"

Why was he being so confrontational? She was clearly doing what any employee of Hope Children's Hospital should be doing: Holding the patient's needs first and foremost in their mind. At all times.

Take it down a notch, man. She's trying to do right by the kid.

He shrugged the tension out of his shoulders and adopted what he hoped was a less confrontational pose. "I see what you're saying. The kid's been through a lot. But the one person he's got to trust is me." He let it sink in a minute. He was the one who would be holding the scalpel tomorrow. He was the one who would be changing Adao's life forever.

"You're the one who will help him live. I'm the one who's going to help him rebuild his life," Naomi shot back.

Wow. The pronouncement was so loaded with barbs he could take personally he almost fell back a step. Good thing he didn't take workplace slanging matches personally.

The surgery and recovery Adao required was a step-by-step process. And they weren't anywhere near rehab. No point in popping on rose-colored glasses at this stage. Whether she liked it or not, Adao had a *long* road of recovery ahead of him, and the first step was the operating table. Finn's operating table.

"You got the order right," Finn said. "Life first."

And that was the simple truth of the matter.

Naomi didn't respond verbally. But the pursed lips followed by a swift inhalation told him all he needed to know. She knew the facts as well as she did. She just didn't like them.

"C'mon." He steered her, one hand pressed to the small of her back, toward Adao's room. "All the basics should be taken care of right now. How 'bout you sit in while I talk Adao through his first twenty-four hours here at Hope?"

If she was surprised, Naomi masked it well. If she noticed he dropped his hand from her back about as quickly as he'd put it there, she made no sign of it either. As if the moment had never happened.

The tingling in his fingers spoke a different story. When he'd touched her? That flame in his core had tripled in size.

Leaning against the doorframe, having refused Finn's invitation to join him, Naomi had to silently admit the truth.

She was impressed.

As cranky and gruff as Finn was with her...with Adao?...he was gentle, calm and capable of explaining some incredibly complicated facts in a way that didn't patronize or confuse. When Adao spoke or asked questions, she recognized the same lilting accent she'd acquired when learning English from American missionaries or aid workers. Hers, of course, was softened by years in the UK and was now predominantly British English. His was still raw—lurching between the musical cadence of his mother tongue and wrestling with all the new English words.

"We can go over all of this again," Finn was saying, "whenever you want. But the main thing is we're here to help. Okay, little man? Anything you need?"

Adao shook his head now, his small head and shoulders propped up on the big white pillows. He was a collection of bandages with little bits of his brown skin peeking out at intervals. And his eyes...those big brown eyes rimmed with tears...spoke volumes.

Fear. Bewilderment. Loneliness.

He nodded at Finn but said nothing.

She got that.

The silence.

Admitting there was something or someone you missed so much you thought your heart might stop beating was as good as admitting a part of you wished it would. And despite the anxiety creasing his sweet little brow, she also saw fight in him. He wouldn't be here otherwise.

She ached to go to him. Be by his side. Tell him all the things she wished she had been told when she'd arrived in the UK. That these were good people. And while they weren't family...

Her eyes unexpectedly misted over as Finn and Adao did a big fist, little fist bump.

You couldn't ever replace family. Could you?

Finn crossed to her.

"I think it's time we let him get some rest." Finn tipped his head toward the staffroom. "His minder from the charity is just getting some coffee. She'll stay with him tonight. The chair in the corner converts to a bed, so...we'd best leave him to settle in quietly." He gave her a weighted look. "As you suggested."

Nothing like having your own words come back to bite you in the bum.

He was right, of course. And Adao was in the best possible place. But leaving the little boy was tugging at a double-wide door to her heart she'd long jammed shut. It felt wrong.

"Now," Finn mouthed, when the woman from the charity appeared from round the corner and Naomi's gaze inevitably skidded back in Finn's direction as if he were some sort of homing beacon. It was madness, considering Finn Morgan was the last set of arms she'd throw herself into if she needed comforting. It would be like skipping up to a hungry grizzly bear and asking if he minded if they shared a den. Not. Going. To. Happen.

He had his hand on her elbow and was filling up the rest of the space in the doorframe.

There it was again. That cotton and forest scent. And something extra. She looked up into his slate-colored eyes as if they would give her the answer she needed.

Her heart pounded against her ribcage when it did.

That other scent?

Pure male heat.

* * *

Naomi scooped her keys off the ground for a second time.

What had got into her?

She blew out a slow breath, waited until the cloud dissipated, then put the key in the lock and turned it.

See? There.

All she needed to do was blank any thoughts of Finn Morgan and— *Doh!*

There went the keys again. At least she was inside this time.

She jogged up the stairs to her flat, opened the interior door, flicked on the lights and popped her keys into the wooden bowl that rested on the small table she had at the front door.

Home.

She grinned at it.

The studio flat was dinky, but she loved it. Her cocoon. A twenty-minute walk from the hospital. Fifty if she took a run along the river on the way, which, let's face it, was every day. Going to the river had become a bit of a pilgrimage. If only one day she would come back from the river and find everything was—

If only nothing.

She toed off her trainers—against her own advice!— and pushed her door shut with her elbow.

Brightly lit. Simply furnished. Secure. Two floors above a bookshop/coffee shop that catered to students and, as such, was open all night. All the things she needed to get to sleep at night.

She shrugged out of her padded gilet then pulled her hoodie, her long-sleeved T-shirt and her wool camisole off, all but diving into her flannel jimjams that she'd laid out on the radiator when she'd left in the morning.

The one thing about England she'd failed to get used to was the cold. This winter was particularly frigid. Rumors of a white Christmas were swirling around the hospital like…like snowflakes.

She gave herself a wry grin in the bathroom mirror as she let warm water run over her freezing fingers. At least the sub-zero temperatures helped keep her heart on ice.

She shivered, thinking of that hot, intense flare of heat she'd seen in Finn's normally glacial gaze.

Did it mean that he…? No. The man was like a snapping turtle. Don't do this. Do that. Not here. There. Me right. You wrong.

She thought of his athletic build, his bear-like presence. Maybe he was more… Abominable Snowman than snapping turtle. Could one make love to a yeti?

She gave her head a shake. Clearly she'd lost a few brain cells on the cold walk home. Even if Finn wrapped a ribbon round his heart and handed it to her on a velvet cushion… *Pah-ha-ha-ha!* Can you imagine?

She tugged on her wool-lined slipper boots, padded across to her tiny strip of a kitchen and opened the fridge.

Yup! Forgot to go shopping. Again.

She stared at the handful of condiments she'd bought in yet another failed moment of "I'll invite someone over" and wondered what it would be like to open up her fridge and know that she'd be making a meal for herself and her family. She closed the refrigerator door along with the thoughts.

Being in a relationship wasn't on the cards for her. Each time she'd tried…*whoomp*. Up had gone the shields holding court round her heart.

She laughed into the silence of her flat.

At last! She'd found something she and Finn had in common.

Now all she had to do was find a way to get along.

CHAPTER FOUR

"DID YOU MANAGE to get some sleep?" Finn looked over at Adao's case worker from the charity when all he elicited from the little boy was an uncertain mini-shrug.

"He slept a little." She gave the boy's creased forehead a soothing stroke with the backs of her fingers before crossing to him and holding out a sheaf of paperwork. "I'm Sarah Browning, by the way. I'm afraid we're short-staffed and I've got to get a move on." Her features creased apologetically.

Finn nodded and took the paperwork. "Not a problem. We've got plenty of folk who are looking forward to spending time with this little guy. Myself included." He looked over at Adao for any sign of emotional response.

Nothing.

Hardly surprising considering what he'd been through. It was a shame the charity's financial reach couldn't have extended to bringing at least one of the family members over. Then again…from what he'd read prior to the boy's arrival, both the mum and dad worked and his teenage sister was still in school, so…not easy to uproot an entire family.

He slapped the papers against his thigh. Too loudly, from the sharp look the charity worker sent him.

"Right." Finn gave Sarah his best stab at a smile. "Looks like you need to get a move on and I need to assess Adao before we get him into surgery this afternoon."

He went to the doorway and called to the small team of doctors and nurses who would be in surgery with him. "Righto, mateys. Let's get a move on, shall we?" A twinge of déjà vu hit him as the team moved toward the door as one solid mass. Naomi had been right. Too many people standing around Adao might render the kid less responsive than he already was.

"Hey, mate." He looked Adao in the eye. "We've got a bunch of people who are going to come in, but they're all here to help you, yeah? We're all on your side."

The little boy pursed his lips and then nodded. He understood. He didn't like it. But it wasn't exactly as if he was in a position to argue.

Finn's heart went out to the little man, but he needed to keep his cool. Clean, clear precision was what was required when he stepped into surgery today. Anything less wasn't acceptable.

Finn went out into the corridor as the team crowded into the smallish room to hear the details of Adao's case and help set up a battle plan for the afternoon's surgery.

Battle plan.

The cruel irony of it…

He heard a laugh and his eyes snapped to the nurses' station. The hairs on his arms prickled to attention and a deep punch of heat rocket-launched itself exactly where it didn't belong.

Dammit.

Last night's gym session clearly hadn't drilled his body's organic response to her out of his system.

Who knew a woman's scent could linger in the physio gym hours after she'd left the hospital?

He did, that's who. He didn't know if she wore perfume or body spray or what…he just knew that jasmine and vanilla were forever lost to him as plain old smells now.

"Mr. Morgan? I was wondering if I could have a quick word."

"Yes?" Grabbing his work tablet from the counter, he looked back up at her then instantly regretted it. Those dark eyes of hers were blinking away his brusque greeting as her hands rose to tug on each of her loosely woven, below-the-shoulder plaits.

They made her look fun.

And sexy as hell.

"Hi. Um…hello." Naomi stepped behind the high counter of the nurses' station, putting a physical buffer between them.

So she felt it too. Or was avoiding the "back off" daggers he was sending her way.

Fair enough. He'd hardly been Prince Charming last night. Or the day before that. Or…yup. Patterns. He saw it, but she messed with his focus and he didn't like his highly honed "this way trouble lies" vibes being messed with.

"What is it? I've got the team waiting for the pre-surgery assessment."

"I…um…" Something flickered in those dark brown eyes of hers. Had he ever noticed they were flecked with gold?

Yeah. Just like she'd probably noticed his eyes were

flecked with amber when the sun hit them. Not. Can it, Romeo. Those days are over.

"You coming in to listen or is the idea to break up the assessment mid-flow with more of your touchy-feely stuff?"

Why are you being such an ass?

Naomi's dark irises flashed with disbelief at his narky question. Even the ward sister shot him a sharp look. Great. Just what he needed. More fodder for the nurses to continue the tar-and-feather job they no doubt had begun in the break room.

And it was deserved.

All of it.

If Naomi turned on her heel and marched straight up to HR to report him, he wouldn't blame her.

He was at war with himself and no one was coming out the victor. His body wanted one thing, his head wanted another. His heart was being yanked from side to side and therein lay the crux of the matter.

Good thing he didn't do feelings. Or poetry, for that matter. Ode to a smashed-up, battered heart didn't have much of a ring to it.

To his surprise, and the charge nurse's, Naomi shook her head and gave him a gentle smile. "No, no. Please. Go ahead. I'm here to listen."

He gave her a curt nod. "Fine." Then he turned and walked into Adao's room.

"Looks like someone's gunning for a lump of coal in his stocking this Christmas."

Naomi willed herself to smile back at Amanda, the charge nurse, who was always ready with a quip. She could tell from Amanda's expression it looked as forced as it felt. It appeared all she needed to do to rile Finn Morgan was exist!

"Don't let him get to you, Naomi." Amanda gave her shoulders a quick squeeze as she handed her a mini gingerbread man. "We all bank on you and your sunny smile to keep us cheery, so don't give him the satisfaction of taking it away."

Naomi blinked in surprise.

"Don't look so shocked. We're all in awe of your energy."

"My energy?"

"Of course. Who else around here runs up the stairs after running to work and running round with patients all day. Just watching you is exhausting! We all call you the Fizzy Physio." Amanda laughed then leaned in close after giving a swift conspiratorial look around the reception area. "He's all grizzly on the outside and perfectionist on the inside. We've all decided there's a bit of gold in there somewhere but someone has yet to unearth it."

"Unearth it how?"

"The usual way." She performed a teensy sexy dance. "Romance."

Naomi blew a raspberry. As if. The last thing she could ever imagine Finn engaging in was a hospital romance. She winced. She was hardly one to judge.

"Maybe you could be the one to tease it out of him."

"What? Me?" A solitary laugh escaped. "I don't think so." Her eyes did a quick flick in his direction and in the millisecond she allowed herself to look at him she did think…well…he's not *all* bad.

"Hmm. Well, it's not exactly as if anyone catches him

out on the razzle anyway." Amanda picked up a tablet and started tapping away with some patient information.

"What do you mean?"

"He never—and I mean never ever—accepts invitations to go out. And that's weird."

"It's not that weird," Naomi said, instantly realizing she was defending her own penchant for staying in at night. She'd gone out for the odd night, but had always sneaked off early. She never seemed to be able to let herself go the way the other women did.

"'Course it is!" Amanda protested. "New hospital. New staff. New chance to meet friends, fall in love if you want— Oh. Uh-oh! Did I hit a nerve?"

"Ha! No."

Yes. Definitely yes.

Amanda inspected her for a minute then grinned as if she'd pocketed a state secret.

"What are you doing up here on the surgical floor anyway? Adao won't be ready for physio until after the surgery."

"I know. I— Well, I..."

Amanda's entire demeanor changed, her expression softening with compassion. "Ah. One of *those*."

Naomi bit down on the inside of her cheek. Hard. She needed that "Fizzy Physio" cover more than anyone here knew.

"Hey. Don't worry. Some of them get to you more than others." Amanda tipped her head toward Adao's room. "Just don't let Mr. All Work and No Play rile you. He's all right as long as you wear your crocodile skin when you're in the same room."

"Got it." Naomi smiled, relieved to have dodged more questions about Adao.

"Collins!" Finn barked from the doorway. "Are you going to join us or are you too busy with the gossip brigade?"

Amanda gave her hand a quick squeeze then nudged her toward the room with a whispered, "Don't worry, his bark is worse than his bite."

She followed Finn into the room, staying put at the doorway as he shouldered his way through the seven or eight physicians and nurses already around the little boy's bed.

Finn obviously didn't want her there but that was tough. She'd seen Adao arrive last night and wanted him to know she would be there for him when he came out of surgery. After all, she and Adao would be working intimately together in rehab.

Rehab wasn't just tough physically.

It put many of her young patients through an emotional mangle. Adao was bound to have a truckload of emotions come in wave after wave as they worked together.

He had numerous cuts and nicks on his face. None were so brutal they had blinded him or reduced his facial motor function, but there would be scars. Inside and out.

"Right, everyone!" Finn gave a theatrical throat-clearing noise as he took pole position at the head of Adao's bed. "Adao Weza, seven years old and fresh in from Kambela on the west coast of Africa."

He gave the boy a nod and...well, she guessed it was a smile. Hard to tell, coming from someone who clearly had gone to the Neanderthal School of Social Skills.

Ugg. Me surgeon. Me have no feelings. Ugg.

Naomi tucked herself behind one of the junior doctors so she could hide her smile as she pictured Finn wielding a wooden club while wearing a caveman's leopardskin ensemble.

She could still see Adao but was just out of that steel-gray eyeline of Finn's. Meeting his piercing gaze was too unnerving when all she really wanted to do was focus on the little boy.

Perhaps Finn was every bit as upset by Adao's case as she was and this whole Cro-Magnon act was just that…an act. He definitely wasn't the touchy-feely type.

She gave her head a quick shake, her plaits shifting from shoulder to shoulder as she did so, looking up only to catch Finn glaring at her before he rattled off the facts.

Adao had been in a field when his playmate had stepped on an anti-personnel mine. The mine had instantly exploded. She pressed her eyes closed tightly as he continued. She knew, more than most, how easily landmines could go off. The rebels in her own country had taken particular pleasure in littering them throughout the small vegetable patches most families had behind their homes. Two-for-ones, they called them. The blasts knocked out the women and the food supply in one cruel blast. Each morning she and her sister had gone out to the vegetable patch with a long stick, poking and prodding any upturned earth…hoping…praying that today they would be safe.

"Am I boring you, Miss Collins?"

"Sorry." Naomi snapped to attention, horrified to see all the eyes in the room were on her. "No. Not at all."

"Then can you please indulge me and the rest of the team with what you would see as the best solution for the tissue damage Adao has sustained?" Finn's eyes were bright with challenge.

If only he knew. She hadn't been blocking out his words, she'd been trying to block out her own memories.

She pressed her heels into the floor and looked him straight back in the eye. "Well, as you know, I am a physio, not a surgeon, but my understanding is that free tissue transfer can aid with repairing extensive soft tissue defects if the limb has endured serial debridement."

Finn nodded. He wanted her to continue.

Murmurs of curiosity rippled through the team as they cleared a little space around her.

"After a series of pre-operative diagnoses—'

"Which diagnosis? Be specific."

He wanted specifics? Fine. He could have specifics.

She rattled off the list of tests she knew Adao would have to go through prior to surgery—all of which were geared toward finding just how much of his arm they could save while providing his body with optimum chances of healing. She concluded with the overall goal, "The greater the blood flow, the better the healing."

Finn nodded. "So we're looking at measuring his blood flow. What else?" He scanned the room."

"Oxygen tension," said a nurse.

"Good. What else?"

"If the pressure is zero, no healing will occur," jumped in one of the surgical interns. "Ideally, we're looking for the pressure to read higher than forty mils."

"Excellent." Finn scanned the room. "What else?"

Naomi's eyes flicked to Adao's. The pain and fear she saw in them as the medical terminology flew across the room pounded the air out of her chest. A fierce, primal need to do everything she could for this little boy seized every cell in her body, giving her the extra jolt of courage to cut in again.

Finn had been through a trauma of some sort. Surely he had some compassion for this little boy.

Eyes locked with Finn's, she suddenly felt as though they were two prey animals, each wondering who would be the first to pounce. "What's most important for Adao is getting him to a place where he can begin gentle physio—'

"Yes. Fine." Finn cut her off. "We're not there, yet."

"But…" Wasn't giving Adao something to hope for every bit as helpful as doing a skin fluorescence study to measure his microcirculation? He was a little *boy*! A terrified little boy!

"But nothing. We've got the theatre booked in a few hours' time, Miss Collins. He's got to be as strong as possible going into surgery and time's awasting."

Finn gave the back of his tablet a few swift raps with his knuckles and carried on talking his team through the finer points of the surgery, fastidiously ignoring Naomi's shocked expression.

How could he have done that? Interrupting her was one thing, but making that noise?

He didn't even notice how Adao had started at the sound, but she had.

The sharp rat-a-tat-tat had the same effect on her nerves as it obviously did on Adao's.

To them it wasn't knuckles on plastic.

It was the sound of gunfire.

Finn felt Naomi's presence up in the viewing gallery before he confirmed it with a quick sidelong glance.

Her fingers were in prayer position up at that full mouth of hers. A line furrowed between her brows as he meticulously worked his way through the initial phase of the operation before he began shaping what remained of Adao's arm in preparation for a prosthetic device.

What was it with her and this kid? It wasn't as if the hospital hadn't had amputees before. It was, after all, his specialty.

He blanked the gallery viewing room and returned his focus to Adao's small form.

"Skin temperature's slightly different." He nodded to the nurse by the instrument tray. He really didn't want to have to take off more than he had to, but he knew better than most that providing a solid foundation for the prosthesis was crucial.

There'd been no way to save the elbow joint. A layperson could've figured that out. But he had been hoping for an elbow disarticulation rather than the more blunt approach of a proximal amputation. By employing a fastidious millimeter by millimeter approach, he prepared Adao's arm for separation at the joint, thereby providing a solid platform for his prosthetic device. He'd read about some electric elbow prostheses that could potentially set the boy up for a relatively normal life. He might not become a pianist, but…

With any luck, he'd be ready for some gentle physiotherapy in a handful of days.

An image of Naomi massaging Adao's shoulder with her slender fingers blinded him for an instant. Blinded him because it wasn't Adao he was picturing receiving her sympathetic care. It was him.

It may have been a millisecond but it was a millisecond too long.

"Clear the gallery!"

His growl of frustration sent everyone from the gallery flying. If there was one thing that held true in Hope Children's Hospital it was that the surgeon got what the surgeon wanted when it came to offering a child the best care possible.

Pop music?

No problem.

A favorite scrubs cap?

Same again.

A gallery free of invested onlookers?

That was fine, too. As long as everything came out good in the end.

Muscles, connective tissue, skin all played a role in creating the foundation of what would be Adao's arm from now on.

Sometimes he thought he got the easy part and the physio was actually the one who took the brunt of the patient's pain. Thank God his own physiotherapist had been unfazed by blue language because he had painted that therapy gym the color of a sky heading toward the blackest of midnights for his first few sessions. If by "few" he meant six months. Anyone and everyone who'd crossed his path—and that included family—had been soundly pushed away. The only way he'd survived those dark days had been with grim determination.

Phantom limb pain.

A poor-fitting prosthesis.

Infection.

A second surgery.

He'd had them all.

And he hadn't wanted anyone who claimed to love him within earshot. If ever he'd felt like a wounded animal—made of little else other than rage and fear—it had been then.

It was what had driven him to retrain as a pediatric surgeon after he'd finally got out of rehab and had pushed his past as far away as he could. No one—especially children—should have to go through what he had. And under his watch they wouldn't.

Which was why he did the hard part—the part that required a methodical, emotionless approach—and positive, forward-thinking people like Naomi did the aftercare.

Two or three back-achingly painful hours later he stood back from the surgery table, knowing he had done his best.

"Good work, everyone." He pulled off his surgical cap and threw it in the laundry bin by the swinging theatre doors. "Make sure I'm paged when he wakes up, yeah? One of you stay with him at all times. I don't want the little guy on his own. Not tonight."

His eyes shifted up to the empty gallery.

Idiot.

He should've let her stay.

His gut told him she was the one Adao should be seeing as he blinked his eyes open when he woke from the anesthetic.

His head told him to just butt out and carry on as always. No attachments. No guilt. He was already dragging around enough of the latter, thank you very much, and the last thing he was going to do was add a leggy physio to the list of people he'd wronged.

That list was already full up.

CHAPTER FIVE

NAOMI BURIED HER face in the dog's curly coat and gave him a hug. Much to her delight, he sat back on his haunches and put his paws on her shoulders as if giving her a proper hug.

"He's gorgeous!" She looked up at his handler… Alana, was it?…and opted to ask the surgeon beside her instead. "What's his name, Marco?"

"Doodle," Marco Ricci answered, as if it was patently obvious that the golden-brown labradoodle should be called Doodle. The surgeon gave the pooch's head a quick scrub then wished Alana well.

The pair of them watched as Doodle and his trainer made their way along and out of the hospital corridor.

"Alice thinks he's brilliant. Would use him for all her patients if she could. Whether they needed them or not," Marco said, as they disappeared round the corner.

"Wow." High praise indeed, coming from Alice Baxter, one of the most driven, dedicated surgeons she'd met at Hope Hospital. Then again, having recently fallen in love with Marco, it was little wonder Alice was loving life and seeing the positive side of everything.

Unlike Finn Morgan…the Caveman of Doom.

Naomi shook the thought away—along with the

image of Finn back in his caveman togs—and pulled out the small notebook she always carried with her. "That sounds amazing. I think I know someone who would really benefit from a therapy dog session."

Finn, for one.

Might help the man grow a heart.

Not that she was still smarting from being kicked out of the surgery. Or was acutely aware that she was the reason it happened. Flashes of connection didn't strike like lightning then just fade away. They burnt.

"Who's it for?" Marco asked. His tone was friendly. Curious.

Unlike Finn, who would've flung the question at her combatively.

Urgh! Stop thinking about Finn!

"Adao. You know, the boy in from Kambela for an arm amputation."

"Yes. Of course. Yesterday, wasn't it? I heard the operation went well."

Naomi gave her best neutral nod. "That's what I hear."

"Sounds like we all *heard* and none of us *saw*. Rumor has it the Beastie Man of Orthopedics kicked everyone out of the observation gallery." He laughed as an idea struck him. "You sure you aren't booking the therapy dog for him?"

"Positive." The more space between Mr. Finn Morgan and her, the better. She'd popped into Adao's room a couple of times after checking the coast was clear. The first time he'd been asleep. The second she had given his shoulders a gentle massage, eyes glued to the door in case she needed to make a swift exit. Official physio wasn't meant to start until tomorrow, but when she'd drawn up enough courage to go to Finn's office and check if that was still the plan, he'd already gone for the night.

The deflation she'd felt at not finding him there had shocked her. It wasn't as if she'd been actually looking forward to seeing him.

Well.

No one liked conflict.

Besides, the man was clearly battling demons on his own. She dealt with hers by putting on an extra-cheery façade and pretending she didn't have a past and he... Well, he growled at people like a grumpy grizzly. So to each his own. Who was she to judge?

"If you're after booking some time with Doodle and Alana, the woman you're after is..." Marco rocked back on his heels and did the air guitar version of a drum-roll. "Evie Cooper! The source of all wisdom at Hope Hospital."

Naomi smiled. Evie. Of course.

"I'll go hunt her down."

"Two guesses as to where you'll find her."

"NICU or PICU?" Naomi smiled. Evie was not only the resident elf, she was the hospital's resident baby whisperer. The whole staff had swelled with pride when word had gone out she was going to fulfil a lifelong dream of finishing her nursing degree.

"Or wherever Mr. Walker might happen to be." Marco smiled then glanced at his watch. "Speaking of which, there is a certain blond surgeon who's no doubt wondering where I am. Good luck with the therapy dog. Hopefully he'll be the secret weapon you were hoping for."

She gave him a wave and headed for the stairwell,

jogging up the stairs to see if she could find Evie before she headed off.

Everyone's schedules had gone absolutely haywire with the arrival of the holiday season. No one was waiting for the first of December to get their holiday groove on. It was as if the opening gala at the hospital had unleashed an entire year's worth of magic fairy dust. Half the hospital seemed to be falling in love and decorating Christmas trees or piling nurses' stations with gingerbread men while cross-checking diaries that drinks dates, department dinners and Secret Santas were all accounted for.

And the other half?

Her own evening diary was as pristine as a snow-covered field. Not that she minded. Much.

The truth was, she had only ever dated men with whom she'd known she had no future. They had tended to be serious, more interested in science than sex. Which was fine with her.

Being with someone…being *happy* with someone… *physical* with someone…it didn't seem fair. Not when everyone she'd loved had had their lives cut so short.

On the flipside, she saw just how unfair life was every day at work and, for the most part, her young patients just got on with it. They accepted that life threw grenades at all sorts of people. There was no rhyme or reason to it. That was just the way it was. So they chose to focus on the positive.

She did on the outside. But inside? It felt as though she was frozen. And in order to survive she needed to stay that way.

When she pushed through to the NICU reception area there was scarcely a soul about.

She looked at her watch. It was after seven. It explained why Finn hadn't been in his office. Not that she'd seen him wandering round the hospital after hours, as she had a tendency to do. What sort of life did he lead after hours if he wasn't part of the "meet for a drink" set? Was he hacking piles of wood to bits with a huge, hand-honed axe?

Or needlepointing tapestries of intricate flower patterns to help him with the delicate art of surgery at which he so clearly excelled?

Pah! Yeah, right.

"Can I help you?" The nurse manager, Janine, looked up from her computer screen where she was updating some charts.

"I was just looking for Evie. I wanted to see if I could get some contact details for Doodle." She laughed and corrected herself. "Alana, his handler, I mean."

"Evie's gone for the night, I'm afraid."

Naomi must have looked downcast at the news because Janine quickly added, "You know, a bunch of the nurses have headed down to the White Hart. If you're looking for something to do…"

Naomi pretended to consider the offer. Maybe it would be a good way to distract her from her thoughts. "It's just off the King's Parade, right?"

"That's the one! Go on," Janine urged. "They're a friendly group. They'd love to have you join them. I think the city's even turned on the Christmas lights so it'll be a lovely walk." She peered over the edge of the nurses' station at Naomi's "uniform" of trainers and athletic wear. "Or cycle? Or run?"

"Walk sounds nice." Naomi smiled. They had turned on the lights. She actually lived nearby and had heard all of the oohs and ahhs as the lights had been switched on, followed by a good hour of excited chatter and laughter.

It would do her good. Even if she just went to see the lights. Give her a reminder of life outside the hospital. She looked down at her trainers. Not really going-out gear, but…why not give it a go? Who knew, maybe she'd take a new route and discover something else about Cambridge to tell Adao about when they began their proper treatment the next day.

Twenty minutes later Naomi was lost. With the medieval twists and turns of the city center and all the twinkling lights, she'd allowed her thoughts to drift away and had lost track of where she was.

She could hear laughter and the sound of a ball game being played nearby. A group of children were obviously playing footie, with someone teasing and cajoling them from the spirited yelps and guffaws traveling round the corner. A sports center, maybe? A small green?

She made a promise to herself to ask the first person she laid eyes on. What she didn't expect was to discover the laughing, fun-loving man powering along the floodlit football pitch with a child hanging off each of his well-built arms was Finn Morgan.

She froze, unable to reconcile the dedicated curmudgeon she knew from the hospital with this bright-eyed, chuckling human climbing frame! He looked positively alight with joy.

Spurring herself into action, she turned to go just as he lifted his head and met her eyes. Their gazes crashed together and locked tight.

Naomi's heart pounded against her chest as she saw

his eyes brighten, then just as quickly turn dull with recognition as the smile faded from his lips.

"Naomi! Hang on a minute."

She looked as surprised as Finn felt. And the look of dismay on her face when he had let his features fall into a frown had touched something deep within him.

He knew hurt.

He knew pain.

And he'd caused both in Naomi.

"Don't go." He scanned his ragtag team of footie mates looking up at him for guidance. He'd never brought a "stranger" to sports night. Hell. He'd not brought anyone anywhere for years.

"Do you think she wants some hot chocolate?" asked Ashley. She was the undisputed leader of the group. One crook of her arm and every single one of those kids followed in her wake.

He glanced back across at Naomi, who was still rooted to the spot.

Yeah. She'd "caught him" in his private place, but it *was* a public playing field. That, and he really had to do something to break the ever-increasing tension building between them. There were only so many alternative routes a man whose patients all required physio in a hospital with one exquisitely talented and beautiful-without-knowing-it physiotherapist could take.

"C'mon." He waved her over, two scrawny six-year-olds still hanging from each arm and—he looked down—yup, two kids on his good leg. At least they had the sense to leave his "robot" leg alone.

The uncertainty in her eyes got to him. He wasn't an ogre.

Well.

Not all the time.

"It's freezing out. Let's get you a cup of hot chocolate. What do you say, lads and ladettes? Hot chocolate all round before I beat you all in the second half?"

Cheers erupted round him and he couldn't resist joining in. These kids were awesome. Some of them had special needs. Some of them were just lonely. For all the beauty and brains Cambridge had on offer, there was also a poorer, lonelier side. Parents working overnight caretaker shifts. Single mums earning just enough to pay the rent and not quite enough to get food on the table. More latchkey kids than there should be. More pain than there should be.

If he could put a two-hour dent in their loneliness and give their cheeks a flush from a bit of a run-around and get some healthy grub into their bellies, then he was all for it. The hot chocolate was just a bonus. So week in, week out, this was his home away from home.

He probably needed them as much as they needed him. They kept him from falling back into that pit of self-loathing that he'd used to ill effect. It had turned out that driving everyone you loved away had a flipside. You were on your own when the demons attacked.

He looked across at Naomi and took an invisible punch to the chest when her features lit up with a genuine smile. A grin, actually. Had he noticed she had dimples before?

Damn. That smile of hers pierced right through to bits of him that hadn't so much as shown a flicker of interest in years. He was no monk, but even his home—a houseboat he'd picked up when he'd been retraining in

London—was something he could unmoor and just…
float away.

It's hot chocolate, you idiot. Not a proposal.

He gently shook the boys off him, doing his best to
avoid Naomi's inquisitive looks. His hand was itching
to reach out to the small of her back, see if touching
her with fourteen layers of clothes on still elicited fireworks. Instead, he grabbed a little curly-haired moppet
under his arm and gave him a quick fist bump. That
sort of contact he could deal with. "All right, matey.
Time to learn a little something about showing some
hospitality."

Finn steered everyone directly toward the sports center's kitchen, which had its own outside entrance. There
was a game going on in the gym he didn't want to interrupt.

"All right, everyone. To your stations!"

The children all ran to their pre-assigned spots and
Finn couldn't help but feel a surge of pride. Not because he wanted to show off in front of Naomi or anything—well, maybe a little—but it was nice to see these
kids so keen to please. When he'd met them, most had
lacked the social skills that would help them on a day-
to-day basis.

"Excuse me, miss?"

Finn grinned. His star "pupil," Archie, was standing in front of Naomi with a little pad of paper in his
hand as if he worked at a Michelin-starred restaurant.
"Please, miss. May I take your hot chocolate order?"

Naomi squatted down so she was about the same
height as Archie.

It was a nice move. Not many people treated these

kids with respect. He shouldn't have been surprised Naomi would be one of them.

"What are my options?" she asked, her eyes twinkling with delight.

"Well…" Archie looked up at Finn with a flash of panic on his face. There weren't really options. It was hot chocolate or…well, hot chocolate. Squash never really got a look-in this time of year.

"Why don't you ask the lady—whose name is Miss Collins—if she'd like it hot or cold, and whether or not she might like marshmallows on top?"

"There are marshmallows?" Archie looked around at his playmates in disbelief. A ripple of excited whispers turned into a sea of high fives and whoops when Finn reached up above one of the cupboards where he'd stashed a tin of Christmas-tree-shaped marshmallows and revealed them to the children.

Wide-eyed, Naomi reached to the floor to steady herself.

What? A man wasn't allowed to indulge in a bit of home economics?

A soldier—an *ex*-soldier—had to feed himself. Especially when he'd told everyone who was dear to him to bugger off.

Turned out water biscuits and cheese did not maketh the man.

"But, Finn!" Archie shook his hands in exasperation. The kid had Asperger's and always had to get things exactly right before he could move forward on any project. Even putting home-made marshmallows into hot chocolate. "Marshmallows are made from horses' hooves, which also bear a similarity to reindeer hooves, which, if you consider the season—"

"Whoa there, mate." Finn gave his shoulder a reassuring squeeze then lifted one of the little tree-shaped confections and popped it into his mouth. "These little babies are as pure as the driven snow. No horse hooves. No reindeer feet. Get your pen ready. I used vegan gelatin." He ticked off the ingredients on his fingers slowly because he knew Archie would want to write them down. "Water. Sugar. Fairtrade." He threw a look in Naomi's direction, not entirely sure why he cared that she knew he bought Fairtrade, but…whatever. Proof he had a heart, he guessed. "Icing sugar. Salt and vanilla."

"My mother says sugar is evil," one of the children jumped in.

"Only evil if it's your only food group." And he should know. He'd survived off a stale box of party rings for a week once when his knee had been giving him jip. Weeks like that one had been the beginnings of finding the fight again. The will to live versus survival.

So he'd cracked open a recipe book and—*voilà*. Turned out he could cook.

"Extract or flavoring?" asked Archie.

"Extract. Only the good stuff for you lot."

He reached up again and pulled down another tin, revealing a couple of dozen flapjacks dotted with cranberries and dried apricots and whatever else he'd found in his cupboards before his shift this morning.

Archie cleared his throat and started again. "Miss Collins, would I be able to interest you in one of Cambridge sports club's finest instant hot chocolate sachets with a topping of home-crafted marshmallows?"

Naomi gave the ends of her red woolen scarf a tug and gave a low whistle. "Wow. That's quite an offer. I would be delighted. Now…" she reached out a hand to Archie "…what did you say your name was? Mine's Naomi."

Archie looked up at Finn—a clear plea for permission to shake the pretty lady's hand. Finn nodded.

"Can I make it?" Ashley shot her hand up into the air as far as it would go.

"I don't know, can you?"

"*May* I make it," corrected Ashley. *"Please?"*

"I want to pour the water!" Jimbo—their littlest warrior—leapt to the hot water urn.

"Whoa, there, soldiers. Who's the only man on campus who does the boiling water?"

"You!" all the children shouted, their arms moving as one toward him followed by a little cheer that always cracked him up.

These kids were nuts.

He gave a couple of their sweaty little heads a scrub and as he turned to get to work caught Naomi looking at him with an expression of pure warmth. It disappeared so quickly when she saw he was looking at her it was akin to seeing a falling star.

Little short of a miracle.

Naomi felt as if she'd walked into an alternate universe.

Finn Morgan made marshmallows and flapjacks?

She tried to picture him wearing a frilly pinafore and oven mitts and came up with… Oh, my, that was all she pictured him in.

Unexpected.

Was that what a glimpse of the "heart of gold" could do to a girl? Turn a man naked in her imagination?

Crikey.

She gave her head a shake and watched as all the children fell into place for what was obviously a finely tuned routine.

The littlest kids pulled out mugs from the lower shelves of the sports center's kitchen. Bigger ones emptied packets of hot chocolate into the mugs—about a dozen all told. One—who seemed to be the mini-matriarch of the pack—slotted herself in and around them to wipe up any stray chocolate powder.

One scuttled up to Finn, who was holding court at the hot-water urn—wise, considering the sign on the metal urn warned that the water was at a boiling temperature at all times—and beckoned to him that he wanted to whisper something in his ear.

Finn knelt down, his eyes shifting up to the ceiling as the little boy cupped his hands round Finn's ear and whispered. Finn's gray eyes traveled to the two mugs in the little boy's hands and said something in a low rumbling voice then tipped his head in Naomi's direction. "Go on."

The little boy shook his head and pressed the mugs into Finn's huge hands. Had she actually noticed how big his hands were?

He rose to his full height and turned to her.

Gulp.

About as big as the rest of him.

"Miss Collins, would you like the flowery mug or the ladybird mug with a chip in it? Jamie is sorry in advance about the chip, but he can recommend use of the ladybird mug from personal experience." He held them out to her, his features looking as serious as if he were offering her a choice between food for the rest of the month or famine. From the look on Jamie's face, it was on a par.

"Well…" She rose so that she could examine the mugs with proper consideration then gave Jamie a serious nod. "I think I'd like the ladybird mug, if that's all right? Seeing as it comes so highly rated."

The little boy's face nearly split in two with an ear-to-ear grin as he tugged at Finn's shirt. "I told you."

"Well, then, Jamie. Maybe next time you can be brave enough to ask her yourself."

Finn's eyes never left hers as he spoke.

Next time?

She was astonished there was a first time, let alone… Was this an olive branch? His way of saying he was sorry for raking her over the coals at the hospital?

Her heart skipped a beat.

"Finn, look." A little boy came over to him, a marshmallow stuck on each of his index fingers. "I am the ghost of Christmas past!"

And just like that the moment was gone and a new, sillier one had begun. Naomi didn't know whether to be grateful or wistful.

After a few minutes of fussing about with stirring hot chocolates into mugs, doling out the remaining marshmallows and filling kitchen towel squares with a flapjack each, the motley crew were told to head toward the benches in the gym to watch the game.

"Game?"

Finn was shuttling a couple of the children past her as she asked. He dropped an unexpected wink her way.

"You'll see."

When the door to the gym was pushed open, Naomi's eyes widened with delight.

A full-on game of wheelchair basketball was under

way complete with heated banter and the non-stop squeak and squeal of wheels on the gym floor. It was mesmerizing.

About a dozen men and women—all in low-slung, wide-angle-wheelchairs—were careening round the gym with all the focused intent of a professional sports team. The atmosphere was absolutely electric.

"All right, chaps and chapesses." Finn issued a few instructions to his team, holding a couple of the steaming mugs of chocolate aloft as they clambered onto the benches to watch the game. From the gleams of excitement in their eyes this was clearly one of the highlights of their night out.

"Want to grab a pew or are you happy here?"

Finn stood beside Naomi, eyes glued to the game, but his presence… It was weird to say, but…it felt like their bodies were *flirting*. Which was completely mental.

Particularly considering she didn't flirt.

She did happy.

She did bubbly.

Flutter her eyelashes and blush like a maiden on the brink of a kiss?

Nope. That wasn't her. Not by a long shot. Because if she were to allow herself to feel good things, she'd inevitably also feel all the bad things, too. And she never wanted to go back there. Because the bad things came cloaked in a bone-deep fear that was too terrifying to even consider confronting. Once had been more than enough.

"Naomi?"

"Happy here, thanks." She took a sip of her chocolate and gave Finn a bright grin. "These marshmallows are amazing. You should sell them at the hospital café."

Finn barked a laugh. "Yeah. I'm sure Theo would love me upping the obesity rate right there on the hospital mezzanine."

Stung, she looked away. "I was hardly suggesting—" She stopped when she felt Finn's hand on her arm, the heat of it searing straight through the triple layers of her outdoor wear.

"Sorry. I didn't mean it like that."

"You never do, do you?"

Finn stepped back and shoved his free hand through that tangle of dark, wavy hair that was all but begging for someone who looked a lot like her to do the same. He never broke eye contact and it took just about all the willpower she possessed not to look away.

"No," he finally said. "I don't."

She had absolutely no reason to believe him. But she did. Something about the flashes of light hitting those steel-gray eyes of his…they spoke volumes. He knew pain. He'd seen it in her eyes just as she'd seen it in his.

At least she now knew they shared some common ground.

His home-made marshmallows were also ridiculously lovely.

Silver linings and all that.

They watched the rest of the game in silence. It was a revelation, watching the hard-core stamina of the wheelchair users in action.

A few minutes later when the whistle was blown he strode across to a man with a pitch-black buzz cut and piercing blue eyes. When both of them looked her way she checked behind her to see what they were looking at. When she looked back, Finn was beckoning her to come over.

"Naomi, I'd like you to meet one of my oldest—'

"Hold up!" The man interrupted. "Longest term—not oldest. Let's keep this accurate." He laughed good-naturedly. "You may continue."

Finn gave his friend a punch in the arm then, still smiling, began the introduction again. "Naomi the Physio meet Charlie the Basketball champ." The change in his tone and demeanor was as warming to her belly as the hot chocolate had been. The two men obviously shared a deep friendship. It was nice to see Finn had so much more to him than gruff bluster and, of course, his incredible reputation as a surgeon.

"Champ?" she asked, truly impressed.

Charlie waved off the title. "Just a couple of regional matches where we beat the pants off the other county teams. Funding's always a problem, but we're hoping to get to the Commonwealth Games next time they come round in the UK. I might be a bit long in the tooth by then, but some of these whippersnappers might still be up to it." He raised his voice and aimed it in their direction. "So long as they all keep listening to my outstanding coaching!"

They sent back their own set of razzes then took the children up on their offer to pour water for them all from the big cooler at the end of the court.

Naomi stood with Charlie as Finn jogged across to oversee the "catering."

"You two together?"

Naomi sucked in her breath and gave an incredulous laugh. "No. I was just walking past and saw them playing. We work together. That's all."

"Huh." Charlie pinned his bright blue eyes on her,

as if to say, *I'm more than happy to wait it out until you come clean.*

It didn't take long.

"Honestly. We don't really know each other. The hospital's still relatively new. I do my thing. He does his."

"Yeah, well. I think there might be a little bit o' the lady protesting too much." He chuckled and gave the beads of sweat on his brow a swipe. "I've known Finn a long time and he's never brought anyone in here to see him do his thing before."

"Oh." Seriously? Then again…the man played his cards so close to his chest she sometimes wondered if he'd even seen them. But the only one to ever see him do this amazing work? "Well… I did just happen to be walking past, so…"

"So nothing. I haven't seen him look at anyone like that since the divorce went through."

"Finn was married?"

You could've knocked her over with a feather.

Maybe that explained why his male-female relations were so…rusty. Not that she wanted him to flirt with her or anything. Her eyes traveled across the gym to where a gaggle of children were clamoring to get his attention.

Her heart did a little skippity-hop as their eyes met and he dropped her a quick wink before returning his focus to the children.

Maybe she did.

"Oops. My bad. Open mouth, insert foot!" Charlie grinned unapologetically. "Look. Finn and I go way back. Did our basic training together when we were fresh out of school. Never met anyone who wanted to be an army man more. He started young with everything, precocious upstart that he was." Charlie grinned, his voice warm with genuine affection. "Finn comes from a long line of army men so the second he could enlist he did. Would have lied about it if that sort of thing were possible these days. He married young, too. Then got himself blown up after just a couple of tours in the Middle East, but…" he paused for effect "…not before he saved my life."

What?

An action hero on top of everything else?

Still waters did run deep. At least in the case of Finn Morgan.

"That one?" Naomi pointed across the gym to where Finn was teaching the children how to turn their hands into "pilot goggles" then scanned Charlie's face for signs of a wind-up. "That Finn Morgan saved your life?"

"Too right he did." He gave her a quick glance as if trying to get a gauge on her "combat story readiness."

He wheeled his chair closer to her, looked her straight in the eye and said, "If Finn Morgan hadn't thrown himself on top of me that day, I wouldn't be here."

His tone was enough for Naomi to decipher what he was really saying. Finn Morgan had sacrificed his leg to save his friend's life.

She was about to ask how he'd ended up in the chair but Charlie beat her to the punch. "This happened later. On my next tour. I shipped out while Finn was in rehab. He took it hard. Pushed everyone he loved as far away from him as he could."

Naomi could hardly get her head around the fact that Mr. Grumpy liked to play footie with kids with special needs who he handcrafted seasonal treats for, let alone take in the huge news that not only was he a hero, he was also a broken-hearted divorcee.

"Including his wife?"

It felt such an intimate question to ask.

"Including his wife. She moved on but Finn hasn't. May never forgive himself. He was a seething ball of fury by the time I came back for my own stint in rehab." He shrugged it all off. "He just poured all of his energies into retraining as a pediatric ortho king and…' he blew an imaginary trumpet fanfare from his hand '…*voilà*! Look who is one of the country's top limb specialists. An amazing guy."

This was more than peeling away the layers, like an onion, and finding out there was a diamond in the rough. It was like opening up an enormously intimidating book, only to find the binding and outer layers disguised an enormous and generous heart.

CHAPTER SIX

"FINN! ARE YOU coming along to the Christmas quiz night at the Fox and Hounds?"

Finn scrunched the paper he was drying his hands with into a ball and threw it into the nearby bin. "Nope."

"Now, there's a surprise." Amanda rolled her eyes and laughed good-naturedly. "Don't think a handful of 'nopes' is going to stop me from trying, though."

Finn bit back his usual retort—*good luck with that*—and did his best to give her a better-luck-next-time smile before heading toward the stairs. It wasn't her fault that ducking out of social gatherings was his forte. Especially at this time of year. Everything seemed infused with extra meaning. Intent. He figured Amanda would catch on soon enough. Finn Morgan wasn't a social creature.

So what the hell was he doing, heading down to the physio gym with a bit of extra fire in his step?

No prizes for guessing the answer there. A sweet, soft smile.

He was hoping for a dose of both.

He may not win Hope Children's Hospital's Most Sociable Doc Award, but it seemed as though he'd done a one-eighty on how he felt about "Naomi run-ins."

The encounter at "his" sports center had changed everything. Letting someone see his private self, the side he allowed to have fun—to *care*—hadn't been the horror show he'd thought it would be.

His world hadn't shattered into bits. He hadn't flared up in anger as he had at his family and wife. His heart still beat. Beat faster, if he was being truly honest.

And, of course, it wasn't just any old someone.

It was Naomi.

Instead of rubbing him up the wrong way, he was experiencing an entirely new breed of agitation.

He actually caught himself *smiling* when their appointments overlapped. Feeling concern when he saw her shoulders tense up in advance of going into Adao's room. Actual, honest-to-God pleasure shot through his veins when she clapped and hugged a patient who'd achieved a new benchmark.

Curiosity teased at his nerve endings. What would it feel like to be on the receiving end of one of those hugs? One of those smiles?

Which was why the deserted physiotherapy gym was getting a bit more after-hours attention from him than usual.

One man. One gym. A perfect night. The best way to pummel all the feelings straight out of his system.

At least that's how it had worked in the "before Naomi" days.

Now that he'd let himself see beyond the beautiful, chirpy façade of hers, and he'd realized she seemed to have every bit as much going on beneath the surface as he did, the gym felt empty if she wasn't there. He'd almost grown to anticipate the quiet way she had of looking at him when he'd been a bit too gruff. The slip of her gaze from his eyes to his hips then his knee on days his leg was giving him jip. The way her cheeks had pinked up when he'd winked at her that night at the gym.

Winked!

What the hell? The last thing his ex would've accused him of was being soppy and yet…each time he walked through the deserted corridors and pushed through the doors to the physio gym, he caught himself hunting for signs of her. A stray clipboard, a little cloud of her perfume, a Hope Hospital hoodie hanging in the small office she used in the corner of the gym.

True, he could've gone to any gym, anywhere in Cambridge, but something about coming to the playground atmosphere of the hospital's physio ward appealed to him. A reminder that if children could push themselves to work harder, achieve their goals, then he could, too.

There were the standard weights and cardio machines any adult physiotherapy center would have. Running machines. Static bicycles. A small set of steps. Massage tables.

But the walls were painted with colorful murals. There was a climbing wall. It was too small for him but it never failed to capture his interest. All of the "rocks" were shaped like dinosaurs. Each time he came down here he traced a new path to the top. And there was also— Ah! A zip wire. And tonight it was in use.

"That's right, Ellie." Naomi was helping a blonde ponytailed girl establish her grip on the bar. "Now, off you go and hold, hold, hold, hold… Hooray!"

Naomi applauded as the young girl—maybe around ten—landed on the huge gym mats at the far end of the zip-wire run.

"Looks like fun."

Naomi snapped to attention, obviously unaware he'd been watching them.

"Yes." She looked at her young charge for confirmation, as if she wasn't entirely sure whether to be happy or wary to see Finn. Wow. That stung. Guess he only had himself to blame.

"What do you think, Ellie? Have you been having fun?"

"Definitely." The girl's eyes shone with pride. "Especially now the distal radius epiphys...epiphysss..."

"Epiphysititis," Naomi and Finn said as one.

Ellie laughed and called out, "Snap!"

Finn just stared. Naomi's eyes were about as deep brown as a woman's eyes could get. A man could get lost in them if he had nothing but time.

She drew in a quick breath and turned back to her young charge.

"I think there should be a rule that until you can say the word, it's not completely gone." Naomi nudged the girl with her hip and Ellie giggled.

"Okay. It's not *gone* gone...but now that the cast is off and I can use my wrist again, I can get back to gymnastics practice, right?"

"Well...that's what we're here to establish, young lady."

The way Naomi's dark eyes twinkled and the corners of her mouth were twitching, it was easy to see she was teasing the girl. He liked that. Having patients think they're playing rather than working was half the battle on the rehabilitation side of things. Naomi was obviously excellent at her job—and enjoyed doing it.

"C'mon, please?" Ellie put her hands into prayer position. "That's the first time I've done the zip wire without letting go."

"A zip wire's one thing. Vaulting is another."

Ellie scanned the room, her eyes alighting on Finn. "I bet I could vault him."

Naomi's eyes widened and a hit of the giggles struck her hard and fast.

"What?" Finn gave a mock frown. "I put Ellie's cast on, if memory serves." With a huge grin, Naomi nodded. "I also took the cast off, which would indicate it was healed. So…tell me, Miss Collins, what exactly is the problem with Ellie here using me as a human vault?"

"Er…health and safety for one?" She crossed her arms playfully and gave him her best what-are-you-going-to-say-to-that-one-pal? look. "Her muscle strength would have deteriorated."

"Not that much!" Ellie pointed at the zip wire as if it was proof she was ready for the next phase. "Look! I can do handstands on the mat, no problem."

They watched and, yes, she could indeed do handstands perfectly well.

"Well." Finn turned to Naomi when Ellie put her hands into prayer position again and gave them both a doleful round of puppy-dog eyes. "I doubt she was planning on vaulting all six foot two inches of me, were you, Ellie?" He pressed himself up to his full height and actually—oh, good grief—he'd actually swelled his chest a bit. Like a cartoon character.

Why are you showboating like this?

Mercifully, Ellie was oblivious to his lame attempt at flirting with Naomi. She was already dragging a mat over alongside the ball pit. "Look, Naomi, I won't do the splits version. I'll just do a simple handspring. If Finn kneels on here…" Ellie eyeballed him for a minute and he tried not to laugh. He'd never really been considered as gymnastics equipment before. Ellie pointed at Finn to relocate himself. Stat. "Mr. Morgan, you have to kneel here and then I'll do a quick run-up on the mats here and when I do the handstand over you, I'll land in the ball pit so it'll be totally safe."

Naomi tilted her head to the side and stared at him. If he thought he was being considered for anything more than a stand-in vaulting horse he would've read something into it. But this was work and it was easy enough to see Naomi's focus was one hundred percent on her patient's safety. As his should be. Which did beg the question…

"You ready, Finn?"

"If we have Naomi's stamp of approval."

Finn and Ellie turned to Naomi as one and the smile that lit up her face at both of their expectant expressions was like the sun emerging from a cloud on a summer's day. Pure light.

Damn, she was beautiful.

"Fine!" She threw up her hands. "Under two conditions. One…" She gave Naomi a stern look. "I will stand by to spot you. And two…" She looked at Finn and then quickly shifted her gaze to his knee. "If you think you're up to it."

He did a squat, as if that was the ultimate proof he could kneel on all fours.

Hmm… That was what her expression said. She drummed her fingers on her lips for a moment then put up a finger. "Hang on a minute." She jogged to the far end of the room and rummaged through a drawer for a minute. She brandished an elasticated wrist brace as if it were a long-sought-after treasure. "Put this on first."

"Thank you, Naomi!" Ellie threw her arms around

Naomi then pulled on the brace and eyed Finn with the cool acuity of a girl who knew her way around a competitive gymnastics tournament. "Are you ready, Mr. Morgan?"

"As I'll ever be." He went down on all fours and steadied himself, wondering how the hell he'd gone from wanting a quiet workout on his own to being part of a ten-year-old's gymnastic ambitions.

He looked straight ahead of him to where Naomi had relocated herself to spot Ellie if she needed it.

Her dark eyes shimmered with delight for Ellie as she executed the move to perfection and, much to his satisfaction, when he rose to his full height in front of Naomi, there was an extra flash of pleasure just for him.

After Ellie's mum had come and collected her and she'd been signed off to go on her gymnastics tournament— "using the brace!"—Naomi returned to the gym, surprised to find Finn was still there.

"Did you need anything?" She'd not been alone with him since he'd bitten her head off before Adao's arrival, but seeing him at the sports center the other day seemed to have softened the tension that often crackled between them. Further evidence that gold heart the charge nurse had alluded to wasn't a myth.

"Nope." Finn looked around him as if sizing up the place. "I sometimes sneak down here after hours for a bit of a workout, but having stood in as a human gymnasium was good enough for tonight."

Naomi laughed. "I suspect it wasn't really on a par with your normal workouts."

She saw him start to say something, his eyes alight

with fun, and then bite it back, his expression turning back to the thunder face she was more used to.

She turned away so he wouldn't see the disappointment in her eyes. And the shock. Who would've thought a chance sighting at a sports center and a brief encounter in the gym would've brought out a side to him that made him…well…really attractive. If she hadn't been mistaken, he'd been on the brink of flirting with her. But the part that had shocked her? It was that she had wanted him to.

Flirt! With *her*. The one woman in the whole of Hope Children's Hospital who seemed to rub him up the wrong way just by appearing.

She dug rhe fingernails of one hand into the palm of the other. The woman who liked to keep her own heart as locked away as he seemed to.

Whether she liked it or not, they just might be birds of a feather.

At least it explained the tension.

"Here. Let me help you with that." Finn reached out for the same mat Naomi was lifting and their hands brushed. He pulled his hand back as if she'd branded him with her fingers. She rolled her eyes.

Here we go. Back on familiar territory.

The Mark of The Evil Physiotherapist.

She pulled the mat over to the stack alongside the wall, laid it in place and tried to shake off the grumpy thoughts.

Maybe it was simpler than like attracting like.

Maybe it was a case of a man dealing with his own frailties. Someone as physically capable-looking as Finn—an actual war hero—would not like to be seen as weak, and she'd caught him in an incredibly private

moment the other day. Or maybe he'd had an evil physiotherapist back in the day. Not that she was going to
ask but physiotherapy wasn't always as fun as it had
just been with Ellie. And recovering from an amputation surgery was tough. Just seeing the abject misery
on Adao's face brought tears to her eyes.

Finn was a big, strong, physical man. Before his injury she could just imagine how fit he must've been.
A young man at the height of his strength and fitness,
only to have it taken away by the horror of war. What
the man deserved was compassion—not huffs of frustration. It didn't stop her from smarting that he'd rolled
back on the flirty behavior he'd shown when Ellie had
been in the room. Maybe having her there made it safe.
A buffer to ensure nothing would ever really happen.

She knew that feeling. Keeping people at arm's
length was her specialty. Except her patients. Her patients *always* went straight to the center of her heart.

"I'm good here if you wanted to get on," she eventually said when all the mats were back in place.

"I was thinking of heading down to the sports center. I owe Charlie a pint after the game the other day."

"Ah." Was she supposed to be inviting herself along
or telling him to get a move on?

"You live in town, don't you?"

Was he feeling as awkward as she felt? Because this
whole chitchat thing was… Neither of them was really
excelling at it.

"Yes."

*Why don't you invite yourself along, you idiot? He's
clearly trying to ask you if you want to come.*

"Would you like to walk into town? Together?" He

shifted his weight and kicked up the pace. "And then, of course, I'll go and meet Charlie."

She smiled. It was strangely refreshing to be with someone as awkward at the "making friends" thing as she was.

"Sounds good. I'll just grab my jacket." She jogged across to the small glass office, willing it to magically get curtains or one-way glass so she could bang her head against the wall. *What was she thinking?*

Her heart was pounding against her chest as white noise filled her head.

C'mon, c'mon, c'mon! Behave like a normal human.

It was a walk.

Just a plain old walk. As she stared at her thickly padded winter coat she smiled. Plus point. It was cold enough that they didn't even have to talk if they didn't want to.

Oh, good grief. If they lived at the North Pole maybe. Not Cambridge.

What on earth was she going to talk to Finn Morgan about for twenty whole minutes? How he made her insides turn into an entirely new weather system? How she didn't normally blush when men winked at her? Or how, even if the blush led to something more, he could never follow through because she'd left her heart behind in Africa?

"Everything all right in there?"

"Yeah. Great!" Wow. She didn't know her voice went that high. "'Course. Why?"

"Well…" Finn looked at her through slightly narrowed eyes. "You're just…standing there. Have you lost something?"

My sanity.

"Nope! All good." She pulled on her hoodie and then her puffer jacket over it, yanking the zipper up so fast she nearly caught her chin in it when she hit the top. "Ready to go?"

Finn was really beginning to question his own grip on reality. What was he *doing*?

First, acting like a first-class show-off idiot in the gym.

Second, asking to walk a girl home like he was a nineteen-fifties teenage boy.

And, third, making up a story about meeting Charlie for a drink when he knew damn well his friend was at home, helping his children decorate the Christmas tree.

What a doofus.

Way to show the pretty girl you like her. Walking mutely along the festively lit streets of Cambridge as if you couldn't wait to shake her off.

Which he couldn't.

He pretended he had to scratch his chin on his shoulder so he could see if she looked as uncomfortable as he felt.

Yup! Pretty much. Romeo of Cambridge strikes again!

Not that he was courting her or anything like that. They were just colleagues, walking down the cobbled streets of a particularly attractive-looking university city on a frosty, clear-skied, festively lit night. Just the type of night that would be perfect for holding one of her mittened hands.

If he liked her that way.

Which he didn't. Not least of all because his dating track record after his ex totaled a handful of one-night stands that never should've happened. Turned out the chicks didn't dig a surly one-legged bastard intent on becoming the best pediatric limb specialist in the UK.

He gave his face a scrub and groaned.

"Oh, my goodness!"

Though she whispered it, Finn heard Naomi's exclamation.

He dropped his hand, hoping she hadn't seen his what-the-hell-am-I-doing-here face. The last thing he needed to introduce into his life was romance. Saying that, he'd be little short of an idiot to ignore the chemistry between the pair of them.

Then again, he was pretty skilled at being an idiot.

What a nightmare.

"Is that…? Is that *Santa*?"

Finn looked to his left and saw Santa appear around a corner. He turned back to Naomi, only to see she was looking the opposite direction…at another Santa.

They and the Santas were just entering Market Square in the city center. The temporary vendors had taken the "deck the halls" edict to the fullest definition. There were long swags of evergreen caught up in bright red velvet ribbons twirled around the lampposts, giving them a North Pole effect. The shopfronts all glittered and twinkled with their own festive displays. The daytime vendors had handed over to the temporary Christmas market stalls that were positively bursting with seasonal delights—edible and otherwise. Someone was roasting actual chestnuts over a crackling fire and from just about every street that led onto the small square was a Santa. And another and another until it finally dawned on them.

"We're in a Santa flash mob!"

They blinked at one another.

Again they'd spoken in tandem. And something about the synchronicity of the moment felt like fairy dust and kismet. Just like the atmosphere in the square. Someone had put on some music and was piping it through speakers Finn couldn't quite locate. Maybe in the vicinity of the huge Christmas tree lit up in a swirl of tiny golden lights.

"C'mon. If we go over here, up onto the church steps, you should be able to see."

"See what?" Naomi jogged a few steps to catch up with him.

"The dancing. I've seen this type of thing on the internet. The Santas all get together, do a dance or sing a carol."

Naomi stopped and blinked her disbelief. "You watch flash mobs on the internet?"

"Moi?" He feigned horror at the thought then shrugged a confessional, "Yeah, maybe…"

Naomi was more than familiar with his roughty-toughty grumble-guts routine. Not that he put it on or anything, she just…there was something about her that spoke to him and somewhere along the way he'd lost his ability to speak back. Growling was a go-to reaction. Overreaction, from the look of things. When she smiled…something he'd seen far too little of…it felt as though his whole world was lighting up from the inside out.

"C'mon." He held his arm out to block the crowds so Naomi could get through and find a good spot to watch as the Santas did, in fact, fall into formation and perform a street dance to a new Christmas song that had whisked its way to the top of the pop charts.

Finn was enjoying watching Naomi every bit as much as he was enjoying the Santas. Her smile was bright and genuine. She clapped along with the crowd when all the Santas encouraged them to do so. She even threw in a few "Woos!" when the dancing elves who'd joined the Santas pulled off a particularly athletic dance sequence. At one point, she dropped her hands after a brisk rub together and one of them shifted against Finn's. Her eyes sped to his as if she'd felt the exact same thing he had when they'd touched. Fireworks.

Naomi was grateful to have found mittens in her pocket for a number of reasons.

One. It was freezing.

Two. They gave her something to fiddle with when Finn looked at her so intently she thought those gray eyes of his were going to bore a hole straight through her and see the myriad sensations that went off in her head when their hands had brushed.

And, three…

There wasn't really a three, other than they were a similar shade of gray to Finn's eyes, which she could not stop staring into, so she needed to make her excuses and go.

"I'm really sorry, I need to—"

"I suppose Charlie's probably waiting for me at the—"

They stared at one another for a moment, their breath coming out in little white puffs, the music and excitement of the flash mob buzzing around them like a blur of fireflies.

"Neither of us are particularly good at finishing sentences tonight," Finn finally said. He tipped his head toward the opposite end of the square but didn't explain why.

"No." Naomi's lips remained frozen in the "O" they'd formed as she looked up at him.

It would be so easy to close that small gap between them. If she just rose up on to the tips of her nearly frozen toes...

"I guess you'd better get to your meeting," she said.

"What?"

Yeah. What? You were having a moment.

"With Charlie? Aren't you meeting Charlie for a drink?" she reminded him.

What are you *doing*? The man was obviously trying to get to know her. He probably just needed a friend. It would be mean to shut him down. Especially since she could do with someone to talk to as well. Someone who understood the types of feelings patients like Adao elicited.

Guilt.

Fear.

Bone-deep sorrow.

Finn shoved his hands in his pockets and cleared his throat. "Yes. Absolutely right. Charlie's probably on his second pint by now." He flicked his hand toward the dispersing Santas. "Easily distracted tonight."

His gray eyes returned to hers, his look so intense she blinked and had to look away.

"Right, well. Thanks for the escort. I mean...company walking back."

"You're all right to get to your flat on your own?"

She looked at Finn as if he'd grown wings and popped on a halo. What was he doing? Going for boy scout of the year to make up for being such a grouch the other day? Or was he actually a genuinely nice guy outside the hospital walls? Maybe he was a bit like her. Wore a mask to work and took it off once he was alone. Only they seemed to have chosen opposite masks to cope. He'd looked so content, so happy with the children at the sports center and even now there were glimmers of that guy standing right in front of her, waiting for her to say something. Do something.

She simply didn't know how to access the "old" Naomi. The one who had never once imagined a world without her parents or boyfriend in it.

"I'm fine." She gave him a tight smile and a little wave and left before they drew out what was quickly becoming a shambles of a farewell.

It wasn't until she'd run up the stairs to her flat, opened the door, thrown her keys into the bowl on the table by the door, just as she'd done every night ever since the hospital had opened, and flicked on the light that she realized she wasn't fine at all.

She had been thrown off balance.

By the unexpected fun of the flash mob.

The impending session she was going to hold with Adao, who still had to crack a smile.

But most of all by Finn.

It had been a long time since someone had unnerved her in this way. And she wasn't entirely sure which way she was hoping it would go.

CHAPTER SEVEN

"DON'T WORRY, ADAO. It's still early days." Naomi rubbed her hand across the little boy's shorn head and tried to coax a smile out of his somber little face.

She'd been giving him a massage and manipulating his shoulder joints to try and prevent any blood clots. This type of physiotherapy was critical at this phase of his recovery. And painful, too.

Adao dropped his head and it all but broke Naomi's heart to see two fat tears fall onto his blanket.

"I want Mama and Baaba." Adao's voice caught on the final word and he barely managed to stem a sob.

Naomi ached to pull him into her arms. Tell him everything would be all right. His loneliness and grief tore at her chest with a ferocity she hadn't felt in years.

She wanted her mother and father, too. Not a single day had passed since they'd been stolen away that she hadn't ached for their presence in her life. And that of her boyfriend. All lost to a foolish war that had, ultimately, come to nothing. Her country was run by the military now. It was a place she'd never be able to call home again.

"I know, love. I know." She gave his head a soft caress and before she could think better of it dropped a kiss on top of his head and pulled him to her for a half-hug, doing her best not to put any pressure on his loosely bandaged wound.

"Hey!"

They both looked up as Finn appeared at the doorway. His hair looked like he'd just come in from a windstorm and his eyes were bright with energy. He gave the doorframe a couple of polite knocks after he'd quickly taken in the scene. "Mind if I come in?"

Adao didn't even bother to disguise the tears now pouring down his gorgeous plump cheeks.

Finn's eyebrows instantly drew together and he crossed the room in three quick long-legged strides. "Are you in pain, little man?"

Adao shook his head. Then nodded. Then shrugged as the tears continued to fall. It was all Naomi could do not to burst into tears herself.

Physio was often difficult. Often produced tears. Tears of frustration. Tears of pride on a good day, but this was different.

He was a lonely, lost, terrified little boy who wanted his parents.

"Naomi's not been putting you through her torture chamber, has she, mate?"

A few days ago Naomi would've taken umbrage at the question, but now, having seen a new side of Finn, she took it for what it was. A playful attempt to draw a smile from a frightened child. To be honest, she was grateful for the intervention as she was struggling to find anything to say that would make him feel better.

Finn pulled a chair up alongside Adao's bed across from Naomi. He held out his hand for Adao's. When

Adao didn't move his, Finn took it in both of his own, ducking his head so he could catch the little boy's eyes.

"Listen, bud. I know this is tough. You know I know, right?"

Adao nodded.

"I showed you mine…and pretty soon you'll be able to show me yours."

"But…all I have is…is…" Adao whispered, tears falling everywhere as he turned to look at his heavily bandaged shoulder. He was still a good week—maybe even a fortnight—away from trying out a prosthesis.

"I know." Finn shot a quick look at Naomi, who pulled a fresh packet of tissues out of her pocket and put them in Adao's lap, keeping one for herself. Just in case.

Definitely, more like. She was already scanning her brain for a private corner just as soon as was humanly possible.

"Bud, look at me. You're talking to someone who's been there and has come out on the other side. The good side. You've got a while yet with the compression garments. They'll support your arm—"

Adao let out a small whimper and then began to cry in earnest.

Just then one of the local hospital volunteers— a lovely grandmotherly type called Mabel—came in with a cup of steaming tea cradled in her hands. She'd assigned herself the task of reading Adao stories since the charity that had brought him here was unable to provide "on the ground" support.

"Oh, Adao!" She threw a quick inquisitive look at Naomi and nodded at the spot where she stood. Obviously it was "her" spot. "Do you mind? I think maybe we need a bit of quiet time."

A swarm of responses jammed in Naomi's throat. All of them were a muddled ache to help and the conflicting, urgent need to push everything back into place that this moment was unzipping.

"Of course." She stepped away from the bed. There was no point in telling Adao she'd be back the next morning. And the next. He was leaning into Mabel's arms and giving himself over entirely to his grief.

Finn took up Adao's charts and quietly explained to Mabel about when to call the nurses for pain management or, if things took a turn for the worse, when to call him.

Naomi felt invisible. Worse, actually. She felt powerless.

Just as she had on *that* day nearly fifteen years ago when her heart had pounded so loudly she could barely hear the shouts and screams. Shame washed over her as the memories slammed to the fore. Her hiding place. The gunfire. The stench of hot metal filling her nostrils as she'd clenched her eyes tight against what she'd known was happening.

Everyone she loved had gone when she'd found the courage to open them again. Fear had turned her into a coward—not a hero like Finn. And with that knowledge came another bitter home truth. She did not deserve unconditional love. She'd thought she'd loved her parents and boyfriend unconditionally, but she had failed at the first hurdle and had just saved herself. And for that solitary selfish act, she could never forgive herself.

"Naomi! Wait." Finn jogged to catch up to her. Damn, she could crank up the speed when she wanted to. No doubt all that running she did along the river.

Not that he'd clocked her doing her stretches outside the hospital most days before shift. No…he didn't do things like that. The less you knew about someone, the easier it was not to care.

And yet here he was, actively avoiding his own advice. Maybe Christmas was a time of miracles.

"Let me take you to lunch."

Her eyes went wide. He fought not to do the same. He didn't ask women to lunch.

Colleague.

A colleague wrestling with the age-old dilemma. Getting too close to a patient. Most of the time the essential emotional distance needed just clicked into place. It didn't take a brain surgeon—or someone who'd been forced to go through a shedload of PTSD counseling as he had—to see this little boy had wormed his way straight into her heart. And he knew he wasn't the only one to have noticed.

"I've already had a sandwich, thanks." Her tone was apologetic rather than dismissive. And if he wasn't mistaken, the swipe at her eyes wasn't a bit of primping. She was fighting tears.

"Coffee, then." He steered her toward the elevators and put on his best stab at a jaunty salesman's voice. "I hear they've got some festive pastries down in the atrium café. I could grab some and meet you down by the river."

"What?" she snapped, dark eyes flashing with a sudden flare of indignation. "So you don't have to be seen being nice to me in public?"

"Hey." He lifted his hands up in protest. Talk about wrong end of the stick!

She carried on over him, clearly having found her

voice again. A very cross voice. "There's no need. I'm more than happy to carry on working. Unless you think I'm not up to the job." She squared herself off to him, eyes blazing with challenge.

"You're crossing a line." He cut her off cold, the smile dropping from his face. He knew she was upset, but he'd never questioned her professional skills. "No one's doubting your ability to do your job."

She harrumphed. "Are you sure about that? This little talk of yours isn't actually some sugar-laced ploy to let me down easily? Tell me you've decided to put someone else on the case?"

"I will if you carry on like this." Finn meant it, too. There was more than an impassioned plea to do her job crackling in her eyes. Adao's presence here had turned her normally chirpy demeanor raw with emotion.

"Are you *kidding* me?" For a moment Naomi struggled to come up with the best retaliation. "This is what I *do*. It's *all* I do. No hidden talents here. No secret skills in the kitchen. Or special volunteering projects. Sorry to disappoint, *Mr.* Morgan."

"Finn," he corrected her, trying to shake the defensive reaction that shot his shoulders up and around his ears. "And let's leave the sports center out of it, shall we? Those kids are…"

They meant the world to him. Reminded him he had a heart.

"What I do there is different. There's no need to try and rack up bonus karma points to prove you're good at your job. You already are."

She wheeled on him as the elevator doors opened then closed. "You mean you can act like an actual living breathing human being with them but not with me?

Fine. Suits me. Once these elevator doors open feel free to take it in whichever direction you like—except *mine*."

Where the hell had that come from? He'd only been trying, in his usual clumsy way, to… Wait a minute. This was all-too-familiar terrain.

Defensiveness. Evasion. Flare-ups followed by pushing the ones you cared about away while deep inside all you really wanted was to be pulled into a deep, reassuring hug and told everything would be okay because you were in a place so dark it was impossible to believe in anything good ever happening again.

She was at war with something that lived deep within her.

Had he become her "someone" she could rail against? The one she was testing?

Despite the fact her entire body was radiating fury, Finn didn't move. He knew how lonely it felt when a person finally succeeded in pushing everyone who cared about them away.

Damn. He cared.

Despite the twitches to fall back into old habits, he held his ground.

His patience paid dividends.

As quickly as Naomi's temper had detonated, a few moments of "I'm not going anywhere" eyes from Finn saw the remaining sparks fizzle and all but disappear. She dropped her head into her hands and huffed out a full-bodied exhalation. After a deep breath in, she let them fall.

"Sorry. I—I didn't mean…" She floundered, trying to find the right words.

His heart softened another notch. Flare-ups were inevitable when the stakes were so high. And there was no doubt about it. Something about Adao had got right under her skin.

Just the same as she had slid right under his.

Two lost souls doing their best to make the world a better place. Sometimes they did good. And sometimes they made a hash of things. Sometimes they did both at the same time.

"C'mon," he said. "Coffee." He punched the elevator button again before tipping her chin up so she was looking him straight in the eye. "And a festive pastry. Doctor's orders."

He turned back to the elevator, trying to disguise his pleasure at eliciting a smile from her. A small one. But it was a smile, nevertheless.

Naomi was one part mortified to one part mollified.

Thank goodness they were outside, walking along the river where there were all sorts of other things and people to look at besides the tall, dark-haired, increasingly intriguing doctor she'd just verbally flayed.

Whoops.

Having a meltdown in front of someone—especially a surgeon—wasn't really her style. Particularly as it hadn't even been about something to do with a patient. This was a hundred percent personal and he knew it. He hadn't rubbed it in, though. For someone whose forte wasn't "cuddly bear"—at least at the hospital—it touched her to see that kind heart she knew he buried under his bluff and bluster rise to the surface.

She blew on her latte before taking a sip of the cinnamon-and-nutmeg-sprinkled drink, sighing as the warm liquid slid down her throat.

"Hit the spot?" Finn asked.

"Yes. And thank you. I'm really sorry—"

"Uh-uh." Finn tutted. "You've already apologized seven times. That's my limit." He stopped and pointed off the path toward a wooden bench made of green sleepers nestled in a sun-dappled copse of silver birches. "This is a good spot."

"You know all the good ones?" A feeble joke, but he gave a little laugh nonetheless. Generous, considering she'd not been showing her best face for the past half-hour. A rare slip.

He gave a vague wave along the towpath. "I live a bit further down the river, so I do actually know all the good spots."

"You live on the river?"

"Literally." He grinned. "Houseboat."

"A houseboat?" She didn't even try to hide her shock. "You."

"Yup. My family moved a lot when I was a kid—military—and I guess life on the move suited me."

"A houseboat?" Naomi couldn't even begin to picture it. Finn was so tall and powerfully built and…well…it was easier to picture him striding across the sprawling slate floors of a huge stone castle than a houseboat.

Finn laughed a full, rich guffaw. "What? You don't think little old me could fit on a houseboat?" He gave her a quick scan then dropped his volume a notch. "You'd be surprised what I can do when I set my mind to it."

Naomi flushed and looked away. Courtesy of Finn Morgan, she'd been surprised quite a few times recently. She had little doubt he could achieve whatever he wanted when he put his mind to it. He'd already pulled at the seams of her perfectly constructed life and exposed her weak spots. No one had done that since she'd arrived in the UK. Not even the emergency refugee staff who'd seen her at her shell-shocked worst when she'd arrived from Zemara. It was as if from the moment she'd arrived she'd had to prove she was worth even the tiniest kindness.

Her foster mother, Charlotte Collins, had been the only one in those early days who she'd felt hadn't been judging her. Her compassion and support had meant so much to her it was why Naomi had legally taken her surname. At that point, to survive, she had needed to look forward. And Charlotte had given her the strength to do so.

Which had been why standing by and doing nothing when Adao had been crying had near enough destroyed her. Little wonder she'd gone on the defensive when Finn had followed her out. She'd been braced for all sorts of words to come hurtling at her: coward, failure, weak, worthless.

But he'd not said a single one of them. Instead, he'd shown her patience. Kindness. And now this…a chance to talk without any pressure.

Following his lead, she took a seat on the bench and sat back to take in their surroundings.

The little woodland nook looked as though it had been designed by Hollywood. Frozen beads of water clinging to the silvery bark shone in the watery sunlight. The river quietly susurrated in the distance as joggers wove their way around couples—old and young—walking alongside the river's towpath. A hoar frost had coated everything overnight and it had yet to melt. Even though the sky was a clear blue today, it was cold and everyone was wearing hats with fuzzy bobbles or silly Christmas jumpers. Or both. No doubt about it. There was a festive buzz in the air. So different from the chaos swirling away in her chest.

"He got to you." Finn's voice was warm. Kind. "Sometimes that happens."

He fell silent, clearly waiting for her to fill in the blanks. Explain why Adao in particular had rattled her otherwise happy-go-lucky cage.

She couldn't go down that path. Not when it already felt as if she was being sucked into a black hole that would lead her straight back to that horrible day when her entire life had changed forever. A hit of iron-rich earth and palm fronds filled her nostrils so powerfully she bit the inside of her cheek and drew blood.

After a few minutes of sitting in silence, Finn, no stranger to keeping himself to himself, realized he wasn't going to get her life story. He hitched his good knee up on the bench and propped his arm on the back of the bench, chin in hand, so he was facing her.

"Next time you need to lash out at someone, maybe you can leave my baking skills out of it? I don't want that secret getting out onto the hospital's gossip train, otherwise the entire surgical staff will be demanding marshmallows like clockwork."

His comically stern expression teased a smile out of her. The second since she'd lost the plot.

How embarrassing to have just snapped like that. And in front of *Finn*, of all people.

"I'm really sorry—" She stopped herself. "I've never done that before."

"It's okay. Better in front of me than in front of Adao,

right? And look." He reached out and laid his hand on her arm. "Like I said, it happens."

She stared at his hand, wondering how such a simple touch could have such a powerful effect on her. Just a colleague giving another colleague a bit of kindness.

But this was Finn Morgan they were talking about. Resident grumpy bear and…well…she was seeing all sorts of differing hues in his "rainbow" these days. In fact, he *had* a rainbow…not just a set of crackling thunderclouds!

She stared out toward the towpath and tried to collect her thoughts. What he'd said was true. It was impossible to be completely neutral at all times. After all, he'd cleared the entire viewing gallery during Adao's operation. Even so, she wasn't feeling particularly proud of herself right now and being on the receiving end of his surprisingly gentle touch was disconcerting. She shrugged her arm away from his hand, disguising the move as a need to give her arms a brisk double rub.

"Cold?"

"No. I mean yes." She rolled her eyes. "I'm always cold here."

"Cambridge or the UK?"

"Both." She frantically thought of a way to nip the direction this conversation was heading in the bud. "But I have an affection for thermalwear so, really, living here suits me to a T!"

Thermalwear? What are you talking about?

Finn didn't press. Either he was completely repulsed by the idea of her in woolen underwear or…oh, no. Was he thinking of her in her underwear? Worst conversation dodge ever.

"So…how do you deal with it?" Naomi tucked her hands into her pockets.

"What? Not let my heartstrings get yanked out of my chest each time I deal with an emotional patient?"

He wasn't patronizing her. He was stating a bald reality of being in the medical profession. Emotions were high. Keeping one's cool was essential. They were health care providers, not family.

"Tell me. What's the 'Morgan Technique'?" She genuinely wanted to know. For the first time in her professional life it seemed impossible.

He didn't even pause to think. "Easy. I think of my dad."

Naomi's heart squeezed tight at the faraway look in Finn's eyes. He didn't elaborate, but he didn't have to. It was enough to hear the warmth in his voice to know he loved him.

Her dad was the reason she'd pushed herself so hard when she'd moved to the UK. "Me too."

The admission was out before she thought better of it. What an idiot. Saying something like that only invited more questions.

"Mr. Collins?" Finn asked. Inevitably. "Was he a physio as well?"

Naomi shook her head. "And Collins wasn't his name."

Why do you keep telling him private things?

"Wasn't?" Finn asked quietly.

Yes. Past tense. She was the only surviving member of her family.

She ignored the question and instead said the family name she'd not spoken in over a dozen years. "Chukwumerije."

"That was your original surname?"

Yes. It had been.

"A tough one for the British tongue to force into submission," she said, doing her best to keep her tone light. She put on an English accent and mangled her name a few times. Finn's laugh echoed throughout the little clearing. He had little crinkles by his eyes. She'd never noticed those before.

An intense need to tell him the whole story took the laughter from her voice.

"There was actually a woman. A lovely woman. Charlotte Collins. She was my foster mother when I came here. Without her…" Naomi's voice cracked and she pressed her fist to her lips to stem a sob of gratitude.

Finn nodded. He got it. She didn't need to spell out just how important compassion was. Kindness.

"Say it again," he asked gently. "Your Zemarian surname."

It was strange, feeling the taste of her own name on her tongue.

For years using the new name had felt like the worst kind of betrayal and also the most generous of blessings.

She'd been granted a new life. A chance to become everything she'd ever dreamed of. But it had only come to pass because of the deaths of those she'd loved most.

Now? Here with Finn? The name felt like a disguise. All part of the chirpy, got-it-together facade she wore day in, day out to keep the demons at bay.

Finn had been mulling over her name. He gave a few aborted starts on mimicking her pronunciation before miming throwing in the towel.

She laughed softly. "When my mother said it, it sounded like poetry. Stella Chukwumerije. She used to say it as if she were royalty."

He raised his eyebrows. The question in his eyes asked one thing and one thing only: Where were they now?

The fact she'd probably never know haunted her dreams every single night.

"My mum's name means star, so sometimes…" She let the rest of the thought remain unsaid as her gaze lifted upwards. Looking up at the stars and believing that maybe, just maybe, her mother was looking down at her offered her solace. Most of the time.

At least Adao's family was alive and well.

An idea sparked. "What if we went onto the internet? Or asked the charity if they have a picture of his parents—maybe them all together as a family. We could put it in a frame for him. I could run and get something from the charity shops now."

Finn smiled as if she'd just handed him a present. "That's a great idea. I'll leave you to the running bit." He pointed at his knee.

"Is it acting up?"

He tipped his head side to side.

The gesture could've meant any number of things.

Yes. No. It always hurts, but I'm a man, so…

"You know—" An offer to give him a massage was just about to fly off the tip of her tongue when he held up a hand.

"I know. I *know.*" Unlike the last time she'd offered help, his defenses didn't fly into place. There might have even been a bit of gratitude in those hard-to-read eyes of his.

In this light they were like sparkling like ice crystals with amber hits of flame…

Oh…

Naomi's body heat shot up a few degrees as their gazes caught and snapped the pair of them into a heightened awareness that blurred everything around them.

Heart. Lungs. Throat. Breasts. Lips. Her *hair* was aware of Finn. Even more so when he turned toward her on the bench, his knee gently shifting against hers.

It was one of the most sensual feelings she had ever experienced.

Which was ridiculous.

Right?

But it didn't feel ridiculous at all. Not with his face so close she could reach out and trace a finger along the fullness of his lower lip before—

No.

She didn't do this. She didn't *deserve* this. And especially not with a man who came with a complicated past.

His gaze on her own lips was virtually palpable. Her body responded against her will, the tip of her tongue dipping out and licking her lower lip, vividly aware that the only thing separating them was a handful of centimeters and air.

Abruptly, she swiveled so that she was facing the towpath and pressed her knees together.

"It must be nice to have Charlie to confide in after all you've been through."

"What?" Finn shook his head as if not entirely understanding what had broken the spell.

An all-too-familiar deadweight of anxiety began gnawing at that indescribably beautiful ball of heat in her belly and turned it into a churning mass of guilt.

"You know." She heard herself continue, regretting each word as it arrived. "After things changed with your wife."

"*Ex*-wife," Finn bit out, his body language instantly registering the change of mood. "We're divorced."

A cold wind blew in off the river, grazing the surface of her cheeks. A welcome sensation as they were burning with embarrassment.

Finn pushed himself off the bench, his good leg all but launching him toward the towpath.

She remained glued to the bench, in shock at her own—what was it? Stupidity? Common sense?

No. It was worse than that. It was fear. Fear of allowing herself to feel true happiness.

"I'm heading back. Going to do a quick check on Adao before I go into surgery for the rest of the afternoon."

He didn't ask her if she was going to join him, but he didn't power ahead as she'd imagined he might.

Silently they headed back to the hospital.

"Aren't you going in?" Amanda flicked her head in Finn's direction as he went into Adao's room.

Naomi shook her head. She was more off kilter than when she'd left the room half an hour earlier.

Had she and Finn almost kissed?

"He's not been Captain Grumpy again, has he?"

"Finn? No. Not all. He's—"

"Uh-oh… I see the tides might've shifted where Mr. Morgan is concerned."

Naomi gave Amanda her best "are you crazy" look then went to hover at Adao's doorway, where Finn was talking with Mabel.

"Absolutely we do, Finn. What a lovely idea. I'll just send a little message through on this thingamajig here and see if they can't do it today." The gray-haired woman pulled a mobile phone out of her cardigan pocket and held it out to him, clearly having no intention of sending the message herself.

Finn gave Naomi a quick nod where she was hovering in the doorway. "You still up for getting Adao a frame?" He looked at the little boy whose tears had now dried. "Would you like that, pal?"

Adao nodded, his tear-laced eyes wide with anticipation.

"Right. I guess we'd better send the office a message."

She watched as he made a show of trying to get the tiny phone to obey his large fingers, even managing to draw out giggles from both Adao and Mabel.

When he was done, he handed the phone back to Mabel then chatted a bit more with Adao. Told him how he was still toying with the idea of becoming an astronaut one day. Pointed out what fun going through airport security was now that he had an "iron" leg. Told Adao how lucky he was they were both lefties. Some of the best people he knew were lefties, he said with a wink, before turning to give her a meaningful look.

She was a leftie.

Was there anything the man didn't notice?

Finn was so good with him. It was mesmerizing to watch the pair of them as Finn ever so casually noted Adao's heart rate. Blood pressure. A little bit of swelling that had developed around the joint. There were multiple factors to consider in these early days after the surgery. Joint contracture. Pathological scars. Cardiovascular response to what had been, ultimately, a traumatic event. Residual limb pain. Phantom sensation, edema, and the list went on. All of which Finn nimbly checked while keeping up a light-hearted conversation about Adao's favorite British football players.

It turned out Adao didn't have any. His heart lay with the Spanish.

"What?" Finn feigned receiving a dagger to the heart and only just managing to pull it out. "Not *one* British player?"

Adao shrugged and grinned. He liked who he liked.

Standing there, watching the pair of them banter, Naomi felt an acute sense of loss. She could've kissed this man. This gorgeous, warm-hearted bear of a man.

Would it have been a mistake?

Most likely.

She didn't deserve a fairy-tale moment like that, let alone the promise of the happiness that could follow in its wake. From what little she knew about Finn, and the stony silence he'd maintained as they'd walked back to the hospital from the river, he wasn't exactly in the market for love. Neither was she, for that matter.

Lust. That's what it had been. A hit of seasonal lust that had taken them both by surprise.

That he was able to treat her as if absolutely nothing had happened between them was proof he compartmentalized his life. Just as she did.

Work.

The sports center for him. The riverside runs for her.

Home.

She tipped her head to the side and scrunched her eyes tight, trying to imagine him in a houseboat, and came up with nothing. The first thing that popped into her mind was a huge man cave carved into the side of a soaring mountainside. Accessible only by foot. Or yak. She easily pictured it all decked out in shaggy woolly mammoth hides and zebra skins. Did it make sense? No. But then again… A huge fire would be roaring in the center of it, with Finn presiding over the place as if he were the king of the jungle. Or the mountain range?

"What's got you so smiley?"

"What?" Naomi shook her head, startled to find both Finn and Adao looking at her as if she'd lost her marbles.

Oh, crikey. She'd gone all daydreamy right in front of the man she was meant to not be daydreaming about.

"Nothing. Just thinking about…" Her eyes darted across the ward to where a Christmas tree was merrily blinking away "I was just thinking about the Christmas party and how much fun it will be."

"Christmas party?" Adao spoke the words as if he'd not let himself imagine such a delight.

Naomi grinned.

"Absolutely." Evie was really outdoing herself if the rumor mill was anything to go by. "It's in a couple of weeks, I think. And…" she held up two sets of crossed fingers "…if everything goes well with your recovery and we get your physio under way, I don't see any reason why you wouldn't be able to go."

Adao looked to Finn for approval.

Finn smiled and gave the little boy's short head of hair a scrub with one of his huge man hands. "You heard the lady, mate. You focus on getting better and in a couple of weeks' time you might be showing Santa your new prosthesis."

For the first time the mention of the false arm elicited a smile from Adao. "I would very much like to shake Santa's hand," he said.

"Well, then." Naomi's heart was buoyed at the fierce

determination lighting up the little boy's eyes. "That's what we shall focus on."

Her gaze shifted to Finn, whose eyes were already on her, his expression unreadable. What had she expected? Him to be all doe-eyed? Hardly. She'd turned him down. He was getting on with his life as if it had never happened and what lay deep in those moonstone-colored eyes of his would remain a mystery. No matter how much curiosity was getting the better of her.

She gave Adao a quick wave goodbye and headed toward the stairwell, fighting the growing sensation that running away from Finn could be one of her biggest mistakes to date.

CHAPTER EIGHT

AN EMPTY GYM.

No music.

Just the pounding of his heart and the sound of his breath.

The best part about an exhausting workout was that there was no room in Finn's head for anything other than the weights in his hands and the resistance his body was or wasn't giving as he pushed himself to the next level.

There wasn't one spare second to consider just how close he'd come to kissing Naomi the other day.

Or if he'd been counting: six days, twelve hours and a handful of minutes ago.

But he hadn't been counting.

Or popping round when she was giving Adao one of his physio sessions, taking careful note of how gentle she was with him. Sensitive to how lonely and lost the boy was feeling.

Neither had he been so much as giving the slightest thought to those beautiful, full lips of hers. The slight tilt of her eyes rimmed by lashes so thick and long he could almost imagine them butterfly-kissing his cheek.

Almost.

But he wasn't thinking about things like that.

He wasn't letting himself notice that when she walked into a room the world felt a little bit nicer.

Or the soft curve of her neck.

How watching her work with patients was seeing someone answering a calling, not doing a job.

Or the gentle swoops and soft curves her body revealed even in the athletic gear she almost always wore to work.

Finn strode over to a press-up bench and took off his prosthesis. A challenge. That's what he needed. He dropped to the floor and did a few press-ups, unsuccessfully trying to rid his brain of that instant—that bit of other-worldly time and place—when he'd been absolutely sure they'd both moved toward the other.

Two lost souls finding solace in each other.

Only he had no idea if she really was a lost soul or not. Something about Adao had well and truly shot her emotions up to explosive level. Then again, he never saw her raise her voice or offer anything less than a smile to every other member of staff.

Maybe it was him. Maybe it was the combination of the pair of them. Maybe it was the fact he'd never come to terms with pushing his ex-wife so hard the only choice she'd had in the end had been to leave him.

"Mr. Morgan!" The door to the gym was pushed open and Theo appeared. He was dressed in running gear. In his usual swift, efficient manner he took in a sweaty senior surgeon, a discarded prosthesis, a look that could kill and said, "Want a spotter?"

No. He wanted to be left alone to wallow in his misery. Only…he didn't really.

Blimey. Since when did misery *actually* love company?

Theo crossed to the press-up bench and eyed the weights Finn had loaded on the bar. He clearly knew better than to wait for an invitation.

"Looks like you're weighted light tonight."

Theo had the world's best poker face and he was playing it hard right now. He knew Finn only pressed weights that challenged him at the highest level.

"I could lift this with my pinky," Finn grunted, not even caring that Theo was his boss. Not right now anyway.

"Well, then. Show me."

Finn craned his neck before lying back on the bench. Rather than address the obvious—his unusual decision to work out stripped back to his true self—he threw a question at Theo. "You look like you could pound out a few frustrations yourself."

Theo sucked in a sharp breath. "That obvious?"

"Only to a seasoned doctor."

Theo huffed out a mirthless laugh. "You mean like all the other doctors we've got wandering round Hope?"

"Something like that." Finn lay back on the bench and wrapped his hands round the bar. "Only…to…the… rest…of…them…you…look…achingly…handsome."

To Finn's relief, Theo took the jibe as it was intended and chuckled. Something to break the tension that had added more than a silver hair or two to Theo's temples.

Ivy wasn't getting any better. Quite the opposite, in fact. No amount of testing, Doodle visits or letters to Santa Claus were making a blind bit of difference.

Theo's hands floated just under the bar as Finn cranked out three rounds of three lifts before pushing himself up. "You want a go?"

Theo eyed him for a minute as if he were being asked to a duel then did the standard guy response. "Get up, then. You're on my bench."

"Your bench?" Finn guffawed loud and hard then made a show of wiping it clean and presenting it as if it were a throne. "Your majesty."

Theo flicked him a look that said, *Enough with the servitude, mate*, then settled on to the bench.

True. It was Theo's bench. His gym. His hospital. But the last thing he'd ever seen the man be was proprietorial or smug about his financial status. Billionaire. What the guy was was a worried dad. And letting off steam had to be hard when your little girl's health was deteriorating right in front of your eyes.

"How's the diagnostician getting on?"

"Madison?" There was a bite in his voice when he said the name and he ripped off three quick rounds, pressing the same weight Finn had.

Impressive.

Or emotion-fueled.

Easy to see there wasn't much point in asking him if Madison had made much progress. His heart went out to Theo, seeing his little girl, the only one left in his family, go through so much pain right in front of him and feeling utterly powerless. It was one of the reasons he'd stripped himself of his own friends and family. No one to lose. Then, of course, there was the flipside… nothing to gain.

"Want to do another round?"

Theo lifted the bar and began pressing again. The determination on his face reminded him of his own once he'd decided to retrain as a pediatric surgeon. He'd poured everything he'd had into becoming the best.

Apart from work, he'd barely imagined wanting to properly live again—let alone love again. And while he was nowhere near loving Naomi, he barely knew the girl, he felt more connected to her on a visceral level than he had with anyone.

Maybe it had taken this long for him to figure out who the hell he was. His whole life he'd worked toward becoming a soldier. Then he had been a soldier for five incredible years. Then in one solitary instant everything he'd thought he'd become had been taken away from him.

Why would his wife and family want a fraud?

And then this beautiful, mysterious, happy, sad, talented and obviously conflicted woman had walked into his life and another bomb had gone off.

For the first time in over a decade, taking the risk seemed better than going back down that soul-sucking rabbit hole he'd swan-dived into after his life had changed forever.

Theo clanged the bar back into place, sat up and stared right through Finn.

Um...

"Christmas plans?" Finn asked.

What the—?

King of casual chitchat he was not.

"You're looking at them," Theo said, lying back down, pressing out one more round then getting up and whirling round on the bench. "This, and trying to find my daughter a Christmas miracle. What about you?" He glared at Finn as if daring him to have better plans.

"Ditto." He opened his wide arms to the gym.

They stared at one another then laughed. "Couple of real players on the social circuit, aren't we?" Theo pushed himself up from the bench, gave it a swipe with the towel he'd grabbed on the way in. "I'm going for a run." His eyes flicked to Finn's good leg. "Want to come?"

"Nah." He had a prosthesis that was great for running, but he wasn't in the mood. He'd come here to test himself. See if he was ready—not just physically—to move away from the past and see how he got on with the future.

Naomi heard the weights drop to the rubberized gym floor before she entered the room. It wasn't unusual for staff to use the large physio gym, but it was definitely rare to hear such heavy weights in use. Aware that being startled could throw whoever was in there off their stride, she slipped into the gym as innocuously as she could.

The sight she saw actually took her breath away.

Finn Morgan.

Bare-chested.

Athletic shorts exposing a leg so toned it would've made Michelangelo gasp.

She pressed her fingers to her lips to stop herself from doing the same.

Finn's body glowed with exertion as, without even wearing his prosthesis, he alternated between single leg barbell lifts and pull-ups.

His back was to her, but she could see his focused expression in the mirrors on the far side of the gym. She'd never seen such a display of precision and resolute determination.

Despite the use of heavy weights, Finn's body wasn't

over-pumped, like some of the zealous gym rats she'd seen throughout the years.

No. Finn's tall form had heft, but it was toned to absolute physical perfection. She could see clear definition in his shoulders and biceps as he pulled himself up and over the pull-up bar with the fluid grace of a gymnast. The muscles in his back rippled with the lithe strength of a lion.

Parts of her own body lit up as if she were a freshly decorated Christmas tree. She hadn't felt warm tingles of response below her belly button in just about forever and now Finn seemed to have some sort of remote control on her internal fireworks display—just one solitary glance could detonate an entire evening's worth.

When he dropped to the floor and took a double hop across to where he'd laid the heavily weighted barbell, she watched quietly as his internalized focus manifested itself in an extraordinary show of physical strength and courage. Not every man would put himself to the test like this. Not every man would win.

He'd obviously been working out for a while and when he crouched to pick up the barbell she saw him hesitate before heaving the sagging bar up and over his head. As he held it aloft and looked toward the mirror to monitor his form, his eyes shifted across to her and he threw the weight to the floor with a crash.

"I'm sorry, I didn't mean to interrupt. I was just going to set something up for a patient."

Finn turned to her and said nothing as he reached out an arm to steady himself.

He dipped to the floor and scooped up a white towel and wiped his face.

She'd never seen him without his prosthesis. Well. Not glossed in sweat and half-naked, anyway.

He certainly didn't need it, or anything else to prove that he was anything less than a powerfully driven man.

She'd never wanted to touch someone more in her entire life.

"Do you need these for your next patient?" Finn asked.

"No." Naomi held up her wrist as if her timepiece-free arm would remind him it was well after hours. "I thought I'd just get a head start on tomorrow and set up some equipment for my first appointment."

Neither of them moved.

Tension crackled between the pair of them as if a power line had been torn from its stable housing and set loose in a wind storm. Sparks flying everywhere. No clear place to hide.

"I've got a trick that might help you with your dead lifts."

Finn arced an eyebrow. Go ahead, the gesture read. Improve on perfection if you can.

He wasn't smug. He was just right.

Well. Almost right.

"Your hips. You're not using them as the power thrusters they're designed to be."

Naomi flushed as she spoke. If he were a patient she would normally move up behind them and…well…they would go through the motions together, but…

Her throat tickled. She was suddenly feeling really *parched*.

Her hand moved along the length of her throat as if it would ease the dry, scratchy sensation. A drink of water would be good about now.

As if mirroring her thoughts, Finn dipped to the floor again and grabbed a bottle of water, unscrewed the cap and, eyes still on her, began gulping down the water as if he'd just emerged from the desert.

Her eyes were glued to a solitary trickle of water wending its way through his dark stubble on his throat, shifting along his clavicle, heading toward that little sternal dip between the bones, only to be swiped away by a towel.

She caught Finn's grin as he dropped the towel on a nearby bench and shot her a surreptitious glance. He'd seen her ogling him. And he'd enjoyed it.

"That's a pretty intense workout you have there."

"No excuses," he said.

Wow.

It was that simple.

Of course it would be. For a man who worked with amputees, not to mention his time at the sports center where the wheelchair-bound athletes pushed themselves to achieve more, do better, try again, and never give up, no excuses sounded like a pretty solid motivator. He was making himself an example for his patients.

Only…she wondered if they could see the dark shadows flickering across those eyes of his. The man knew loss. The man knew pain. Whether or not she wanted to admit it, they were kindred spirits. But could two souls who had known devastation create something good?

He hopped over to the press-up bench and strapped on his prosthesis. When he rose again, squaring himself off to her as he pulled on his long-sleeved T-shirt, about a million butterflies took off, teasing her body's erogenous zones as if he were tracing his fingertips along the surface of her skin as his eyes drank her in.

"Well, then." She gave her hands a brisk let's-get-to-it rub. "If you're up for it, let me add some notches to your bow."

Finn stood absolutely still, his eyes cemented to hers. "I don't think that's what you meant to say."

"Of course I—" Naomi stopped. Had she?

Sometimes, even though it had been over ten years, she still muddled up British expressions. Her eyes widened as she realized how the expression could have been taken. Sexually.

"Oh, I didn't—"

Before she could form a coherent thought, Finn crossed to her and she was in his arms, his mouth descending on hers as if the world's most powerful magnets had drawn them together. When he first came up for air he looked into her eyes as if this had been the moment he'd been waiting for. The moment when his life would change forever.

She recognized the fire, because she felt the very same heat incinerating her every intention to remain immune to him. To protect her heart.

Her hands flew to his face, the pads of her fingertips enjoying the contrast between the hot, needy demands of his mouth and the masculine prickle of his stubble.

There was not a single cell in her in body with the power to resist. Neither did she want to.

One of his hands slid round her waist and pulled her tight to him. As if she wasn't already arching into the solid heat of his chest. No one needed to tell them her body had been designed for his.

Finn slid his free hand up the nape of her neck and pulled back for a moment, looked deep into her eyes then changed tack, descending once again, to taste her in slow, luxurious hits of teasing kisses. He threaded his fingers into her loosely woven solitary plait and tipped her head back, dropping heated kiss after kiss on her throat.

Staying silent wasn't an option.

It was the first moan of pleasure she had ever heard roll from her throat.

These were no ordinary kisses. This was no ordinary connection.

Desire. Hunger. Need.

They were slaking all of them, their bodies and mouths moving intuitively as if the universe had aligned its entire history for this very moment.

In the center of her fiercely pounding heart Naomi knew this moment would be forever branded on her soul.

And she also knew it could never happen again.

Not unless she made peace with her past—and fifteen years on it still seemed an impossible task.

Finn sensed the change in Naomi's body language before she pulled away. They were the matching pieces of the puzzle of his life. He knew that in the very marrow of his bones.

When she stepped back, he didn't try to stop her. He couldn't.

His entire body was jacked up on adrenaline and hormones and one single move toward her might betray just how powerfully—how *intimately*—she had touched him. Had touched his heart.

"Don't let me keep you if you need to set up your equipment."

Naomi shook her head as if he were speaking a foreign language.

"No. It's fine. It can wait. I was just being hyper-prepared."

"Avoiding your life, you mean?"

Her expression became shuttered, her eyes protectively dropping to half-mast.

"I do exactly the same thing, Naomi. Take every shift going. Work out here just in case my phone goes. Tell myself, *Look. Someone needs me.* I'm trying to find proof, I suppose." He looked her straight in the eye. "Proof there's a reason why I exist."

She didn't even bother to protest. Didn't need to. He could see it in her eyes. She shared exactly the same fears he had.

A gut-clenching fear that he hadn't done enough to be worthy of the life he had.

It was the most honest he'd been with anyone in years. And every word he'd uttered was nothing less than the plain truth.

Hard to confront. Abrasive even. But *real*.

The door swung open and Evie appeared with an elf's hat on her head and a Christmas wreath dangling from her arm. She was all smiles these days and today was no different. "Hey, you two! Coming upstairs for the carol concert in the foyer? Free mince pies and mulled wine for the over-eighteens who aren't on duty!"

Naomi just stared at her as if she were a ghost.

Mercifully, Evie whirled around with a wave and a merrily trilled "Fa-la-la-la-la" before registering the shock of being interrupted on their faces.

"Carols?" Finn asked, as if it were the natural progression of snogging the woman of your dreams— Wait. *Woman of his dreams?* That was going to take some processing.

Naomi shook her head and pointed vaguely to another part of the hospital. "I've got to check on someone."

No, she didn't.

The message was clear. She was saying something, *anything,* to get as far away from him as possible.

"Fine."

His stiff, abrupt movements as he pulled on his outdoor gym clothes spoke volumes. He didn't want this to end. He wanted it to be the beginning. The frustrated yanks he gave his hoodie as he pulled it over his head and down across his torso—yes, he caught her looking when his shirt hitched up, *ha!*—were all far too familiar reactions for him. He'd behaved the same way with his ex-wife. Pushed her away when the going had got tough.

Well, he wouldn't give Naomi the chance. Not tonight. Not ever.

He pretended not to watch as she went over to the duffel bag she'd brought in and pulled out a bright red picture frame with a tropical theme embossed along the edges. She turned around with a shy smile and showed him what looked like a family photo. "For Adao."

Ah...

She actually was going to see someone.

He pressed his fingers to his eyes and gave his head a good shake. What an idiot.

He raised a hand to wave goodbye, but when he looked toward the doorframe she had already gone.

CHAPTER NINE

Pacing on a houseboat wasn't much of a tension-reliever.

Finn loved the place even though he near enough brained himself on the doorframes every single day. The warm wooden planks. The compact but modern kitchen. The old leather sofa he'd wrangled in through the small rooftop hatch by sheer force of will.

The ability to untie himself from the mooring and set off whenever the mood struck.

It's how he'd ended up here in Cambridge. He'd bought the portable home when his stint at rehab and his marriage had come to mutual and abrupt endings. He'd stayed in the Manchester area for a while to keep up with his rehab. But really? Once he'd cut ties with his past, he'd liked the idea that he could just cast off whenever he wanted and just go.

He stared at the phone for a minute, then picked it up, checking that he still had his ex-wife's number. His mum had sent it to him "just in case." She never nagged, but about once a year she asked if he'd "heard anything on the grapevine."

The way he'd treated Caroline gnawed at his conscience.

They'd not been a match in the end. They'd been

kids who'd married too soon, all caught up in the romance of him going off to war. The last thing they'd been equipped for had been for him to come back at the ripe age of twenty-four with one good leg and a seething ball of fury where the other one had been.

He'd been angry with everything and everyone back then. Most of all himself. But his immediate family had taken the brunt of it.

His parents had retired to Spain a while back and, before they'd gone, the three of them had made their peace. They got it.

It wasn't simply the loss of his leg. It was losing the army as well. It was his family's chosen profession. His family's *history*. And for the first time ever…a Morgan was stepping away from the front line.

Sure. It had been bad luck. No one looks to get injured.

But Caroline…bless her…she hadn't been who he'd needed at his darkest hour.

And now, fourteen years after coming out of that pitch-black tunnel, he was beginning to think he'd found the woman he could open his heart to.

Someone who understood a core-deep sense of loss.

When Naomi looked into his eyes she seemed to see all of the trauma he'd endured and more. The pain. The doubt. The urgent, primal need to do better. To *be* better.

All the things he saw when he looked into Naomi's eyes.

She *knew* him.

And for the first time since he'd cleared his social calendar of anything more than a casual fling he wanted more.

He wanted Naomi.

He stopped his pacing and snorted out a laugh as he remembered Theo warning him about wearing through the floorboards at the hospital. To do so on a houseboat would be little short of a disaster. He scanned the cabin, looking for something, anything, to do.

A stack of cookbooks lay front and center on his dinky kitchen island.

When in doubt?

Bake.

And while whatever he'd decided to rustle up was in the oven, he'd call Caroline. It was about fourteen years overdue, but…maybe he'd needed the time.

He began pulling ingredients out of the cupboards.

Excuses. Everything he thought up to say to her was an excuse.

The truth was, he'd met someone.

And if he were going to be in any sort of place to even try having a relationship, he needed to make peace with his past.

A quick look at the ward clock showed it was just after eight.

Naomi had ended up getting wrangled into listening to a few of the carols by a very happy Alice and Marco who'd let it slip they'd set their wedding date for just before Christmas.

She hoped they hadn't noticed her fingers leap to cover her kiss-bruised lips as they'd spoken of their excitement about spending the rest of their lives together.

She'd made her excuses, something easily done in the hospital, and had come up here to see Adao. Chances were he was asleep, but even if she was able to tiptoe into his room and place the framed photo of him with his family near him, it would be nice for him to wake up to.

It wasn't as if she was going to get much sleep tonight.

Kissing like teenagers!

No.

She shook her head.

What had happened with Finn had been two consenting adults ripping open a pent-up attraction. And from the looks of things, neither of them had any idea what to do next.

She'd had a couple of boyfriends, but nothing with this level of passion. If the gossip was anything to go by, Finn was a renowned lone wolf so... He was such a mystery to her and yet...a part of her felt like she'd been waiting her whole life to find him because she'd known him all along.

Those *kisses*.

Fireflies danced around her belly at the thought.

She'd kissed like a teenager with her boyfriend back in Zemara. It had been sweet. Innocent. Two young people focused on school, getting into university and then, when war had broken out, surviving.

She glanced at the photograph she'd managed to get from the medical charity.

In it Adao's face was alight with an ear-to-ear grin. He was holding a puppy in one arm and had his other arm flopped round his big sister's shoulders from his perch atop a large wooden barrel. His parents were behind the pair of them, also smiling. It was a perfect family photo and reminded her so much of how happy she had been with her own family that a prickle of impending tears teased at her throat.

She shook it away as she approached Adao's room. She was here to comfort him, not cry about her own past.

Her eyes shot wide open when she reached the room. Far from asleep, Adao was wide awake, with a huge, cuddly labradoodle sprawled across his lap.

Alana, Doodle's minder, was sitting in a chair a couple of meters away, reading a book.

Naomi tapped on the doorframe.

"Okay if I come in?"

Alana nodded toward Adao. It was up to him.

He looked at Doodle and the dog wagged his tail so he smiled and nodded.

"I've brought you something I thought you might like to put by your bed."

"Really?"

The astonishment in his voice tugged at her heart.

She pulled the photo out from behind her back and showed it to him.

Tears instantly sprang to the little boy's eyes. Naomi held her breath, suddenly worried it was the worst possible thing she could have given him. She hadn't been able to look at any photos of her own family since they had been taken away that horrible day. They existed. In an envelope buried deep in the back of her cupboard. But to look at their smiling, beautiful faces every day and know she'd never see the real things again? She didn't know that she had the strength.

"I love it. I love it so much. Thank you, miss."

"Naomi," she gently corrected.

He repeated her name as if tasting it, his eyes still glued to the photo. He pulled the photo close to his chest and hugged it, then lifted it up to his face and gave each of his family members a kiss.

Out of the corner of her eye Naomi saw Alana reaching for the box of tissues near her chair.

She didn't blame her. The moment was about as powerful as they came. She was struggling to keep her own tears in check.

Adao's face brightened as an idea struck. He showed the photo to Doodle. The dog sat up and listened as Adao pointed out his mother, father and sister. Then listened to a detailed explanation of where the picture had been taken—outside their home—when it had been taken—after they'd come home from church—what they had eaten afterwards—a huge meal with the rest of the members of their congregation—and how he had played and played with his friends that day. Played until the sun had gone down, when all their mothers had called them in and made them go to bed so they would be fresh for the next day at school.

His voice had cracked a bit at the end, but it was the happiest he'd ever sounded.

In fact, it was the most Naomi had ever heard him speak.

From the astonished look on Alana's face, it was the most she had heard as well.

"Good idea," the blonde woman mouthed.

"Naomi?" Adao was holding the photo out to her. "Could you please put this up so Doodle and I can see it from the bed?"

"Of course." She made a bit of a to-do about rearranging the scant items on top of his bedside table and put the photo front and center as Adao lay back on his pillow. "Is this good here?" She gave it a tiny shift closer toward him.

He looked at Doodle for confirmation. The dog lifted his head and tilted it to the side as if checking it from the same angle as Adao, then gave a little woof.

Adao beamed. "Thank you."

"You're welcome. I'm so pleased you like it."

There was a light knock on the door. Navya, one of the night sisters on the ward, was wearing The Look. It was gentle but firm, and it meant it was time to go now.

Naomi dropped a kiss on Adao's head. "See you tomorrow, okay?"

For the first time he didn't look at her fearfully and a huge warmth wrapped around her heart.

She walked to the elevator with Alana and Doodle, amazed at seeing the change in the little boy.

She gave the dog's head an affectionate rub and smiled. "Does everyone tell him their secrets?"

"A lot of people do. Mostly the children," Alana conceded with a smile. "But you know what they say."

Naomi shook her head and entered the elevator along with the pair of them. "What do they say?"

Alana cocked her head to the side at the same time as Doodle. "A problem shared is a problem halved. Or something like that. Maybe it's burden." She shrugged and grinned. "Better out than in is what it boils down to. Isn't that right, Doodle?" She gave the dog a loving stroke. "This guy knows far too much about me. I'm surprised he doesn't put his paws on his ears and start to howl half the time."

Naomi laughed along with her, but the words were hitting home. She'd never shared her story with anyone. Not even the girls and women she'd first bunked with at the refugee facility she'd stayed in when she'd first moved to the UK. She'd nicknamed the facility "The House of Secrets."

Naomi had convinced herself it was best to keep her story close. Hidden. But between kissing Finn and watching Adao pour out his life story to this adorable pooch…it was like the universe was offering her sign after sign that now was the time she needed to share her story.

And she knew exactly who she wanted to share it with.

The elevator doors opened and Alana and Doodle began to head toward the main exit. "Are you walking to the car park?"

Naomi shook her head. "I think I'm going to take a little walk along the river."

"It's freezing out there. Make sure you wrap up warm."

Naomi watched as the pair ambled out of the hospital and toward the car park then set off with a gentle jog along the riverbank.

She'd know Finn's place when she saw it.

Something told her the universe was working in her favor tonight and it was time to start reading the signs.

Finn was pulling the cake out of the oven when he heard the knock on the door.

What the—?

No one visited him. Ever.

He opened the door, feeling almost as shocked as Naomi looked to see him there.

"I need to tell you something. To explain." She spoke

low and urgently, as if she might implode if she didn't get whatever it was she had to say out soon.

"I have one cake, two forks and a bottle of red."

Wow. He was a real Romeo, wasn't he?

Her brows drew together as if he'd just told her he was from the planet Zorg. Her short, quick breaths told him she was running on adrenaline. Maybe he should've offered the standard cup of tea and a biscuit. The rest could wait.

"Come on in."

A few minutes later, coat off, but with a woolen blanket wrapped round her shoulders, Naomi sat across from him at the small wooden table with a fork in her hand, a cup of steaming tea in front of her—she'd refused the wine—and a cake between them.

"Um… This all right?" Finn gave his dark tangles a scrub. "I don't really do hosting. No one really ever calls round."

"I've never been offered an entire chocolate cake before."

"Guess this is a day of firsts."

They looked at one another, their gazes catching and clasping tight. Of course it was a day of firsts.

First kisses being the most memorable of all.

But she wasn't here to talk about kissing, so he sat back and waited.

The air between them was alive with pent-up energy and yet…somehow it felt right, Naomi being here in his man cave.

"I saw Adao just now."

"The picture? How did that go?"

"He loved it. Alana was there with the therapy dog, Doodle. He told Doodle all about his family. His life…"

Her gaze shifted down to her hands where she was rubbing her thumb along the spine of the fork as if trying to remold it into an entirely new shape.

Something clicked. He saw where this was going. She wanted him to be her Doodle.

"I'll take the first bite, shall I? Save you the embarrassment."

"Embarrassment?"

"Of wanting to wolf down the entire cake in one go." He took a huge forkful and made a show of really enjoying it. Which, even if he had made it himself, didn't require much acting. Who didn't like warm chocolate cake?

Following his lead as he plunged his fork into the large cake, Naomi took a daintier portion, her eyebrows lifting as she tasted the cake. "Oh, wow! Mmm… This is delicious."

"I've been competitive baking with a television show," he confessed. "So far I think I'm winning."

Naomi put her fork down, her expression sobering. "I need to explain why Adao means so much to me."

"You don't need to explain anything you don't want to."

"I want to." Her gaze locked with his and everything he saw within those dark brown eyes of hers seared straight into his chest cavity. She was a kindred spirit. A fellow lost soul who, if he was strong enough for her, just may have found her mooring.

He pulled his own mug of tea toward him, took a drink, sat back and listened.

"Many years ago…fourteen and a bit…"

He nodded. It was about the same length of time since he'd lost his leg.

She stopped, drummed the table with her fingers then backtracked. "When I was seventeen, my country was disrupted by civil war. Up until then I had lived a happy childhood. Just like anyone else. Maybe just like you."

Finn nodded as confirmation. He'd had a great childhood. Military through and through. Moving every few years. New countries. New parts of the UK. Always "on mission" to make himself the best possible candidate for army recruitment when the time came…

"It all changed so quickly. One day my boyfriend and I were going to school like normal teenagers—"

"Your boyfriend?" Finn prompted. There was no point in editing her story on his account.

She gave him a weak smile. "It was a teenage romance."

"Hey." Finn raised his hands. "I'm not going green-eyed monster on you. Everyone has a past. I have mine. You have yours." He laid his hands on top of hers and gave them a light squeeze. "The only thing I am here to do is listen."

And learn. And something told him right then and there he'd stay and be there for her as long as it took. Everyone had a past. And everyone had a future. It took moving on from one to get to the other, and that was precisely what he was hoping to do.

CHAPTER TEN

NAOMI SEARCHED FINN'S intense expression for any fault lines.

Not a single one.

Just a solid, warm-hearted, generous man sitting across from her with nothing other than her own well-being in mind.

It was painful. But she began to speak.

"For the most part, the rebels hadn't been around our small town. It was about the size of Cambridge, actually. It had a river. And a hospital." She suddenly became lost in memories of just how much she had taken for granted before the war had begun. A quiet, bustling market town where her father had run a hardware store and her mother had been a teacher. She'd always had food. Clothes. They'd had a happy, perfectly normal life.

"Had you always wanted to be a physiotherapist?" Finn asked, dipping his fork into the cake and indicating she should feel free to help herself.

She smiled but shook her head. She couldn't eat cake and tell this particular story. "I knew I always wanted to help people, but I wasn't sure how. I used to volunteer at the hospital as... I'm not sure what you call them here. In Zemara we had a lot of American missionaries, so we were called candy-stripers. We worked in pinstripe pinafores to identify us as volunteers. It was good fun. I loved it whenever I could help a patient smile or laugh."

"I bet you were great at it."

Her smile faded. "I had only done it for about a year, but it was long enough to discover physiotherapy. I really enjoyed seeing the rehabilitation side of working with patients."

"Sometimes that's the hardest part."

"Exactly!" She felt the original spark of passion for the job still burning bright within her. "That's what drew me to it. The challenge of instilling a sense of pride in the patient. Changing the parameters. Looking at things from a new perspective."

"That's how it works all right." Finn put his fork down and took a gulp of tea. "There were about a thousand times I wished I could've unscrewed my head from this old lunky body of mine and screwed a different one on it."

She gave him a sidelong look. From where she was sitting he was looking pretty close to perfect.

"One with a positive attitude," he explained.

Ah. Well. "Everyone has their down days." She took a sip of her tea and lifted her gaze to meet Finn's. He really was an extraordinary man. A flush crept to her cheeks but she ploughed ahead and said what she was thinking. "For what it's worth? I'm glad you kept the one you had."

They looked at one another in the soft light and if Naomi hadn't come here for another reason entirely she would've been hard pressed not to lean across the table and start kissing him all over again.

Though she'd seen his fiery side, she knew now his

temper was usually directed at himself. He was fiercely loyal. That was much apparent. And brave. Her thoughts skipped to Charlie and the look of true respect and admiration he'd given Finn when telling Naomi how Finn had saved his life.

She hadn't saved anyone's life.

And therein lay the crux of the matter.

He was a hero. She was a coward. No wonder she was drawn to him.

She played with her fork for a minute. Took a sip of her tea. She wasn't here to talk about physio. Or her childhood. She was here to explain to Finn why she'd become so emotional about Adao. Too much emotion fueling too many memories.

"The rebels came when we were least expecting it."

Finn nodded, showing no sign of being surprised they'd changed from talking about his head to her home town being invaded by armed rebels.

"I was down at the river, seeing if there had been a catch that day. Food had been…scarce in the previous weeks. We weren't starving but the country had slowly been falling under their reign of terror."

A shiver juddered down her spine at the memory of the helicopters flying overhead, the wild-eyed recruits practically hanging out of the open doors and firing their machine guns indiscriminately. Men, women, children. They hadn't cared. Most of the rebels' so-called cavalry had been poor men bribed with alcohol and drugs. Men who, in another world, could have been convinced to turn their energies to doing good had they been offered food and shelter instead. She tugged the edges of the soft cashmere blanket Finn had draped round her shoulders closer together.

"C'mere." Finn rose and gestured to the comfortable-looking sofa. Worn, golden leather. When she sank into a corner and pulled a cushion onto her lap she felt protected, safe. Finn threw a couple of logs into a small wood burner she hadn't noticed earlier. An image of Finn chopping the precisely cut woodpile by hand flickered through her mind before his silence reminded her she needed to get through this story.

"I heard the helicopters first. My instinct was to run home. I'd asked my boyfriend to meet me there so that we could all eat together that night, but when I heard the shooting and screaming… I…" She pressed her hands to her ears, still hearing the cries of disbelief and fear coming from the normally tranquil country town. "I hid." The words came out as a sob. "I hid underneath some palm leaves I found drying at the edge of the forest because I could see from there. They were loading everyone they could into trucks. Men in some. Women and children in others. They were screaming at everyone to hurry. Telling lies. Saying that they were taking them to refugee camps where they would be safe, but everybody knew where they were really going."

"The mountains?" Finn asked softly.

She nodded, swiping at the tears cascading down her cheeks. From the grim look on his face he knew exactly what a trip to the mountains would have meant for her family and the rest of those other poor, innocent people. The excavation of the mass graves that had been found there only warranted one or two lines of mention in the newspapers these days, but Naomi lived with the knowledge that those she had loved most dearly were very likely amongst the bodies slowly being recovered.

Finn handed her a handkerchief from his pocket. "It's clean."

Their fingers brushed as she accepted the cotton square and the hit of connection felt like a lifeline. A chance to believe in the possibility that one day the weight of guilt might not be as heavy as it was at this very moment.

She swiped at her tears and when she'd steadied her breath she finished her story as quickly as she could. "I hid under the palms for three days."

His eyes widened. "What about food? Water?"

She shook her head. "I was too terrified to move. It rained at night anyway…a warm rain…so I drank what I could from the palm fronds. Even if there had been food I am sure I would have not been able to eat it." Her hands balled into two tight fists in front of the cushion she'd been hugging. "My stomach was tied in knots that day. Permanent knots of guilt and sorrow and shame that I did nothing to help my family."

"Do you still feel that way?"

Pain lanced through her heart. "Of *course* I do. They're still gone. I know the chances of them ever re-appearing are minimal. No. They're not even that." She scrubbed her hands through her hair and looked Finn directly in the eye. "They will never come back. And I will have to live with that guilt for the rest of my life."

"Guilt for what? You wouldn't have been able to save them. If anything, you would've been killed trying or…"

He didn't finish his sentence. He didn't have to. If she'd run and joined her mother on the truck, she would have died with her. But what was the point in living if everyone you loved died knowing you did nothing?

"Have you spoken to anyone else about this? There

are professionals who deal precisely with this kind of trauma."

He should know.

"When I first moved here there was counselling." She rattled off a few truisms from those early days. "There wasn't anything I could do. I would've been killed, too. Look at all of the good I've done now."

"You *do* know all of those things are true." Finn's eyes were diamond bright with emotion. With compassion. It wasn't pity. And for that she was grateful.

"I do. On an intellectual level." She pressed a hand to her chest. "It's knowing it here that I find just about impossible."

Finn reached across and took Naomi's hands in his own. He looked into her eyes so intensely she was certain he was seeing straight through to the very center of her soul.

"Naomi Collins," he began, his voice gruff with emotion. "There is so much that is wrong with the world. You have seen more of it than anyone should have to. Take it from someone who's seen more than his fair share too. But let me tell you this. The light and the joy that you bring to your patients and to the people who work with you—hell, to anyone who's lucky enough to see that beautiful smile of yours…"

He paused, giving one of her cheeks a soft caress with the back of his hand while rubbing the back of her other hand with the pad of his thumb. Her stomach was doing all sorts of flips and it was just as well Finn opened his mouth to keep on talking, because she was positively tongue-tied with disbelief.

"The light and joy you bring to *me*—and, let me tell you, I'm a pretty grumpy character, so that takes some doing—is more than enough to lighten the burden of any guilt that you bear."

The tangle of emotions that, for so long, had been a tight knot in Naomi's chest felt the first hit of relief. A slackening in the constant tension that she should be doing more, or better. Telling her story to someone who understood and who didn't judge or blame her for the decisions she'd made all those years ago released something in her she hadn't realized was locked up tight. For the first time in fourteen years she felt it just might be within her power to receive affection.

"Finn?"

He cupped her cheek in one of his broad hands, the edge of his thumb gently stroking along her jawline. "Yes, love?"

"Thank you." And she meant it. With every pore in her body she meant it.

Finn didn't know if it was he or Naomi who had leant into the kiss, but semantics didn't matter at this point. Neither did the fact that finally being able to hold her in his arms was lighting up every part of him like the center of London. One minute they'd been holding hands and the next they'd been kissing and he'd pulled her up and onto his lap. She was straddling him, one hand cupping his face, one hand raking through his hair as if she'd been made to be there. Made to be with him. Gone were all the shy inhibitions he'd thought he'd seen in her earlier.

The same fierce attraction that had pulled them together at the gym was alight. Touch, taste, scent were all threatening to overwhelm him as their kisses moved from tentative and soft to a much deeper exploration of their shared attraction. He wanted this. He wanted *her*. But it had to be right.

What mattered was Naomi and ensuring she wasn't letting the powerhouse of emotions she'd just shared with him lead her into doing anything she would regret.

Using all the willpower he possessed, Finn pulled back from the deep kiss then tipped his forehead to hers, vividly aware of Naomi's soft, sweet breath on his mouth as he spoke. "Are you sure this is what you want? That *I'm* who you want?"

She put her finger on his lips. "Yes."

He captured her hand in his and gave the tips of her fingers a kiss. He wanted this—he wanted her—but not if it was misplaced emotion fueling her desire. "And you'll feel free to stop or tell me if there's any point you don't want to con—"

She dipped her head to kiss him lightly on the lips. "I will." She spoke again, her lips still brushing against his. "There won't be."

She pulled back so he could see her eyes. They shone with certainty. And desire.

Finn's internal temperature ratcheted up a hundred notches as he ran his hands down her sides, enjoying the shift and wriggle of her body's response as he pulled her in close. Two people reveling in the simple pleasure of holding one another. It had been so long since he'd done this and had been emotionally present. She ran her cheek along his stubble then nestled into the nook of his neck for a few slow kisses along his throat.

He heard himself groan with pleasure. And they weren't anywhere near naked yet. As far as he was concerned, they could keep going as slowly and luxuriously as the long winter's night would allow.

"Do you have a bedroom hidden somewhere around here?"

Her smile was one part timid, another part temptress.

"Yes, I do." He rose and took her hand in his, laying a kiss atop her head as he showed her the way to the bedroom in the stern.

This wasn't pure lust at work. He *cared*. He genuinely cared for this woman and all the beauty and pain she held in that enormous heart of hers.

The night might be a one-off. It could be the start of something more. Either way he would finally know what it was like to be with her after months of wondering. He'd deal with the fallout in the morning.

As she opened the bedroom door and turned to him, eyes filled with questions, he knew that from this moment on, starting with the softest of kisses, the most tender of caresses, he would do everything in his power to make sure she never felt heartache or fear again.

When Finn entered the bedroom, the two of them stood for a moment, frozen between fear and desire. Need trounced tenderness. Hunger savaged restraint. The air crackled with electricity, as if the space between them was a taunt—a dare to see who would be brave enough to make the first move.

Finn's touch was powerful enough to fill the void Naomi had ached to fill ever since her family had been stolen away from her. As he turned the distance between them to nothing, his scent—a heady wash of pine and man and baking—unleashed a craving in her for more.

His caresses, more tender than she had ever known, told her she was no longer alone.

With Finn, she felt invincible. Like a queen who had finally met her true intended after years of isolation and loneliness. With the invincibility also came an unexpected sensation of peace. Cell by cell, her body registered the change.

Their kisses were weighted with intent. With longing. As if they'd known one another far longer than the handful of months Hope Children's Hospital had been open. Their bodies seemed to know one another as if this whole union had simply been a matter of time. Kismet.

She'd never known what it was like to feel whole again.

And when they lay back upon the pillows, a tangle of limbs and duvet and satiation, the tears came. Tears of relief that she still had it in her to love. To believe in a future. Tears of sorrow for the family she would never see again. And through it all Finn held her tight, the beat of his heart keeping time with her own.

A few hours later, Naomi tucked the thick duvet close round Finn's sleeping form, doing her best to work with the gentle sway and rock of the houseboat to quietly tiptoe out of the bedroom, scooping up her discarded pieces of clothing from the floor. Atop a lamp. Hanging from the door handle. Her pants had somehow ended up latched to a hat-rack shaped like a pineapple attached to the wall.

Wow. Finn had some aim.

A slow shimmer of sparkles rippled its way through

her bloodstream as she pulled on layer after layer of out-door clothing in advance of going back to the real world.

Dawn wasn't anywhere near appearing, but already what had happened felt like a moment preserved in aspic. A moment so magical she'd picture it in one of those magic snow globes in her heart because there wasn't any chance something like that could happen again.

Not because she didn't want it to.

In the few hours they had shared in the night she had felt complete. And it terrified her. It felt like leaving her family behind all over again.

She couldn't burden him with her history. Finn clearly possessed the strength to forge ahead, see the future for what it was—a kaleidoscope of possibility. She wasn't there yet. Not by a long shot. And Finn deserved someone stronger. Someone able to forgive themselves for valuing her own life above others.

She pulled the zip up on her puffer jacket, tugged on her woolly hat and slipped her fingers into her gloves before realizing she was hardly breathing. As if exhaling would make part of the magic of what she'd shared with Finn go away.

She forced herself to breathe out and in again. Reality was only a few short steps away.

She slipped out of his houseboat, crossed the gangplank and urged herself into a gentle run. The cadence of her feet pounding on the footpath drummed in reminders of who she was. Physiotherapist…survivor…

The next word was usually coward. It was her daily process of building herself up only to break herself down again, only this time…this time she kept hearing

Finn's soothing words ease away the sharp edges of the accusation she usually hurled at herself.

And yet…trusting that…believing she could still honor the memories of her family and loved ones as well as open her heart to someone and experience such *joy*…it didn't seem possible. It didn't seem *right*.

She pushed herself to run harder, faster. Until she could no longer feel the touch of Finn's fingers on her bare skin. The tickle of the bristles on his chin against her stomach. The warmth of his lips pressing against her own.

Until all she felt was that familiar ache of loss. Only this time it was bigger. This time it wasn't only for what she had lost. But what she would lose if she couldn't release herself from the guilt of having survived what her family had not.

CHAPTER ELEVEN

FINN WOKE UP HAPPY.

Head to toe.

Realizing he was on his own had come as a bit of a shock, but he brushed off Naomi's absence since, for the first time in years, he'd actually slept in. She'd always struck him as an early to bed, early to rise type. Neither did she seem the type to show up in the hospital wearing yesterday's clothes, so…fair enough. Hospital gossip was hard to shake and it had been one night. It was hardly as if they were at the adorable notes on the kitchen table phase of things.

After a brisk shower, he dressed and went back out to the main room, where he stared at the empty kitchen table again. Had he really convinced himself he was cool with the one-night-only thing? Or was this the seismic shift Charlie had warned him would come one day?

Once he'd heard Naomi's story…understood how deep the waters ran beneath that eternally kind smile of hers…he'd known their paths had crossed for a reason. She was the beacon he'd needed to shine a light on his own life. Show him the bridges he still needed to cross. The truths he needed to confront.

He hit the towpath and walked quickly toward the

hospital. An urgent, primal need to see her possessed him. He hunched against the wind and pressed forward. It was cold out. Cold enough to snow if the weather report on his phone was anything to go by.

He followed a group of nurses into the main hospital doors, wondering when he'd last felt this hyped up.

For a surgery?

Months.

Years, maybe.

For a patient?

More recent, but this was different.

For a co-worker he'd just crossed the line from professional to personal with?

Never.

But he'd cross it a million times over if it meant holding Naomi in his arms again.

He knew it as a truth like he knew the thump of his own heartbeat in his chest.

He walked through the hospital's front doors and scanned the huge atrium at the entryway to the hospital. There was no escaping the fact the festive season was creeping up on them fast and furious. Just over two weeks until the big day and the hospital was, courtesy of Evie and her magic elves, reveling in the lead-up.

Two enormous Christmas trees flanked the large glass sliding doors, giving the impression visitors and patients were walking into something more akin to Santa's grotto than a children's hospital, which—he scrubbed at his freshly shaved jaw—he supposed was a good thing.

These poor kids. None of them wanted to be in hospital. Especially at Christmastime. Despite the early hour, he'd bet Naomi was seeking refuge here for exactly the same reasons he'd thrown himself into retraining as a pediatric limb specialist. To forget about herself and pour her energies into her patients.

"Are you planning on making yourself part of the scenery or are you actually going to work?" Marco gave him a jolly thump on the back as he and Alice took off their winter coats and joined him in soaking up the festive atmosphere.

"I don't know. I'd make a pretty cute Santa's helper, don't you think?"

Both Marco and Alice looked slightly surprised to see Finn waggle his eyebrows and do a mini-jig. Well. It was a stationary jig but, hey, he was new at this "jolly chap" thing, so…

"Hey, Finn. While we have you here, you've not got yourself booked up before Christmas, have you?"

He shook his head, though he had a fair few things he knew he'd like to fill his social calendar with and they all sounded a lot like Naomi.

"Go on." Marco gave Alice a loving squeeze. "Show him."

"He doesn't want to see this."

"See what?"

"This." Marco held out Alice's hand just as the sun broke through the clouds. It hit the ring to glittering effect.

Finn pretended to be blinded by the ring's brilliance. "So it's official, then."

"It will be even more so by Christmas. Here…" Marco scribbled a date and a location onto a sticky piece of paper and pressed it on to Finn's chest. "Consider this your early invitation."

Alice laughed and rolled her eyes. "There will be

something a bit more official than a sticky note in a few days."

Finn took off the note, put it in his pocket, watching as Alice and Marco wandered off toward the wards, arm in arm. It looked nice. It looked…solid.

"Finn!"

He whirled round and saw a grinning Evie. She was wearing a silly reindeer jumper complete with glowing nose on it.

Why was everyone so *happy* today?

Wait a minute.

He was happy today.

Evie brandished her watch at him. "Countdown to Christmas is officially under way!"

He resisted the curmudgeonly urge to point out that the countdown to Christmas was *always* under way… that was how time worked…and smiled instead.

"Are you still planning on helping out at the Christmas party?" She scanned her clipboard as if suddenly doubting herself. "I've got you down as a yes."

He gave her a distracted yes, not entirely sure if he remembered when the long-awaited party was.

"Bringing anyone?"

That got his attention. There was only one person he'd like as a plus one. Not that he knew where she was. The entire staff of Hope Children's Hospital seemed to be swirling in and out of the atrium, buying coffees, getting first dibs on the fresh-out-of-the-oven mince pies, admiring the decorations. Everything but telling him where Naomi was.

"Finn?" Evie prompted. "Are you bringing anyone tomorrow or are you lending a hand on your own?"

"Why? What's tomorrow?"

Evie gave a faux sigh of exasperation. "What we were just talking about. The Christmas party? For the children?"

"Yes. Right. Of course. No. Maybe." He looked at Evie's list, which appeared to be as long as Santa's list of toys. "Does it matter?"

She gave him a curious glance then shook her head and smiled. "No. Of course it doesn't. Just as long as we're all there to show the children just how big the Christmas spirit is here at Hope."

"Count me in. You've done an incredible job, Evie. The place is looking magical."

And he meant it, too. The whole world looked different today. Now, if he could only find the person who'd helped change his perspective.

Finn could feel Evie's curious expression on his back as he strode away toward the surgical ward. He had a full roster today and needed to get his head screwed back on straight.

This whole "looking forward" thing was not only messing with his ability to focus, it was adding a bit of a kick to his step.

"Hey, Alana. You and Doodle are looking well today. Hi, Adao."

Naomi waved to Adao from the doorway, waiting for Alana and Doodle to finish their session. Adao's demeanor was still pretty forlorn, even with the curly-haired pooch nestled up beside him on the bed.

Her spirits sagged.

The photo of his parents might've done the trick for a minute or two, but the little boy, now that she had a moment to watch him talk with Doodle, wasn't much chirpier than he'd been that very first day. And who could blame him? He was in pain. He was adjusting to an entirely new way of dealing with his body. The whole hospital was bedecked and beribboned with all the Christmas festivities and he was here all alone.

She knew that feeling so well and yet…for the first time in her adult life she knew she didn't have to. Finn had thrown her a lifeline. A chance to live and see life from an entirely new perspective.

A flight of butterflies took off in her belly as she thought of Finn. His big bear body all tucked in under the duvet looking more peaceful than she'd ever seen him. His arms tightly around her as they'd slept. Well, *he'd* slept, she'd fretted.

The last thing she was going to do was set herself up for more loss.

"I'm afraid it's our time to go, Adao." Alana picked up Doodle's lead and clicked it onto his collar.

Tears welled in the little boy's eyes. "Can't he stay?"

"Not all day, I'm afraid. We've got to go visit some other children and then Doodle's got to go for a walk. Perhaps…" The therapist looked to Naomi for support. "Perhaps when you're feeling a bit stronger, you'll be able to come out for a walk with us."

Naomi smiled. "As long as we get you wrapped up nice and warm, that sounds good to me." She grinned at Adao. "What do you think of that?"

He gave a lackluster shrug.

Poor little guy.

Perhaps going outside was exactly what he needed. Her runs along the river were far more therapeutic than just a bit of physical exercise. Maybe if she could get Adao outside at the party tomorrow…

Alana and Doodle stopped in the doorway so Naomi could give the pooch a cuddle. His furry face was so lovely and open it was little wonder the children felt safe telling him their secrets. She was seriously beginning to think of getting her own dog, seeing how wonderful Doodle was with the children.

Then again… Finn was easy to speak with. And he gave good advice, too, whereas Doodle's talents peaked at furry cuddles. She buried her face in Doodle's curls for a moment, trying to turn her own expression neutral. It was almost impossible to believe the Finn she had just spent the night with was the same man who'd practically bitten her head off every time she'd seen him over the past few months.

To think…all that time it had been attraction holding him at bay.

Mutual attraction.

And it went so much deeper than the physical. Last night she had wanted nothing more than for him to know her. Understand her.

And when she'd taken that risk and told him the raw truth about her past—how shamefully she'd behaved— he'd painted an entirely different picture. He had been so thoughtful. And kind. Not to mention the best kisser she'd met. A ripple of pleasure shimmied down her spine at the memories. Kissing on the sofa. In the kitchen. In his bedroom.

What had possessed her? She'd never behaved like that before with a man. She'd never been so open with *anyone*. Urgh! She wasn't meant to have let herself fall head over heels—

Wait a minute.

Was she in love with Finn?

The thought threatened to overwhelm her so completely she shut it down immediately. Of course she wasn't. She barely knew the man.

Well, that wasn't true. She knew a whole lot more about him now than she had just a handful of days ago. He was generous. A good listener. Amazing with children. Had an ex-wife. Had saved a life. Had an excellent reputation as a surgeon.

What on earth was he doing, wanting someone like her? Someone who'd let her entire family down at the time they'd needed her most?

"Naomi? Is everything all right?"

Alana was peering down at her as she all but kept a stranglehold on the poor therapy dog.

Naomi popped up to standing and gave her leggings an unnecessary swipe. "Yes. Good. Perfect." A crazy laugh burbled up and out of her throat. "Clearly in need of a hug."

"Who needs a hug?"

Her spine slammed ramrod-straight as her heart started jumping up and down as if it had just won the lottery.

Finn.

The man had a way of being there exactly when— when she did and didn't need him.

"No one." She smiled, doing her best to ignore the confusion in his eyes. Steering clear of that intense gaze of his might be the only way she could get through this day. "Adao and I were just going to have a session and Doodle was kind enough to give me a hug on his way out."

"Very generous of the old boy." Finn's tone had slipped from congenial to neutral and, despite the fact

Naomi had hoped for things to stay professional, she already missed the warmth in his voice. "Mind if I have a quick word with the lad about his prosthetic casting before you begin?

"Not at all. Adao?"

Adao nodded somberly as Finn talked him through how a team from the prosthetics department would be coming in and taking off his bandages. "But it's nothing to worry about, all right? They're going to cast a mold of your shoulder area and measure your residuum."

"Residuum?" Alana whispered to Naomi.

"It's what's left of his arm. They'll need to measure the shape perfectly so that his prosthesis works well with what he's got left."

"Such a brave little boy." Alana absently stroked Doodle's head as she spoke, but to Naomi the gesture spoke volumes. She was seeking comfort. Seeing someone you cared about endure pain—no matter how big or small—was hard. Just as her instinct had been to go to Finn when she'd seen him that first time without his prosthesis. Everything in her head had all but screamed out for her to go to him. To help. To help him through his pain.

Now that she actually could go to him—to talk, for a hug, for another one of those spine-tinglingly perfect kisses—acting on it was even more frightening than it had been when he was a virtual stranger.

Because now it mattered if she lost him.

"Right, then. I'll leave you to your session with Naomi, but we'll see you in an hour or so, all right?"

Finn crossed the room to Naomi, who was shifting

some paperwork around in a folder. Presumably something to do with her session with Adao.

"Hey." He kept his voice low. "Everything okay?"

"Yes, of course. Why?"

We spent the night together and you disappeared.

"Nothing." They were at work. He wasn't going to press it. "Hey." He gave the door a light pat to get her attention before she began her session. "Do you fancy meeting up for a coffee later or something after work?"

She gave an apologetic shake of the head. "Sorry. Full day today and I promised Evie I'd help get things ready for the party tomorrow." She reached for the door as if to shut it.

"The Christmas party?" He held it open. She nodded, her eye contact hitting all the points around him but never solidly meeting his gaze.

Had he done anything? Said anything to upset her? If so, he wanted to fix it.

"I've really got to get on." She pressed the door again and this time he dropped his hand and watched it shut. How was that for poetic justice? A door closing right in his face just when he'd thought a new path in life had just opened to him.

Right.

He glanced at his watch. An hour until his next surgery. A poor little girl born with curly toes. Sounded cute. Was actually very painful. Now that they had exhausted all the physiotherapy routes and waited for her to reach the ripe old age of four to see if her tendons were going to offer her any relief, he was hoping to put an end to that pain today.

He headed to his office, mulling over Naomi's cool reaction to seeing him after last night. He suspected there was a lot more to Naomi's lack of eye contact and polite thanks but, no, thanks to his invitation to meet up than a simple case of "buyer's remorse."

Quite the opposite, he was suspecting.

Intimacy was the one thing he'd been unable to bear when he'd been hurt. A lot of his mates from the military had also struggled to make a start on a relationship—or, even more to the point, hold onto one. Help it flourish and grow.

He grabbed the back of the wheeled chair in his office and let it take his full weight as he picked up his phone from his desk and thumbed through the address book. There was one person who knew exactly what it was like to be an open and loving soul on the receiving end of a person going through hell.

He stared at the phone for a moment then, after years of promising himself he would press "call," he pressed down on the little green receiver icon and lifted the phone to his ear.

Hearing her voice say hello was like being yanked straight back in time—except this time he had perspective. This time he wasn't a raging ball of fury. This time there was gratitude she had been as kind to him as she had.

"Caroline. It's me. Finn."

The line was silent for a moment and he was just about to explain who he was again when she spoke.

"You think I wouldn't recognize your voice after all these years?" There was no acrimony in her voice. No bitterness. He heard children's laughter in the background and a dog bark, followed by Caroline's muffled instructions to take the dog outside while she spoke on the phone. An old friend was on the line.

An old friend.

Generous of her.

"You've got kids."

"Observant as ever." She laughed easily then gave a little sigh. "I've landed on my feet, Finn. I hope the reason you're calling is to tell me you have, too."

"Tell me about you some more first." He pushed his chair back from his desk and threw his good leg up onto his desk and gave his knee a rub as she told him how she'd transferred schools after things had fallen apart with him so she could be closer to her family in the Cotswolds. She was a primary school teacher and had stuck with it. After keeping a close guard on her heart for a while, the gentle persistence of a certain black-haired, blue-eyed teacher across the corridor from her classroom had eventually persuaded her she should let herself love again.

They had two children now—Matty and Willow— and a dog named Mutt.

"So-o-o-o...." Caroline persisted. "I'm presuming you're not calling me to tell me bad news or you would've said it by now. Are your parents all right?"

He smiled at the receiver. Even all these years later she still knew him pretty well. As for his news? He was...*by God*...he was pretty sure he was in love again.

"The parents are fine. Tanning like lizards down in Spain." He'd rung them last week and would ring again. Let them know he finally had news on Caroline and that things might have changed for him a bit as well. "I'm sorry," he said.

"For what?" Caroline's hand went back over the receiver as she issued some more instructions to her children, who had burst back indoors again. He heard something about Santa keeping close tabs on them followed by a sudden, obedient silence.

"That usually keeps then in check," Caroline said in such a way he could practically see the smile on her face. She'd always wanted to be a mother and he'd always wanted "just one more tour" before they began a family. Sounds like things had panned out for her just as she'd hoped. Eventually, of course. What was the saying? After the storm came the rainbow. Something like that. Whatever it was, he hoped her rainbow was a double.

"I'm sorry I was such a git," he said. "After…you know…everything."

"You weren't exactly seeing silver linings when you got back, Finn." Caroline's voice was soft. Forgiving. "And it's me who should be thanking you."

"What? For being a right old ass and pushing away the one person who loved me most?"

"Your parents probably had the market on that one." Caroline laughed then fell silent for a moment. "Look, we were kids when we were married. Did I hope and pray it would work out? Of course I did. I loved you."

"Loved?" He knew he was being cheeky, but it was nice to know the vows they'd taken had meant something. They'd meant something to him, and tearing them apart as he had—ruthlessly—had been like destroying part of his own moral code.

"You know what I mean. I'm happy now. Really happy. And I wouldn't be married to this great guy or have these fabulous, extra-noisy kids of mine if things hadn't gone the way they had with us. It took a while, but I see now that I wasn't the person to help you get back up. You were the only one who could do that and you were determined to do it alone."

"That I was." Finn huffed out a laugh. "Turns out it takes a lot longer if you do it on your own."

"Yes, it does." He could picture her nodding and smiling in that endearing way of hers and was heartened to realize the place he had in his heart for Caroline was very firmly in the "cherished friends" section.

"Are you in love, Finn? Is that why you're ringing? I hope to God you're not going to ask my permission, because you've always had my blessing to find joy."

He barked a laugh. "How the hell did you figure that out from a few 'what's been going on for the past twelve years of your life' questions?"

"Ha! I'm *right*. Love that. Totally easy to figure out." He heard her blow on her knuckles and knew she was giving them a bit of a polish on whatever top she was wearing. Most likely a goofy Christmas jumper if she was anything like she used to be.

"Easy how?"

"Easy because you've never rung me before and your voice has a certain puppy-dog quality to it."

"What? Roughty-toughty me? I don't think so."

"I do," Caroline said firmly. "So what's holding you back? You'd better not say it's me, because that ship sailed long ago, my friend." She spoke without animosity and Finn knew she was doing her best to tell him that whatever guilt he had about the past wasn't necessary anymore. She was in a great place and she wouldn't be there if he hadn't left her.

Finn thought for a moment. Losing his leg had ripped him from his past in one cruel instant. He'd never be the lifelong soldier he'd planned on becoming. But it was different for Naomi. She'd not had any sort of closure as far as he could make out. Her internal life still seemed dominated by what she thought she *should* have done. An impossible position to live with when your choices had been life or death.

"I think she might be afraid that if she lets herself love me, she'll lose her link to the past." He didn't tell her Naomi's story. It wasn't his to tell, but it gave Caroline the lie of the land.

"Well, then. I guess someone had better find himself a way to prove to her that it is possible to love again, and still be true to yourself."

"Good advice, Caroline."

"Yeah, well…" She could've said a lot of things here. She'd learned from bitter experience. Life could be cruel when you least expected it. But she didn't. Because she obviously also knew that life could be kind and full of richly rewarding happiness that made near enough anything seem possible. Even convincing the woman he loved that she wasn't betraying her family by opening up her heart again.

"Happy Christmas, Finn," Caroline said.

"Happy Christmas to you, my friend. And thank you."

"Couldn't think of a nicer Christmas present than to hear you've finally found yourself again."

"Took long enough."

"Well, you're tall," she said. Then laughed. They garbled a farewell as her children's quiet time erupted into a spontaneous round of "Jingle Bells."

He said goodbye, not even sure if she heard him, but the warm feeling he had in his chest told him all he needed to know.

Caroline had forgiven him and moved on. All the proof he needed that miracles existed.

Now all he needed to do was show Naomi she could trust him to be there for her. He was ready now. Ready to live his life to the fullest. And the one way it would be the best life possible was to know he would have Naomi by his side.

CHAPTER TWELVE

NAOMI PUSHED HER tray along the counter of the hospital cafeteria, not really seeing the food options. Normally she loved it here. The social atmosphere. Doctors, families, hospital employees all taking a break from "the medicine business" to enjoy a meal. When it wasn't absolutely freezing out, like today, the cafeteria's concertina doors opened up to a small garden that was scattered with picnic tables.

"Do you mind if I take that?"

Naomi turned to see Madison Archer, the diagnostician from America, reaching for the last bowl of Christmas pudding drowning in a puddle of custard. Truly healthy fare for a hospital.

Her shoulders hunched up around her ears as she inhaled and let out a sigh. It was Christmas. People deserved a treat.

"It's all yours," she said to Madison, even though it was a bit of a moot point at this juncture. "Enjoy." She tacked that on to make herself sound cheerier than she felt.

"Is that what you're eating?" Madison asked as they shuffled up the queue a couple more steps.

Naomi stared at her tray as if seeing it for the first

time. A bowl of applesauce. A plate of spaghetti. And a yoghurt.

"Nothing on there really looks like it matches." Madison reached across Naomi toward the fruit bowl and pointed at a banana just out of reach. Naomi handed it to her. "So. Are you pregnant?"

Naomi's eyes went wide. She and Finn had used protection and it wasn't like she wanted children right away anyhow— Wait. No. This whole line of thought was completely going in the wrong direction.

Madison unleashed a triumphant smile. "Am I right?" She gave a little air punch. "God, I needed a win."

Naomi winced an apology. "Sorry. I'm just distracted. Not pregnant." She stared at her tray of mismatched food and bought it all anyhow. She could put the yoghurt in the staff fridge for later when she was filling up gift bags for the children...also known as avoiding Finn so he could forget about her as soon as possible.

She gave Madison a quick smile then wound her way through the lunchtime crowd to the one free table in the room.

A bite or two into her spaghetti she laid down her fork. Nothing was right today. Ever since she'd left Finn's houseboat without leaving so much as a note, the entire day had felt off kilter.

"Sorry. All the other tables are full and I've not really found an office to claim as my own yet. Do you mind?" Madison was already settling down in the chair, so Naomi scooched her tray over a bit to make room for her. More quizzes on whether or not she was pregnant were definitely not what she was after. She would've eaten in the gym, but every time she'd walked in there today all she'd been able to think of was Finn…a shirtless Finn…and being kissed by him and held by him and— *Urgh*.

Stop. Thinking. About. Finn.

"Enjoying your stay?" Naomi asked, to cover the fact that she was playing with her food and the few bites she had taken had tasted like cardboard.

"Not particularly," said Madison, stabbing at one of the small roast potatoes that had come with her chicken and vegetables.

Naomi sat back in her chair and looked at the forthright woman across from her, then laughed. "You've definitely not let the English way of covering up how you really feel get to you, then."

Madison shrugged. "Why would I do that? Wastes time. And energy." She cut off a piece of chicken and brandished it in Naomi's face. "If I could just get disease to be as forthright as I am, I would be one happy customer." She ate her chicken.

"If only life could be that simple."

"But it isn't, is it?" Madison pounced on the statement. "It's a complex, difficult and solitary business." The diagnostician didn't seem angry about it. That was just the way life was. She stabbed another potato with her fork and popped it into her mouth.

Naomi was about to protest when she realized she had actually been living her own life precisely as Madison had succinctly put it. Definitely the solitary part. But who at the end of the day was she protecting? Certainly not her family. Whether she was happy or sad, single or falling in love, it would never change what had happened to them.

"Do you think it has to be? Solitary?"

Madison's green eyes widened at the question then softened. "Maybe not. I just find it's easiest." She stared at her plate for a moment then stood. "I think I'll finish this pudding thing on the ward. See if the ensuing sugar high gives me any insight."

"Ivy?" Naomi asked.

"Hmm." Madison scanned the room as if looking for an escape route.

"The trays go over there. Against the wall." Naomi rose with her own tray. She didn't have much of an appetite either.

"Too many mince pies?" Madison asked, as her final stab at conversation.

"Something like that," Naomi said to Madison's back as the redhead slid her tray onto the rack and headed toward the cafeteria's main doors where an all-too-familiar figure appeared.

"Butterflies, more like," Naomi whispered, as she turned and headed for a side exit. "Definitely butterflies."

Finn glanced through the glass doors into the gym and saw Naomi putting away some equipment from a session with a patient. A pretty strong one, from the looks of the weights she was hoiking about. Now that he was finally being honest with himself, admitting that he loved Naomi, it was a true pleasure to watch her pootle about the gym, slipping things into place, having little conversations with herself—presumably about one patient or another.

When she looked up, those warm eyes of hers lit up when she saw him, and just as quickly dulled.

He pushed through the swinging gym doors. No point in standing outside like a creepy stalker. Besides, he had to get down to the sports center.

"Hey, there."

"Hi." Naomi started rearranging the weights he'd only just seen her settle into place. Unnecessary busy work.

"I'm just going to put it out there. It seems like you're avoiding me."

A nervous laugh formed a protective bubble around Naomi, telling him all he needed to know. "No. Of course not."

"So…" He sat down on one of the large balancing balls in the room and stared at his hands for a moment. "Why am I getting the opposite impression?"

"I'm not avoiding you," she said, dodging meeting the clear gray of his eyes as she spoke. "I just… It's been busy."

"Too busy to come out for a mug of hot chocolate?" He pointed in the direction of the atrium. "My shout."

"No. Sorry. I…"

Finn watched as she floundered for an excuse and decided to put her out of her misery. He rose from the balancing ball and cupped her shoulders in his hands. "I liked what happened between us the other night. Did it scare the hell out of me? Absolutely. Do I want it to happen again? Definitely. Will I encounter some stumbling blocks in unveiling the true Charm Machine that lives somewhere under this grumpy bear exterior? I hope so. For you. For me. For what I think could be an 'us'… I really hope so."

Naomi wriggled out from beneath his hands. "Thank you. I've just— I've got a lot to do tonight."

"This wouldn't have anything to do with feeling guilty about letting yourself actually enjoy your life, would it?"

From the sharp look of dismay that creased her features Finn knew he'd hit the nail on the head.

"Hey." He brushed the back of his hand along her soft cheek. "I know what you're feeling. And if you believe you can trust in that, trust in me. I will be here for you when you're ready."

An hour later, down at the sports center, the feeling that he might've pushed too hard kept losing Finn point after point.

"I hope she's worth it," Charlie called out as he threw the basketball through the hoop with a fluid swoosh.

"Who?"

Playing dumb had been one of his fortes during the dark years. But it didn't always work with Charlie.

"The woman giving you a taste of your own medicine."

"And what medicine is that exactly?" Finn grunted as Charlie threw the ball at him. Hard.

"The kind of medicine a man deserves when he's pushed and pushed every woman who's ever tried to get close to him as far away as he can and then, when he falls hook, line and sinker, is made to work for it."

"That obvious?"

"That obvious."

Charlie wheeled to the side of the court and chalked up his hands then came back to give Finn a quick once-over. "You've got The Look."

"The Look? What the hell is that?"

"All doe-eyed and soppy-faced—"

Finn punched him in the arm. "There isn't a doe-eyed cell in my body."

"Rubbish. You're one of the most romantic men I've ever met. It's why you fell to bits after…" Charlie tipped his head toward Finn's leg, his expression as sober as a judge's. "You wanted things to be perfect. Your vision for how you saw your life, army, marriage, the whole shebang had been all planned out. You hadn't planned on this happening. Not ever again. Well, my friend, it's happened. So how are you going to deal with it? Fight or flight?"

Despite himself, Finn laughed. There was no point in acting the fool in front of Charlie. He dropped onto the bench next to where Charlie had wheeled his chair. "All right, then, O Wise One. What do you prescribe to make sure I don't follow old patterns?"

Charlie leaned back in his chair and stroked an invisible beard. "Listen, my son, to the wise man who has been married many years. To win this woman's heart, you must be there."

"Be there?" Finn had been prepared for a half-hour lecture on understanding the finer points of a woman's psychology, but this was clearly all he was getting.

"That's the one." Charlie nodded, the idea of a beard clearly growing on him as he continued to "stroke" it, waiting for the light bulb to ping on with Finn.

Finn scrubbed a towel over his head and draped it across his shoulders.

Be there.

Charlie was right. Naomi had not only lost her family and boyfriend that day. She'd lost her home town. Her country. Her birthright.

No wonder it was hard to commit to him. Falling

in love with someone so different, so far away from the life…the light bulb went on…*the life she'd thought she'd have*. To fall in love with him, Naomi would have to let go of every single childhood hope and dream and allow herself to believe in a new Naomi. A new life. A new set of dreams. All at the expense of everything she'd ever believed would be true.

He snapped Charlie with his towel. "Who made you so wise?"

Charlie gave his invisible beard a final stroke then grinned. "A really good friend saved my life once. Puts a lot of things into perspective." He popped a wheelie in his chair. "That. And I married a woman who told me if I so much as thought of checking out on her when the going got tough I was going to wish I was dead once she'd got through with me!"

They laughed.

"You got a good one," Finn said.

"And so is Naomi. I could tell that the moment I set eyes on her."

Finn gave him a how-the-hell-did-you-know-it-was-Naomi? glare and Charlie guffawed. "Mate. Your face was puppy dog from the moment she entered this sports center. You are a goner." He wheeled around him and pointed at him. "But not in the real sense. Remember. Be there. That's the most important thing."

CHAPTER THIRTEEN

Despite all the confusion knocking around her head about Finn, Naomi couldn't help but feel a growing fizz of excitement over the Christmas party at the hospital today.

Evie had seriously outdone herself. She had stayed with Naomi for two extra hours at the hospital last night to sort out some of the final decorations. Naomi had watched, transfixed, as she'd handed over her precious little one, Grace, to Ryan with a thousand words of warning on how to care for her. He'd laughed and kissed her, reminding his future bride he was a doctor and, as a pediatric heart surgeon, had a rough idea how to care for infants.

Naomi pulled on the silly Christmas jumper Evie had given her last night in thanks for helping. When she pulled on the ivory top, edged round the sleeves, hem and neckline with holly-berry-red stitching, she had to admit, she'd drawn the lucky card.

Where other doctors were being doled out jumpers complete with blinking lights or designs that made them look like miniature elves or pot-bellied Santas, hers was almost elegant. A pair of gold antlers was stitched into the fabric and "floated' above a perfect red nose.

She considered her reflection in the mirror, twisting this way and that, only stopping when she realized she was being this vain because she was wondering what Finn would think.

Her heart was already telling her. Finn was looking to the future…a future with her…if only she would take his hand and join him.

Had he spelled it out? No. Had she seen it in his eyes each time she'd dodged his attempts to talk? Without a doubt.

This was up to her now. She looked into the mirror again. Without having even noticed, she'd woven her hands together in front of her heart as if they were providing some sort of shield. But what was it she really wanted protection from? Happiness?

It seemed ridiculous and yet… Allowing herself the true happiness of falling in love and all that could follow in true love's wake, was that bigger than living with the constant fear that she'd never be entirely present? That part of her would always be in Africa?

Her phone buzzed on the little table by her front door.

Evie. She was already down at the hospital, wondering if Naomi fancied coming along to help get the ball rolling.

A few hours later and Evie finally admitted there was nothing left to be done, apart from have the actual party.

The small green in front of the hospital had been utterly transformed from a frost-covered, plain expanse of grass to a winter wonderland.

"All we need is snow," Naomi sighed.

"That," agreed Evie," would be the icing on the cake."

Together the pair of them looked up at the sky then

took in the party scene spread out before them. A bouncy castle shaped like an ice palace was nestled in amongst about a dozen stalls all giving away warm, spiced apple juice or hot chocolate. Others had platters filled with amazing glittery cake pops shaped like miniature Santas and snowmen. There were star-shaped cheese crackers and even a huge Christmas-tree-shaped vegetable platter with a pretzel "trunk" surrounded by all sorts of tasty-looking dips. An enormous tray of reindeer-shaped sandwiches was already doing the rounds with curly pretzels standing in as antlers and a perfect roundel of red radish taking the role of the nose. At the far end of the smattering of stalls hosting games for the children was a carousel! Where on earth Evie had magicked that up remained a mystery. Whenever Naomi asked, Evie would just tap the side of her nose and say, "I've got love on my side. Anything's possible when you're in love."

Anything except changing the past.

It felt discordant to have such a gloomy thought when everything about her was all sparkles and glitter and twinkling magic. Maybe a bit of Evie's "love magic" would rub off on her.

Only if you let it, you numpty.

And she wasn't ready to let go. Not yet. Maybe not ever.

"Want a gingerbread man?" Evie held out a cheerily decorated biscuit to Naomi, dancing it toward her with a zany jigging movement. She looked every bit as excited as the children who were starting to arrive from the main entrance of the hospital, all bundled up in their warmest winter clothing, with nurses, parents and scores of others.

Naomi laughed and took the biscuit, holding it slightly aloft as Evie shot past her to attend to a red baubles or silver baubles crisis while Naomi went through the age-old conundrum of deciding whether to bite the gingerbread man's head off or start with his foot.

"I bet you go with the foot first. Then he'll look like me."

Finn's deep voice crackled like a warm hit of electricity along her spine and, despite the urge to run away, Naomi forced herself to turn around and smile. She couldn't imagine him making a joke about his leg a few weeks ago.

A few weeks ago she hadn't been able to imagine him being *nice* to her, let alone setting her entire body alight with a single brush of his hand. The least she could do was afford him a festive smile. She made a show of biting the hand off, knowing it was a contrary move, but he was disarming her. His gray eyes seemed to hold an extra luster today, jewel-bright against the dark clouds gathering in the distance. He was wearing a scarlet-colored hat that made the dark curls peeking through seem even more mahogany rich than they did without it.

He had what looked like a hand-knitted scarf, dark blue, wrapped round his neck and was wearing a light blue jumper with…gold antlers and a single red nose.

"We match." Finn stretched out his jumper as proof.

Oh, yes, they did. In so many ways.

A warmth lit up her belly as her body took its time remembering just how much they did match.

Unable to hold his gaze, her eyes flicked away from his, scanning the large green, hoping an excuse to run away would jump out at her.

"This is all looking pretty spectacular."

Finn reached out and put his hand on the small of her back as a woman led an immaculately groomed Shetland pony past them and toward a small trap that had been reconfigured to look like a sleigh.

A part of her was desperate to bolt and seek refuge somewhere quiet and solitary, while another part of her wanted to feel that lovely, large hand of his touch her back until the end of time. Despite the layers of fabric between them, heat radiated from the spot where he held his hand and it took all the power she possessed not to lean into it. Heck. It took all the power she possessed not to go up on tiptoe and throw her arms around him and tell him she knew she was being strange, but she was scared and her fear was her problem and hers alone.

"Naomi." Finn shifted round so he was facing her. "I know things have been a bit awkward between us since…" His eyes flicked down toward the river with enough meaning in them to indicate the night they'd spent in his houseboat. "What do you say we start again with a clean slate?" He performed a courtly bow. "Would you do me the honor of coming to this afternoon's party with me as my date?"

Her heart skipped a beat at the invitation. The warmth in his eyes told her so much. He was willing to take it slowly. Go at her pace. *Be there for her.* That someone could be so kind, so generous threatened to change the cadence of her racing heart. It was a risk she simply found too terrifying. Patients came and went. That she could cope with. But loving and losing again?

Is it worth losing him without having even let yourself try loving him?

The ache in her heart threatened to tear her in two.

She simply didn't know and choosing to be alone seemed the safest option. Always had been. Always would.

"I've got to go and get Adao," she finally said apologetically, when the intensity of Finn's gaze became too much. "I promised him I'd be his date."

A flash of something all too easy to read shot across Finn's eyes.

Hurt.

It twisted her heart so tightly she could barely breathe. "Excuse me." She gave his arm a quick squeeze then set off at a jog toward the hospital entrance, weaving in and out of the crowds of children, their parents, their doctors and nurses, all wreathed in smiles and bathed in laughter as they saw the magical world Evie had created for them.

Questions assaulted her with each step she took.

Why couldn't she let that joy into her own heart?

Why couldn't she allow Finn to shine some light into her world after such a very long time of living cloaked under the weight of guilt and sorrow?

Because they were your family *and you left them behind.*

"Oops. You going in or coming out?" Alice Baxter was wheeling a child out of the front door.

"In. To get a patient," she hastily explained, stepping out of the heavy flow of traffic heading out to the green. From where she was standing, there was already a queue forming at Santa's grotto.

"Have you seen Marco?"

Naomi smiled. She knew Marco Ricci was the one who had put that non-stop smile onto Alice's face.

"I'm pretty sure I saw him with a set of twins. Twelve-year-old boys, both of them on crutches."

A slip and fall on the ice hockey rink in a spat over a home goal, if she remembered correctly. They were both scheduled to come in to have some physio when their casts came off.

"Excellent. See you out there!" She dropped Naomi a quick wink as she passed. "With any luck, I'll find Marco under the mistletoe!"

Wow. Everyone seemed to have sunbeams shooting out of their ears today.

Little wonder.

Alice was in love.

Evie was in love.

Obviously the same was true for Marco and Ryan.

It was as if the mistletoe fairy had come and sprinkled her fairy love dust over the whole of Hope Children's Hospital…

Was there anyone in this place who wasn't in love besides…?

Her shoulders drooped as her spirits plummeted to the bottom of her boots. *You could be too if you let yourself.*

She gave herself a quick shake and slipped through the traffic coming out the main door.

Adao.

She needed to get Adao and spend the day with him. That would keep her nice and distracted. No more thoughts about love or tall, gorgeous, ex-servicemen turned surgical geniuses needed here. Especially not ones with hands that drove her body wild when—

Naomi pressed her lips together hard and jabbed the elevator button so hard it hurt.

Served her right.

For everything.

Her focus should be on Adao. And after that there'd be another patient and another and another until… How long would she have to keep paying penance for something she couldn't have changed?

Fourteen more years?

Never?

Forgiveness came in many forms. She'd said that once to a parent chastising themselves for taking their eye off their child who had fallen and broken their arm.

Forgiveness comes in many forms.

The question was, would she ever be ready to forgive herself? Until that happened, she would always be alone.

Finn lifted the three-year-old off the carousel and gently deposited her in her mother's arms.

"Have a lovely afternoon."

What the hell? He sounded like one of his mum's friends after they'd popped round for tea.

"Thanks so much." The mum smiled and whirled around, both her and her daughter's cheeks pink with a combination of the fresh winter air and the exhilaration of the afternoon. If they were giving out medals today, Evie deserved a gold. No doubt about it. The party was a through and through success.

"Oops. Easy there, Adao."

Finn whirled round at the sound of Naomi and Adao's voices.

"Need a hand getting onto the carousel?"

Naomi's dark eyes flicked up to meet Finn's. He hated seeing the panic in them when she saw it was him.

"Yes, please, Mr. Morgan," Adao piped up. "May I ride the black one?"

Finn smiled down at Adao. It was nice to see the little guy up and about. Apart from the rumored smile when he'd received the picture of his parents, he remained as somber as ever. His arm was healing nicely and within a few days he should be fitted for the prosthetic that was being made at a special factory that supplied them.

"Absolutely. We just need to let it come to a stop so we can get you safely up there and then you can have a ride. Sound good?"

Adao nodded as if he had just agreed to accept responsibility for Finn's most prized horse.

Finn enjoyed watching Naomi interact with the little boy. Kneeling down when she spoke to him so they were eye to eye. Assuring him that "proper riders" only used one hand for the reins.

When the carousel came to a halt again, Finn helped Adao up and onto a glistening ebony stallion, avoiding jogging his arm as much as he could. The stallion's mane was painted a shimmering gold with a saddle painted on in shades of deep reds and oranges.

Naomi walked round to the far side to help offer Adao support if he needed it, but for now he was holding on tight to the stallion's reins, his face serious as the carousel began to turn and the horse began to "gallop" up and down.

Still avoiding eye contact with Finn, Naomi began to jog in place, pretending to try and keep up with Adao as his horse "galloped' forward.

"I'm just about there! I'm coming to get you."

The corners of Adao's mouth began to twitch as Naomi carried on with her jape, dropping her hands to her knees to pant for a moment then straining to "catch up" as the horse leapt and dipped with the rhythm of the festive music.

Finn watched, delighted, as, at long last, Adao's face lit up with a genuine smile. His smile spread like sunshine and lit up Naomi's features as well. He knew it had only been a few days since he'd seen her share a genuine laugh with someone, but it felt like it had been weeks.

Naomi leant in to ask Adao a question.

He didn't quite catch what she'd said, but the words "Christmas" and "wish" leapt out at him.

He could've told Naomi in a second what his was. But this was Adao's time so he watched as the young boy's expression grew very still as he considered his options.

The music began to slow, along with the movement of the carousel, just as Adao seemed to make up his mind.

"For Christmas," he began, "I would love to see my parents. And I would love to see snow."

Tears sprung instantly to Naomi's eyes when Adao mentioned his parents. It was a wish neither of them could grant. And no doubt was doubly painful for Naomi to hear, knowing she would most likely never know what had happened to her own family.

As for the snow… He looked over his shoulder at the gray clouds moving in from across the fens. He looked straight up to heaven and threw in a silent request that at least one of the boy's two wishes could come true. As for Naomi…he needed her to know the truth about him. See how far he'd come before she completely wrote him off. He was living proof that life was full of second chances.

"Let's get you off there, mate." Finn lifted Adao up and off the horse, noting how light he was, and how receptively he responded when Finn pulled him in close for a bit of a hug before he put him down.

Evie rushed up all smiles and twinkling eyes. "Adao! Just the man I was looking for. Do you think you'd like to come along and meet Father Christmas?" She shot a quick look at Finn and Naomi. "Would it be all right if I steal him for half an hour? We could meet at, say… how about at the Pin the Tail on the Reindeer stand at half-past?"

"Absolutely." Naomi's voice was bright, though Finn sensed a note of reluctance to let the little boy out of her sight.

"How 'bout I take care of this one?" Finn pointed to Naomi. "And you take care of this one." He pulled his own knitted cap off his head and tugged it onto Adao's. "And we'll meet up for apple cider doughnuts and a warm drink after."

"Sounds great." Evie grinned at the pair of them then stuck out a mittened hand to Adao. "Ready to meet the big guy?"

Adao's eyes shone with delight as he slipped his hand into Evie's.

"Right!" Finn clapped his hands together and gave them a brisk rub before putting them gently on Naomi's shoulders. "You and me. We need to talk."

CHAPTER FOURTEEN

NAOMI TRIED HER best to look relaxed as she and Finn strolled away from the party and down toward the river.

"From the look on your face people are going to think I'm kidnapping you!" Finn gave her a playful nudge with his elbow and tried to rouse a smile.

He wasn't successful.

She felt nervous and as if her heart was being yanked from one side of her chest to the other.

Sure. The angst was all of her own making, but... why couldn't Finn just let sleeping dogs lie?

"It's so cold I think we'd better forgo the bench and just keep on walking, if that's all right."

"Of course." She glanced back at the party scene behind them.

"Don't worry, love." He wrapped an arm around her shoulders and gave her a light squeeze. "I'll get you back to Adao." He dropped his arm from round her shoulders and instantly she felt the loss of contact.

"I want to tell you a bit more about me after my accident."

"You don't have to," Naomi quickly jumped in. She knew how painful trips down memory lane were and yet…she'd wanted him to know about her past. "I'm sorry. Please. Go ahead."

Finn gave her a thin smile of thanks, clearly already halfway back on his journey to the past. "After I lost my leg I was in a rage with the world. As you know, I was married at the time and the truth of the matter was I didn't handle it well. Not at all. From a young age I had everything all planned out. I would be in the army like my dad. I would teach my kid brother to do the same so I could look after him—"

"You have a little brother?"

Finn's smile was tight and his eyes didn't meet hers, so she knew the memories were painful. "I do. And there are still some fences that need mending on that front. He's a career military man. Always traveling. Mostly peacekeeping tours, but…he's out there, doing the family thing."

Naomi shook her head. "What do you mean?"

"Morgans have always been military. As far back as we can trace. When I became the first one to drop the baton—"

"You didn't 'drop the baton'!" Naomi was indignant. He'd sacrificed himself to save a fellow soldier. A friend. A life.

Finn took her hand in his and gave it a squeeze. For the first time in days it felt right and she gave his fingers a squeeze back so he would know she was there, listening.

"It felt like it. I thought I'd let my family down. And my wife. It wasn't the future I had promised her. Wasn't the future I had promised myself, and the only way I thought I could deal with it was on my own so I pushed and pushed until there wasn't anyone around me any-more and I'd got exactly what I'd wished for."

"And?" Naomi knew there was a big "but" linger-ing out there and felt a twitch of nerves, wondering what it was.

"But…" Finn grinned at her as if he'd been read-ing her thoughts. "Being alone, going through what I'd been through on my own was about the dumbest thing I think I'd ever done."

"So…do you regret getting divorced?"

"Yes. No." He quickly shifted course. "Our vows meant a lot to me. To both of us. And not coming good on them was a lot to face up to. So, for a long time, I didn't. Just pushed her and everyone else who mattered away." He looked up to the sky for a minute before con-tinuing. "Caroline's in a great place now, and to be hon-est? I don't know that she and I would be a match…the people we are now. We were married very young and neither of us was ready to take on the challenges that my injury brought along with it. The minute I'd decided to retrain as a pediatric surgeon, that was all I had room for in my life. I simply shut her and anyone else who cared right out of the picture."

"What about Charlie?" Naomi was completely lost in Finn's story now. She knew exactly what he meant. The same drive he'd used to retrain as a surgeon sounded so similar to how she'd poured herself into her physio-therapy studies. Like it had been a mission. And yet… she had a feeling Finn's tale came with a lesson. One she might benefit from learning herself.

"Charlie?" Finn laughed. "Charlie was the one who knocked me on the head and demanded I start being more sociable. As far as I was concerned, doing surgeries and skulking round my houseboat were good enough for me. But when he introduced me to those kids and the lads on the wheelchair team, I slowly began to see what an idiot I'd been. But I was still compartmentalizing."

"Until…?" There had to be an "until" because Finn was completely different from the gruff, standoffish man she'd met at that first staff meeting.

He turned and faced her, eyes alight with emotion. "Until I met you."

"Me?"

"Yes," he said softly, stroking her cheek with the back of his hand. "You. You made me want to live again."

"What are you talking about? You're the one who went to the sports center. You…you…made marshmallows!"

"That wasn't living, love. That was going through the motions. Charlie used to harangue me like an old harpy. 'Come down to the gym! Do this! Do that! If you don't come for tea the trouble and strife'll have my head!'"

Naomi laughed at his spot-on imitation of Charlie, then looked up to the sky, trying to collect her thoughts. "Why are you telling me all this?"

"I think you know damn well why I'm telling you," Finn said gently. "I'm in love with you and I think you feel the same way, but you're scared."

Tears sprang to her eyes and she was half-tempted to ask if he'd also been retraining as a psychic. "How do you know?"

"Because I know what it feels like to carry a burden of guilt around. I know how terrifying it feels to let yourself be happy when you hold yourself responsible for causing the ones you loved so much pain."

He took her hands in his and dropped kisses on her knuckles. "Naomi, what happened to your family is not your burden to carry. What you can and should carry in your heart are all the happy memories. The joy."

Tears began to trickle down her cheeks. Finn tugged a handkerchief out of his winter coat pocket and held it out to her. "I brought extras just in case."

She giggled through her tears, despite herself. "You came prepared?"

"I try to always come prepared." He gave her a cheeky grin.

"Army boy," they said in tandem then stopped, frozen in each other's gazes as if they'd been given a heaven-sent reminder that they were and should be together.

"You're right, you know," Naomi finally admitted.

"About what?"

"All of it. The guilt. Not wanting to let go. Not wanting to let myself admit that…" A hint of shyness overcame her. Finn, once again, seemed to read her mind and dropped a kiss on her forehead.

"It would be the first time in a long time anyone admitted I was worth loving."

"I want to be that person." Naomi spoke in a rush, acutely aware that if she let this pass with Finn—this love that really could grow into something wonderful—she would be letting an enormous part of what it meant to be alive pass her by. Because what was the point if there wasn't love?

"I love them so very much," she admitted. "But I can't do anything to change what's happened."

Finn nodded along as she spoke. "It's the double-edged sword of loving. Loving and losing," he clarified. "Look, I was determined to spend the rest of my days on my own. I didn't want to hurt anyone the way I'd hurt Caroline ever again, but you know what? I rang her the other day and wouldn't you know it? She's as happy as Larry."

"Who's Larry? How do you know that he's happy?"

Finn threw his head back and laughed a full-bodied laugh. A warmth grew in her chest, a happiness that she'd been the one to set him off.

He pulled her close to him, so close she could feel his heartbeat through his winter coat. "Larry is a very happy guy," Finn said. "And I will be too if you'd agree to give this thing a shot with me. I want to live again, Naomi. I want to love and laugh and…" his voice went all rumbly "…make love. And I'd like you to be the woman I do all those things with." He held her out at arm's length. "You deserve happiness, Naomi. You deserve to live a full, rich, incredible life. What do you say? You and me doing our best to make our peace with the past and give ourselves a shot at a happy future?"

She stared up into Finn's gray eyes and knew she could look into them forever. He truly understood her. Her fears, the terrifying experiences she'd been through. Her reluctance to let herself experience unfettered happiness. And yet…he was willing to try it. And when she was with him, she felt brave, too. She'd already had a glimpse into the joy of being with someone who made her insides fluttery and her heart skippity. She already knew she was in love. It was simply a question of saying… "Yes."

Finn stared at her as if in shock. "Yes?"

Her grin widened along with his. "Yes!" She shouted it out and a pair of swans took flight from the river.

"Well, then, my little flower blossom…" Finn pulled her close to him and cupped her face in his big hands "…I think we'd best seal this deal with a kiss."

"You think?" Naomi teased.

"I know," Finn growled, kissing her with a sensual confidence that came with truth and honesty and love.

"He's over here!" Finn hadn't felt this happy in he didn't know how long. A beautiful woman by his side, a chance to look forward rather than dwelling on the past and, best yet, snow!

"Adao!" Naomi waved her arms when the boy turned to them, a cup of steaming hot chocolate in his hands.

"Finn! Naomi!" Evie waved them over. "I jumped the gun when the snow began and ordered some hot chocolate. You in?"

"Of course." Finn looked up at the sky, enjoying the sensation of the big, fat flakes falling on his face, then knelt down so he was eye to eye with Adao. "What do you think, little man? Does it live up to its reputation?"

"Even better."

Naomi laughed and gave the knitted cap on his head a bit of a tweak. "Looks like it's definitely a day for Christmas wishes to come true."

She laughed, enjoying the comforting sensation of Finn nestling in close to her, then leaning in even closer so that he could whisper into her ear.

"Was I *your* Christmas wish?"

"Something like that."

He feigned looking affronted. "Just something?"

"Exactly." She gave his hand a squeeze, already excited for the next time they could be alone and share more of those luxurious, life-affirming kisses. "Exactly what I wished for."

And he was. Finn had helped her see the only person she was hurting was herself. She scanned the party area as she sipped her hot chocolate and listened to Adao tell Finn all about his time with Father Christmas. The only thing she needed to do now was find a little sprig of mistletoe and then all her Christmas wishes would come true.

CHAPTER FIFTEEN

A year later

"Mum... Baaba..." Adao beamed at his mother and father as they stepped into the hospital's foyer, which was decked out with two huge trees the hospital had decorated in their usual incredible fun-loving style. "This is Naomi. And this is Mr. Morgan."

"Finn," Finn corrected, as he stepped forward to shake hands with the couple who had just been flown in. "Lovely to meet you, Mr. and Mrs. Weza. And you must be..."

"Imani." Adao's sister didn't suffer from shyness in the slightest. She shook hands with Naomi and Finn and beamed. "I can't believe it is snowing!"

"These are just the types of miracles that happen here at Hope Children's Hospital." Naomi shrugged and grinned. The place was magical. Especially under a thick blanket of snow.

"It's amazing to see you here in your working environment," said Mrs. Weza. "After the village, I mean. You seemed so at home there as well."

Finn wrapped his arm around Naomi's shoulders and gave her a kiss on the cheek. "That was an amazing trip. I don't think I've ever had such incredible sea-food before."

"It was wonderful of the charity to organize for us to come out and work with Adao. He's progressed so much with his prosthesis. And grown, too!"

Adao beamed. "Nine centimeters in one year!"

"Well above average. In many ways," she added, giving his head a scrub. Seeing his parents again had really brought out the spark in him.

Naomi smiled up at Finn. She couldn't believe how much the pair of them had changed in just a year. Evie had even taken to calling them the Grin Twins.

Well…

When one was in love, why not spread the joy?

The prosthetics specialists spotted them and joined their group. After a quick discussion about what Adao would have to do to get the mold for his new prosthesis, they suggested his family join him so they could all see.

"It was really lovely meeting you."

"We'll see you again before we go, right?" Adao threw his arms round Naomi's waist and gave her a huge hug. His new prosthesis seemed a part of him now. Proof, as if she needed any, of just how important their work at the hospital and overseas was. She smiled down at him. "Of course we'll see you again. And next year when Finn and I come out again with the charity, we'll see if you can manage to grow as much as you have this year."

"As tall as you!" whooped Adao. "Then the next year as tall as Finn!" The thought struck his entire family as hilariously funny and Naomi felt nothing but warmth and joy in her heart as she watched them laughing their way down the corridor.

"They're a lovely family." Finn slipped his hand round hers and gave it a squeeze.

"That they are."

"Want to go out and have a snowball fight with me?"

Naomi looked at him in disbelief. "I bet you think you'll win."

"I think a lot of things," Finn riposted playfully as he pulled her into a hug.

"You do, don't you?"

"Yes," Finn said airily. "And I'm usually right."

Naomi went up on tiptoe and gave him a quick kiss. "You have been right about a lot of things."

"I know."

He tried to keep a straight face for as long as he could, but Naomi knew the trick to make him break now.

"Tickle fight!"

She ran out the front door, chasing him as he begged her not to tickle him. His weakness, she'd discovered one day when she'd worn nothing but a feather boa to bed.

Finn tripped when he reached the green and Naomi fell on top of him breathless with laughter and joy.

When they had caught their breath, she beamed at him. "I love you, Finn Morgan."

"I love you, too, pretty lady. You make the world— my world—a better place."

"And you helped me see what a lovely place the world is."

They shared a tender kiss before getting up and shaking the snow off themselves. She hoped Finn knew how much she had meant what she'd said. Over the course of the year he had shown such patience and tenderness that sometimes it was hard to believe he was the same man who'd barked at her to leave him alone.

Finn knew her inside and out. Her fears. And now, more importantly, her hopes and dreams.

"Fancy a cup of hot chocolate by the Christmas tree before we get back to work?"

"Absolutely."

Finn reached out his hand and took Naomi's in his. This was the moment he'd been waiting for all year.

Luckily, the hospital "fairies" had waved their magic wands over the green outside the hospital yet again and… Yup! Just over by the enormous candy cane…a mistletoe stand.

"C'mere, you." Finn led her over to the stand.

"What are you up to, you rascal? I thought we were going for hot chocolate."

Finn tipped her chin up and looked straight into her eyes. "I can do you one better than that, my love."

"Better than hot chocolate on a snowy day?" She laughed. "I don't think so."

He reached into his pocket and pulled out a little light blue box. "How 'bout an early Christmas present?" He flicked open the box and showed her the diamond solitaire he'd been carrying around in his pocket for the last three months.

"A—? What—?"

Finn dropped to one knee, not caring who saw him.

"Naomi Collins Chukwumerije…" He stopped and grinned, clearly pleased with his pronunciation of her surname. "Would you do me the honor of marrying me?"

Her heart stopped for an instant then did a happy dance all its own.

"Oh, Finn… I… Of *course* I'll marry you!"

He leapt to his feet, pulled her into his arms and would've kissed her until the sun went down if some of the other doctors hadn't started wolf-whistling.

"She said yes!"

A huge roar of cheers and applause rose up around them as he pulled Naomi close to him. "You said yes."

"You're the love of my life," Naomi whispered as he slipped the ring onto her finger. "I can't wait to let the whole rest of the world know."

Together, smiles lighting up their faces, they entered the hospital with their eyes solidly on the future, knowing they had each other to help them in whatever came their way.

* * * * *

THE BILLIONAIRE'S CHRISTMAS WISH

TINA BECKETT

MILLS & BOON

To my family.
You bring me joy each and every day.

CHAPTER ONE

"THEO—IVY IS asking for you."

Theo Hawkwood's heart dropped into the acidic pool in his stomach as the nurse's voice came through his cellphone.

"Is she okay?"

Of course she wasn't. His daughter hadn't been "okay" for months. Which was why she'd been moved to a room a short distance from his office.

"There's no change. I think she just wants to see you."

A familiar nagging ache went through his chest, filling the space his heart had just vacated. His wife's sudden death four and a half years ago had left him with a hole in his life and an infant daughter to raise. And now Ivy was sick. Very sick. And no one could tell him why. If he lost her too…

You won't. You have one of the best diagnosticians in the world on the case.

Except even she was stumped.

"I'm on my way. Can you find Dr. Archer for me?"

"She's already there. She's the one who asked me to call you."

Shoving his phone into the pocket of his jeans, he

pushed away from the desk and the pile of requisitions he'd been studying. Once on his feet, he dragged a hand through his hair. It had been months. And still no definitive diagnosis. They knew what it wasn't but not what it was that was making Ivy's arms and legs grow weaker by the day. As unfair as it was, he'd been pinning all his hopes on Madison Archer, only to have them dashed time and time again.

Striding across the bridge that joined his section of the hospital with the area that housed the family suites, he tried to avoid looking at the festive ribbons and lights that twinkled with the joy of the season. Joy? He just wasn't feeling it. As much as he tried to put on a cheerful face for the sake of his daughter, the storms raging inside him were anything but cheerful. How long before Ivy noticed?

Maybe she already had.

He took his gaze from the decorations and fixed them straight ahead until he came to Ivy's room. He didn't bother knocking, just pushed quietly through the door then stopped in his tracks. Madison was seated on the side of his daughter's bed, their heads close together, and they were…laughing.

Had he ever actually heard Madison laugh?

He didn't think so. She was professional to a fault. He'd even overheard the word "Scrooge" attributed to her after she'd refused to give an opinion on the lights on the banister leading to the family suites. A quick glance from him had silenced the comment in mid-sentence.

And now? The deep copper highlights of the diagnostician's hair cascaded in waves that covered the side of her face so he couldn't see her, but she was writing something in a small notebook. She giggled again. "Are you sure?"

"Yes," his daughter replied.

Something in his gut gave a painful jerk.

"What's going on in here?"

The second the gruff question came out of his mouth the laughter came to an abrupt halt, and Madison slammed the notebook shut.

He wished he could take the words back. Wished he could take a whole lot of things back, but he couldn't.

Madison's face came into view as she shook her hair back to peer up at him, her indrawn brows causing tiny puckers to form between them.

Hell, he needed to get a grip. The nurse's message a few moments earlier had made him think something was wrong, and he'd buzzed in here like some kind of hornet, looking for something or someone to strike.

Only there was no one. Only some mystery illness that refused to poke its head out so it could be seen for what it was.

A stealer of life. A stealer of joy.

For Theo, the feeling of helplessness was the worst sensation in the world. Worse than the loss of his wife to a drunk driver over four years ago. At least that had been something concrete that he could understand. He'd known exactly where to place the blame that time. But this time there was nothing.

"Are you okay?" Madison's smile had morphed into professional concern, her fingers balancing her pen over the notebook. Scrooge? Hell, he was the Scrooge, not her.

"I'm sorry. You called me down here, and I thought…" His voice trailed away and a lump formed in his throat when Ivy didn't immediately jump off her bed and squeeze his legs in a tight hug, like she used to.

She couldn't. Ivy couldn't even walk now.

The diagnostician tucked the pen and book into the front pocket of her long gray tunic and then got up and stood in front of him. Those long legs of hers brought her almost to eye level. She still had to tilt her head a bit, but she didn't have to crane her neck like Hope used to do.

He swallowed and threw another log onto the fire of guilt.

"Hey." Her fingers landed on his arm with a quick squeeze that sent something skittering up his spine to his brain—a flash of something he had no intention of analyzing. "Don't you quit on me."

She didn't have to translate the meaning for him, and Theo was smart enough to nod at her subtle warning not to scare his daughter unnecessarily.

But how about him? He was scared out of his mind right now.

"No quitting involved." His voice sounded a lot more sure than he felt. Even so, he softened his tone for the next part. "So I'll ask again. What's going on?"

"We were just making some plans for… Christmas."

He blinked. There had been an awkward pause before she'd added that last word. And the way she'd blurted it out—like she couldn't wait to fling it off her tongue—made him wonder.

Was it because she wasn't sure Ivy was even going to be around to celebrate the event, which was a short two weeks away? That thought sent icy perspiration prickling across his upper lip. "Plans for?"

Ivy, who had been silent for the exchange, said, "For Sanna Claus. And your presents."

Her mispronunciation of good old Saint Nick's name made him smile, relief making his shoulders slump. It had become a running joke between them, with him correcting her and Ivy persisting in leaving out the "t" sound with a nose crinkled in amusement.

He glanced at his daughter and then at Madison. "The only present I need is for you to get better, sweetheart."

He put a wealth of meaning into those words and aimed them at the diagnostician.

Uncertainty shimmered in the green depths of the other doctor's eyes and his relief fled in an instant. Theo knew how she felt, though. Before he'd founded the hospital—back when he'd been a practicing surgeon—there'd been a few cases where he'd been unable to promise the family a good outcome. He'd still done his damnedest for those patients despite seemingly impossible odds. Was Madison feeling that same pressure? Worse, did she think Ivy's case was hopeless?

Unable to face what that might mean, he turned his attention to Ivy. "Have you been out of bed yet today?"

"Yes. Madison helped me." Ivy took the rag doll she carried everywhere with her and struggled to lift it to her chest in a hug. "I had to leave Gerty on the bed. She was too heavy today."

The ache in his chest grew. Hope had made that doll for their daughter a few months before she'd given birth to Ivy.

"Wheelchair? Or walking?" He kept his eyes on his daughter, even though the question was directed at Madison.

The other doctor went over and laid a hand on Ivy's head. "I'm going to have a chat with your dad outside, okay? You keep thinking about that list."

Right on cue, Ivy yawned. "I will."

Madison led the way through the door. Once it swung shut, she said, "She'll be asleep in five minutes."

Was she avoiding answering his question? "Wheelchair or walking?"

"She hasn't walked in a week, Theo. You know that."

"Yes. But I'd hoped…" His eyes shut for several long seconds. "Tell me again what we've ruled out."

"Did you get the list I emailed you? Your staff had already ruled out most of the obvious conditions before I arrived." She tucked a lock of hair behind her ear, fingers worrying the ends for a second or two before continuing. "There is no brain tumor. No lesions that suggest something is going on with the synaptic connections. And the results of the muscle biopsy I ordered came back yesterday. There's no sign of limb-girdle muscular dystrophy."

She must have seen something in his face because she hurried to add, "That's a good thing."

"Then why are her arms and legs getting progressively weaker?" As relieved as he should be that there was no sign of the deadly condition, his inability to help his daughter made his voice rough-edged yet again.

"I don't know." She pulled in a deep breath and blew it back out. "But I'm still going down a list of possibilities. I just don't want to rush through them and overlook something and then have to double back. Wasted time can't be recaptured."

No, it couldn't. What was gone was gone.

He did his best to ignore those last words and tried

to focus on the positive: she hadn't exhausted everything. Not yet, at least.

"Multiple sclerosis?" Although MS normally affected adults, he'd researched everything he could think of and had found cases where children were diagnosed with it.

"Again, there's no sign of brain lesions. I went over the MRI scans with a fine-toothed comb. I saw no anomalies at all."

"Damn."

A tug at his sleeve brought his eyes back to hers. "I told you I'd tell you when to worry. We're not there yet."

"Yes, we are. I can see it in your face."

"It's not that I'm worried. I'm just frustrated I don't have an answer for you. I'm exploring every avenue I can think of." Her fingers tightened.

"I know you are, Madison. I'm treating you like Ivy is your only patient, and I know that's not true."

"I'm here for her and for patients just like her. She has a great team of specialists fighting on her behalf, and I'm grateful to be included in that. Ivy is a big part of Hope Children's Hospital."

Named after his late wife, who'd waited patiently in the wings for him to break ground on his dream, even putting her own career on hold to look after Ivy while he'd worked day and night. She'd died before seeing the fruits of their labor or being able to practice medicine again. And he damned himself every single day for not spending more time with her and Ivy while his wife had still been here.

"Wasted time can't be recaptured."

Truer words had never been spoken.

He leaned a shoulder against the wall and turned

to fully face her. Her fingers let go of his sleeve in the process.

"Anything I can do to help?" he asked.

"Just throw out any ideas that might help—even if they seem farfetched. I sent a panel off looking for some markers of Lyme disease or any of the co-infections that might be related to it. I should have something back in a few days."

"Lyme. Is that even a possibility? I keep going back to it being a brain issue."

Madison's brow puckered the way it had back in Ivy's room. She was either thinking or irritated. Maybe she thought he was challenging her readings of the MRI scans. He wasn't. He just couldn't get past the possibility that something in Ivy's head was misfiring or inhibiting signals. The condition mimicked one of the muscular dystrophies. But the biopsies said it wasn't. So if it wasn't in the muscles themselves...

"I thought for sure it was too. But there's nothing there, Theo."

Every time she used his name, something coiled inside him. Lots of people called him by his given name rather than his professional title, but that husky American accent, devoid of the crisp consonants that peppered the speech of those in Britain, warmed parts of him that had been frozen in time and space.

She provided hope. A fresh perspective. She was unconventional, could think outside the box. Her files listed one of her weaknesses as being her hard-nosed approach. She had difficulty being a team player, and she wasn't afraid to question findings or demand a test be run again if it wasn't done to her satisfaction. He didn't see that as a weakness. In this case he viewed her reputation as a strength, which was why he hadn't insisted she attend the staff meetings related to Ivy's care.

She'd made a few enemies back home—and even here in Cambridge. But she'd also made friends. And one of those friends appeared to be his daughter.

"Where do you look next? She's had no headaches. No symptoms other than the growing weakness in her limbs. And wondering whether that weakness is going to progress to her breathing or autonomic nervous system is making me—"

"Crazy? I know. It's making us all a little crazy. That kid has a lot of people wrapped around her little finger."

"Yes, she does." He smiled. "Including her father."

Her fingers toyed with the edge of his sleeve again, not quite touching him, as if she wanted to give comfort but was afraid of skin-to-skin contact. "We're going to figure this out."

Right now he was *glad* she wasn't touching him. Because the warm flow of her voice was doing what her hand wasn't. It was permeating his pores and meandering through his bloodstream, where it affected his breathing, his heart rate and his thoughts—taking them into dangerous territory. Territory that only his late wife had occupied. He couldn't afford to let Madison trespass there. If he did, it could spell disaster for both him and his daughter.

"I'm sure you will." In a deliberate move, he tugged his sleeve from her grasp. "I'm counting on it. And so is Ivy."

Then he was walking away, before he could ask exactly what she and Ivy had been planning for Christmas, or ask if Madison was including herself in those plans.

* * *

Once back in the tiny office she'd been given while Dr. Camargo's office was being renovated, Madison fingered the notebook in her pocket. She was glad that Theo hadn't asked her to hand it over to him. He'd seemed pretty upset to find the two of them in there laughing, but it hadn't been easy to pretend when her heart was aching over the little girl's revelation. Because the first thing on Ivy's wish list was for her father to like Christmas.

Her eyes had burned. It seemed that she wasn't the only one with an aversion to the season. And the last thing she could promise anyone was that she'd help them learn to like a holiday she detested. Maybe she should put that on her Christmas list too.

Except Madison had no interest in changing her ways at this late date. She did what she could to get through the last month of the year, closed her eyes as she passed the festive trees and lights, and then breathed a sigh of relief once the calendar rolled over into a new year.

Fingering the thick file folder on her desk, she flipped it open to the first page, where Ivy's vital statistics were listed in bold clinical letters. The child was far wiser than her five years. And she saw things Theo probably didn't even know she was aware of. Or maybe his daughter had already shared her longing with him. Madison didn't think so, though.

She knew he was widowed, from the hospital grapevine. And his ring finger no longer held a wedding ring, so he'd gotten over the loss. Or had he? Some people never really got over that kind of life change.

Another thing Madison could relate to. Although

her loss had nothing to do with a husband, or even a boyfriend.

Shaking herself free of her funk, she pulled the notebook from her pocket and dropped it onto her desk. She'd have to figure out a way to get a few of the things on Ivy's list without making her dad suspicious. Or angry. He had to know how fortunate he was to have a daughter who was worried as much about him as he worried about her. She was small and so very ill, and yet her determination to do all she could to get better—for her dad's sake—was one of the most touching things Madison had seen in a long time.

She flipped the first page open and perused the list, forcing her glance to leap over that first item. The rest of the things ranged from sweet to hilarious.

A new stethoscope—in purple, if Santa has one, because that is Ivy's favorite color.

A book about horses so he'll fall in love with them like she has.

An adult coloring book. One of Ivy's nurses talked about how every grown-up should have one.

Somehow, Madison couldn't picture those big hands clutching a crayon—although he was very much a paint-by-numbers type of person. No coloring outside the lines for him.

Macaroni and cheese. Evidently Theo's favorite food. Santa must carry casseroles around in his toy sack.

*A puppy. Ha! Wouldn't Theo love coming home
to find a puppy under the tree.*

That was all they had so far on the list. Except for that
very first thing. Her eyes tracked up to it against their
will.

Make Daddy love Christmas.

God, even the real Santa would have a tough time
granting that wish. The rest was doable. Well, maybe
not the puppy. But everything else could be gotten for
a relatively inexpensive price, wrapped and listed as
being from Santa.

Why did she even care? She wasn't here to buy anyone gifts. Or to make a little girl happy.

She was here to help solve difficult diagnoses. That
was it. And to fulfill a lifelong dream of visiting the
UK. She should be on cloud nine. Instead, she felt itchy
and slightly uncomfortable, like wearing a new wool
sweater without anything else beneath it.

*You need to get out and see more of England. Staying
around this hospital day in and day out isn't healthy.*

But there was something about Ivy...

She'd found herself spending more and more time
with the little girl, almost succeeding in convincing
herself it was to help figure out the child's condition.
Except she knew it was a lie. She was here for Ivy, even
if being around her dad made her squirm in discomfort.

She wasn't exactly sure why that was, but she'd better figure it out before she did something stupid. Really
stupid. Like wish Ivy were hers, maybe?

She stood in a rush and clasped her hands behind her

back, lifting them away from her body while bending forward at the waist, hoping the resultant stretch would help clear her head of its current thoughts. Higher and harder she stretched, vaguely aware of her door opening with a couple of light taps.

"Dr. Archer?"

Madison froze in place. Oh, Lordy. But at least the voice was female and not the man who'd jerked away from her a couple of hours earlier. How humiliating had that been? She'd just been trying to help.

Letting her arms drop back to her sides, she stood and saw Naomi Collins, one of the physical therapists at the hospital. Her romance with pediatric surgeon Finn Morgan was the stuff dreams were made of.

"Hi. Sorry about that. I had a kink in my neck and was trying to work it out." More like a kink in her head, but it was pretty much the same thing.

Naomi chuckled. "It's fine. You should see the things I do when I'm alone." Another laugh. "Forget I said that. I didn't mean that quite the way it sounded."

"I didn't think it sounded odd at all." She smiled to reassure her. After all, if Naomi could have gotten a good look at what was rattling around in her head, she might be a little more than shocked. "Can I help you with something?"

"I just wanted to talk with you about Ivy. What you wanted me to work on with her tomorrow."

With her clear complexion and deep gorgeous skin tones, Naomi was beautiful. And she was a huge hit with all her young charges, including Ivy.

"I'm not her only doctor, you know."

Naomi entered the office and closed the door behind her. "Maybe not, but right now everyone—if they're smart—is deferring to you and hoping you'll solve whatever is going on with her."

"And if I can't?" The words that she hadn't dared say aloud in the hallway with Theo came tumbling out before she could stop them. She dropped into one of the metal chairs that flanked her desk.

The physical therapist came over and sat in the other one. "It's a bit of pressure, yes?"

"Yes. And I want to figure it out. But I'm at a dead end at the moment." She didn't know why she was suddenly voicing her fears, but there was something in the other woman's eyes that said she'd known fear— intimately—and had come out on the other side.

"Sometimes we just have to give ourselves a bit of space to regroup. And that's when it normally comes to us. That realization that's been in front of us all along."

Were they still talking about Ivy? Or about something else?

"I hope you're right."

"I am. You'll see." Naomi leaned forward and captured her hands. "Just give yourself permission to take a step or two back and look at the problem with a wide-angle lens."

Something about those words caught at an area of her brain, which set to work in the background. "Thank you. I think I needed to hear that." She squeezed the other woman's fingers before letting go. Gently. Not the way Theo had done in the hallway. "How are things with you and Finn, if I may ask?"

Naomi's smile caused her nose to crinkle in a way that was both adorable and mischievous. "You can. And it's great. Better than I have a right to expect."

"It's exactly what you *should* expect. And what you

deserve." From what Madison had heard, Naomi had had a hard time of it, losing loved ones in a terrible conflict in her home country. But she'd overcome it and had learned to live her life in the present.

Maybe Naomi should write a how-to book on how to do that. Madison would be one of her first customers if that ever happened.

"Thank you. Finn's a good man." Naomi sucked down a deep breath and squared her shoulders. "Now, about Ivy…"

Madison went over what she would like to see happen with Ivy's therapy tomorrow. Although she couldn't walk or even hold herself up on the parallel bars they used to help people learn to walk again, they could still try to utilize what muscle strength she did have to its best advantage. Having her kick a large exercise ball and do some resistance bands to hopefully keep things from atrophying any faster than they already were was the biggest goal at the moment.

"I agree. That's the perfect thing for her. I did a little work with the bands today, in fact. Right now the hope is to slow that downward spiral as much as possible, to buy ourselves time to find whatever's going on."

"Yes, and thank you. Do you want me to check with Theo to make sure he agrees?"

Naomi shook her head. "He'll agree. He's desperate to find anything that will work. As are we all. We all want her to beat whatever this is."

With that she stood to her feet. "I think I'll check in on her on my way out."

"Thank you. And thanks for the pep talk."

The physical therapist fixed her with a look. "It wasn't a pep talk. It was the truth."

She showed herself out, leaving Madison to think about what the other woman had said. Maybe she was right. Maybe she was going about this the wrong way. Maybe she really was using a microscope and focusing very narrowly when she should be casting a wide net and seeing what she could haul to shore.

Ha! That was easier said than done, but the more she mulled over the idea, the more it felt right. Now all she had to do was figure out what it meant. And then how to go about implementing it.

And she'd better do it soon. Before that slow downward spiral increased its pace, becoming something that no force on earth could stop. Before a child's modest wish list was nothing more than a memory, and a father's last hope was pulverized into dust.

CHAPTER TWO

She wasn't in her office.

Theo had knocked and then peeked into the small space before moving inside. He felt a little bit like an interloper, but figured he could as easily wait for her in here as go looking for her. The fact was, he was half-afraid of going to Ivy's room and finding them in a cute little huddle like he had three days ago. Since then he'd forced himself to let Madison alone to do her work. If he hounded her every moment of every day, he would do more harm than good.

Or so he told himself. In reality, he wasn't sure he was ready to face her after his panicked flight the last time. And he wasn't sure why.

He dropped into one of the little chairs, wondering why her office was so spartan when most other doctors' spaces were decked out with squashy leather chairs and the personal touches of its occupants.

It was because this hadn't been an office at all. It had been a supplies cupboard, but it was all they'd had available, since the renovations on Dr. Camargo's office were running behind schedule. But she hadn't offered one word of complaint or acted like they'd set her in a place that was beneath her status. They were damned lucky to have someone like her, and Theo knew it.

He glanced at her desktop, finding it neat and mostly empty except for the stack of file folders on the left-hand side, at the top of which was Ivy's chart. His fingers brushed across the cover, the temptation to open it coming and going. There was nothing in there that she wouldn't have already told him. Then he spotted a small notebook. It was on the right side of the desk toward the back. He was almost sure that was the same notebook she'd tucked into her pocket after her *tête-à-tête* with Ivy. What was in it? Notes about the case?

No, she'd been scratching in that when he'd caught them giggling. They'd been making plans, Madison had said.

About Christmas.

The notebook was on her side of the desk, so he'd have to stretch across to reach it.

It's not like it's a personal diary, Theo.

And if it had anything to do with Ivy, didn't he have a right to know what was in it?

His palm slid across the smooth wooden surface of the desk, and he had to lean slightly to reach it. His fingertips landed on the cover, preparing to drag the item toward him, when a slight breeze swept across his nape, sending the hairs rising in attention.

He pulled back in a hurry, turning to face whoever'd entered the room.

Damn.

It was Madison, and she'd caught him red-handed. Well, not really, since he hadn't got a chance to crack the cover on that book.

"Theo, this is a surprise. Were you looking for

me?" Her voice was slightly breathless, and she hurried around to the other side of the desk and opened a drawer, sweeping the offending item into it.

There was definitely something in there she didn't want him to see. And that just made him want to look even more.

Dressed in a black cowl-necked sweater that hugged its way from her shoulders to the tops of her slender thighs, it set his senses on high alert. Just like the last time they had been together. He swallowed and tried to regroup and remember his reason for coming here. It certainly hadn't been to ogle her.

"I was, actually. I wanted to know how Naomi fared with Ivy. She told me you changed tack a bit on her therapy. You're no longer actively trying to get her to walk?"

"Not at the moment." She dropped into her office chair and explained her reasoning pretty much the same way Naomi had described the plan to him. And he had to admit he agreed, even if it felt like they were giving ground to some hidden monster—one that was busy pulling a rope from the hidden safety of a screen. It might be out of sight but the effects were apparent to anyone watching the display. They couldn't use brute force to overpower the lurker so they were simply trying to stop it from gaining traction.

"What's our next step?"

"I'm not quite sure. The treatment team is meeting today. I'll digest their findings later."

"I'm aware of the meeting. So what are you bringing to the table?"

"Table? I've been to one or two of the meetings, but wasn't planning on going to today's."

Theo's heart chilled in an instant, even though he'd

been the one to say she wasn't required to go to them. "Reason?" Maybe this was where she conceded that she was giving up.

"I wasn't invited."

That made him sit back for a second. "You're always invited. And they'll want you there. *I* want you there. If you're waiting for a formal, gold-foiled envelope to arrive on your desk, that probably isn't going to happen." He forced a smile he hoped reflected reassurance, although it certainly didn't match what was churning around on the inside. What if she decided she wanted to focus on other cases and not spend the bulk of her time on Ivy anymore? Or, worse, what if she'd noticed the tugs of interest he'd felt—even just a minute or two ago—despite his efforts to sweep them under the rug and out of sight? Would she think he was using his position to try to pressure her to prioritize Ivy's treatment above anyone else's?

His instinct as a father was to do exactly that. Help his child in any way he could. Use whatever means he could.

And yet he knew he had to push all of that aside and hold tight to his professional ethics. He'd started this hospital as a way to help people. If he chucked that aside and gave anyone preferential treatment, he would be flying in the face of his convictions.

Madison pulled her hair to the side and let it flow over her shoulder, the golden highlights contrasting with the dark knit of her sweater. And there it was again. That tickle in his midsection that was wreaking havoc with his objectivity.

Dangerous territory. Yes, it was. And his earlier thoughts about her trespassing? If he was the one putting out the welcome mat, he could hardly accuse her of wandering where she wasn't invited.

She leaned forward, some of those silky strands of hair brushing across the surface of her desk.

He swallowed again, trying to think of something to say to cover the moment. She beat him to it.

"I know this is going to sound strange, but I've been sending my findings to the group, and they've relayed any information they wanted me to have. It's how I've always worked, even back at my own hospital in the States. I look at all the pieces and try to put them together to form a diagnosis. It's hard for me to do that with a bunch of voices and emotions tangling with each other."

Like the ones going round and round his head right now?

Maybe this was why she wasn't getting on with one or two of the doctors at the hospital. He knew some of those sessions could get heated, with specialists vying for a chance to be heard, but Theo had always thought that was a healthy atmosphere. Hope Hospital emphasized working as treatment teams with the idea that more input was better for the hospital's patients. He was finding out that Madison's file was right. She preferred prowling around the outskirts.

But she was much sought after in the States. So maybe they shouldn't try to stuff her into a box she didn't fit into. Even if Theo himself had created that particular box.

"I understand. And I'll respect that decision. To a degree."

What had happened to not pushing Ivy's needs to the forefront? Or telling her that those meetings were optional?

"I'm sorry? What does that mean?"

"Just that the hospital uses these meetings not only

as a chance to bounce around ideas but also to provide accountability to all the players."

"Accountability." Her palms pressed against the surface of the desk, an edge of tension beginning to infuse her words. "As in you don't think I'm carrying my weight here?"

She was getting angry, and hell if he didn't like the little hints of emotion: the sideways tilt of her head, the color sweeping up her cheeks…the way her gaze remained riveted to his face.

Especially that last part.

Damn. So much for keeping this cool and impersonal.

"I phrased that badly. Let's call it curiosity. I would like to know your thoughts on their thoughts. I was hoping to get to that meeting today as well."

Her hands dropped into her lap and the tension seemed to flow out of her.

"I'll be happy to share my thoughts. I just don't want to waste my…" She smiled. "Sorry, badly phrased. I don't want to spend two hours in a chaotic team meeting when I could be looking down other avenues. I promise I do glance over what the team discusses. It just takes me a while to get into my work mode, and having my day cut into pieces with meetings makes it doubly hard, especially if I'm trying to piece together a complicated list of symptoms."

"Understood." Theo, whose days were often "cut into pieces," as she put it, often wished he could just put a "Do Not Disturb" sign on his door and get in eight hours of uninterrupted work. "Would you prefer to just write up your findings and send them to me?"

"I think it would be faster to tell them to you directly,

if that's okay. It can be a voicemail, if you're too busy to take my call."

He was never too busy to discuss Ivy. "I'll make time. But if you want to pass on information directly, why don't we set up our own face-to-face meeting of sorts? You tell me the time that works best for you."

"Okay, that's easy. The end of my official work day. Six o'clock or so?" She sat up, so the ends of her hair no longer brushed along the top of her desk. As hard as he tried, he couldn't stop the image of that hair sliding across his skin—skin in an area that was suddenly shifting upward at an alarming rate.

She tossed the offending locks behind her shoulder, going back to that professional demeanor he'd come to recognize, while he struggled to regain control of thoughts that were anything but professional.

"That works for me. I was just getting ready to head down and see Ivy. Do you want to go with me?"

He shouldn't. He should put some distance between them for a while—at least until his strange reaction to her had a chance to power down.

Then his gaze went to the right-hand side of her desk, where that little notebook had sat. Was she taking that with her?

That made his decision. "I haven't checked on her in a couple of hours, so I think I'll join you."

A buzzing came from the other side of the desk and she lifted a finger, asking him to wait. Lifting her cellphone, she looked at the readout and then put the device to her ear. "Dr. Archer here."

She listened to whoever was on the other end of the line, frowning slightly. "And the others?"

Her chest lifted and she expelled an audible sigh.

He could fairly see the tension that had gathered in her shoulders. "Okay, thank you for letting me know."

Setting the phone on the desk, she pressed her fingertips against the surface for several seconds.

"Was that something about Ivy?"

"The test results came back from her Lyme panel."

"And?" He waited, his heart in his chest. Was this the answer they'd been looking for?

"I'm sorry, Theo, but they're negative. All of them. Ivy doesn't have Lyme disease."

Sitting on the side of the bed a half-hour later, listening to her little patient talk about what she'd had for lunch, caused a lump to form in Madison's throat. It looked like Santa was going to have a hard time delivering the first wish on Ivy's list.

Had Theo peeked inside that book before she'd come into the office? She should have written the list somewhere besides the first page, but she'd had no idea at the time that the girl's first request would be something of such a personal nature.

Looking at the stiff way he stood in the corner, watching them, it was hard to imagine him ever liking the holiday, especially since the news they'd been waiting for hadn't materialized. She had pinned her hopes on Lyme disease being the culprit, especially since the symptoms of it were often vague and could appear like those that Ivy had. They were back where they'd started yet again. She should be used to it. And she was. The challenging nature of her work had always energized her.

But not today.

For each terrible disease that was ruled out, another waited in the wings.

And right now Theo looked pretty exhausted, the smile lines around his eyes now tinged with white.

She ached for him. Wished there was something she could say or do that would make this easier.

She'd been surprised to find him in her office earlier. Surprised at the way her heart had jumped to attention.

Was that why she'd agreed to meet him personally to review the details of the case?

Not smart, Madison.

There was something about the man that touched a spark within her, though. Maybe it was the brave front he was putting on for his daughter's sake. Or the fact that he'd walked through some hard years, something to which she could relate. She'd struggled through some heartache of her own as a kid. Since reaching adulthood and graduating from medical school, though, things had been smooth sailing.

Sure they had. Because she was on a roll as far as the dating scene went.

Actually, things were pretty dry. Men weren't exactly lining up to go out with a diagnostician. Then again, she wasn't scrambling to go out with them either. Her days had been too full of work and…work. She was busy. Which made the lonely nights a little easier to bear. Right?

Her glance tracked back to Theo, and she swallowed.

"Did you get to see Doodle?" she asked, forcing her thoughts back to Ivy.

Doodle, the labradoodle, had been a regular visitor around the hospital, thanks to Evie, the ICU reception-ist who was slated to return to nursing school after the holidays. She'd come up with the idea of bringing in a Pets as Therapy dog. He'd been such a hit with the children that the dog and his handler, Alana, came by most days to visit the different pediatric areas. The family suites were probably some of the last on the list today. But Evie had said the pair would be by soon.

"Yes, this morning. He was so sweet and nice. I really would love…" Ivy's eyes went to Theo, and then her shoulders slumped. "Oh, well."

Madison's heart cramped. The little girl had almost blurted out that she wanted a dog. Maybe she should have. It was better for Theo to give her a definite answer than for Ivy to pine after something she might never have.

Like the love of a mother?

Madison's breath stalled for a few painful seconds.

Ivy's mom had died, but surely she'd loved her daughter.

That didn't make the loss any easier. But at least she hadn't simply wandered in and out of Ivy's life, until one day she hadn't been there at all—leaving a heartbroken child to wonder what she'd done to make her mother go away.

Was she thinking of Ivy? Or herself?

Madison had done the rounds in various foster homes after her mom had disappeared. Finally, she'd been sent to a group home when she'd been a teenager, where she'd stayed until she'd graduated from high school.

The chaos of moving from place to place had made it hard to develop long-term friendships. Maybe that was why she preferred working on her own. And why colleagues saw her as aloof and unfriendly. She'd relied on herself for so long that she didn't know how to ask for help. Or to trust that someone would catch her if she fell.

"I didn't realize they brought the dog in here." Theo's low voice was neutral. A little too neutral.

"They did, and I loved him so much. He even fell asleep on my bed while I was stroking him." She pulled her covers up to her thin chest. "Do you think Doodle can come and see me again?"

Theo moved from his position against the wall to sit in a chair beside her bed. "I'll have to see how those visits work, exactly, but I think it can be arranged if you would like that."

"Oh, I would!"

Theo glanced at Madison with brows that went up slightly. In accusation? Had Ivy shared with him her desire for a puppy of her own, or…and here went her wandering thoughts once again…had he looked inside that notebook after all? She gave a slight shake of her head to indicate she hadn't put Ivy up to it.

"They've been trying to bring him by to visit all of the children before Christmas. He's been wearing his elf hat, since he's one of Santa's helpers." She hoped he'd understand what she was trying to say, that they were linking the visits with the man the hospital had hired to play Santa. "I guess it was just Ivy's turn for a special visit."

"I guess it was. An elf, huh?" His voice, like his eyes, had a speculative sound to it. So what if he thought she was behind Doodle's visit or that she was inserting herself where she wasn't welcome? Once they were alone, she would set him straight. Or maybe she would ask Evie to make Ivy a priority and have the labradoodle stop by more often.

Although why she wanted to make him uneasy, she had no idea. A little quid pro quo for the way he hung around in her thoughts—where he most definitely was *not* welcome?

"Yep, an elf. It seems Santa sometimes uses locals to help him do his work."

"And sometimes he uses people from a long way away to do his miracles." The graveled plea behind the words made her tummy twist and turn.

So much for a quid pro quo. Any desire to make him uncomfortable vanished, replaced by a plea of her own.

Please don't pin all your hopes on me.

And yet he was. She knew it. Knew he'd called her to come to the hospital because of this very skill set. Normally Madison thrived under that kind of high-pressure atmosphere, the urgency making her job exciting and unpredictable. Her mind seemed to revel in taking a scattered array of seemingly unconnected symptoms and somehow fitting them together.

Only she'd never been colleagues with a parent before. Or connected with a child the way she had with this one.

Her fingers tweaked Ivy's hair and she forced a smile, pretending the wordplay hadn't suddenly become deadly serious. "Miracles can come from many different sources."

"Will Pablo get a miracle?" The little girl glanced up at her.

Madison saw Theo go still at the mention of the little boy diagnosed with muscular dystrophy who'd been a couple of doors down from Ivy's room until they'd moved him to PICU.

Madison swallowed. "Pablo left today." She tried to

put enough subtle emphasis on the word "left" that Theo would realize she wasn't talking about going home.

A muscle went to work in his jaw, pulsing a couple of times before going quiet. He got it.

He lowered himself into a nearby chair, elbows on his knees, head down.

Thinking about how Pablo could just as easily have been his daughter?

Unwilling to leave him to figure out a way to respond to Ivy's question about miracles—or the lack thereof—Madison spoke up. "Why don't we see if we can challenge your dad to a game of Go Fish?"

Up came Theo's head, eyes fixed on her. "Go Fish?"

Those two words had never sounded as elegant as they did in that accent of his. It forced a smile from her.

"It's a card game that uses a special deck." She never knew what kind of cases she might be called in on, so she'd gotten used to carrying a pack in one of her pockets. Sometimes getting someone's mind off an illness helped calm nerves, whether it be children, parents, or anyone else. She'd been kind of famous for producing that deck of cards at her hospital in the U.S., had often being called on to help calm a child who was being prepared for surgery. It was the one time she'd felt wanted—needed—for something other than her skills at diagnosis.

"I know what it is. I'm just not sure how you're going to manage—"

Out came the pack of cards. Theo's head gave a funny little tilt as if he couldn't believe his eyes.

"Now I've seen everything." His glance landed on her. "Madison the magician."

The way he'd said that…

A shiver rolled over her that she did her best to suppress.

"It's good therapy for cognitive and fine motor skills."

And it gave Madison a way to observe her patients, looking for any tiny changes that she might miss otherwise. If she played a quick game over a period of a couple of weeks—or months—she could see disease progression. The first game gave her a base from which to compare progress or deterioration. In this case, she prayed she wouldn't see the latter.

She let the magician comment stand, instead of going into that kind of explanation. Maybe later.

Nodding at the spot on the bed next to her, she said, "Move closer, Doc, so I can deal."

There was a moment's hesitation, but he finally got up and sat on the mattress, watching as she dealt the first hand and placed the rest of the deck face down between them. She hoped he didn't see the slight tremor in her hand as she did so.

Although she'd come prepared to play, Theo's presence was threatening to derail her. And although she'd invited him to sit next to her, she was now wishing she hadn't. She was hyper-aware of everything about him. His scent. The way the fingers of his left hand rested on his thigh.

The way he was avoiding looking at her.

Lordy. She was in trouble.

When dealing with children, she sometimes adopted rather goofy voices as a way to make her patients laugh. Ha! There was no way she was going to do that today.

Ivy picked up her hand, although it took some effort

to do so. The little girl's struggle poured an icy dose of reality over her. Madison tensed, resisting the urge to offer help, and when Theo looked like he might intervene, she spoke up. "She can do it. Let her."

"Yeah, Daddy, I can do it." She carefully separated her cards, fumbling a little and dropping one of them in the process. There was silence as she recovered and picked it up again.

"Player to the left of the dealer goes first." She would have had Ivy go first, no matter which side she'd been on.

The girl's eyes swiveled between the two of them before focusing on her father. "Do you have any threes, Daddy?"

Theo handed over a card. "I have one."

Ivy's grin lit up the room. "I knew it." She asked for another card, this time from Madison, who didn't have the requested item. Then it was Theo's turn.

"Madison, do you have any aces?"

"Go fish."

He didn't move for a second. "How about up your sleeve? Do you have any there?"

She froze as his eyes finally met hers. Nerve endings crackled as she stared back at him.

"Daddy! That would be cheating, and Madison doesn't do that."

Madison snapped her gaze back to her cards, none of the numbers coming into focus.

She would cheat in a heartbeat if it meant outsmarting whatever was going on inside Ivy's small body.

It took them fifteen minutes to declare Theo the winner, and to Madison it seemed like an eternity. All she wanted to do was retreat to the safety of her office, lay her head down on her desk and try to come up with some kind of answer. For Ivy. And, heaven help her, for her father.

Especially after seeing slivers of change in Ivy over the course of the game. Her cards appeared to get heavier and heavier, the young girl having to set them down in between hands. But her mind was as sharp as ever. In fact, she seemed to make up for her deteriorating condition by memorizing what was in her hand. And when she said, "Go fish," without even looking, neither Madison nor Theo challenged her. By the end the girl was yawning, even though it was only six in the early evening.

"Tired, kiddo?" she asked.

"No."

Theo gathered the cards into a neat stack then leaned over to kiss his daughter's head. "Why don't you rest for a little while, and I'll help Dr. Archer put these away, okay?"

"Will you tell me a story later?"

"Of course."

Ivy lay back against her pillows, her face pale, the muscles in her thin arms lax and still. She made no move to hug her dad. Or wave goodbye. For a child who was normally so affectionate, it struck a chord of fear in Madison.

If she felt it, then that chord had to be a million clanging gongs going off in Theo's head.

God, why couldn't she figure this out?

A hot wave of nausea seared up her esophagus as she pictured Theo tucked in next to his child, reading her a bedtime story.

How many stories did she have until that bed was empty? Just like Pablo's.

Twenty? Ten?

Two?

The pain grew, engulfing her with a terrible sense of responsibility.

She needed to fix a picture of that bed in her head and stare at it. Force herself to get to grips with the reality that this was life or death.

Wasted time can't be recaptured. Hadn't she just said that not very long ago? Yes, and it was true. It couldn't.

Neither could lost opportunities.

She straightened her backbone. So she needed to do something about it. Needed to work faster. Harder.

Theo led the way from the room and handed her the rest of the cards. "I gather there was a reason for that. Quite clever, actually."

It took her a few seconds to realize he hadn't read her thoughts but was talking about the game.

She drew a careful breath, trying to tamp down the chaotic emotions that had been racing through her a few seconds ago. "I wondered if you would figure it out."

"Only after I caught those eagle eyes studying Ivy as she played. After the third or fourth time it hit me that you were monitoring her." He sighed. "She's getting tired more quickly."

"Yes."

"What else?"

"Theo…"

He shook his head. "I want to know."

And he deserved to. She just didn't want to be the one to tell him. But she owed it to him to be honest.

"Her arms have developed a tremor when holding

them in front of her." Muscle wasting from lack of use. The problem was, no one had any idea what was causing them to atrophy. "By the time we were ready to leave the room she was completely spent. I have a feeling she forced herself to keep going. For you."

"Hell."

Theo put his hands behind his neck and stretched his arms out to the side. A pop sounded in one of his joints, the sharp sound making her flinch slightly.

"Sorry. Bad habit."

She could understand that. She had her little quirks as well. But they were more along the lines of insomnia when she was dealing with a puzzling case. She'd had more than her share of nights doodling symptoms on a whiteboard and looking for something that would ring a bell. Ivy's symptoms were plastered on a board she'd propped in the dining room of her apartment. And she had definitely spent more than one sleepless night searching for a clue.

"Her treatment team wants to do more blood tests," he said.

"I know. I asked that the report be sent down. The list of what it's not is growing longer, which is good in that the list of what it could be is getting shorter."

"Is it?" His arms went back to his sides. "How long can she go on like this? At some point it's going to reach a point of no return."

Hadn't she thought something very similar moments earlier?

Fighting through the catch in her throat, she turned toward him, wrapping her fingers tightly around his wrist. She wasn't sure if she was clutching him to reassure herself or to lend weight to what she was about to say.

"Hey. We're not there yet. She's still breathing." *Not* the best way to word it. She hurried to add, "The weakness is only in her limbs and hips at the moment."

"Thank God for that." The second he reached up to cover her hand with his, she knew touching him had been a big mistake. The heat from his skin was electric, unseen calluses scraping across her nerve endings and bringing them to life.

She should move. Tug her hand free. But since she'd initiated the contact, she had no one to blame but herself.

"I'll take as many of those 'at the moments' as I can get," he murmured. "Until we can figure this out."

The hallway was completely empty. There were fewer people staying in this section over the holidays, since everyone who could go home to be with their families did.

Ivy could probably have a great team of caregivers if she went home as well, but Theo wanted her here. Near him. They had an amazing bond. One she'd never had, growing up.

A tightness in her chest warned her that her emotions were venturing far too close to the surface.

She glanced up and caught him staring at her. She wanted to promise him miracles and happy endings and anything else he was looking for. But she couldn't. "Sometimes we just have to do our living in those moments."

"Yes. I agree."

The seconds stretched into minutes. Neither of them

moved. Until—real or imagined—his thumb brushed the back of her hand.

Her body erupted instantly, nipples drawing tight inside her thin bra. God, she hoped he couldn't see them. Hoped he couldn't—

"Madison…"

A sharp *ping!* signaled the arrival of the elevator. Jerking free, she took a hurried step back. Then another, struggling to catch her breath.

She needed to escape while she could. "I'll see you tomorrow for our meeting."

"And another game of cards?"

"Cards?" Her brain was a huge mudslide of buried thoughts and emotions at the moment, and so it took her a second for the words to make sense. "Oh. You don't have to be here for that, if you don't want to."

The less contact she had with him the better. At least it was looking that way. What had she been thinking?

She hadn't been.

Evidently neither had he, if his response to her living-in-those-moments comment was any indication. It had certainly veered away from the professional and into the personal.

Her lack of dating life had shown its ugly face. She'd lapped up the attention like a lovesick teenager.

"I'd like to be, if it's okay. It gives me a chance to measure her abilities as well."

Two people stepped off the elevator, one of them giving Theo a wave that asked him to wait before heading toward them.

Madison did not want to hang around. Her face was already burning. Someone was sure to notice, since she had the worst poker face in history. Theo seemed to be thinking the same thing. "I'll see you tomorrow. Call me when you know a time."

"Okay."

And with that, she fled down the hall in the opposite direction of the approaching staff members. It would take her longer to get back to her little cubicle this way, but she didn't care. Right now, all she was worried about was how she was going to face Ivy's father tomorrow. Or keep herself from doing something else stupid. Like hurtling down a road that led from professional courtesy toward unprofessional crush.

CHAPTER THREE

"WE WOULD LIKE to congratulate Naomi Collins on moving in with Finn Morgan. He is one lucky devil."

Madison, who'd been talking to Naomi about Ivy, saw the woman's eyes widen in surprise as the voice continued over the hospital PA system.

"Oh, my God," the physical therapist muttered. "Is that Finn?"

Madison's lips curled in a smile. She knew Finn and Naomi were an item, but had had no idea their relationship had progressed to this point. "It certainly sounds like him."

"He said he wanted to keep it under wraps."

That made her laugh. "Well, he's evidently changed his mind."

"So it would appear. That man has some explaining to do." Naomi didn't sound angry, though. She sounded…in love. Completely and madly in love.

And the fact that Finn was announcing to the world that they had moved in together? It was dreamy in a way Madison had never experienced. The quick fumbling in the back of her prom date's car had been anything but a dream. It had left her feeling empty and confused. And the guy had never called her for another date, something that had hurt almost as much as her mother's abandonment. She'd been wary of relationships ever since.

So why was Theo affecting her the way he was?

She glanced at Naomi. She didn't seem empty. Or confused. She seemed very, very sure of what she wanted. And what she wanted was Finn.

And that, my dear, was love. The kind that real dreams were made of. The kind she'd never found.

"Congratulations, honey." She gave her new friend a quick hug. "If anyone deserves this, you do."

Naomi waved a hand in front of her face. "Stop or you'll make me cry. Or he'll make me cry. Or someone will."

"I'd go find him if I were you, before he adds to his story and says something really embarrassing."

"Good idea." She gave Madison's arm a quick squeeze. "Can we continue this another time?"

"Of course. Go."

With that, Naomi hurried down the corridor in the direction of the elevators.

Madison watched her go until she disappeared into a small group of people.

What would it be like to find someone like Finn and settle down?

She wasn't likely to ever settle down, wasn't sure she even knew how to stay in one place longer than a few months or a year. Even her job changed repeatedly. Well, not the job itself. Just where she practiced it. She seemed to gravitate toward the hardest of the hard cases. Her last hospital had been different in that regard. She'd been there for two years. And now she wasn't. But she'd left there expecting to go back. Hadn't she?

Or had coming to England put something into motion

that felt both familiar and unsettling? Like pulling up her tent stakes and wandering to a new city with new faces and new challenges.

Was she really bored so easily?

Or was she too afraid to get attached, expecting what was familiar to be yanked away from her at any moment?

Like her prom date? Or her mother's love? Or all those foster homes she'd lived in?

One thing was for sure. No one would be announcing she'd moved in with them over a hospital intercom. She'd made sure of it.

The universe had tricked her one too many times. She no longer wanted to play the relationship version of Go Fish. There was no card out there that matched hers.

She swallowed, not liking her train of thought. She was single because she chose to be single, not for any other reason. She certainly didn't need to be looking for wisdom in a child's card game. Time to go back to her little cubicle and lose herself in Ivy's case or someone else's.

Once there, she sat behind the desk and opened the drawer that contained the little notebook she was using for Ivy. Flipping open the cover, she saw that infamous list again. Her pen paused in front of the first item and stared at it for a moment or two. Then she drew two straight slash lines underneath the words *Make Daddy like Christmas*.

Maybe while Santa was at it he could figure out why she had just as much of a problem with this season as Theo did. Maybe even more. But until then, she would just keep chugging along until all the baubles, trees and Go Fish games were packed away and life became normal again.

* * *

Theo pushed off the couch in his office and dragged his hand through his hair, trying to bring to mind the positive affirmation the hospital chaplain was always going on about. What was it?

Today was a new day, with new hope and new possibilities. Don't dwell on days past.

Which day was that? The day when Hope had died, taking joy and love with her? Or the more recent one where he'd put his hand over that of another woman for the first time in a very long time?

Madison had done something his late wife had loved to do to get his attention when confronting an important matter. She would wrap her fingers around his wrist and grip it tightly. The second the diagnostician had done that it had triggered an automatic response. Only it hadn't been his wife's hand his had reached to cover. It had been Madison's. And within seconds Theo had been acutely aware that he wasn't touching a ghost but flesh and blood. She was warm and alive, her touch reaching inside him and coaxing something to life. Something he'd thought long dead.

His gaze had scoured Madison's face, looking for something. Her cheeks had blushed bright red, something Hope's had never done. And Theo had liked it, had found his attention drifting toward her lips. And then he'd said something stupid. And when her blush had deepened, he'd known he was going to kiss her.

The sudden arrival of the elevator had broken the spell.

Thank God.

He and Hope had been colleagues as well as lovers. And good friends. And she'd put her career on hold for him, something he now regretted bitterly. He didn't regret Ivy's birth. Or the hospital's founding—Hope had been just as excited about that as he'd been.

No, he regretted neglecting her. Putting both of their lives on pause while he'd pursued his dream. And, yes, the hospital did good work. But had it been worth sacrificing a part of his life he could never get back?

He would never know.

What if Madison decided to leave the hospital because of what he'd done? He'd taken a friendly gesture on her part and read something into it. Or had he? Either way, he'd turned it into something more.

He couldn't afford to have her pack up and take off. Even though she hadn't come up with a solution to whatever was happening with Ivy, he had a feeling that she would. Or at the very least she would put them on the right track. And if he'd ruined that out of some maudlin trip down memory lane…

No, it had been more than that. Within seconds of touching her he'd been acutely aware that it had been Madison he'd been touching and not Hope. And hadn't wanted to break that contact. Had wanted it to go on.

Was it about sex? It had been a long time since he'd been with anyone. But even if it was just a physical reaction, then of all people for that to happen with…

He needed to find her and set things right, if possible. And if she hadn't even been aware that sparks were igniting inside him?

He'd just be subtle about it. *Really?* He wasn't exactly known for his subtlety. Hope had often rolled her eyes at him because he pretty much said what he thought. He'd tempered that in later years, learning that to run a hospital took more than a bull-in-a-china-shop approach. So he'd learned tact. Of a sort.

Madison was supposed to meet him to discuss Ivy's treatment and to play cards.

Hell, since when had his duties included playing children's games?

Since his daughter had become ill, that's when. And he respected Madison's ingenuity in assessing her condition without making Ivy uncomfortable. She'd made it fun. And he was damned glad of it.

Hmm. Madison was supposed to set up a time to meet with him. He glanced at his watch. It was still early, just before six a.m. There was time to go down to the hospital cafeteria and grab a bite for him and Ivy and figure out his strategy. Maybe he would gauge the diagnostician's behavior and decide whether he needed to address the issue or not.

And if she blushed again?

He would damn well keep his hands to himself.

A few minutes later he was balancing a tray containing a bowl of warm porridge, fruit and a French omelet and headed back to the elevator, trying to push the button inside with an elbow.

"Need some help?"

He glanced up to find the very person he'd been thinking about standing just inside the doors. Not a trace of red graced her face, and her voice was as steady as the day was long. Maybe he'd overreacted. "I was just taking some breakfast up to Ivy."

"That's an awful lot of food for one little girl." Up went her brows.

He smiled, his insides relaxing. "I was planning on

joining her. Ivy hates eggs." He nodded at his own plate, where the clear cover revealed its contents.

"Ah, so she has the oatmeal and fruit?"

He smiled at the American term for porridge. "Yes, she loves…um…oatmeal."

"She has good taste." Madison pressed the button for the fourth floor and the elevator headed up. She didn't push a second button.

"Were you going to her room as well?"

"Not until a little later, but I wanted to talk to you."

Oh, hell. Maybe he hadn't overreacted. Was this where she said she was catching the next flight out?

"Something with Ivy?"

"No. I wanted to apologize for getting too personal outside her room."

It was then he realized that her voice was a little too steady and her face was not only *not* blushing, it was deadly pale. And her hands were clasped behind her back where he couldn't see them.

What kind of irony was that? He'd been worried sick about how his behavior had come across, and here she was worrying about her own.

"I was upset and you were trying to reassure me. Nothing more. Nothing less."

It sounded ridiculous. And a little bit condescending. He also wasn't happy with the fact that he hadn't admitted to his own part in what had happened. It would be a whole lot easier to let her take the blame and leave it at that, but it didn't sit right. It was time to set the record straight. "If anyone needs to apologize it's me. I actually woke up this morning worried that you might have thought I was being too forward yesterday. But, again, I was upset. And concerned."

"I know. Really I do." Her hands came out from behind her back, and at first he thought she was going to touch him again, and had to force himself to stand still. All she did, though, was reposition the porridge container, which had slid a little too close to the edge of the tray.

"Thank you. I appreciate that. I wouldn't want to do anything that would…" He gave a half-shrug.

Her head tilted. "That would what?"

"Make you leave the hospital." There. He'd said it. His biggest fear was laid out for both of them to see.

"I'm not going to leave. Not yet. So if you're afraid I won't help with Ivy's case anymore, you can rest easy." Her brows went up. "I've dealt with worried dads before."

That made him frown. "You've had men make passes at you before?"

There was a moment or two of silence as she stared at him. "Is that what you were doing?"

Hell, he hadn't meant to say that. And he actually hadn't got to the pass part yesterday, although it had definitely been on his mind.

The doors to the elevator opened as he was casting around for something to say. They both stepped off and into the corridor, where Theo stopped and faced her.

"Not exactly. I forgot who I was with for a second."

She blinked. "I'm sorry?"

"Hell, I'm mucking this up completely. Let's just say I shouldn't have done what I did. And it won't happen again."

He needn't have worried, if her expression was anything to go by. He'd probably just earned himself a knee to the groin if he even looked in her direction ever again.

"Then we're both agreed. We were both worried about Ivy and not acting the way we would normally."

"Yes, that's it exactly."

And if she wanted to believe he had been thinking of Hope that whole time, it would be easier on everyone. Including him.

"I'll help you get her breakfast situated. I want to peek in on her anyway."

"No card games this morning?"

"I'll be back a little later to play, once I've checked on my other patients."

That's right. It was too easy to forget that Madison wasn't at this hospital solely for him and Ivy. His mind scrambled around a bit before rephrasing that internal thought. She wasn't here solely for Ivy. She'd been flown in because the hospital's own diagnostician had suddenly been offered a six-month medical mission to Africa and had left unexpectedly. Dr. Camargo had been texted about Ivy's case a couple of months ago, but he was just as stumped as everyone else. He was the one who'd suggested bringing in another set of eyes. Thankfully Madison had agreed to come.

His phone vibrated in his pocket. Reaching for it with the tray still in his hand, he glanced at the screen. "That's strange."

Motioning to her to wait a second before going into his daughter's room, he pressed the talk button and put the phone to his ear. "Hawkwood here."

"Theo, this is Marco. We've got a couple of cases down here we could use your help on, if your surgeon's hands are still up to the task."

It was very unusual for them to call him in on anything nowadays, so this had to be urgent. "Alice?"

Marco Ricci and his fiancée Alice Baxter were both pediatric surgeons and handled a lot of the general surgeries in the hospital.

"She's tied up with an appendicitis case right now, and I need to scrub in on a suspected ovarian torsion."

Both of those were medical emergencies. "Okay, what do you need help with?"

"We have an eighteen-month-old who is also presenting with right side lower quadrant pain, fever and vomiting."

"Another appendicitis?"

"We thought so at first because of the location. But the scans actually show a probable intussusception. Ryan is doing a heart cath right now, so we're running out of available surgeons."

"Air enema?"

"Already tried it."

"Okay, I'm on it." A fairly straightforward surgery, intussusception was where part of the intestines telescoped in on itself, causing blockage and restricted blood flow. Timing was critical, since the sooner they could free the affected bowel the better the prognosis.

He pressed the phone against his hip to mute it. "Are you interested in scrubbing in on a surgical case? Suspected intussusception in a toddler. We're running out of surgeons."

"Of course. I'd be happy to help."

"Thanks." Putting the phone back to his ear, he said, "On my way. Dr. Archer will assist."

"Great. Tell her thank you."

"I already have. What suite?"

"Seven is open. I think it's been cleaned up after the last case."

"I'll check on it. Get back to your patient. We've got it from here."

He rang off and after putting Ivy's food in front of her Theo left his own on the counter for later. They hurried back to the elevator, arriving at the second floor—where all the surgical suites were located—ten minutes later. Theo went to the desk. "Intestinal intussusception patient? We're here to scrub in."

The young woman's eyes widened. "Right away, Mr. Hawkwood. Let me just check for you."

He frowned. He hated how his position caused some people to treat him differently than other doctors. Yes, he was the CEO of the hospital, but he was also a doctor…would always be a doctor. His inheritance hadn't changed any of that.

A minute later, the nurse came back. "They're getting her prepped for surgery."

"Great, I'd like to take a look at the contrast scans if I could."

"Of course. Here's her chart number." She wrote it on a sheet of paper, handing it over to him. Was it his imagination or had she just batted her lashes at him?

Your imagination, Theo. You're seeing things that don't exist.

"This is Dr. Archer. She'll be scrubbing in as well."

Madison reached over to shake the woman's hand with a murmured greeting, then they both headed toward the small conference area to access the computer. A few seconds later they were looking at Meghan Pitruscki's scans. Madison found it first with an exclaimed, "There!" as she pointed to the computer monitor.

The area was in the lower right quadrant, just as Marco had said. "We'll have to get in there to see how compromised the intestines in that area are."

"Once we get them separated they might be fine."

"We can hope." He switched the computer off. "Ready?"

"Yes. It's been a while since I scrubbed in on a surgery so I don't know how much help I'll be."

"Right now, another set of eyes is exactly what I need." Those were almost exactly the same words Dr. Camargo had used when suggesting they bring another diagnostician in.

He'd have surgical nurses to assist, but he'd like Madison there to make sure he didn't miss anything. It had been a while since he'd scrubbed in on a surgery as well.

Once they got the call that the patient was prepped and waiting, they gloved up, Theo using his shoulder to push through the door that led to the surgical suite. The patient lay on a table, her tiny body barely taking up any of its length. The anesthesiologist was already at her head, monitoring the sedation. Theo would meet with her parents after surgery, which was how he preferred it. It was hard to remain objective in the face of anguished pleas and tears. Hell, it was hard to remain objective under the best of circumstances. Somehow operating on a toddler was so much more difficult than treating an adult. There was so much life they hadn't yet got to experience.

Like Ivy?

Nope, not the time to be thinking of his daughter or her problems right now.

"Hello, everyone. Let's get started, shall we?"

Making the first incision with Madison standing beside him, he called out his movement, step by step for the overhead recorder.

Then he was inside the abdominal cavity, carefully making his way through myriad folds of intestines, laying them aside as he continued to search for the affected area. "I see it."

"I do as well," Madison said. "It's red and inflamed, but I don't see evidence of necrotic tissue at this point. We'll know more once you're able to free the trapped portion."

Carefully checking for tears or perforations that could contaminate the abdominal cavity and cause peritonitis, he used his gloved fingers to try to ease the telescoped part out of the confined area. It didn't budge.

The surgical nurse on the other side moved closer, handing over forceps when he asked for them. He tried again.

"It's not coming loose." The intestines were small and slick and, since he was having to be delicate in handling them, he was stumped. "I may have to resection the affected portion." It was a small enough piece that it shouldn't affect little Meghan's digestion, but cutting and removing bowel always carried an added risk. He tried again, using a tiny bit more pressure, but it was still wedged tight.

Madison's low voice whispered past his ear. "Can you try getting some saline in the space between the two and moistening it? Maybe it's adhered."

It was a good idea.

Without needing to be asked, the nurse loaded a syringe with the solution and placed it in his hand. Theo then nudged the plastic tip into the space and slowly pushed the plunger. He made his way around the area, centimeter by centimeter, until he reached his starting point. He handed the syringe back to the nurse, then repeated the separation attempt. This time the trapped portion of the intestine popped free. Theo heard audible sighs of relief come from various parts of the room.

The affected tissue was blue from lack of oxygen, but hopefully they'd caught it before it went necrotic. He'd give it a few minutes before closing up to make sure. In the meantime, he felt along the length to make sure there wasn't another section that they'd missed.

"It's pinking up." Madison's voice broke through. He finished his inspection, though, before going back to look. It was indeed returning to the pale pink of the rest of the intestines.

"It looks good. Thanks, people, great work today," he called out to everyone in the room.

Returning everything to the abdominal cavity, he glanced up. "Let's get her closed up and back home for Christmas, where she belongs."

Over the next twenty minutes he sutured muscle and skin and then placed a layer of sterile gauze over the area, taping it in place. Meghan would have a little war wound on her lower belly, but that was much better than the alternative.

"Done." He nodded to the anesthesiologist. "Let's wake our little patient up."

"Gladly."

When he glanced at Madison, the corners of her eyes had crinkle lines and she nodded at him. "Thanks for asking me to come."

He should be the one thanking her. She was the one who'd suggested he try saline to lubricate the tissues. It had worked beautifully.

"Thank you, you were a big help."

"Just glad to work on something that is a little more straightforward."

"Something other than Ivy?"

"No, of course not. It's just different from what I normally do."

He shut his eyes for a moment. Why the hell was he putting words into her mouth?

Moving up to the girl's head, he watched as the other doctor adjusted the dials that would send oxygen to her body, replacing the gases that had been used to keep her under sedation.

Twenty minutes later the trach tube had been removed and the toddler's eyes flickered, pure blue irises struggling to focus on his face. He put his hand on her forehead. "Hi, sweetheart. Welcome back."

And just like that it was over and people were moving to do their jobs, and Meghan was wheeled away to the recovery area to finish waking up.

"I need to speak to her parents. Can you wait for me?"

"Of course. How about if I meet you in my office?"

Her tone didn't sound as sure as it had a few minutes ago. Afraid of being alone with him? Well, she should be. Although he'd kept his mind on surgery as it had been happening, now that it was over he found himself wanting to study her, from those cute little smile lines all the way to how her hair drifted in different directions when freed of its normal clip.

Except her hair was covered by a surgical cap at the moment, so there was no hair to see. Just those beautiful clear green eyes and the straight length of her nose.

High cheekbones. Smooth forehead. All things he had no business noticing.

"Thanks, I'll try not to be long."

Turning, he forced himself to stride away, ruing the fact that he'd asked her to wait for him. To talk about Ivy's case. That was all. Otherwise he would while away the hours worrying about every little detail of her condition. Better to just talk about it and be done with it. Maybe in the same way that two pairs of eyes had been better than one, two minds might be able to figure out a solution when his was stuck in limbo. A fearful limbo that was stealing his soul just like the disease that was stealing his daughter's ability to move. He had no idea which side would succumb first. His soul. Or his daughter.

"The symptoms look like appendicitis. But it's not. It's something completely different."

Theo's words as they'd walked down to the surgical suite a couple of hours ago stuck in her head and wouldn't leave.

It looks like appendicitis. But it's not.

A tickling at the back of her brain was slowly gaining strength. Slowly consuming her other thoughts.

Reaching into her desk, she grabbed her little notebook, flipping a couple of pages past Ivy's wish list, and wrote down her thoughts.

"Add to whiteboard at home: It looks like appendicitis. But it's not."

She didn't know what they meant. Not yet. But she knew from experience that her brain would be fiddling with those words in the background, much like a computer program might work behind the scenes until you opened it again and saw what had happened.

She just hoped it wasn't another rabbit hole.

A quick knock, and then Theo poked his head in. "Thanks."

"I was tempted to go on up to check on Ivy, but I did this instead." She nodded at some food on the desk. "Hope that was okay."

She'd stopped by the cafeteria and bought some fruit for herself and another omelet for Theo, since the one he'd left upstairs had to be stone-cold by now. "I wasn't sure what you had in it, so I just had them add some cheese and seasonings."

His brows went up. "You didn't have to do that."

She smiled. "I know I didn't, but since I was getting something for myself anyway, it only made sense. I called upstairs, and Ivy ate most of her oatmeal and all her fruit. How were Meghan's parents?"

"Relieved. Thanks to you and your saline idea."

"There was no guarantee it would work. It was pure luck."

"It was thinking outside the box." He lowered himself into one of the metal chairs with a groan. "I need to find you some better furniture."

"It's fine. I won't be here forever."

The reminder was more for herself than anything. She was feeling a little too comfortable in her tiny little space, metal chairs and all. Only she didn't want to feel comfortable here. This had never been intended to be permanent.

"I'm aware of that."

There was a hint of something in his tone that made her take a second look. Was he thinking about Ivy and how she might not be here long enough for them to come up with a diagnosis?

She wanted to find a solution as much as he did. Madison did not like leaving things undone. She liked everything tied up with a neat bow, unlike her childhood where things had never been neat and had rarely ever been followed through to completion. Those insecure years had turned her into a fanatic about finishing tasks and making sure she had closure. One way or another.

And closure with Ivy and her dad? What would that look like? She had no idea.

She pushed the plate containing his omelet across to him, placing a fork on top of it. "I'm not leaving until we figure this thing out, Theo, if that's what you're worried about."

His eyes closed for a second. "Sorry. I haven't been getting much sleep lately."

"I can imagine. But you can't help her if you're completely run down yourself."

His hands went behind his neck, and she braced herself for the popping of that shoulder joint. It didn't come as he seemed to catch himself just in time. "I forgot that you don't like that."

How did he even know that? Was she that obvious?

Lord, she hoped not, because that might mean he saw a whole lot more than she wanted him to.

"It's not that I dislike it. It just surprised me that first time. Go ahead if it helps."

"I can do it later. When you're not around." Then he smiled before his eyes tracked to the desk and his head tilted before he opened his box and cut into his omelet. "What are you writing?"

For a split second she thought she'd left the book open to Ivy's wish list, but then remembered what she'd been doing. "I was writing down something that struck me during Meghan's surgery. I'm just not sure why yet."

"You're not sure why it struck you, or why you wrote it down?"

"Both."

She turned the book to face him so he could read it.

"I don't understand."

"Neither do I. Yet. It might mean nothing. Or it could trigger a thought."

He took a bite, his strong throat contracting as he swallowed. "About Ivy's case?"

"Yes, I think so." She felt the need to warn him. "I do this a lot with cases. Many times, it ends up being a dead end. But there are enough times that it's not to keep me doing it."

"You think Ivy's symptoms could be something related to appendicitis?"

"No. I'm not sure why it seemed important. I have a board at the apartment with all Ivy's symptoms on it. It helps me visualize what's happening inside a patient. And if it's staring me in the face at every turn, it can help a diagnosis leap out of nowhere. I'm going to add this to that board."

"You have one made up for Ivy?"

"I do."

They ate in silence for a minute or two, and Madison wished she'd gone ahead and eaten before he'd arrived. Because this companionable silence was disconcerting. It didn't feel as awkward as it should have. In fact, it felt kind of good to be able to sit and talk through a problem with someone. Which was also weird. She usually

preferred to work alone, not sharing details with anyone, which was another reason she was loath to go to
the meetings upstairs. She preferred to keep her clut-
tered thoughts to herself. Adding someone else's to the
mix was just too confusing. Oh, she could sit and listen to others' ideas, but she rarely wrote them down or
added them to her lists. Theo's comment had been the
exception to that rule, evidently.

"I'd like to see your board."

She froze. "What?"

"The board you've worked up about Ivy."

Suddenly she was backtracking like crazy. "It's just
a mishmash of symptoms." The idea of having Theo in
her home threw her into a panic, and she wasn't sure
why. She'd had other visitors and it hadn't seemed like
a big deal. Hadn't she just wondered about what that
closure would look like? If she complicated it by allowing him to walk around her home…

"I know, but I've seen the rest of the team's thoughts
and ideas. But not yours."

Yes, he had. "I've talked you through them."

"I'd like to see what you've written down. The order
and placement."

"Why?"

"I don't know. But it's important to me. Is it a problem?"

Yes. It was. But there was no way she was going to
say that to him.

"If you really think it will help." She was not stupid
enough to keep the list from him if he insisted on seeing it. And she could understand being so desperate for
any clue that you would do anything to find one.

She'd done that with her birth mom, gone through all

kinds of hoops and verbal gymnastics with bureaucrats until she'd discovered a truth she hadn't wanted to find.

But find it she had. And once she'd opened that box, there had been no closing it. She would have preferred to think her mom was out there somewhere, maybe even looking for the child she'd abandoned all those years ago.

She took a deep breath and threw out one more feeble attempt at self-preservation. "I could always take a picture of the board and send it to you."

"If you don't want me in your house, I'll understand."

"It's not that…" It was that. Exactly that. Only there was no way she was going to admit it. "I just didn't want you to drive all that way to look at something that won't make sense to anyone except me."

"I would like a picture for the team, if that's okay, but I'd also like to see it in person, if you don't mind."

"Of course." Now that she'd admitted to having the board at home, she was a little embarrassed for anyone but her to see it in all its chaotic glory. "But I'm warning you, they've already mentioned almost everything that's on there."

He nodded at the notebook as he finished the last bite of his omelet. "Not things like that."

"My brain doesn't always work in an orderly fashion. It could just as easily be erased by tomorrow morning."

"Understood. I actually came by to see when to meet you in Ivy's room."

"I'm just going to play cards with her. Are you sure you want to be roped into that?"

"I'm not being 'roped' into it. Anything that can give insight into what's happening to her will be welcomed with open arms."

"Okay, then let's plan on dinnertime. Unless you need to go home before that."

"I've been sleeping in her room to stay close to her, so that's fine. My housekeeper's bringing me fresh clothes periodically."

Housekeeper. Okay. She knew he was wealthy, since he'd been the one to open the hospital, but evidently he had a lot more money than she'd realized. That explained his comment about the lack of luxurious chairs in her office. Well, she'd grown up at the opposite end of the spectrum and tended to be pretty frugal in a lot of ways. So those metal chairs were just her style. She wasn't poor anymore, per se, but she still didn't like to waste money. So her apartment here was spartan. Just like her apartment back in the States.

Oh, well, he could take it or leave it. She certainly wasn't going to apologize for her taste in decor.

And now that the decision had been made, she was kind of anxious to see his reaction to the space she'd carved out for herself. Would he turn his nose up like some kind of aristocrat?

That didn't seem to match the man she was learning more and more about. But you never could tell. Actions could be deceiving.

Like her own actions yesterday in front of Ivy's room? She'd said it had meant nothing but in her heart of hearts she knew she was deceiving not only him but herself. She was attracted to him.

Only like the anesthesia that had been administered to Meghan before her surgery, she'd better find a way to reverse it. And fast. Or she was setting herself up for a whole lot of heartache.

CHAPTER FOUR

"MUMMY DIED AND went to heaven."

The bald words floating from his daughter's room stopped Theo in his tracks. Delayed almost an hour by an emergency meeting of the board, he could hear the sound of cards being shuffled. There was a pause before it resumed.

"I know she did. But she would be awfully proud of the big girl you've grown into."

A hard lump formed in Theo's throat and his fingers curled into his palms, biting deep. Ivy hadn't mentioned her mother in over a year. It had been last year at Christmas, actually, when she'd asked him if Hope was opening up presents in heaven and if God was like Santa Claus. He'd been hard-pressed to answer those questions so he'd redirected her the best he could and had buried his own heartache deep inside his chest, hoping she couldn't see it.

"Daddy still gets sad sometimes."

"We all get sad sometimes." Another ruffle of cards being shuffled hard. "My mommy is in heaven too."

Madison's mother had died as well? Something about the matter-of-fact way she'd said that made the hair lift on the back of his neck.

He realized he actually knew very little about the diagnostician other than her professional credits. She liked to work alone—as she herself had admitted—and she'd sometimes run into trouble with the hospital administrators back in the States because of the bull-headed way she went about her work. But she got the job done. And since she avoided being involved in treatment meetings, she circumvented some of the bureaucracy hospitals—even Hope Hospital—were known for.

"Did your mum die at Christmas?"

His daughter's young voice asking such hard questions caused a prickling sensation behind his eyes. One he quickly forced back. He knew he shouldn't be standing here eavesdropping on their conversation, but since they so rarely talked about Hope, he couldn't bring himself to interrupt them.

"She didn't *die* at Christmas. I don't know when she died, actually. I just know she did."

"That's sad. What about your daddy? Is he in heaven too?"

He wasn't sure why Madison hadn't cut off this topic before it got this far, but she'd offered up the information about her mother without his daughter asking about it.

"I never knew my father, so I don't know if he's in heaven or not."

Hell.

"How did Santa find you to give you your presents, then?"

That was his cue to put a stop to the prying. He knocked on the door a little louder than necessary and went on in to find the pair of them on Ivy's bed. There was no sign of giggling this time, though.

Madison was seated at the foot, across from his daughter, her legs drawn up and tucked beneath her thighs, her shoes on the floor beneath the bed. It was an incredibly casual and intimate scene. He could picture Hope doing exactly the same thing.

Only this wasn't Hope and he would do well to remember that. Madison was a temporary fixture in his daughter's life. He needed to remember that too, and he needed to find a way to let Ivy know she would be leaving eventually.

But that could wait until later. When she was better.

"Santa knows where everyone is." By bringing the conversation back around, and forcing a lightness to his voice that he did not feel, he hoped that Madison would think he'd just come in on the tail end of their conversation. When she tilted her head to glance up at him, her eyes said she knew exactly what he'd heard. But she didn't seem angry that he'd been standing there. If anything, she seemed relieved.

"Hi, Daddy!"

"Hi, sweetheart." He came in the rest of the way and gave his daughter a kiss on the head, frowning slightly. Did her brown hair seem a little less lustrous than it used to? Or was that his crazy thoughts leading him down dark paths again?

The little notebook Madison seemed to like so well was half-tucked under her left thigh. Writing down ideas? Or measuring Ivy's reflexes and drawing an arrow that was slowly angling down and gaining speed?

He was killing himself here. Ivy seemed in fairly good spirits, even after talking about her mother being in heaven. Of course she was too young to really remember Hope, even though photos of her peppered his apartment and office as a reminder.

The pack of cards was back in its box. Theo frowned. "Aren't we playing cards?"

"Sorry," Madison said. "I wasn't sure when you were going to be free, so we played without you, and we just finished up, actually."

"And I won, Daddy!"

"You did?" He smiled a question at the diagnostician he hoped she could decipher.

"She did very well." Madison gave a slight nod of her head. "Naomi was in earlier to do her therapy. Tomorrow good old Doodle will be coming in."

The therapy dog. Ivy seemed enamored with the dog already. Just like she was enamored with Madison. The thing was, neither of them would be sticking around in her life, and Theo wasn't sure it was a good idea for his daughter to get attached to either of them. He didn't want another scenario where something that was a constant in her life was suddenly snatched away.

Maybe it was time for him to set a few boundaries, much as he disliked doing so. "Can I speak to you outside for a moment?"

Madison frowned, but she uncurled her legs and stood, tucking her notebook into her pocket. His eyes lingered on the book. His curiosity about it was getting out of hand. As were a lot of other things.

Like noticing how her bare feet were pink from being tucked underneath her, with the little toe on her right foot having a small crook to it. And nail polish. Glittery silver that seemed so out of character compared to the short plain nails on her hands. As if realizing she'd revealed something she preferred no one see, she hurriedly shoved her feet back into her low-heeled black pumps and tweaked a strand of Ivy's hair before preceding him out of the room and heading for the waiting area. He half expected her to go to his office, but maybe it was just as well that he address this in a public setting. Especially after being caught staring at her toes.

She dropped into one of the plush leather chairs, a luxury, yes, but Theo figured if parents were going to have to sit for hours and wait for potentially devastating news, they deserved something other than hard plastic. The leather could still be disinfected, with nooks and crannies kept to a minimum, while still being comfortable with supportive cushioning on the back. He moved to sit in the one across from her, leaning to prop his elbows on his knees.

Fortunately, no one else was there at the moment, since the bulk of the procedures would have been done earlier in the day. Most of the family suites had two rooms, one with a pull-out couch where parents could sleep near their children. There was also a playroom down the hallway with educational toys and movies for parents who had other children with them.

But none of that was important right now, and Madison was sitting with tightly clasped hands, waiting for him to get on with whatever he wanted to say to her.

"She's doing okay?"

"Yes. She hasn't gotten any worse over the last couple of days, so that's a good thing."

Yes, it was. At least the arrow he'd pictured taking a plunge wasn't a reality. But that wasn't why he'd asked to speak with her.

He decided to start with what he'd heard of their conversation. "I hope Ivy didn't ask a lot of personal questions in there. If so, I apologize. She doesn't always understand the concept of boundaries."

"About my parents? No, it's okay. And after she'd shared about her mom, I thought it might help her to not feel like she was the only child in the world who'd lost someone. I'm sorry if you'd rather I hadn't said anything."

"No, not at all." And he hadn't even thought about that being her reason for sharing. His reasons for asking her to come out here now seemed petty and mean. The woman was trying to figure out what was wrong with his daughter, for God's sake, and he wanted her to back off? Yes, Ivy was getting attached, but did he really want her growing up in a world that didn't form connections? Would he have rather never loved her mother?

Madison didn't know when her mother had died, or even who her father was. How was that for not having a good foundation?

The words came out before he was aware they'd formed. "I'm sorry about your mother."

"Thank you. But I didn't grow up with her. At least, not my whole life."

"You were adopted." Talk about prying questions.

"No, I wasn't that lucky." She sat there for a few seconds and then continued. "My mom overdosed on Christmas Eve when I was ten. I didn't realize it until I got up the next morning and there were no presents under the tree. We were poor, but there was normally a gift or two."

Damn. "You said you didn't know when she died."

"That overdose wasn't fatal, but it was the last one I experienced with her. I found her on the floor in the kitchen. There was a needle on the counter and a roll of wrapping paper where she'd evidently been trying to wrap a Christmas gift for me. It was a bracelet-making kit." She shrugged. "I don't know what happened to that. It didn't come with me."

"To the hospital?"

"No. I was put in foster care. I remember sitting in a police car for a long time while they tried to find a place for me—not an easy task on a holiday, when gifts had already been purchased. The female officer was really nice, though. She bought me a fast-food meal and hugged me as I cried and asked a million times about my mom.

"My mom lived. That time. And I saw her periodically for about a year as I went from one set of foster parents to another, until it was finally a group home for me." She smiled. "Believe it or not, I was a little difficult to deal with as a child. I bet if you ask anyone at my other hospital, they'll tell you I still am."

She may have been trying to make light of a difficult situation, but it didn't work. "I have a feeling it made you tenacious—not difficult."

"A nice way of saying the same thing." Her smile faded. "Anyway, Christmas doesn't hold the best memories for that reason. I actually have the perfect career imaginable for someone like me, since most doctors have to work at least some Christmases. I simply choose to work them all."

Christmas was hard for him too, but he did the opposite because of Ivy. He would have liked to work his way through that particular holiday as well, but he wanted his daughter to have good memories, even if he didn't. "I understand that completely. My late wife died at Christmastime."

"Ivy said you were sad this time of year."

"My daughter is far too wise for her years."

"Children like us don't have a choice." She stopped suddenly. "I didn't mean that the way it sounded. You're a great dad. Ivy is very lucky."

Right now it didn't feel like either of those things was true. As much as he tried to make time for his daughter, he still worked long hours. His housekeeper had stepped in to help time and time again. And as far as being lucky, looking at Ivy and her condition, it didn't feel like she was very lucky.

"I can't be with her as much as I'd like to, but Judy helps fill in some of those gaps."

Her eyes widened slightly. "Judy?"

"Sorry. She's our housekeeper. She also plays nanny more often than I would like."

"Is she the older lady who has been in to visit? I assumed she was Ivy's grandmother."

That was another way Madison and Ivy were connected. Neither of them had grandparents. Well, he assumed Madison didn't since she'd been in foster care and had only mentioned visits from her mother and not grandparents. "No, my folks passed away when I was in medical school, and Hope's mom has Alzheimer's and is in a care home."

"I'm sorry." She hesitated. "You mentioned having a housekeeper. I never associated that with having someone to watch Ivy while you work."

"It's not an ideal situation, and I will be the first to admit it. I don't have time to cook and clean like some fathers do."

"I wasn't criticizing you. I just…" She let her voice trail off.

She sounded almost apologetic, although he had no idea what she had to be sorry for.

"I didn't take it as criticism." His elbows were still planted on his knees, but somehow he had leaned in, the long curtain of Madison's hair close enough to touch. And hell if he didn't want to.

To keep from acting on that impulse, he twined his fingers together and used the resulting fist to rest his chin on.

He'd brought her here to ask her to be careful of how attached she was letting Ivy get, and here he was thinking about toying with strands of that silky hair.

"Can I ask you something?"

"Of course." Even as he gave her permission, something in him tensed up.

"It's personal. And hard."

The tension turned into rigid muscles and a frozen brain. "What is it?"

"Your wife's name was Hope?"

Damn, the last thing he wanted to talk to her about was his late wife. "Yes."

"Is there any way I can get a copy of Hope's medical records? And yours?"

"I'm sorry?"

"That came out badly. I want to see if there's anything in there I can spot. Maybe a genetic component that's been overlooked."

She thought he or Hope had passed something to Ivy that was making her sick? "Didn't they do that when they were looking for muscular dystrophy?"

"Yes, but there are other things. How did your wife die?"

"She was hit by a car while out walking Ivy." His

voice was a little harsher than he'd meant it to be, but she was right. These were personal questions.

Her chin went up a bit. And her words about being a difficult child came back to him. He had a feeling she wasn't going to back down until she got whatever it was she was after.

"Did you notice any unsteadiness in her before it happened? Any changes in her behavior?"

Had there been? He cast around for the last time he'd seen his wife. It had been that morning when he'd left for work. They'd made love the night before, and she'd made him breakfast before he'd left the house the next morning. No unsteadiness. Just a loving woman who had been far too patient about his long hours.

"No. She was perfect. In every way."

Madison didn't move for a second. Then she reached a hand toward him. "I'm sorry, Theo. Really I am."

He allowed himself to capture her fingers, while he tried to process his thoughts. "What do you expect to find in her records? In mine?"

"It's not what I expect to find. I've just hit a brick wall time and time again with the test results. I thought maybe I could look at each of you separately and see if there's anything I could use as a springboard." Without unlinking their hands, she moved to the chair next to his and turned to face him. "Is there any possibility Hope could have had Huntington's?"

A degenerative brain disease, it showed itself in uncoordinated muscle movements, followed by cognitive decline. It was inherited and deadly, passed from mother to daughter. If Ivy had that...

Well, he didn't want to think of the ramifications. Any hope he'd had of a cure would go out the window.

And how would he know if Hope had had it, really? Could she have fallen in front of that car rather than the other way around? The driver had been arrested and convicted, but what if there had been something insidious he'd missed?

How far would Madison be willing to go to follow her hunches? How far would he let her go? All thoughts of Doodle and attachments disappeared.

"Look at her records. Look at mine. But I don't want to exhume Hope's body."

Madison squeezed his fingers. "I don't either. I'd just like to chase this rabbit for a little while." She paused. "But only as long as I think it's useful. I'm not at the point of throwing spaghetti against a wall and seeing what sticks."

"And if I'm ready to do just that?" Would he actually allow them to dig up her body? He wasn't sure.

"Do you really want Ivy to go through a battery of unnecessary tests?"

No. He didn't. She'd already gone through her share and more. "I'll have Hope's records pulled. But I'd like to go through them with you."

"Of course." Her eyes searched his. "And yours?"

"Yes. I'll make sure you have those as well." He had nothing to hide. At least nothing in his medical history. As for his current history… Oh, yes. He had things he would rather Madison not know about. Like the way her hand in his felt reassuring. And unnerving. And anything except platonic.

"Do you really think it could be Huntington's?"

"No, but I'd rather not leave any stone unturned. Like multiple sclerosis, Huntington's is normally found in adults, but it can appear in young children on rare occasions. I don't see any mental decline in Ivy, though. Quite the contrary. That little girl is a card shark. She bats those big innocent eyelashes at you, all the while waiting for an opportunity to do a smack down."

"A smack down?"

"You know."

"No, I really don't." But it was a good confusion. Something that felt shared.

"It's an expression."

"I see." He paused, trying to get back on track, but not enough to let go of her hand. "So what other genetic conditions could it be?"

"I need to do some research. Huntington's was the only thing that came to mind, but her wobbliness made me think of that. Which led me to think of genes. The dystrophies are normally genetic, but the muscle biopsy ruled that out. But there are lots of other possibilities."

"Lots is not a word I want to hear."

"I'm not looking at it like that. There are lots of possibilities, yes, but all it takes is one. And that one is what I'm eying at the moment. I just ruled out polymyositis. She's developed foot drop in her right ankle, which is what made me think of it, but her torso and neck flexion seem normal."

An inflammation of muscle tissue, polymyositis could affect the heart and/or the lungs, so he was glad she'd ruled that out. Although a Huntington's diagnosis would be as bad, if not worse.

She jiggled his hand, and touched her shoulder to his, bringing his mind back to her. "Hey, I'm just trying to be thorough. We can't help her until we know what it is. A steroid for a few days might not be a bad idea, though."

She turned her head to look at something and the scent of her shampoo floated toward him, along with some lighter, more feminine fragrance.

He swallowed. He'd been doing okay. Until now.

She was still talking but the words began to flow together into a long incoherent string of sound as his mind zoomed in on the warmth of her fingers in his, her grip tightening and relaxing as she worked through another thought. Within seconds, the sensation eclipsed the rational side of his brain, leaving it open to attack from other areas. And attack they did.

The pleasure centers went on the prowl, cruising along the aisles of awareness. An awareness that had been simmering in the background ever since they'd met.

"…we could also try activating some of those neural receptors and see what happens…"

His fingers tightened on hers. She was already activating some of those neural receptors and it was pretty obvious—to him—what was happening.

Her head tilted as she studied his face. "Theo? Are you okay?"

This was the moment of truth. Admit it, or pretend there was nothing wrong. Only she'd already noticed something wasn't right. If he tried to lie, he could end up making things a hundred times worse.

Was he crazy? How could they be any worse than they already were?

"Theo?"

"Actually, I'm struggling with something." Maybe it was the revelations about her mom that cast Madison in a different light—the reasons for the slight standoffishness he'd noticed from time to time suddenly making sense. Or maybe it was the stress of dealing with Ivy's illness that had his senses out of whack. But he found himself wanting to do something crazy and impulsive, something he hadn't analyzed from every angle before acting on it.

"With what?"

"The way your thoughts dart from one thing to the other so fast that I can barely keep up."

"I—I'm sorry."

"Don't be. I like it. But it also drives me…insane. In ways I should be able to control." Letting go of her hand, he curled his fingers around the nape of her neck, his thumb sliding just beneath her jaw to where he knew her pulse beat. He let his fingers trail down the side of her throat, along skin that was incredibly soft. "But right now I don't want to control it. And that's the struggle. So… I need you to tell me to back off."

She moistened her lips and started to say something, then stopped. Her eyes met his. "I don't think I can."

Something inside him leaped to attention and he lowered his voice, aware that they were still completely alone. "You *can't* tell me to back off, or you don't want to?" He leaned forward, employing light pressure to bring her nearer until their lips were a mere centimeter away.

"I don't want to tell you…want you to…" Her hand went to his shoulder, fingers pressing through the thin fabric of his button-down shirt. Warmth bloomed and traveled. And then, with a feeling of déjà vu, her mouth touched his.

Senses that had been dormant for years erupted in a huge array of lights that rendered him blind for several seconds.

When he could see again, he was kissing her back and Theo knew at that moment he was in big trouble. He should stop this before it went any further, but his limbs wouldn't co-operate. Neither would his mouth.

So there was nothing else to do but sit back and enjoy the ride. Because any time now Madison was sure to realize what a mistake this was and call a screeching halt to it.

All of it.

And when that happened, Theo had no idea what he was going to do.

CHAPTER FIVE

MADISON'S BODY WAS turned at a weird angle, but she didn't care. She would have stayed there until her muscle strength totally deserted her. In fact, she dragged herself closer, even as something about that last thought tugged at her.

No. She didn't want to think. She wanted to feel. How long had it been since she'd been in someone's embrace?

Far too long.

The men who found her aloofness attractive at first were soon disillusioned when that didn't magically shift into something softer. She wasn't capable of softness. To be soft was to be vulnerable, and to be vulnerable was to be hurt.

Except her softer side showed through around one little girl.

And now around that little girl's father.

His hands came up and cupped her face and a sound rumbled up in his chest, a half sigh, half groan that had her reacting in ways that were foreign to her. She didn't normally stick around long enough to form attachments. But Madison suddenly wanted to set this man's world on fire, and she had no idea why. Her tongue slid forward, catching her first real taste of his mouth.

Heaven, pure heaven. Just like she knew he'd taste.

But how?

Her muscles weakened further, sending her thoughts skittering back to another place. A place she didn't want to be. Her hand slipped off his shoulder as a pressure grew behind her eyelids.

Muscle weakness.

Wheelchairs.

Possible...

Ivy!

She dragged her mouth from his in an instant as reality swamped her. What was she doing? This was her patient's father.

No. Ivy wasn't solely her patient.

Did that matter? She might have a string of doctors as long as her arm, but Madison was definitely on that list.

"Sorry, Theo. I'm sorry." She tried to suck down a few deep breaths to ward off the light-headedness that was doing wonky things to her thought processes.

He stared at her for a second, then dragged the back of his hand across his mouth. Trying to wipe away her touch?

Her heart slammed against her ribs in protest, even as he shook his head.

"I'm the one who should be apologizing. God, Maddy, I have no idea where that came from."

She swallowed hard. No one called her Maddy. No one. Not since the last time she'd seen her mom. It was part of the problem she'd had in foster care, lashing out anytime someone had tried to shorten her name to something more familiar.

She hadn't wanted familiar. She'd wanted distance. After her prom disaster that need had grown.

But this time?

Trying not to acknowledge the little thrill that went through her at hearing him call her that—and trying to reject the kernel of an idea that Theo's kiss had sparked an indefinable change between them—she sat back in her seat. "It was me. Or maybe the struggle to find an answer to Ivy's condition. We're both tired. Stressed. And definitely not ourselves."

At least, Madison wasn't herself. Whether Theo was acting out of character or not was for him to decide.

"No, not ourselves." He glanced around. "That was unprofessional, especially since I wanted to mention an item of concern."

"Besides the kiss?"

He gave a visible grimace. "Yes. Ivy has suffered one terrible loss in her life. I wonder whether allowing her to get too attached…" There was a huge pause in which he seemed to be searching for something.

Oh, God. He thought Ivy was getting too attached to her? Was he going to ask her to back off the case? And if he did? As Ivy's father, he certainly had the right to do whatever he wanted.

He finally continued his thought. "Whether getting too attached to Doodle—is that his name?—is a good idea. What happens when he no longer comes back to visit her."

Theo might be genuinely worried about that, but his words made her sag into her seat in relief. She'd been so sure he was going to point that accusing finger at her.

And he might be right, if he had. She had been spending a lot of time with the little girl. But then she spent a lot of time with all her patients. It was how she did her job.

"I was afraid you were going to say I was the problem. And I want to assure you that I do the same thing with each and every one of my patients. It's not that Ivy isn't special. Of course she is. It's just my process. I do whatever I have to do to come up with a diagnosis."

Even as she said the words, Theo flinched. Damn. She'd made it sound like she kissed all her patients' fathers.

"That's not what was behind that…" She couldn't even bring herself to say the word. What if that was why *he'd* kissed *her*? Because he was desperate and willing to do anything to help his daughter?

So what was her excuse?

Just what she'd told him. She was stressed at not being able to come up with an answer for him. Strong emotions needed a pressure valve or they exploded. So had his kiss been the valve? Or the explosion?

Something she didn't want to look at.

But someday, Madison, you're going to have to. Because unless you actually remove yourself from Ivy's case—ha!—emotions are bound to get out of hand again, eventually.

Not a good thing. She needed to figure out how to contain them enough to avoid getting into another situation like this one.

"That's good to know. It was a simple misstep on both of our parts. You are an attractive woman who is smart and funny and who my child seems to enjoy being around. And I let things spiral out of control." He paused a beat or two. "I think you hit the nail on the head earlier. There are a lot of unknowns right now. That kiss was one of those unknowns. Hopefully now that we're aware of the possibility, we won't let ourselves be drawn into situations where one—or both—of us might react without thinking of the consequences."

"Consequences?"

"What it might mean for Ivy if someone thinks you're getting preferential treatment."

She forced a laugh. "Exactly what kind of preferential treatment would that be? Getting to kiss the mighty Theo Hawkwood?"

The comment might contain a hint of snark, but it was only to cover up how shaken she still was. And how being this close to him was still working on her nerve centers. Which wanted to kiss him all over again, damn them.

"How about if someone saw us and thinks you're playing some kind of angle?"

Her soul froze. What if someone actually did think she was trying to work her way up some corporate ladder—or angling for an invitation to stay in Cambridge and continue to work at Hope Hospital? It happened all the time, didn't it? What if Theo himself thought she was doing that? Could that be why he'd mentioned it?

The frozen spot inside her grew. Madison had worked hard her entire life. She'd never had anything handed to her. And certainly not because she'd tried to manipulate someone into it. "I—I would never—"

"I know you wouldn't, Maddy. I wasn't trying to say that. People could just as easily think I'm abusing my position and sexually harassing you."

"Which I would *assure* them you weren't." The ice was turning into a block that encased her heart. The same one that had surrounded it when her first set of foster parents had asked to have her transferred elsewhere. She'd soon figured out that nothing in her life was permanent. So why bother trying. Thank heavens she'd finally channeled all that anger and despair into her studies once she'd hit college and medical school. Her stubborn unwillingness to bend or give in had served her in good stead. And as a diagnostician, she had taken what had seemed like a personality defect and turned it into an asset.

Theo held his hands up. "Okay. Let's both acknowledge our part in this fiasco and work to fix it."

"Agreed."

"We can start by going out on the town. I have a day off coming up a week from Thursday on Christmas Eve and a couple of half-days before that."

"Going out on the town…together?"

"Yes."

Her brows shot up. "Are you crazy? Or just plain nuts?" That was a little over a week away. Not nearly enough time to section off the memory of what had just happened into a different part of her brain.

He grinned. "It would seem both. But maybe if we get away from the hospital for a couple of hours and do things that don't revolve around patients or tests or the millions of other things we do on a daily basis, we could unwind in ways that are a bit safer."

"Safer. What about Ivy?"

"As long as she's having a good day, I don't see how it can hurt anything. She doesn't require twenty-four-seven nursing care."

Not yet. But if Madison couldn't figure out what was

wrong with her, it could very well come to that. She pushed that thought away. "I don't know."

"I'm not trying to pressure you, but I think it would do us both some good, and I know for a fact that you've spent almost all of your free time in Ivy's room."

That was true. What if Theo was right, and that kiss had been caused by being pulled one way and then the other until she'd gone past the breaking point? It would be stupid to turn him down in that case, wouldn't it?

"Well, as long as Ivy is doing okay, I guess it wouldn't hurt."

He pulled out his wallet. "In fact, I happen to have an extra ticket to a carol service at King's College, compliments of the parents of a patient, if you're interested." Producing a ticket, he held it out to her.

"A carol service? As in Christmas carols?" A tense note entered her voice, but she wasn't sure how to get rid of it.

"You've never heard of Carols from King's?"

"Yes, but I thought that was pre-recorded earlier in the month."

He nodded. "The actual program is, but the college also holds a carol service on Christmas Eve at three o'clock."

She wrinkled her nose. "I'm not much of a Christmas person, for the reasons I explained earlier. I tolerate the season, but would rather not attend anything dedicated to it."

"It's a church service. Santa Claus doesn't even make an appearance." He took her palm and placed the ticket in it. "It's extra. I have my own ticket. So keep it in case you change your mind."

Her fingers closed around it, trying to ignore the

warmth from his body that permeated the piece of card. "You won't be offended if I decide not to go? Maybe someone else can use the ticket."

"No, I normally go by myself. The extra ticket has gone to waste for the last four years."

Because he'd taken his wife before that? That made her heart ache, and she couldn't bring herself to refuse to keep it. How many of those extra tickets had he tossed in the garbage?

"Thank you." She took out her notebook and slid the ticket inside it before replacing it in her pocket.

Just then the elevator doors opened and Marco Ricci emerged. He started to turn left then stopped and glanced their way. He gave a half-wave. "I was just getting ready to head to your office," he called to Theo.

"Is the surgery docket full again?"

"What?" Then, as if he realized what Theo was asking, he headed over toward them, reaching out to shake his hand. "No, today we have it all under control."

He glanced at Madison. "By the way, I heard you lent a hand in the surgical suite the other day. Thank you."

"I did more observing than anything, but you're welcome."

He smiled again. "Actually, it's good that you're both here. Alice and I are planning a private little soirée on Saturday evening." He cleared his throat. "Actually, we're getting married. We're going for a big celebration in Italy later, but neither one of us wants to wait. And…we need two witnesses. We would be honored if you would do that for us, if you can. You've come to mean a lot to Alice in the time you've been here, Madison, so she really wants you to be there. She was going to come and ask you directly, but she's been swamped with work and with plans for the baby."

Alice was pregnant and positively glowing with health and happiness.

Looking at Theo, she suddenly didn't care if he agreed to do it or not. If anyone deserved to be happy, it was Alice and Marco. "I'd love to. What time?"

"Six in the evening. Will that do?"

"Yes. Absolutely."

Marco stuffed his hands in his pockets. "And you, Theo. Are you game?"

"I would be honored. Just let me know where."

"It'll be at Hotel Cambridge du Monde."

Theo gave a quiet whistle. "Flying high nowadays, are we?"

"In more ways than one." He clapped Theo on the shoulder. "I can hardly believe my good fortune. Alice and our baby. What more could a man want?"

"What more indeed." There was a wistfulness to Theo's voice that made sharp tears prick behind Madison's eyelids. Was he thinking about his late wife and all he'd lost?

"It's going to be a very small ceremony, but Alice wants her colors to be green or red, since she'll have red roses and green ivy in her bouquet. So, if you can scrounge up one of those two colors, that would be great. If not, just come as you are."

Madison racked her brain, but she hadn't brought a dress at all, much less a green or red one. Which meant she'd have to go out and buy something in town. Instead of spending a whole day with Theo, and feeling like she needed to go to that carol service with him, maybe they could just roll the wedding and a quick shopping trip into one joint venture. Hopefully that was one of his half-days off.

It would help keep her mind focused on a task rather than the man she was with. The timing was perfect. And Theo would know the town much better than she did. "Is it formal?"

"Not black-tie formal, but we're doing dresses and suits."

So not long dresses but something short. And a fascinator? Did they wear those to less formal events? She would wait and ask Alice the next time she saw her. Or Naomi. Wow, she just realized that people were falling in love and getting married all around her. She was on the outside, looking in.

Just like always.

The way she liked it.

"I'm really happy for you both," she said. She hadn't gotten up from her seat like Theo had because her legs were currently shaky and she felt a little out of sorts after everything that had happened.

"Thanks, we're quite over the moon ourselves." Marco glanced at the elevator, which had long since traveled to some other floor. "Well, I've got a surgery to scrub for. I just wanted to come up and ask you in person rather than ring you. Alice will be thrilled you've both agreed to come. If you have any questions, call her. She's the boss."

They said their goodbyes and then Marco was gone, off to his next stop in a full and happy life.

"I have nothing to wear to a wedding. Any chance we can skip Thursday and shop for something before the ceremony? I can just change at the hotel before that. Unless you can't get the time off."

"It won't be a problem. I'll get a tie to match your dress while we're at it. It wouldn't do to have Alice be cross with me. Because that would make Marco cross and probably everyone else at the venue."

So much for them each going their separate ways in town. It seemed that they were stuck shopping together. But since they had a destination afterwards, their day would be pretty much programmed down to the last second. Which left no time for anything else to happen.

Like kissing.

Or worse.

Because when they'd been kissing, she'd definitely wanted it to lead to something worse. Thank God they'd come to their senses before Marco had come up here. Because that would have been a disaster in the making.

And with Ivy's life hanging in the balance, that was something neither she nor Theo could afford.

Thursday evening, Theo had gathered his and Hope's medical records and spread them out on his desk for Maddy to see. She pored over them page by page, her green eyes slowly perusing charts and tests, down to the smallest details such as blood types. "Your mom had diabetes. No sign of anything in you, though."

"No. She had type one. I don't."

And diabetes certainly wouldn't be behind whatever was happening with Ivy. It was a lost cause. She'd already been through Hope's records and found nothing. No hint of a genetic anomaly, although it still couldn't be ruled out. Theo could have told her that, but he understood why Maddy wanted to see it for herself. No muscle-wasting diseases in either of their family histories that they knew of. And definitely no Huntington's disease.

Having Hope's records on his desk hurt, but not in the sharp, unfathomable way it once had. It was more of a wistful longing for his daughter to have known her mother. He'd loved Hope, there was no doubt about it. But she was gone. It had taken him a long time to accept the fact that she wasn't going to walk into the room one day and wrap her arms around his neck the way she once had.

Was he okay with that?

He'd accepted it, if that counted. He would always carry a part of her with him. Ivy was the greatest gift she could have given him. And he would always be grateful for what they'd had. His biggest regret was not having been a better husband to her. He had the same regret with his daughter, although he had learned his lesson and made a conscious effort to spend more time with Ivy. Not as much as he'd like, but her illness had been a wake-up call to focus on the truly important things in life.

With fewer distractions.

Like the beautiful distraction sitting on the other side of the desk?

Yes, he had been distracted ever since she'd set foot in his hospital. That seemed to be growing worse by the day. He was hoping that going shopping together would fix the shock of awareness that happened every time he ran across her in unexpected places. Like sleeping in his daughter's room.

Which reminded him. "Are you spending the night in Ivy's room?

She blinked, her teeth coming down on her lip. "Not

every night, no. Sometimes if I'm working on a case late at night, I stop in to check on her, and I'm too tired to go home. I end up falling asleep in the chair next to her bed."

He knew. He'd come into Ivy's room and caught her curled in a ball in that chair beside his daughter's bed, her hair flowing down the dark fabric. As hard as he'd tried not to stand there and watch the pair of them, he'd been held in the grip of some strange emotion. It was like seeing Hope and Ivy together again. Only Madison didn't look like his wife. She wasn't Ivy's mother.

And right now she sounded a little defensive. He hadn't meant it as an accusation. Time to put her mind at ease, even if he couldn't do the same for his own.

"I wasn't criticizing. I've just been sleeping on the pull-out couch in the next room and have tried not to wake either of you. That chair can't be comfortable. I was just going to offer the couch in my office on the nights you work late."

"I had no idea you were going in and sleeping there—I'm sorry for intruding."

"You weren't. I'm normally out of there early in the morning. But I didn't want you to think she was alone at night, if that was part of the reason you were staying there."

"I know. And she has nurses check in on her regularly. It's just quieter there than in the staff lounge, and the chairs in the rooms aren't that uncomfortable."

"For sleeping? Yes, they are. Just stretch out on the couch in my office. It is quiet, and I promise I won't disturb you." He grinned. "You can hang a sign on the door if you want."

"Thank you. I may take you up on it. There are days I could fall asleep anywhere."

"Please do. Like I said, since we moved Ivy into the room, I've been sleeping on the couch in there, so the office is unoccupied at night."

And seeing her dozing in that chair, looking so soft and vulnerable, also did a number on him. Maybe the subtle hint would move her out of reach. Or at least out of his sight. Several times he'd been tempted to offer the guest couch in the adjoining room. But Ivy was his daughter, and his place was there with her, not in his office.

"Thank you again. That sounds like a great idea." She turned her head to the right. "And maybe I can get rid of this crick in my neck."

A quick stab of guilt went through him, even though he knew she hadn't meant it that way.

"I'm sorry about that."

"Don't be. It was my choice to sleep there." She straightened a row of papers on his desk. "I, um, didn't realize you'd been coming in at night. The couch is never unfolded in the morning. I hope I wasn't snoring or anything when you walked by."

"I try to fold everything back up before I leave. As for snoring, you hardly make a peep. Just a tiny snuffle every once in a while."

Which he found adorable and charming.

"A snuffle? Ugh. Don't tell me that." She paused. "You must not sleep for eight hours at a shot, or I would have seen you at some point."

"No, I rarely do. My body doesn't need more than six hours at any given time."

Plus the fact that he hadn't wanted to come face to

face with Madison in the morning with sleepy eyes and mussed hair. So he set his watch for a time he knew she'd be still asleep. Another reason to offer her the couch in his office. Those restless nights were beginning to tell on him.

As if on cue, she yawned. He glanced at his watch and saw it was almost ten o'clock. "Why don't we call it a night? We can leave everything here, if you still need to look at them some more.

"I think I've seen everything I need to see." She hesitated again and then started gathering pages together into stacks. "Are you sleeping in Ivy's room tonight?"

"I am. I was just waiting to finish up here. So why don't you take my couch, like we talked about?" He helped her finish straightening and showed her into the adjoining sitting room, which had the same cozy furniture as the rest of the hospital. "There are sheets and blankets and a pillow in the closet. Are you on call in the morning?"

"Yes. At six."

Which made him feel bad about keeping her up so late, even though this had been her idea. "It's settled, then."

"Are you sure?"

"Absolutely." It was the best solution for everyone. He could sleep in peace knowing she was comfortable. And he wouldn't be kept awake thinking about her being in the next room, with that quiet snuffling to remind him of that fact every couple of minutes. Although he would miss knowing she was close by. More than he cared to admit.

"Okay, then, I appreciate it."

"You can just close the door to the suite and have

complete privacy. There's a bathroom with a shower in there as well." Theo stacked the two medical folders on the corner of his desk. "I'll return these tomorrow."

"Sounds good." She suppressed yet another yawn, and he decided that was his cue to leave. "You can text or call me if you need anything or if you have a question."

With that he gathered his keys and wallet and headed for the door. "See you sometime tomorrow."

"Thank you again."

She waited until he had shut the door before stretching her aching muscles. Leaning over that desk, even from a seated position, had caused her shoulders and neck to cramp. But, more than that, she was frustrated that she hadn't found the answers she'd been looking for. No hint or clue as to what could be behind Ivy's condition. Swiveling her torso from side to side in an effort to loosen things up, she prowled around Theo's office, peering curiously at various medical degrees and awards he'd earned over the years—things she hadn't noticed since she hadn't been in his office very many times.

Moving to get a closer look at a commendation letter on the wall about Hope Hospital, a frame on his desk caught her attention. When she'd been studying their medical charts the frame's back had been to her, so she hadn't known what was in it. She'd assumed it was a snapshot of Ivy. It wasn't. Theo and a woman with a baby were in it. Theo was younger than the man she knew now, and there was no evidence of the frown lines he wore today. She picked up the picture to study it. The woman's peaches-and-cream complexion glowed with happiness as she cradled a baby. It had to be Ivy and her mother. The woman was beautiful, her long blonde hair shimmering with life and health.

She glanced at the wall again, something she'd seen earlier kicking to the forefront of her mind. There. Frame in hand, she moved past the far side of his desk toward the corner of the room. Hope Elizabeth Mueller was listed as having earned her Bachelor of Medicine and Bachelor of Surgery degrees—the equivalent of medical doctor degrees in the States. That had to be Ivy's mom. So she'd graduated from medical school before she and Theo married. And he'd named the hospital after her. She held the picture up and looked at it and the medical certificate together, trying to picture what Theo's and her life must have been like together.

Happy. That's what it had been.

How could anyone get over the once-in-a-lifetime love they must have shared?

A sudden sound behind her caused her fingers to open. The picture crashed to the floor with a sickening sound of broken glass.

She whirled around, already knowing she'd been caught red-handed, her snooping ending in catastrophe.

Theo stood in the doorway, his head cocked to the side as his gaze went to the desk and then to her. Then he frowned.

"Oh, God, Theo. I am so sorry. I saw the picture and was just looking at it and—"

"It's okay, Maddy. It was bound to break at some point."

Madison swallowed. What was bound to break? The frame? Or his heart?

"I had no business looking through your things." She squatted down to hurriedly gather broken pieces of glass, shuddering when she saw a white line down the photo where a shard had slid along the smooth surface. A hard knot formed in her stomach. What had she been thinking?

That she wouldn't have minded being the woman in the idyllic photo standing next to Theo, their baby cradled between them?

No, she hadn't been thinking that at all.

Theo moved to the other side of the desk to help her. "Don't worry about it." He glanced at the picture and carefully picked up some of the larger bits of glass.

She held out the photo. "Do you still have the file, so I can replace this?"

"I do somewhere, but I'll take care of it." He dumped a pile of glass on top of his desk and then turned the frame around to get the back off it.

He slid the picture free and shook it to remove any debris. There was writing on the other side of it. "To my love. A reminder to always come home to us at the end of the day."

She gulped, her vision blurring. It took several blinks to clear it. When she did, she realized Theo had spotted the words as well, a muscle in his jaw working as he stared at them. Then he turned it over and placed it flat on his desk. "I came in to get my shaving kit. Sorry. I thought you'd already gone to bed."

Obviously, she'd been rummaging through his things instead. No, she hadn't. The picture had simply caught her eye. He wouldn't have offered to let her use his office if he was embarrassed or ashamed of anything in here. Or if he didn't want her to see this picture.

But he certainly hadn't expected her to smash it to smithereens.

"That picture has been in the frame ever since she gave it to me. I never saw what was on the back of it."

He'd never looked on the other side of it?

Don't cry, Madison.

"I am so sorry."

"Don't be." He climbed to his feet and held out his hand. "I'll get the rest of it tomorrow."

She let him help her up and looked down at the photo. "She loved you very much."

"Yes." He didn't say anything for a long minute. "She died a week after this picture was taken. Just before Christmas. It was still wrapped and under the tree."

An image of a devastated Theo sitting under that tree and opening those presents by himself sent a stab of pain that was as sharp as any piece of glass twisting through her. "What happened?"

"Drunk driver. I was working. Just like I always was." He walked around to the front of his desk, leaving her to follow him. "We'd planned to share this office once the hospital was up and running. She never got a chance to do that, though. She gave up everything to sit at home and wait for me."

Madison frowned. "I'm sure she didn't think of it like that. She looks very happy in that picture."

He picked it up and studied it. "Does she? I can't tell anymore. I can't even really picture her without the use of a photograph. I keep them up for Ivy's sake."

But not for his own? Did it hurt to see her face staring at him day after day? He'd changed—his face maturing into hard, craggy lines of determination. Did he wonder what she would look like five years later? Or was she forever immortalized as young and beautiful? And hopeful?

Ivy talked about her father being sad. And Madison could see why.

"Let me replace the frame."

"I'll get one tomorrow. It's not a problem."

Maybe not for him. But it was for her. Her stupidity had evidently unleashed a dam of pain he'd had walled up inside him. He'd never even seen that inscription before? What a tragic situation. And now the daughter in that picture was sick, and possibly fighting for her life. And just like with the death of his wife, Theo probably felt helpless to change anything.

So that meant it was up to her. She *had* to find a reason for Ivy's weakness so they could take measures to reverse it, or at least stop its progression. And she would. If she had to work twenty-four hours a day and scour every medical journal known to man, she was going to figure this out. All that channeled stubbornness? This was what she'd been born to do.

And do it she would.

She went over and put her hand on Theo's arm and looked up into his eyes. "I'm going to find that answer for you, Theo, whether it's tomorrow or the next day. I'm going to do it. And it's going to be soon."

CHAPTER SIX

MADISON STARED INTO the microscope and drew in a deep breath. Bacterial meningitis. It had taken all of five minutes to request the test be run and have a read-out confirm her suspicions. She pushed back from the desk and headed out to the ICU department, where the child's worried mom was waiting for her to put in an appearance. Hopefully they'd caught it early enough for the boy to make a complete recovery.

She saw Alice in the hallway. She was in street clothes, so she obviously wasn't on duty today. Not that she'd expect her to be.

"What are you doing here? I thought you'd be getting ready for the wedding?"

"I'm on my way out now. I had a surgery to do."

Leave it to the dedicated surgeon to work until the very last second.

Like Theo used to do before Hope had died?

Ugh! She needed to stop thinking about that picture. But it had haunted her day and night. Two days later, it was still frameless. She'd been so busy working that she hadn't had time to buy a replacement frame. And knowing the picture was still lying on his desk, like an accusation, had kept her from using that couch a second time. Would Hope have considered it a betrayal that Theo had let her in to use his private office? That he'd kissed her?

Great. She was going to drive herself crazy at this rate.

Alice glanced at her face, maybe seeing something there she didn't like. "You and Theo are still planning to come this evening, aren't you?"

"Yes, of course. I have to go shopping for a dress in a little while but, yes."

"Okay, great. We'll see you there around six, then. Talk to you later."

They said their goodbyes and Madison continued on her way, entering her patient's room a few minutes later. Kyle Saunders was hooked up to a ventilator and the sight and sounds of the machines up by his head monitoring blood pressure and respiration had to be a heartbreaking sight for any parent.

"Any news at all?" Shirley Saunders, a single mom of two young boys, got up from her chair, her bloodshot eyes the only spot of color in an otherwise pale face.

"Yes. He has meningitis. We're going to start an IV antibiotic and some medicines that will hopefully keep the swelling in his brain to a minimum."

"Will he get better?"

She glanced at Kyle, whose still form was eerily silent. "Now that we have a definitive diagnosis, we're hopeful. We'll know soon after we start the antibiotics. Do we have your permission to treat him?"

"Of course. I'll sign anything. Just help my son."

Theo had said something very similar to her when she'd first arrived at the hospital. *Just help my daughter.*

"We'll do our best. We have a neurologist who is going to assess him as well and see where we stand."

Shirley clasped her hands in front of her. "Will he be like this forever?"

She assumed she meant in a coma.

"No." She could say that with all certainty, because unless something unexpected happened, Kyle would either get better or he would die. She just didn't want to say that to his worried mom, unless it looked like it would come to that. "A nurse will be here in a few minutes to start the IV medication. And I'll be back to check on him before I leave today." She scribbled her cellphone number on a sheet of paper and gave it to her.

"I want you to call me if you have any questions once he begins treatment. The nurses are here to help as well. So don't be afraid to ask."

"I won't." A hand on her wrist stopped her for a second. "I can't thank you enough. I was warned it could be a while before they worked out what was wrong. It's only been a few hours."

"It's never as quick as we'd like it to be."

It certainly hadn't been in Ivy's case, despite the long hours she'd devoted to finding a cause. But she had a couple of new hunches she wanted to try out before she left to go shopping with Theo, whom she'd barely seen since she'd broken that frame.

She'd gotten up early and vacated the room that morning, hoping to avoid running into him. But first she'd finished cleaning up the glass, using a small hand vacuum she'd found in the same closet as the sheets and blankets. Then she'd folded all her linens and put them back where she'd found them. And his pillow...

She cringed, remembering how the fabric had trapped

his scent from whenever he'd last used it, his musky aftershave melding with the essence of what made Theo unique. It had haunted her the entire night. Unable to resist, she'd hugged it close one last time, inhaling deeply before stuffing the thing into the closet and slamming the door shut.

Finally, she'd used her phone to snap a picture of the frame itself, hoping to run across something similar in their shopping travels this afternoon.

She'd been fairly successful at steering clear of Theo since then. But she couldn't avoid him forever. They had arranged to go shopping at three. She could only hope that she'd find a dress quickly and that she survived the wedding ceremony.

All she could do was take things one hour at a time and hope for the best.

Theo waited in his office for Maddy to finish her last case of the day. Picking up the picture, he turned it over again, just as he had for the last couple of days.

A reminder to always come home to us.

Which he hadn't always done. She'd been home alone many nights before Ivy had been born.

How had he not known that inscription was there? Because Hope had died before he'd opened the present. Otherwise she would have told him to look. He never had. Had never seen a reason to take it out of the safe place that had housed it for the last four and a half years.

Like the place that had housed his heart? The heart that hadn't ventured from that spot since the day Hope had died?

He flipped the photo back to the front and dragged a stack of folders and dropped them on top of it.

A knock sounded at the door, relieving him of his thoughts. He got up to answer it and found Maddy, cheeks pink, a calf-length black coat belted around her waist, a matching handbag over one shoulder. She had a red scarf knotted around her neck and on her head was a black knit hat.

She was dressed for Cambridge in winter. And that fact made him smile as he stepped aside to let her in. Except her glance went immediately to his desk, probably looking for the same picture he'd been staring at. Guilt gnawed at him all over again.

"I'm ready if you are," she said.

"Yes. More than ready. Just let me get my coat."

"Is Ivy okay?"

"She's fine for now. Judy has promised to look in on her in case we're late."

Something about the way the words came out made him stiffen. They weren't some normal couple going out on the town. And they never would be. But if he tried to correct himself it would only make things worse, so he let it stand and headed toward the exit.

Within minutes they were walking along the cobblestones of Cambridge's bustling shopping district, doing their best to dodge the scores of bicycles that whizzed by.

"It always seems strange that there are so few cars."

"It's a university city. Can you imagine trying to navigate through here by car with all the bikes and pedestrians?" He grabbed her hand and hauled her close to avoid another cyclist. She laughed, pulling the strap of her bag higher on her shoulder.

Tiny shops dotted either sides of the streets, which were still full of shoppers trying to get their Christmas gifts. Although the Christmas lights hadn't yet been turned on, they were everywhere, strung from one side of the street to the other, the center of each set sporting a large star. And there were Christmas trees everywhere. In the evenings, after the shops were closed, it was a beautiful sight and one that sent a reminder punch straight to his gut. Here he was out here thinking about what the town looked like at night, while Ivy was stuck in a hospital bed.

"It's gorgeous." Maddy's face was tilted up toward the peaked roofs and the varying facades along the route.

"The town? Or the decorations?" He looped her hand through the crook of his arm, the act seeming far too natural, the pressure of her fingers curling around him sending a warmth through his chest. He was just trying to keep from losing her.

He swallowed. Losing her?

She glanced at him, pushing her hat more firmly onto her head before shoving her free hand into the pocket of her coat. "Both. I can appreciate the beauty of the season, even if Christmas itself leaves me cold. Pun unintended."

"Point taken. So where to first?"

"I'm looking for a dress and probably shoes. I think my handbag will suffice. And you?"

"A tie, and since I didn't think to bring my suit to the hospital with me I probably need to buy one."

She paused and glanced down the street. "So where is the best place to find those?"

"Probably one of these shops. If you're up for walking a bit, we can just window shop until something grabs your attention. It won't take more than about half an hour to see all of it."

"Ha! I'm not the biggest shopper in the world, but I suspect it'll take me a little longer than that."

He had to smile at the way her eyes took everything in. The half-timbered buildings, their creamy white masonry filling in the areas between dark wooden beams. The durable streets that had held up for generations and which now gleamed in the sunlight. The old-world charm of life and a way of living that had been honed over the centuries.

Things that Theo took for granted but were probably new to someone used to a different way of life. Trying to see it through her eyes, a sense of pride enveloped him. He loved this city, he always had, which was why he'd chosen to stay here and build a thriving hospital. It was also a university city, teeming with young people who brought a life and intensity that wasn't found everywhere.

"Can I go in here?"

Theo glanced at the shop next to them and frowned. "I don't think you'll find a dress in there. Just some odds and ends."

"It's okay. I'll just be a minute."

She didn't wait for an answer, just disappeared inside. He wasn't sure whether he should go in after her or just wait for her to re-emerge. He had no idea what she could possibly want here. It was kind of an artsy shop with handcrafted home items. Maybe she wanted a gift for a friend. Within ten minutes she came out with a small package.

"Did you find what you wanted?"

"I did. Thanks for waiting." She didn't enlighten him as to what she'd purchased. Or for whom. She didn't have family, according to what she'd told him. But surely she had friends back in the States.

They walked a bit further and Theo spied a shop that had semi-formal wear for both men and women. "This looks like a likely place."

"Great."

They went in, shedding their winter coats and hanging them on hooks just inside the door. "It looks like dresses are down here, but I don't see any menswear."

"It's upstairs. How much time do you need?"

"Not long."

When he gave her a skeptical look, she smiled. "That looks like a challenge to me. I bet I can find something in less than a half-hour. How about if the last person back has to…?" Her lips puckered in a way that caught his attention and held it. The pucker turned into teeth catching one corner of her bottom lip and holding it for a second or two.

Hell, he could think of a great punishment for being last, but it probably wasn't one that would go over very well with her. Or with him, for that matter.

"The last person back has to…to choose the gift for the bride and groom," she finally said.

"Gift?" Something inside sagged in disappointment. Okay, had he really expected her to come up with something personal? No. But a part of him had been making up possible scenarios, as unlikely as it was that any of those would ever come to pass.

"Do you not buy wedding gifts here?" Her face tilted to look at him, and it might have been his imagination, but he thought he caught the slightest hint of laughter in her tone. Had she somehow read his thoughts and found them hilarious?

No, there was no way she could know. "Are you sure you didn't already buy a wedding gift back at that last shop?"

The laughter faded in an instant. "I'm positive."

So whatever she'd bought couldn't be mistaken for a gift for a bride and groom.

He shook off his thoughts. "Okay. Let's see who finishes first."

"You're on."

They took off in opposite directions, Theo going for the stairs. And although he didn't think they were really racing, he'd never been much of a shopper. He was pretty content with going in and finding what he needed and getting back out. But he also wasn't thrilled about having to choose a gift for Marco and Alice, since he had no idea what they might like or need. So he took his time looking through the racks of suits before finding a black one that he liked.

Then he remembered he'd said he would try to match his tie to Maddy's dress, which now sounded like an idiotic idea. It wasn't like she was his prom date or anything. But Marco had made a point of telling him what the wedding colors were, so it stood to reason that photographs would be taken. They would at least want everyone coordinated a little bit. A black suit, though, he couldn't go wrong there. He found his size and tried it on and deemed it suitable. Then he got dress shoes, a white shirt, and a few other items, paying for them and waiting while they were loaded into a shopping bag.

Then he headed downstairs where he spied Maddy, looking through the racks of dresses.

"Did you already find a suit?"

"I did. Are you having any luck?"

She looked up, brows raised as if in surprise. "I've been done for fifteen minutes."

"You're kidding."

"Nope." She reached down to lift a matching bag and laughed. Probably at the shell-shocked expression on his face. "I tend to be a bit competitive," she said.

"I guess so. I still need to get a tie. What color dress?"

"Green. If we go up and look at them, I can help pick one out."

Ten minutes later, she'd chosen a tie in a deep spruce color with a subtle patterning that only showed up when the light hit it a certain way. "Marco said she was using ivy in her bouquet, so that's what I went with."

"Christmas colors, since she's also using red roses."

"That's what I thought as well." She smiled. "So what are you going to get them as a present?"

"Cash?"

"What?" There was enough outrage in her voice that it was his turn to laugh.

"I'm kidding. But, seriously, I have no idea."

"Hmm. Marco said they're flying off to Italy right after they get married, so maybe something to do with their trip?"

"Like what?"

"I don't know. I thought maybe we could walk a little more and see if something strikes our fancy."

He glanced at Maddy. "How long do you need to dress, so we can plan when to arrive at the hotel?"

"Judging from our shopping times, I'm going to guess not as much time as you need."

"Do you compete at everything?" An image flashed through his head, making him shift. He was not going there.

"I like to win."

"That's obvious."

They bundled back up in their coats.

"I think I have an idea about a present that might work." She ducked out onto the street and was almost lost from sight. The shoppers had increased in number and it took a little bit of maneuvering to reach her. He reached for one of her mittened hands, smiling when she curled her fingers around his. "I thought I was going to be swept downriver for a second. This is fun. You were right. I did need to get away from the hospital for a while."

"I think we both did."

Maddy stayed close to his side as they wandered down the road and turned into another alley. "I can't seem to find what I want."

When she adjusted her purchases for the third time, he took the bag from her and added it to his own. "What were you thinking of?"

"A set of bright matching luggage tags. It was something I wished I'd had when I came, since it's hard to pick out your luggage sometimes on the carousels."

"I like it."

"I hope they do too. I'm just not sure where to…"

He tugged her hand and started back the way they had come. "Actually, the shop you went in at first has all kinds of unique items. I think they carry handmade luggage as well. And it's on the way back to the hotel."

"Perfect."

Arriving back at the shop a few minutes later, they

found a set of eight luggage tags in the shape of shoes. High heels. Trainers. Men's sandals. All in light tan. "The color might not stand out, but the shapes will. Silly and classy all in one package."

"I think you found a winner." And Theo thought he had too. Her no-nonsense determination and quick way of making decisions was just what they'd needed on Ivy's case. Something inside him relaxed just a bit, a feeling of hope growing instead. A hope he hadn't allowed to surface in a long time.

They had the package gift-wrapped and found a gift card that they each signed. Only afterwards did he wonder if they should have purchased separate presents, but time was growing short and he didn't want to have to explain to Maddy why it might look funny. Especially since she obviously hadn't thought so.

Taking her hand again, they headed in the direction of the hotel, a massive cream-colored building with arched entryways and a covered portico.

"Wow, this is it?"

"Yes." He had eaten here a time or two for business meetings and the inside of the hotel was just as impressive as the exterior. "They may have wanted a small wedding, but they went all out on the venue."

"I don't blame them. It's not every day you marry the love of your life." There was a wistfulness to her voice that made him pause for a second, her hand still in his.

Theo had married the love of his life once, but he wondered if that was all there was. Was one chance at love all you got? Or was there the possibility that love could reset itself with someone new?

Not something he wanted to be thinking of right now. Especially after the way he had enjoyed Maddy's company this afternoon. The way he liked the feel of her hand in his, the way her laughter trickled over him like a warm breeze sweeping through icy corridors.

They made their way up the steps with an hour to spare. They checked in at the reception desk and found a note from Marco telling them which floor they were on. Maddy was supposed to go straight to Alice's room to help her dress, while Theo was going to hole up with Marco. Knowing his friend, he would be champing at the bit to get the ceremony underway. They were a great pair, and Theo was glad they'd found happiness together. Although he'd heard rumors of the pair butting heads in the beginning, they had obviously worked out their differences.

"You go on ahead," he told Maddy, forcing himself to finally release her hand and handing her the shopping bag containing her purchases. "I want to call the hospital and check on Ivy before I go up."

"Okay, let me know if there's a problem."

He assured her he would, even though in his heart of hearts he knew there was already a problem. A big one. And it had nothing to do with Ivy and everything to do with him. And a certain diagnostician who was rapidly capturing his daughter's heart. And, worse, she was starting to worm her way into his as well.

Oh, Lord, she wasn't sure she could do this. After helping Alice get into her dress, which was a gorgeous cream sheath dress with tiny matching flowers embroidered into the bodice and hemline, she donned her own dress, which was a lot more form-fitting than she remembered in the dressing room.

They stood there, putting the finishing touches to their make-up.

Alice put her hands on her cheeks and drew in a deep breath. "I can't believe this is happening."

Wrapping an arm around the other woman's shoulders, Madison smiled. Maybe she wasn't the only one feeling jittery, although Alice had a lot more reason than she did to be nervous. "You look gorgeous. And happy."

"I am. Marco wants to have a big ceremony with his family once we get to Italy, which is why we're opting for a small civil service here at the hotel. It doesn't matter to me where it's held, though, as long as we do it before this little one busts free." Her hand slid over her belly, which showed evidence of the life within her.

"I don't think that's going to be a problem at this point." She dropped her tube of mascara onto the countertop. "You look so beautiful, Alice."

"He makes me feel beautiful." She smoothed her dress over her hips. "I think I'm as ready as I'll ever be."

Madison scooped up the bride's bouquet and handed it to her, picking up the smaller matching one for herself. "Let's go find your groom."

"Yes, and his hunky cohort."

"Should you really be noticing the hunk factor in other men?" Madison laughed.

"Are you telling me you haven't noticed?"

"Well, I...I—"

"Joking. I'm joking, silly." Alice gave her a quick squeeze.

All of a sudden Madison was a little reluctant to see Theo. The green dress she'd bought gathered in flattering folds that fell from the waist, but it fit her upper body like a glove, thanks to the clever touch of Lycra in the fabric blend. But the saleswoman assured her it was perfect for her body type. Now she was thinking that was probably some sort of sales pitch that she would have given to anyone. Madison should have at least bought a shawl or something to wrap around herself, but as they weren't leaving the hotel—at least she didn't think they were—she'd figured she would be fine. And her dress had long sleeves, even though it was off the shoulder.

They were supposed to meet the men in the room the hotel had set up for civil ceremonies. As they entered the lobby, a couple of men turned to look as they walked by. Frowning, Madison wrapped her arms around her waist, a little irritated with herself for being as self-conscious as she was. She was normally able to block out anything and walk with her head held high, no matter how squirmy she might feel inside.

"There." Alice practically flew down the short set of stairs that led to the lower level of the lobby, forcing Madison to hurry to keep up. Too late, she spotted Marco and Theo waiting at the bottom, both in black suits. Theo's eyes were glued to her as she slowed her steps, making her even more unsure of her choice in dresses. Marco swept his soon-to-be bride up and twirled her around, while Theo kept his hands behind his back. But his face told another story, a wave of color moving up his neck, a pulse beginning to throb in his right temple.

When she reached the ground level, he moved forward, leaning over to whisper, "*That* is the dress you got?"

Oh, God, did he think it was unprofessional of her to

wear something like this? They *were* off the clock, so why would he even care? "Is there something wrong?"

"Yes. But not with your dress. Or with you."

She had no idea what he meant, but he didn't sound upset. Just surprised, if she had to guess from his voice.

"Your suit looks nice."

And it did. His black jacket hugged his broad shoulders in a way that made her mouth water, and the crisp white shirt and tie looked like something he'd wear to a swanky restaurant to negotiate deals and conquer competitors. So did his proud bearing.

"Doesn't Madison look lovely?"

She blinked back to awareness, realizing that Marco and Alice had joined them, arms locked around each other's waists. Alice stared at Theo expectantly.

"Yes. She looks quite…er…nice."

Ha! He could have been speaking about his sister. Or an acquaintance, for that matter.

But wasn't that all they were? Acquaintances?

A thought that sent her stomach spinning to her feet.

"Do you have the little gift we got for them?" Madison asked to cover the awkwardness of the moment.

"Yes." Theo reached into the inner pocket of his suit jacket and produced a small gift-wrapped package, which he handed to Alice. "We hope this is something you can use."

Even though she'd used "we" a second ago, his use of it made her stomach pick itself up off the floor.

"Thank you for everything, especially coming down here on such short notice." Marco smiled. "You both clean up quite well."

Thanks to a little last-minute shopping.

The hotel lobby was just as gorgeous as the outside,

boasting a huge Christmas tree that rivaled the two at Hope Hospital. Greenery wound down the staircase and dripped from every arched opening. It was a magical atmosphere, even with the tourists that were snapping pictures everywhere.

"You both look stunning as well," Madison said. "How does it feel to be getting married?"

"Like a dream come true." Alice looked up at her groom with a smile. "I am so ready to do this. But first open their present, Marco."

The groom slid the ribbon off the little box and slipped his finger beneath the paper, popping the tape with ease. Alice moved in close to watch as he removed the top. Then he grinned and held up a high-heeled luggage tag. "This is going to look great on the handle of my briefcase."

"Ha-ha." Alice grabbed it from him. "This one is mine. It looks like you have plenty of others to choose from."

She lifted another shoe, a trainer this time. "How about this one?"

"That's more my style, although I'm sure the first one would be a great ice-breaker at parties. Thank you both. They are obviously going to get a lot of use in the very near future." He put the top back on, ignoring Alice's protest to look at the rest of them.

"Getting cold feet?" Marco teased her.

"After it took this long to get you all straightened out? I don't think so."

They made their way to the room set aside for the ceremony and, like the rest of the hotel, it was tastefully decorated with flowers and greenery, but this time there was less emphasis on Christmas, since not everyone celebrated that holiday. The official was already there be-hind a little desk, filling out some forms. He looked up.

"Baxter, Ricci?"

"Yes, that's us."

Standing, he said, "Are you ready to get started?"

They exchanged paperwork and the man glanced up at Theo and Madison. "You're the witnesses?" When Theo nodded, he said, "If you could sign the documents immediately after the ceremony I would appreciate it."

Surprisingly, what could have been a dry, cold recit-ing of vows was anything but. The official had a warm, reassuring voice and a way of moving them along from one thing to the other that was seamless. Madison stood next to Alice and took her bouquet when it was time to exchange the rings.

When she happened to glance up, Theo was watch-ing her, a slight frown on his face that could have meant anything. She lifted her brows in question, only to have him give her a slight smile and an almost imperceptible shake of his head.

She had no idea what that meant either.

And then Alice and Marco were officially married and all the papers signed. "Time to throw the bouquet."

Madison looked around in horror, but of course there was no one else. "That's not necessary."

"Nope, it will be bad luck not to. And I've had enough of that to last a lifetime. Time for a brand-new start."

Marco kissed her cheek. "Absolutely."

"Please?" Alice asked her. "It's all in good fun."

Good fun?

Almost before the words were out of her mouth,

something came sailing through the air. Madison's instincts kicked in and she grabbed at it.

Alice laughed. "See? No harm."

No harm?

Madison looked anywhere but at Theo. It was just a game, like Alice had said. No need to be embarrassed or act like she was taking this thing seriously.

She pressed the bouquet back into the bride's hands. "You'll want to have this preserved."

They hugged. "I can't believe how happy I am. Thank you for making this day even more special."

The air around them seemed to change, negative ions transformed by the power of love. "Do you guys mind if we slide away?" Marco glanced at Alice. "Our flight leaves the day after tomorrow and we have a ton of things to do."

Sure they did. Madison couldn't hold back her smile, squeezing Alice's hand one more time. "Of course we don't. Have a wonderful trip and we'll see you when you get back."

Marco shook Theo's hand. *"Grazie."*

"You're very welcome. Enjoy married life."

There was a wistfulness behind the words that made her heart twist. Thinking about Hope and the life they'd shared?

"I intend to cherish every moment with my *tesoro*." Marco smiled, then leaned in and said something in a low voice to Theo, pressing something into his hand. Something that made Theo frown.

What was that all about?

There was no time to ask since Alice was already saying her goodbyes. A few seconds later the couple walked away, sharing a kiss or two as they went.

Madison sighed. "That was beautiful. They make a great couple."

"Yes, they do." He came to stand beside her. "Would you like to take a walk? We were in such a hurry trying to get things together for the wedding, that I don't think you really got to enjoy the city. Besides, now that it's dark, the lights will be on. Do you want to change first?"

"Oh, I forgot, my things are still up in Alice's room!" She had no idea how she was going to get them, and she didn't want to burst in on anyone.

"No, they aren't. Marco is moving them over to the room he used when we were getting dressed. He said it was ours to use."

Her eyes widened and he must have realized how that sounded because he added gruffly, "To get dressed in, of course."

Embarrassment zipped up her abdomen at having him read her so well. "Of course."

"Are you okay with walking through town a bit more?"

She hesitated, not sure at all that that was the smartest thing to do, but knowing she didn't want tonight to end. It had been the best evening she'd had in Cambridge so far. So with gratitude in her heart for the brief respite from all the crazy hours at the hospital, she said, "I'd like that very much."

CHAPTER SEVEN

HE WASN'T SURE what had prompted him to ask Maddy to take a walk. But he wasn't sorry he had. When she'd glided down those stairs earlier, he had been floored by his reaction. It hadn't been the dress, although that was something right off the cover of some fashion magazine. With her long limbs and delicate features, she could easily be featured there as well.

Something about that simple wedding and Maddy's rapt face as she'd watched the bride make her vows had been...magical. A couple of times she'd caught him staring at her and had lifted a brow in a way that had cranked his engine and got his motor running. She knew. Or did she?

No matter how hard he'd tried to fix his attention straight ahead after that, his gaze had kept shifting back millimeter by millimeter until it had been on her again.

His motor was still running, and all he knew was that he wanted to show her off a little—a purely male reaction that was impossible to completely suppress. And right now he didn't want to even try.

He glanced at her feet. "Are you going to be okay walking in those over the uneven streets?"

"We're not going to be power walking, are we?"

"No. Strolling. And not terribly far. It just seemed like a festive night to walk under the lights. Besides, it's a shame to have spent all that time getting ready just to emerge from the hotel in our everyday clothes."

"Like Cinderella," she murmured.

"Not planning on running out on me at the stroke of midnight, are you?"

"Nope. No mad dash to a pumpkin carriage for this girl."

"You'll need a coat, though. I'll go up and get them."

By the time he got back, she was looking out of the hotel window. He dropped her black coat around her shoulders and handed her her hat and gloves.

"Thank you."

He'd discarded his suit jacket for his thicker wool coat, and couldn't resist taking her hand like he had earlier. To keep from losing her, he insisted to himself.

They walked along in silence, taking in the sights.

"I'd forgotten how chilly it was."

"Do you want to go back?"

"No. Let's walk for a few more minutes, please. It's a beautiful night."

Letting go of her hand and turning her toward him, he buttoned the top button of her coat and wrapped her scarf around her a little tighter. "Better?"

"Yes."

Something about bundling her up against the elements made a rush of warmth flow through his chest. He…cared.

About her. About whether or not she was cold.

Damn. This was getting out of hand. He needed to stop mooning over things that could never be.

That didn't stop him from sliding an arm behind her

back and keeping her close by his side, though. Something any friend would do.

Right, Theo. Keep telling yourself that. Maddy is not your friend.

That was the problem. He didn't know what she was. Didn't have an easy category to file her under.

She seemed to snuggle closer, the arm that had been holding the collar of her coat closed slipping around his waist. He liked the feel of her pressed tight against him. It felt...right.

And Theo had no idea how he felt about that, especially after all that had happened over the last couple of weeks.

It had to be the recent spate of romantic unions around the hospital with Ryan and Evie, Finn and Naomi and now Marco and Alice all finding someone to love.

Was he just lonely?

He hadn't felt the need to be with anyone for almost five years. Why now?

There was no answer for any of those questions.

"Are the university students all going home for the holidays? It's busier than I expected at this time of year."

"It's always busy. Most of the students have gone home, though, although some have flats and stay year-round. King's College, where the carol service will be held, isn't far from here."

Maddy hadn't mentioned the ticket since he'd given it to her. She'd acted like she wasn't interested in going because of her ambivalence over Christmas. But she seemed to be enjoying the lights in the town center. "Does it make you uncomfortable to be out looking at the lights? We can go somewhere else if you'd like."

"No, they're beautiful. I can separate the beauty from the more personal traditions. That's the part I'm not crazy about."

He walked a few more steps, wondering if it was any of his business. But he couldn't stop the question. "Because of your mum."

"Yes. It's easier now. But when I was growing up, I hated receiving Christmas presents because there was only one thing I wanted back then. To be reunited with my mom." Her shoulder moved against his side as she shrugged. "That never happened. And now as an adult I know why. She died."

"I can understand that. After Hope died, I did my best to keep things going and to make Christmas special for Ivy, but for me personally..."

The arm around him tightened. "I get it. Really I do." She sighed as they came to the far edge of the buildings. "But look at that sky up there. Those are the best lights of all. And they're up there all year. No need to put them up or take them down."

Looking up to where a bit of sky was visible, the night was unusually clear and cloud-free, and a few stars were indeed shining, like a small collection of twinkle lights. "There's a better view from Castle Hill if you want to walk there."

"I'm fine right where I am."

Theo felt warm, and happy. And he realized he was fine right where he was too.

Maybe she wasn't the only one who'd needed to get away. Ivy's illness had taken a toll on him, with one day running into the next. Tonight would stand out in his memory as one of the few bright spots during a time of chaos and uncertainty. Could this be the turning point? They would go back to the hospital rested and refreshed and find that breakthrough in her condition they'd been looking for?

Christmas was supposed to be a time of miracles. Maybe he would even find his.

God, he hoped so.

"Are you sure you're warm enough, Maddy?"

"Yes." There was a pause. "Not many people call me Maddy anymore. Not since my mom left."

He blinked. He'd been thinking of her by the shortened version of her name for a week now. He'd never stopped to wonder if it might bother her. "I'm sorry. Would you prefer me not use it?"

"No. I actually like it." She laughed. "As long as everyone else at the hospital doesn't suddenly start calling me that."

So he was the only one allowed to call her Maddy? His stomach did a flip, and he stopped and turned her toward him, his arm still around her. He looked into her face, noting her nose was tipped with red because of the chill. And she was gorgeous. More than gorgeous, because her beauty wasn't only skin deep. "Have I told you how lovely you look tonight?"

Her head tilted back and strands of her hair brushed over the top of his hand. He couldn't resist opening his fingers to let the silky locks sift between them.

"You look pretty good yourself. And thank you for tonight. You could have just let me muddle through the shops and find the hotel by myself. But it was a lot more fun doing it with you."

"Was it?" He smiled, his fingers moved higher, closing over her hair this time and tugging slightly.

"Mmm… Yes. I feel deliciously relaxed and mellow. Even if my feet are starting to grumble a bit."

His smile grew. "I would offer to lend you mine, but I don't think they would be any more comfortable. Shall we go back?"

"Do we have to?"

She linked her hands behind his back, sending his thoughts sliding a little further down a dark road that held wonders…and dangerous curves. Much like the ones that were currently pressed against him.

"We should, yes." Something in him urged him to say what he was thinking. None of them had forever. Hope's death had shown him that. Sometimes you just had to take those bits of joy where you could find them, *while* you could find them. That didn't mean he had to demand forever, or the kind of promises that Marco and Alice had shared.

"I guess you're right." She sounded so despondent that he smiled.

"That doesn't mean tonight has to end just yet." He leaned down and slid his cheek against hers, the chill in her skin making him yearn for warm covers and even warmer bodies.

"My apartment?"

"There's always the hotel. Marco gave us his room, remember? It's booked until morning."

She blinked, looking into his eyes. "And our things are still there, after all, so we do have to get them."

And then do what?

Go out to eat? Or stay *in* to eat.

"What are you thinking?" He needed things spelled out so he could prepare for disappointment if he'd misunderstood her intentions.

"That I don't want this night to end. Not yet." She pressed her face to his chest. "And, like you said, maybe it doesn't have to."

"Are you suggesting what I think you're suggesting?"

"That we utilize Marco's gift? Yes."

A sudden sense of rightness came over him, although he had no idea why that was. Maybe it was just relief at having the decision made. "Are you sure about this?"

"No, but in my line of work, sometimes you just have to go with your gut. And my gut is telling me to let loose and do something dangerous tonight. I can play it safe tomorrow."

"Being with me is dangerous?" Something shimmered just below the horizon, a need that he was going to have a hard time extinguishing, if things took a wrong turn.

She leaned up and bit his chin. "You are the epitome of dangerous."

"Well, lady, so are you. I vote Marco's room." He reached into his pocket and held up an entry card. "He gave me the key."

Somehow they made it back to the hotel, via a late-night chemist to buy protection, but the memory of actually walking there was a bit foggy. It was like they'd coasted along, peppered with small touches of the hand, a palm pressed against her back, a moment spent kissing beside a brightly lit Christmas tree. The journey was winding toward its final destination. And Theo was having a hard time believing this beautiful, kind, intelligent woman actually wanted to be with him.

He knew he wasn't the same person he used to be. Cynicism had become his calling card. Oh, he hid it from patients well enough, but those who knew him well? They'd seen the changes and were warier around him than they used to be.

There. The front doors of the hotel. Finally.

As long as they didn't run into the newlyweds, they were fine, not that they would. Alice and Marco weren't likely to come out of their room, and neither were he and Maddy.

No need to let Judy or the hospital know he'd be a little bit later than he'd planned. He wouldn't be spending the night at the hotel. Just…a few hours. He hoped.

Soon they were on their way to their fourth-floor room. The elevator had several people in it, but Theo couldn't resist slinging his arm around her shoulder. He wanted—no, he *needed* to touch her.

He glanced at the electronic door key in his hand as they got off on their floor. Room 423. To the left, according to the sign on the wall and his own memory. He took her hand and headed halfway down the corridor. The key unlocked the door with a slight snick, a green light displayed on the reader. Theo pushed through the solid barrier and re-entered a room that was on par with what he would expect of a hotel of this caliber.

"It's gorgeous. A little different from the one Alice was in."

Maddy's soft words were filled with wonder as she came out from behind him to survey the space. The huge bed sported a brown damask coverlet that was puffy in a way that could only mean it was filled with the finest down. The walls went along with the style of the city around them, dark bare timbers interspersed with white plaster walls, more beams crisscrossing the high ceilings.

"I know something that's even more gorgeous." He

waited for her to turn and look at him. "Are you glad you came?"

Her eyes met his, shining with something he was afraid to examine. Then she came over and took his face in her hands, her thumb brushing over his lower lip in a way that made him see stars that were even brighter than those in the night sky. "So very glad."

That did it for him. He leaned down and took her mouth, one arm going behind her back and dragging her against him. Soon their surroundings were put out of mind as his hands went to her shoulders, barely able to believe she was his to explore without fear. Without worrying that someone would come upon them and see them.

Without worrying about what tomorrow was going to bring.

Live dangerously, that was what she'd said.

It had been so long since he'd lived like that, or had dwelled in the land of here and now. And he was ready to. With her.

No fears of forever. Or, worse, the lack of them.

Maddy would be going home when her time in England was over. He could kiss her, lie naked with her. Lose himself in her.

Without losing *himself.*

At least that was what he hoped. What he needed to believe.

He didn't have to ease her toward the bed, she was already moving there on her own. Slowly stepping backward and coaxing him to come with her with tiny kisses that he couldn't quite deepen without following her. Not that he minded.

She half turned him and pushed, the pressure of the

bed at the backs of his knees causing them to buckle. But he sat, rather than allowing himself to fall flat on his back. And when he did so he reached and found the hem of her dress and eased it up, his palms gliding up the soft creamy skin at the back of her thighs. Leaning forward, he pressed his lips to her belly, knowing he was going to kiss her there once he'd rid her of her clothes. Then he was going to press his lips against every inch of that gorgeous body. "Come up here with me."

She blinked at him as if not sure what he was asking, so he used light pressure just beneath her bottom to tell her what he wanted.

Straddling his legs, she came onto the bed, her knees on either side of his thighs. He hugged her close, feeling the sweet pressure of her coming to rest against an area of his body that had been dying for this for what seemed like forever.

"Maddy. *Hell.*" He wrapped an arm around the curve of her behind and tugged her tight against him, her slight exhalation washing over his cheek.

He wanted it like this. Just like this. With her rising and falling above him and taking him into the clouds.

As if she knew exactly what he was thinking, she slid down him, still fully clothed, but she might as well have taken him inside her. This was it. The moment they'd been heading toward for two weeks.

Her eyes shut tight, lower lip pursed as she moved against him again. Taking his hands from their perch, he trailed them up her spine until he reached the top edge of her dress, which was just off her shoulders. Tucking his fingers beneath it, he coaxed the stretchy fabric down inch by inch until it slid over her breasts.

Breasts that were contained in a whisper-thin layer of lace. Peach. The color of her skin. A peekaboo effect that he couldn't resist.

Leaning her back slightly, he moved in and closed his mouth over the tight ridge visible at the center of the cup. The nipple was tight and exquisite, and he pulled on it, lapping his tongue over the fabric-covered mound.

Her hands went to his shoulders and she pushed herself closer, and a low whimper was followed by a rub of friction to the front of his trousers. He hadn't lost control while fully clothed since he was a teenager, but there was a real danger right now that he was going to fly over the edge.

He didn't want to do that without taking her with him. So he held her hips still while he continued to tug and kiss and lick, until he could stand it no longer.

"Take it off," he whispered, afraid to let go of her.

Her hands left his shoulders long enough to reach behind her back and unhook the strapless bra, letting it fall to the side of the bed. Then she was bare to him, except when he went to take her in his mouth, she leaned away from him.

"Your turn."

Denied of his prize, he frowned. "What do you mean?"

She climbed off the bed and said. "Unzip them."

He hesitated, noting the lift of her brows.

"Unzip. Them."

Then she did the unthinkable. She reached under her dress and did something. When her hands came back up, there was a lacy strip of cloth that matched the bra.

He cursed softly.

"That makes two things I've given you in exchange

for…" She leaned forward, her palms gliding along his shoulders, breasts tantalizingly close to his mouth. "Unzip your trousers."

One nipple trailed across the seam of his lips and he immediately closed over it, giving a long hard pull that he thought would alleviate some of the growing pressure from behind that zipper. It didn't. It just ratcheted things up until they were at boiling point. He was going to lose it, and it was either with her or without her.

He reached down and grabbed the tab on the fastener and slid it down, undoing the button afterwards. Then he reached in and freed his aching flesh. But not without biting down on her nipple.

She moaned and arched in, before climbing back on the bed, her dress tugged up.

Then they were flesh to flesh, and he was pretty sure this was where it would end. But it didn't. He cupped her face, moving her within kissing distance. And kiss her he did. The way he'd wanted to that first time. Tongue and teeth and snatched breaths, the building of an empire that was going to explode long before he was ready.

Expertly whipping a condom on, Theo lifted her slightly, but she was already anticipating, reaching for him and positioning herself. Then she engulfed him in heat. In sweet, sweet heaven. Taking him to a world where everything was tight and wet and filled with a pleasure beyond anything he could imagine.

It had never been like this before.

Not even with Hope.

A bright flash of guilt stabbed through him.

He gripped her hips and urged her to move, needing to squeeze out everything that didn't involve Maddy. And what she was doing to him.

God. She did it for him.

Her fingers pushed into his hair and gripped the strands as she continued to ride him, holding his face against her shoulder as her breathing roughened.

He wasn't going to last. And he didn't want to. But he also didn't want to go without her. Holding tight to her hips, he lay back until his shoulders touched the mattress, and then he watched. Watched her rise and fall. Watched his erection disappear inside her.

So close.

Pressing a palm against her lower belly, he followed her rhythm, his thumb dipping in and discovering the tiny bud he was searching for. He circled it, touching and not quite touching in at random intervals.

She moaned, a long low sound that was half need and half frustration. But he wasn't quite ready to finish her yet. He wanted to wait. Wanted her to wait. Until they were both ready—until they were wound so tight they were ready to snap—to break into a million pieces.

"Theo," she panted. "Please."

The plea didn't fall on deaf ears. He touched her, applying steady pressure that increased every time she reached the bottom of a stroke. He hoped the little jolt of pleasure would match his own each time her body took him all the way in.

It evidently did, because her eyes slammed shut and she increased the speed and the force of her thrusts as he struggled to hold on.

Just a little. Hell, just give me a little more…

Maddy's body slammed all the way down, and her breath whooshed from her as a strong series of contractions hit him and blew him away.

That was it. Her eruption became his, and he came

harder than he'd ever come in his life, the squeeze of her body forcing his to give everything it had.

Until it was done.

Over.

Tiny ripples still quaking his center, he wrapped his arms around her and pulled her down against him, careful to remain connected. He just needed a few more seconds. A few more whispers of sensation.

Her head nestled in the crook of his neck as he waited for the waves to carry him back to the shore. It wasn't all at once. They pushed him forward and then dragged him back for what seemed like forever, their breath mingling, her hair tickling his chest.

He kissed her cheek.

Tonight was something he would never forget. Would never forget her.

Ever.

There was something final about that word. Something that tugged at a place inside him that was long forgotten. Or was it just buried too deep to be found?

Whatever it was, he was changed.

Marked.

With that realization came a niggle of fear. They were in a hotel room that didn't belong to them, doing something they—

What was he doing here?

He firmed his jaw. Nothing they both hadn't wanted.

She hadn't asked for forever. Hadn't even hinted at it. Which was good.

Wasn't it?

He had no idea.

Maddy shifted for a second, and he thought she was going to pull away and get dressed. He wasn't quite ready for that yet. Wanted a few more seconds to figure this out.

"Don't leave."

She sat up to look at him. "I wasn't going to. My legs are just going to sleep."

He smiled. "We can't have that, can we?"

Moving to the center of the bed, he pulled down the covers and motioned for her. "Lie with me. Just for a few minutes."

A few minutes turned into a few hours of watching her sleep. For real this time. Without fighting it. And then unable to do anything else, he blanked everything out except for the feel of her warmth against him, the soft steady sound of her breathing.

Almost paradise?

The song had it so very wrong.

She *was* paradise. And now that he'd had a taste of it, he wasn't sure he could let it go. No one else would ever come close to where this woman had taken him tonight.

And he didn't want them to.

All he wanted was her.

It scared the hell out of him, but there was absolutely nothing he could do to change it. And he wasn't sure he would, even if he could.

He could worry about that tomorrow. But for the next couple of hours he was going to enjoy having her close, because who knew better than he did that tomorrow wasn't promised? Not to him. Not to Maddy.

Not to anyone.

Maddy opened her eyes and found darkness. But there was sound.

Something.

A ringtone. But it wasn't hers. It was unfamiliar.

A spot of light appeared, and then a low masculine voice abruptly cut the sound off, speaking into the phone.

Then another one went off, one she recognized this time, and a frisson of fear woke her up the rest of the way. She remembered exactly where she was. Who she was with. And what that call might be about. There was no way both of their phones could go off at once, unless...

Ivy!

Stumbling through the darkness, she searched for her phone just as Theo belted out, "When?"

She found hers. "Hello?"

"Madison, this is Naomi. Ivy has taken a turn. We're trying to locate Theo, but so far no luck. You wouldn't happen to know where..." A pause was followed by "What?" to someone nearby. Then her friend came back on the line. "Okay, Dr. Sumner has found him. Sorry to bother you. But do you think you could come in? I know it's late." Out of the corner of her eye she saw Theo grabbing for his clothes, his muscles flashing in the low light of her phone.

"Of course. What's going on?"

"Ivy woke up crying." Naomi's swift indrawn breath told her this was about something far worse than a simple nightmare or bellyache. She waited for her friend to continue.

"Madison. She can't feel her legs. At all."

"I'm on my way."

Ending the call, she tossed her phone on the bed and looked for her own clothes. Not the ones from the wedding but her normal street clothes.

They were still in the bags on the floor. She hurried over and dragged them out, then realized she still needed to locate her panties, which were somewhere in that huge bed. She scrambled onto it, tossing aside bedclothes and sheets, until she found them buried beneath the rubble.

Rubble. That was a very good word to describe the aftermath of last night. Guilt snaked up her spine, lodging at the base of her skull.

Theo still hadn't said a word as he sat on the edge of the bed and pulled on his socks and shoes. She dragged on bra and panties, unable to face him naked, then she turned on the light, blinking until her eyes adjusted. "Was that Dr. Sumner?"

"Yes." The one-word answer was curt with pain and accusation. Probably not at her but at himself.

She went to stand over by him. "This isn't your fault."

"Hell if it's not. I never should have been in this room." He glanced up at her, angry eyes skating down her body and then away. The inference was obvious.

It was like a slap to the face.

He's hurting. This is not about you.

She could tell herself that for as long as she wanted, but it didn't change the fact that he regretted being here with her. Making love to her.

If it could even be called that. Right now he'd looked at her as if he loathed her.

Maybe he did. But probably not more than he loathed himself.

She gathered the rest of her clothes and pulled them on, not bothering with her coat.

When he spoke again, his voice was devoid of emotion. "I'll have the concierge send the rest of our things to my flat if that's okay. I'd rather not arrive with them at the hospital. In fact, I'd rather we didn't arrive together."

Her head could understand all of that. It was quite logical. But her heart cried out as yet another dart pierced her skin. He didn't want to be seen with her.

"It's fine."

It wasn't. But this wasn't about her precious ego, it was about a little girl's life.

She can't feel her legs.

Something about that niggled at the back of her head. Something important. But right now she couldn't separate what was what, or trust her judgement. Not until she was able to get out of this room and forget about what had happened here.

Was that even possible? Madison had no idea, but she needed to at least try.

Within fifteen minutes they had everything bagged back up and were down at the concierge's desk, where someone was ahead of them. She glanced down at her watch. Four o'clock in the morning, and there was someone else checking out? Theo looked at her. "You go on. I'll take care of this."

"No. She's your daughter. You go."

"Are you sure?"

"Yes. Just give me the address to your apartment."

Scribbling something on a piece of paper, and then handing it to her, he nodded at her. "Please don't tell—"

"I won't. Just go."

He nodded, and with a heavy sense of doom and an even heavier heart Madison watched him leave, until he was through the doors and out of sight.

Then it was just her. Alone. An all-too-familiar song in a very familiar life.

He didn't want her to tell anyone about tonight. It was obvious he had no intention of repeating what had gone on here. Even if it had rocked her world and made her realize that maybe even a lone wolf was capable of falling in—

Stop it! This is about Ivy and not your feelings.

The concierge could have asked any of a million questions about why the person checking out of the room was different from the person who'd checked in. But he did neither, just took down the address Theo had given her. He was polite and discreet. And for that tiny gift she was grateful.

She dragged her mind back to Ivy as she left the hotel with only her purse and the memory of all the magic she'd experienced last evening.

She couldn't feel her legs.

What did that mean?

The growing weakness had been the main symptom up until now. She assumed that if Ivy couldn't feel them, she also couldn't move them. Which meant she was now paralyzed from the waist down.

How long before that paralysis began to creep up to other affected areas.

Madison couldn't let that happen, even if she had to spend her days and nights studying every case file from here to Timbuktu.

Until she finally found one that fit Ivy's symptoms. And could put an end to her—and Theo's—agony once and for all. Then maybe, just maybe, Ivy's biggest Christmas wish might come true after all.

CHAPTER EIGHT

"God, why didn't I see it? My legs fell asleep and I didn't see the connection. Until now." She didn't care that Theo might be cringing over that particular memory. None of that mattered.

Madison bent over Ivy, retesting the sensation in her legs, and got the same result Dr. Sumner had. Nothing. Not a flinch, not a contraction of the muscle, not one hint that the nerves in her legs were transmitting signals of any type up the neural pathway. And she bet she knew why. It was the same reason she hadn't been able to feel her own legs after she and Theo had had sex. "I need an MRI. Right now."

"But you already said there were no lesions." Theo's voice was calm. Too calm as he sat by his daughter's bed.

Judy and Naomi had left the room a few moments ago so that Madison could examine Ivy without any distractions. Theo's housekeeper had been distraught, apologizing over and over for falling asleep in the chair next to the bed. It had edged Madison's guilt even higher for keeping the child's father away from his daughter. But if she felt guilty, then Theo felt it a thousand times more deeply, judging from his haggard appearance.

She remembered her earlier words to him. *Don't you give up on me.*

It was as if he already had. As if their night together had sounded a death knell for his daughter.

But he was wrong. So very wrong.

Destiny was not going to punish him for wanting— no, *needing*—a little human companionship.

She felt as guilty as hell for not being here when Ivy's symptoms had progressed. But she wasn't going to allow her feelings to paralyze her—to keep from doing what needed to be done. Unlike the times when she'd been a kid and had sabotaged her chances in one foster home after another, so sure her mom was going to come back for her someday. She'd let her emotions rule her, and they had almost destroyed her.

Not anymore. And certainly not this time. Not when Ivy needed her. Not when Theo needed a miracle.

"I don't want another scan of her head. I want one of her back."

"Her back? I don't understand."

Ivy's voice came up to her. "What's wrong with my legs? Why can't I feel them?"

That tearful voice had asked the same question time after time ever since Madison had arrived at the hospital a half-hour earlier.

The cause had come to her in a flash. She just needed confirmation. And she prayed desperately that she was right.

She leaned in close to the child. "We're working to find out, sweetheart. Do you think you can handle being in that white tube again?"

"Y-yes. If I have to."

"It will help me find out what's going on with your legs. And hopefully make you better."

Theo's grim voice interrupted her. "Madison…"

He didn't want her to make empty promises. But she wasn't. Not this time. And if she was right…

They might be able to reverse the course of Ivy's condition. She'd have to strengthen her muscles to be able to walk, but at least she'd have the chance to be completely mobile again.

She firmed her jaw and faced him. "I know what I'm doing. You need to trust me. In this, anyway."

He might not have trusted their decision about last night, and he'd be right. Everything about what had happened between them had been about a lack of impulse control. But here in this room she was not driven by a decision made in the heat of the moment. Or some kind of crazy attraction that had no logical basis and no possible future.

He'd as much as said it.

They hadn't checked in with the rest of the treatment team as most of them were still at home in their beds, so this was ultimately Theo's call as to whether he let her run with her hunch.

She waited with bated breath as a flurry of emotions crossed his face, and her mind wept as she read each one of them—fear, dread, guilt…pain. And finally resignation.

"Let's do it. We can talk on the way down."

Talk? Oh, God. She hoped it was about Ivy and not about last night. She didn't need anything else clogging up her thoughts. She was having enough trouble filtering pertinent information as it was.

And if he was going to try to let her down easy…

Well, it was too late. Her heart was about to crash to the earth and tear open a crater so deep that no one would ever be able to find it again. Worst of all, it was for the best.

Madison made the call to the imaging department, who said they'd send someone right up for Ivy.

She sat on the bed beside her and held her hand for a long minute, while the child looked up at her with moist blue eyes that brimmed with some of the same emotions visible on Theo's face.

"It's going to be all right. We'll be down there with you in a very few minutes, okay?"

Ivy nodded, glancing toward her father as if for reassurance.

Theo came over and kissed her on the head. "I won't leave you, sweetness. Not even for a second."

He would have to, of course. He couldn't stay in the scanning area with her, but Ivy would already know that. He could wait in the control room and talk to her, though.

Minutes later, Ivy had been whisked away, leaving Theo to explain to Judy what was going on and to ask her to wait here in the room. The housekeeper, her white hair pulled into a bun, nodded. "You'll let me know as soon as you hear anything?"

"I will."

"I'm so sorry for spoiling your evening. You made it to the wedding?"

"You didn't spoil it. And, yes, we… *I* went to the wedding. I'll call you as soon as I know something."

If Judy caught his little slip of the tongue, she said nothing, didn't even glance in Madison's direction. More hurt balled into a lump in her throat. A lump so big it was impossible to dislodge, no matter how many times she swallowed.

Madison and Theo exited the room, heading down the hallway to the elevators. "Theo, I am so sorry."

"Don't." He cut her off. "The blame lays entirely with me. If anything happens to her…"

She caught his hand, forcing him to stop. "If this is what I think it is, there's a good chance we can reverse the paralysis."

His hand tightened on hers. "What do you think it is?"

"Let's see the scans first. I don't want to jump to conclusions without seeing definitive proof. Can you wait just a little while longer?"

"I've been waiting for months, it seems. And…" a muscle in his cheek worked "…it just feels like the clock is running out."

She forced a smile. "I told you I'd tell you when to worry." She shifted her hand and linked her fingers through his, knowing she was letting her impulses reign again. But she was desperate to set his mind at ease, even though she knew it wasn't the time for that yet. "This is not it. But it is the time to hope."

He raised her hand to his lips and kissed it, sending a stream of conflicting emotions streaming through her. "I want you to be right. Heaven help me, Maddy, I pray you're right."

They sat in the room overlooking the MRI room as the machine took detailed pictures of his daughter's body section by section. She'd been given a light anesthetic to help her hold perfectly still during the process, so he was grateful that she wasn't afraid or confused.

Unlike Theo, whose heart pounded in his chest, sending his blood pressure through the roof. It wasn't all due to Ivy either, although right now she was all that mattered.

Maddy had made Theo do something he hadn't done in a very long time. Forget about Hope.

And he damned himself for that. Damned himself that he'd been with her while his daughter had been lying in a hospital bed unable to feel her legs.

He swallowed back a sea of emotions. Even in the hallway a few moments ago, he'd been unable to resist kissing her hand.

As a result of her words, his conscience argued.

No. As a result of last night. And it had to stop. Right here. Right now. Nothing else was going to divert his energy from finding out what was wrong with Ivy. Not even Maddy.

Especially not Maddy.

He'd had no trouble brushing off a woman's interest. Up until now. And the worst part of it was the interest hadn't started with her. It had started with him. He'd been the one who'd felt an immediate attraction to her. And he still had no idea why.

Yes, she was funny and sweet and tenacious as hell when it came to her patients. And she was beautiful beyond belief. But for him to have let down his guard at a time when it should have been at its highest was unforgivable. If Hope knew he'd jeopardized their daughter's health on a night of meaningless sex, she'd be horrified.

Only he wasn't so sure it had been meaningless. And that horrified *him*. He'd been so sure that no one would ever be able to take his late wife's place. And here he was pining over a flesh-and-blood woman who was here, whereas Hope wasn't.

"Okay. That should do it." The tech's voice interrupted his thoughts. "Do you want to sit with her while we read the scans?"

He was looking at Theo.

He was torn. He wanted to be with Ivy, but he also wanted to be there when the tech and Maddy scrolled through those images. He wanted to read the results on her face the moment she realized whether her hypothesis was right…or wrong.

"Can I do both? Can we go through them in the room with her?"

Maddy shook her head, her hand inching toward his before thinking better of it. "I don't think that's a good idea. I don't want her frightened if she hears us discussing the findings. I'll tell you what. Why don't you go down with her to Recovery while we look over the scans? I'll call you as soon I know something."

He had never been on this side of the equation before. He now knew how parents felt as they were forced to wait in a room while people decided what would and wouldn't happen to their child. Or debated treatment protocols and diagnoses. But he couldn't straddle the fence. Not this time. His place was with his daughter.

"Okay. But I want to know the second you have an answer."

"I'll call. I promise."

Theo left without saying another word, meeting the nurse as she wheeled the bed into one of the recovery rooms. Ivy was still sound asleep, her sweet angelic face wiped clean of any traces of worry. Or pain.

And that sent a landslide of fear through him. It was too close to how he pictured Hope's face.

He could not lose her. Surely whatever deity was up there wouldn't take her from him as well.

Hope and Ivy were the only two people he had ever really loved other than his parents.

Really? Was that the absolute truth? Wasn't there…?

He swallowed hard as a horrible, gut-wrenching possibility stole over him. One he shoved aside. This was not the time or the place.

And if he had his way, it would never be.

A minute later, Ivy's voice broke through. "Daddy?"

Relief swamped over him. "I'm right here, baby."

The nurse smiled at him. "She's going to be just fine. And so are you, Dad."

Ha! That was the funniest thing he'd heard all day. Only it wasn't funny. At all.

His phone chirped. He snatched it up and jabbed the talk button. "Hawkwood here."

He had no idea why he did that. He already knew from his screen that it was Maddy. Maybe the desperate need to salvage this situation and put their feet back on professional ground had forced the move.

"Um… Theo?" The confusion in her voice was plain and his gut tightened. He was a bastard. No doubt about it.

"Yes, sorry. Ivy's awake and talking."

"How are her legs?"

"I haven't asked." And he didn't want to ask. Not right now.

"Well, can you get Judy to come up and sit with her? I have something I think you'll want to see."

He gulped down a quick wash of bile. He wanted to

ask her if it was a tumor or any number of catastrophic diagnoses that came to mind. But to do that would just frighten Ivy.

"Yes. Give me a minute to get her up here."

That minute seemed like hours, when in fact it didn't take long at all for Judy to speed up in the elevator and swing open that door. "How is she?"

"She's awake." He brushed Ivy's dark hair back from her face. "Judy is going to sit with you for a moment while I go and talk to Dr. Archer, okay?"

"Why are you calling her Dr. Archer, Daddy?" Ivy's tiny brows scrunched together before she gave a huge yawn. "She wants us…to call…her Madison."

She wanted him to call her Maddy. But he couldn't do that anymore. Not if he had any hope of coming out of this in one piece.

"I know she does, pumpkin. Go to sleep. I'll be back in just a little while."

He needn't have said anything. Ivy's eyelids were already heavy and sinking lower by the second. It had been a long night that had taken a lot out of them all. And dawn was beginning to relentlessly creep up over the horizon.

Judy took the seat next to the bed. "I'll be right here if she wakes."

His housekeeper had been up as long as he had, probably even longer, since he'd been busy having a good old time with Ivy's best hope for a cure.

"I'll be back as soon as I can. Thank you for everything."

"You don't need to thank me, Theo. I love this girl as if she were my own."

And since Judy had never married or had children

of her own, in a very real way Ivy was like a grand-daughter to her. That bond had just grown closer over the last four and a half years.

He slid from the room, closing the door with care so as not to wake Ivy. His legs carried him along, going too fast and yet feeling like he was in one of those nightmares where every step was dragged backward by some unseen force. Still he put one foot in front of the other, wanting to get there and yet not wanting to. What if there was no hope for Ivy? What if it was some incurable disease that would silently steal her away from him?

He gritted his teeth and forced himself to think of something else. She'd told him this was the time for hope, so he needed to hold onto that with all his might.

He found the tech in the scanning booth, but there was no sign of Maddy. "I have another patient coming in, sorry. Car accident victim. Dr. Archer is waiting for you in exam room one, just down the corridor and to the right."

He knew where the room was, but forced himself to thank the guy and head back out again. This time the trip was faster since the room was just around the corner.

The door was open, and Maddy was sitting inside with her back to him, her entire attention focused on the computer screen in front of her. And there it was again. That tug to his gut that appeared every time he was within ten feet of her. He'd thought spending a night with her might erase it, although it had been pure attraction that had brought them together, not a need to banish her from his system. He hadn't thought there'd been a need to do that.

Until today.

The overhead light caught the highlights in her hair, giving them a warm glow that was normally impossible with a harsh florescent tube.

His brain told him to call her by her title. His heart would not let him. Whatever else he did, he didn't want to hurt her or try to deny what had happened in that hotel room. She deserved more than that.

"Maddy?"

She whirled around on the swivel stool. When she went to push a few locks of hair behind her ears, he noticed her hand was trembling.

A cold wind blew across his soul. "What is it?"

"I can't believe I didn't see this before now. Grab that stool and sit down."

Her hand wasn't the only thing that was shaking. Her voice had a quaver to it as well. Only it didn't sound like fear. She sounded almost excited.

Was that a good thing?

He pulled the stool over from beside the exam table and set it beside hers. "Okay. Tell me."

"I'll do better than that. I'll show you. Remember when my legs fell asleep?"

Without waiting for an answer, she began rolling her finger across the laptop's mouse pad and the images changed as quick as lightning.

"Slow down. I can't see what I'm looking at."

"Sorry. Not quite there yet." But she did as he asked and slowed the pace of the changing images as they showed the detailed snapshots of his daughter's spine, vertebrae and blood vessels.

Maddy scrolled back and forth between a couple

of images before stopping abruptly. "There. What do you see?"

There was still that odd intonation to her voice that signaled urgency.

Theo peered at the images, his chaotic brain struggling to make sense of anything he was seeing. "Where am I—?"

"Here." She took her pen and pointed to an area on the screen and his world suddenly went silent.

This section of her spinal cord flowed in a smooth even line until it reached one area where it bulged out a bit. Right next to it was a tangle of blood vessels that looked…enlarged.

When he turned to glance her way, he found her staring at him. She already knew what it was. He was certain.

"Why do people's legs fall asleep?"

He swallowed, realizing now why she'd gone back to that. "Because something presses on the nerve."

"Exactly. And here it is." She circled the area. "This is what's pressing on the nerves that control her legs."

"Her veins have been causing this? The whole time?"

"Yes." She turned to look at the image again. "We'll need an angiogram to be sure, Theo, but I would bet it's an arteriovenous fistula."

"Dural?"

When she nodded, he said, "My God. It's been sitting there in plain sight all along."

Color leached from her face. "I know. I am so sorry I haven't seen it before now."

"How could you have? I would have gone months before thinking to look at the vessels near her spine, and even then it's doubtful I would have found it. Or if

I had, it might have been too late to restore function. If it's not already."

"I don't think it is. A lot of these cases take a year or longer to be diagnosed. It's only been a couple of months."

"But it's progressed so fast."

Spinal dural arteriovenous fistula. He searched his memory for the condition and came up with just snatches of information. The fistula part was easy—it was an abnormal connection between two differing things. In SDAVF, the capillaries that joined arteries to veins were missing. Instead, arteries were connected directly to veins, putting a strain on them until they bulged under the increased load. Those bulges—which were slowly growing in size—put pressure on her spinal cord, resulting in damage that was hopefully reversible.

She'd said they needed an angiogram, but Theo knew she was right. The angiogram would just confirm the diagnosis and give them a definitive location, something not always visible in an MRI.

"What do we do now?"

"We get one of Hope Hospital's excellent neurosurgeons to zap those suckers and shut them down."

The way she said it, in her typical American fashion, made him laugh, although he knew part of that was the sheer force of the relief that was sweeping over him. "You did it. You told me it was a time for hope and you were right."

Before he could stop himself, he took her face in his hands and stared deep into her eyes before his gaze dropped to her lips. "I don't know how to thank you."

"Y-you don't need to thank me."

He leaned closer.

"Dr. Archer?" The sudden sound had him jerking back, sending his stool rolling several inches.

They both looked toward the door where the MRI tech was shifting from foot to foot. "I'm sorry for interrupting."

"You're not." The growled words didn't help. If anything, the young man's face turned ten shades of red before he addressed Maddy.

"Do you still want me to schedule that emergency angiogram for the patient?"

"Yes, please. And have a neurosurgeon standing by." Maddy didn't belt out the words or show emotion of any kind. She stood, smiling at the tech. "I appreciate you getting back to me so quickly."

There was something about the way she said those words that made him think she was glad the man had come in when he had.

Maybe he wasn't the only one who was having regrets over what had happened between them last night. Hell, that hadn't stopped him from swooping in on her the second they found themselves alone in a room again.

Relief. Pure and simple. He would have planted a kiss right on Judy's lips if she'd been the one to come up with the solution.

It would have been a completely different kind of kiss, though, wouldn't it?

Yes, it would have been.

And that's what made this situation so hard to face. He would have to get over it, though. For Ivy's sake. Once all of this was done, he could come back and dissect his feelings all he wanted but right now the only thing that was on the table was his daughter's health.

* * *

By eight in the morning the exams were all done and, as Theo knew it was going to be, Maddy's hunch was confirmed. The location of the fistula fit the area of weakness, which was mostly in her legs and creeping upward as the veins continued to swell. It was also why she suddenly had no sensation in her legs. There had probably been a rapid change in the vessels over the last couple of days. Those kinds of things could progress quickly or move forward and then plateau for a while.

Her arm weakness was probably caused by her upper body trying to compensate for her inability to use her legs to do common tasks—such as using them to shift herself or helping to move from a chair back to her bed. But that had just confused the issue, since everyone had thought it was generalized weakness over her whole body rather than it being confined to her legs.

But Maddy had found the answer. In the end, the sudden paralysis had been the key they'd needed to solve the mystery.

He was grateful. Overwhelmingly grateful. And he had no idea how to express that to her in a way that was appropriate. And the inappropriate ways were out of the question.

That was another thing he wasn't used to. He was used to being on the receiving end of his patients' gratitude. Here he was trying to sort through how to say thanks without it being just words and nothing else.

All of that could wait until Ivy's surgery was over and she was on the mend, though. Then he would work it all out.

And decide once and for all what to do.

CHAPTER NINE

THE SURGERY WAS a success. The neurosurgeon had performed an endovascular embolization, going in through a catheter and injecting a tiny bit of glue into the offending vessels. Like the lights on a runway going out one by one, Maddy had gotten to see the affected veins disappear off the screen as their blood flow was cut off. The body would use other—normal—veins and capillaries in the area to take over for the ones they'd just obliterated.

And hopefully as the swelling in her spinal cord subsided, Ivy would slowly regain sensation in her legs, and with hope and a lot of prayers her atrophied muscles would regain their strength. She was slated to start physical therapy in two days as soon as things started quietening down in her back.

Madison had only seen Theo for a few minutes after the surgery. He'd seemed to be acting strangely, barely making eye contact with her before muttering a quick thank you and taking off to see his daughter.

That was understandable, though. Of course he wanted to spend every second he could with her. It was like he'd been given a new lease of life. One that matched the one Ivy had been given.

She wandered down the corridor of the surgical suite. It was midday and medical staff were flowing in and out of the rooms at a constant rate. Everything had happened so fast. She'd been up for twelve hours already.

Only twelve hours since she'd woken up in that hotel room to the sound of her cellphone ringing. It seemed like a lifetime ago. Theo had seemed to age before her eyes over the day, his sentences getting shorter and shorter. The only time she'd seen a true spark of emotion in him had been when she'd shown him the spinal dural arteriovenous fistula on the MRI scans. She could still feel his palms cupping her face as he'd leaned in to kiss her.

And he had been going to kiss her. Oh, she'd almost talked herself out of believing that, but after reliving the moment a thousand times in her head, she knew if that tech hadn't shown up when he had, Theo's mouth would have been on hers. If that had happened she'd have been just as powerless to stop her reaction to it as she'd been last night. Theo was like a tsunami. One that crashed over the walls that surrounded her heart and knocked down every defense. She'd been a willing participant.

If he asked her up to his office today or a week from today, she'd go and to hell with the consequences.

Except ever since that moment in the exam room, Theo had been the consummate professional, barely speaking to her. During surgery she'd sat in the observation area to watch. Theo had come in and had chosen a chair on the other side of the room. Her insides had squelched in embarrassment.

How could things have changed so drastically?

You came up with the answer, that's why. He no longer needs to coddle you.

No, Madison refused to believe that. That he'd simply been humoring her, hoping that by showing preferential treatment—hadn't he even used that expression one time?—she would work even harder on his daughter's case.

By having sex with her?

Surely not. Unless that's what he'd thought she'd wanted.

And, oh, God, she had wanted it. Had he somehow read her mind and obliged?

She swallowed. She'd gotten it in her head that in the same way Ivy was special to her, Theo was beginning to think she was special too.

But why would that even be true?

She was just a colleague. One that he'd made the mistake of sleeping with.

She had repeatedly told herself that she was not picturing Theo as anything more than a work partner. Until they'd slept together and she'd wondered if they might somehow become more than that.

A family?

Ha! Not very likely. He loved his wife. Didn't the picture that was still sitting on his desk tell her that, along with his late wife's medical degree hanging on his wall?

Maddy was a fool.

A fool who had stupidly fallen in love with a man who was unreachable.

Yes, she could finally admit it. She loved him. And it was impossible. For both of them.

She made her way to the elevator and then to her office, wondering how she was going to finish out the last five months of her stay in England. The last thing she wanted was to run into Theo day in and day out. Unless she could somehow convince herself she didn't really love him. That working so closely together was what had done a number on her—dredging up emotions that were temporary and would fade as Ivy returned to health. As the reasons for she and Theo working so closely together came to a halt.

He was already putting the incident behind him. She could do the same.

At least she hoped she could.

And if she couldn't?

Okay, if she didn't feel more like her old self in a few weeks, she could always resign and go back to the States. It wouldn't look good on her résumé but, then again, she had never really had a stellar reputation in the human relations department. Her hospital would just think that her inability to be a team player had raised its ugly head again and gotten her thrown out.

They'd take her back. Of that she had no doubt. She may have upset some of the staff at her old hospital, but they had kept her on despite it all. And that was obviously not the result of her sparkling personality.

She smiled, feeling a little less wobbly inside. She would give it a couple of weeks and see where things stood. Then she would make her decision. This wasn't a forever job.

And it never would be.

She'd known that from the beginning. Neither would Theo swoop in and declare his undying love for her. He was in love with Hope. And that would never change.

The sooner she realized that, the better off she would be.

Madison poked her head into Ivy's room. The girl was fast asleep. Two days after surgery and all was well. For Ivy and for her.

Sensation in her legs was already returning, along with some tiny movements of her toes. All very promising signs.

Her heart contracted at who else was in Ivy's bed. Theo. Who'd spent every waking moment with his daughter, going with her to her first day of therapy this morning. She'd tried to give them as wide a berth as possible.

Until she could no longer stand it and had to see them…no, not them. Ivy. She'd tried to find a time when Theo wasn't with her, but that seemed to be never.

So she crept over to the bed to check her vitals, hoping beyond hope that she didn't wake Theo in the process. Well, if she did, she could just pretend it was a professional visit.

It was. She would make it one, even if she knew in her heart of hearts that her reasons for being here were far from professional.

Theo was on his back beside Ivy, one arm behind his head, his hand stretching to the opposite side of the bed as if keeping his daughter safe while she slept. His eyes were closed—ha! If they weren't there was no way she would be standing here right now with a lump in her throat the size of Montana.

She missed him. Missed sparring with him verbally. Missed their arguments.

Missed strolling downtown under the Christmas lights.

Most of all, she missed him holding her far into the night. Her eyes welled with tears, making it hard to see, but somehow she made her way over to Ivy's side of the bed, smiling at how small she looked in that long bed, especially next to her daddy.

She missed the little girl almost as much as she missed Ivy's father.

Firming her resolve, she slid closer so she could check her pulse and breathing.

Suddenly Ivy's eyelids flickered open, coming to focus on her.

There was no time to hide or escape to the safety of the hallway. She'd been caught creeping around like a peeping Tom.

"Mummy?"

She was evidently still half-asleep, her small hand scrubbing over her eyes in a way that made her heart break. Soon Madison would fly away and never see Ivy or her father again. There was nothing she could do about that. But she could at least make sure the parting had some closure for the little girl.

Unlike her own life, when her mother had been there one day and gone the next?

Hadn't that happened with Ivy's mom, too?

It was up to her to not add another trauma to the little girl's life. Not that she'd made that big an impact on it.

Ivy was still looking at her, and she realized she was waiting for an answer.

She forced a smile, brushing a strand of dark hair from the girl's cheek. "No. It's just me, Madison. I've come to check on you."

"I wish you were."

"You wish I was what?"

"I wish you were my mummy."

Madison's breath stalled in her lungs, her hand going to her mouth in an effort to stop the words that were clamoring to get out.

I wish I were, too.

The pain was almost unbearable, slashing through her again and again until she was sure there was nothing left of her heart. Her lungs. Her vital organs.

She would never get over this little girl. Or her father.

Against her will, her gaze stole over to Theo.

Open. Open! His eyes were open!

And he'd heard every word they'd said, his brows forming an ominous frown that chilled her to the bone. Here was one person who didn't wish she was Ivy's mother.

She had to get out of there. Now. Before he said something that brought her to her knees.

"I—I... Sorry, I was just here to make sure she was okay." She quickly said goodbye to Ivy and left the room. A second later, her back was against the wall and hot tears were splashing onto her cheeks.

Who was she kidding? She thought she could see Theo for the next five months and act like nothing had ever happened? Act like she didn't love the man or crave him with every fiber of her being?

There was no way. And judging from the pain that still gashed and tore at her, those crazy emotions were not going away. They were only going to get worse.

"Madison? Are you okay?"

At first she thought Theo had followed her out, but it was a woman's voice. She opened her eyes to find Naomi looking at her with concern.

She reached up and scrubbed at the tears and pushed away from the wall. "I'm fine. Have you ever had one of those days where you're so exhausted you could cry? Literally?"

When Naomi gave a wary-looking nod, Madison

chuckled, although it sounded more like the squawk of a pained seagull.

"Well, that's where I'm at. I was just getting ready to head home and sleep for at least eleven hours."

"Are you sure? I could drive you if you wanted."

Her friend's kind words threatened to turn the waterworks back on, so she simply shook her head. "I'm good. I'd rather walk and get some fresh air. I'll see you tomorrow."

Out of the corner of her eye, she saw the door to Ivy's room begin to open.

That was her cue to scram.

Throwing an apologetic smile to Naomi, she hurried down the corridor and didn't stop until she was in the safety of the elevator.

It was then that she knew she wasn't going back to her apartment. She was going to spend a couple of days in a hotel, during which time she was going to type up her resignation—effective immediately—and have it delivered to the hospital. Then she was going to pay someone to have her apartment vacated and cleaned out. But she was not going to set foot inside it or the hospital again.

She was going home. As soon as she could arrange a plane ticket. Getting into a taxi, she asked where she could get a room for a decent price.

When he named a nearby hotel, she asked him to take her there. By the time they arrived a few minutes later, her tears had dried up.

No more crying. Hadn't she learned from her childhood that tears changed nothing? All they did was make her throat ache and her head hurt. The only way she could alter her current situation was with common sense and a firm resolve not to look back.

She took her wallet out and pulled out a few bills to hand the driver. Something fell onto the seat when she did. Picking it up, she saw the ticket to the carol service that Theo had given her a lifetime ago. She'd taken it out of the notebook a couple of days ago, thinking they might actually go together.

That was a laugh.

Handing the driver the money, she got out of the cab, still looking at the ticket. It was in two days' time. The last two weeks had been a whirlwind of activity, followed by a devastation unlike anything she had ever experienced.

Well, she had at least two days until she could get a flight to the States, especially at this time of year. She might as well do some sightseeing while she was here. It might help ease the pain in her heart or at the very least it would fill her time and keep her from thinking about all she'd lost.

Lost?

She'd lost nothing except a thin layer of pride and maybe a little of her self-respect.

Those would come back soon enough. At least she hoped they would. Until then, she would take in some sights and maybe listen to a few carols.

You didn't have to like Christmas to like music, right?

She walked up to the hotel and asked for a room for a few days.

"How many days?" the man at the front desk asked.

Swallowing, she gave the only answer she could think of. "As many as it takes."

He didn't ask her to pin down her dates, and she was actually shocked that they had a room. But maybe there'd been a last-minute cancellation. Why couldn't she have gone somewhere like London for her working furlough?

Because she'd been called in for Ivy.

The man at the desk handed her a key and pointed to the elevator. Here she went again. It seemed like she was forever going up and down in the things.

Kind of like her life.

One minute she was soaring high, and the next she was sliding back to earth with a bump.

Well, she was about to get off this particular carnival ride once and for all. And as soon as she got on that plane, she was going to put her time in Cambridge behind her and never look back.

And that included a certain little girl and her devastatingly handsome and equally dangerous dad.

He'd hurt her. He'd known it the second she'd backed out of Ivy's room two days ago. When he'd been able to finally untangle himself from the sheets on Ivy's bed and rip open the door, he'd come face to face with Naomi, rather than Maddy.

"Where is she?"

Naomi didn't ask who he meant, she just pointed down the corridor.

By the time he got to the elevator, though, she was gone.

He'd acted like an ass ever since the night at the hotel. He'd done his best to avoid her, rather than sitting down and talking about what had happened like an adult.

And this was the result of it. He'd come in to find a resignation note sitting on his desk, delivered by a special courier service. The formal letter had no address on it, and when he'd checked at her apartment later that day, the manager said she'd already vacated the place. In two days' time? How was that even possible?

Maddy was a pretty determined woman. If she wanted something done, she would move heaven and earth to make sure it happened. Just look at Ivy's miraculous recovery. Without the diagnostician's stubborn resolve to find the cause of her condition, who knew if Ivy would be getting one good report after another, like she was now.

Hell, he'd screwed things up so badly. And now there was no way to make it right.

Checking on Ivy and fielding questions about Maddy's whereabouts as best he could, he then headed over to her office. It hadn't been cleared out, but then again there wasn't much here that gave evidence that she'd once occupied this room. He touched a couple of file folders, smiling as he came across Ivy's. All done now. As if she'd been an angel who'd come to help his daughter and had flitted away once her task was complete.

Who knew. Maybe she *had* been sent there by some heavenly realm. Ridiculous. She was a woman. Flesh and blood. He'd seen that first hand.

He went around the desk and opened one of the top drawers, frowning as a familiar notebook came into view. She'd left that here?

Why wouldn't she? She didn't need it anymore, her resignation told him that much.

He flipped the book open to the first page and stopped. His eyes slid over words that made no sense. What did this have to do with patients?

This looked more like a… Like a Christmas list.

We were just making some plans for Christmas.

Wasn't that what she'd said when he'd found her sitting on Ivy's bed with this very notebook?

Which would mean this list was Ivy's.

He re-read the words. His heart lurched to a stop and then took off way too fast, galloping in a way that left him short of breath. This was what Ivy wanted for Christmas?

He sat down in the chair behind Maddy's desk.

No. It was no longer hers. She'd left without a word. Not to him. Not to Ivy.

The list was heartbreakingly simple, with each entry followed by a short explanation as to why Ivy wanted it.

Make Daddy love Christmas. Because he is too sad about Mummy.

A new stethoscope—in purple, if Santa has one, because that's Ivy's favorite color.

A book about horses so he'll fall in love with them like she has.

An adult coloring book. One of Ivy's nurses talked about how every grown-up should have one.

Macaroni and cheese. Evidently Theo's favorite food. Santa must carry casseroles around in his toy sack.

A puppy. Ha! Wouldn't Theo love coming home to find a puppy under the tree?

When had Maddy planned on showing him this list? Or had she just written it to placate Ivy? No, he couldn't see her doing that. What he could see her doing was tracking down each of those items and sitting on Ivy's bed while they wrapped them. Except maybe the puppy. And that devastating first item. He'd done his best to make Christmas special for Ivy and she'd seen right through his efforts. Damn.

Well, he'd made a mistake in not talking to Maddy about what was happening between them. He wasn't going to make a second mistake by tossing this book back in that drawer and acting like he'd never seen it. It was time he started living life honestly. Starting with his daughter.

He went down to her room and found Judy inside. The housekeeper glanced up. Maybe she saw something in his face because she got up from the chair and came over to him, touching his arm. "I'll give you two some time together. I need to go home anyway and do laundry."

Since Judy had only brought his laundry to him yesterday, he doubted that was the truth, but he appreciated her tactful way of sliding out of the room.

Once they were alone, Theo went to the side of Ivy's bed and sat on it before lying down with his head next to hers on the pillow. He got straight to the point. "I found this in Madison's office."

He held up the little book.

"She likes to take notes in that."

"Yes, she does." He flipped through the pages. "She also writes other things down. Like Christmas lists."

"Mine?"

"Yes."

"Then you know what I asked Santa for Christmas." A note of wistfulness crept into her voice.

"I do."

She blinked and looked up at him. "Does it have all of them in there?"

"How many did you have?"

"Not many."

"That's funny. I couldn't tell if this was a list of things for me or a list of things for you."

"It's both, Daddy. I put things I thought we would both like."

Okay, well, the puppy was definitely all hers. And probably the book about horses too. But those other things…

He screwed up his courage before asking the big question. "What makes you think I don't like Christmas, baby?"

She shrugged. "It's when Mummy died. You get sad every year, even though you smile and act all happy and stuff."

"You could tell, huh?"

"Yes." She held his hand, her tiny fingers gripping his tight. "And I was thinking about that. If Mummy's in heaven, does that mean I can never have another one?"

"Another what?"

"Mummy. Because I know someone I would like."

His lungs tightened, threatening to suffocate him. "I know. I heard. But I don't think that would be a very good idea."

"Why? Mummy would like her. And I think you like her too."

He did more than that. He loved her.

Hell, why hadn't he seen that sooner?

Because he'd been too blind to see what had been staring him in the face.

"I do like her, but there's more to it than that. No one can ever take your mummy's place."

"I think Santa has magic. He can make it happen."

"Did you tell Madison any of this?"

"No."

She probably didn't even remember telling Maddy she wished she were her mother.

"Santa can't always grant every wish."

"I wished he would make me better for Christmas and he did. I can almost pedal the bike in the playground."

She'd taken to referring to the physical therapy room as the playground because it was more fun than work.

"Yes, he did. And I am very grateful for that." That hadn't been the work of Santa but the work of the woman he'd driven from his life with his guilt and his own foolish insecurities.

"Well, I think he can make Madison want to be my mummy too. Do you want her to be?"

"It doesn't matter what I want."

"Yes, it does." Ivy's voice went up, her chest rising and falling in agitation. "You have to want it too, or the magic can't happen."

He leaned over her and put a hand on her shoulder, shocked to find she was trembling. "I don't know where Maddy is, Ivy."

"Just ask Santa. He knows. He can show you. I think she makes you happy and can make you like Christmas again."

An icy hand closed over his throat as he realized his

daughter spoke the truth. Maddy did make him happy. Happier than he'd been in a long time.

"How about if I try?"

"Do you promise to try really hard, Daddy?"

"Yes, Ivy. I promise."

He'd wandered the city, going from one hotel to another. There had been no one with the name of Madison Archer at any of those he'd checked. He was almost out of time. And almost out of hope. It was Christmas Eve and in trying to track down Maddy he hadn't had time to buy any of the other gifts on that list. Because he had a feeling that there was only one present that really mattered to his daughter.

I'll tell you when to worry.

"I don't mind telling you, I'm worried. Worried I won't find her. Worried my daughter will have her hopes crushed. Worried that even if I do find her, she'll laugh in my face."

Theo had no idea if he was talking to God or to the jolly old gift-giver himself, but maybe it was both.

He looked up and spotted King's College. The carol service was today. He glanced at his watch. It was close to the time, actually. He hadn't had any luck in finding her and he was out of ideas at the moment, so he may as well go in and rest for a while and enjoy the service. Maybe something would come to him during it. If the worst came to the worst he could ring her hospital in the States and see if they had a revised return date for her.

Making his way to the door, he showed his ticket and went in. There was still half an hour before the service started so he glanced around the pews, looking for a likely spot. His eyes passed over a woman who had hair that looked remarkably like…

He took a step closer. It was the same length, the same sexy waves cascading down her back. And the way the light caught those highlights…

He walked up to the pew and looked past a few other people who were seated there as well. Shock pulsed through him. It was Maddy. She was staring down at the order of service, then reached up to quickly brush something from her left eye.

Tears?

His heart threatened to break in two. He made his way down the pew, apologizing for having to squeeze past the others who were already seated there.

He reached her and sat next to her.

She glanced over and her eyes widened. "Theo?"

"Mind if I join you?"

"Well… Um… I guess not."

The chapel grew silent as the service was about to begin, and he hadn't had a chance to say any of the things he wanted to say. But he'd found her. Somehow. It was a first step. He just hoped she would listen to what he had to say when the service ended.

"Can I talk to you after this?"

"About what?"

He produced the notebook from his pocket. "I may need help with one or two of the items on this list."

Her eyes met his. "I was going to give that to you, and then we kind of got caught up in…"

"Yes. We did." He reached and took her hand, relieved when she didn't immediately jerk away from him. "Will you hear me out afterwards?"

"Do I have a choice?"

"We always have a choice. But I hope you'll let me explain a few things."

A plaintive voice in the group of robed choristers sang the opening words of the first carol. And, like the magic that Ivy had talked about, Maddy's fingers tightened around his.

He wanted to sit here with her forever, but all too soon the service ended and people began to rise from their seats to leave. He'd been here year after year, but he couldn't remember when he'd enjoyed it more. Maybe it was because of the woman seated next to him. She'd healed Ivy and if all went well, she might very well heal his heart. If not...well, that particular organ would never be the same.

"Can we walk?"

"Okay."

They left the chapel and walked back to the front of King's College, facing Market Square. Theo found them a small bench a short distance away.

He turned toward her. "First I want to say I'm sorry for how I acted after that night at the hotel."

"Okay."

It was the second time she'd used that word to answer. Maybe he'd better up his game.

"I haven't felt like that with a woman in...well, ever."

Her head tilted. "Not even Hope?"

He thought back over the years. Yes, he and Hope had shared some wonderful memories, but it wasn't the same. What he'd felt for her was packed away in a box and had been for a long time. "What I feel for you is different from what Hope and I shared."

"What you feel?"

"I love you, Maddy. I'm not sure when it happened, but it did."

Instead of looking relieved, she frowned. "Is this because of what Ivy said the other day at the hospital?"

It took him a moment to figure out what she was talking about.

"You think I'm telling you this because Ivy said she wanted you to be her mother?"

"Are you?"

"No. I would give my daughter the world if I could, but I would never ask someone to marry me just to give her a mum."

Her mouth opened and then closed. "Did you say…?"

"Yes. I said ask someone to marry me." He took both of her hands in his. "What I said is true, Maddy. I love you. And if you feel even a smidgen of love for me, I want to walk down that aisle with you the same way that Alice and Marco did this past Saturday."

Before she could say anything, he went on. "The one thing that can guarantee that I'll like Christmas again, that is if I can spend the rest of them with you and Ivy. And then you, when she's all grown up. Thank you for saving her. And thank you for saving me. For making me realize I've been wearing a funeral shroud that wasn't mine to wear. I belong here…among the living. And I want to spend the rest of that living…with you."

She didn't say anything for a long moment. Was he too late?

He cupped her chin. "Maddy?"

"I'm afraid to believe any of this is real. It's like magic. I was sitting in that chapel thinking about you, and suddenly you were there."

"It is magic. Ivy told me I had to want it or the magic wouldn't happen."

"What magic?"

"The magic of love." His hand slid up to touch her face. "I do want it, Maddy. I hope you do as well."

Her eyes closed, and for a horrible second he thought she was going to turn him down. To get up and walk away and leave him sitting there alone on the bench.

Then they reopened and what he saw shining from the green depths gave him hope like he'd never had before. "Yes, I do want it. I love you too. That night after the hotel, I thought you were feeling guilty, like you'd cheated on Hope. And I already knew that I loved you. It just about killed me. And the way you looked at me in Ivy's room when she said she wished I was her…"

"I was embarrassed that she'd put you in that kind of a spot. I tried to get up to follow you, but I got tangled up in the bed and almost fell out of it, trying to get free. By the time I reached the corridor you were gone. And when I checked at your apartment the next day, you'd already moved out." He leaned down and kissed her. "I was so afraid I'd never find you again."

"I think that's why I haven't bought my ticket back to the States yet. I was going to call yesterday. And then today. Only I didn't. I finally decided as I was sitting in the chapel that I was going to go back to the hospital and have it out with you before buying it."

"Then let's have it out. Will you marry me?" He toyed with her ring finger before lifting her hand and kissing that spot.

"Yes, Theo. I will."

Their lips met, softly, gently and then with growing

passion. By the time they pulled back, Theo's blood was pounding in his ears. "I think we'd better go back before I do something that will get us both arrested."

"Go back?"

"To the hospital to see Ivy, first of all. And then maybe back to my office. Have I ever told you that my couch there is very comfortable?"

"I've slept on that couch so I think we're in agreement as to its comfort."

He smiled and rose from the bench, tugging her up with him. "I mean it's *very* comfortable. It's also large enough for two people."

"Theo! Are you suggesting we do something indecent on that couch?"

"I'm suggesting it's the closest place that I know of."

"Definitely closer than my hotel room."

When she told him the name of it, he laughed. "That is one of the few places I didn't check."

"You looked for me?"

"Yes. I spent a good part of today checking hotel rooms and airline flights. It was like you'd vanished into thin air. I half suspected you were an angel sent to rescue Ivy and me."

"Angels don't do indecent things on office couches."

"They don't?"

"No. But then again I am no angel. I'm a woman in love."

She leaned her head against his shoulder. "Oh, Theo, look at the lights."

The Christmas lights were glowing with hope and the promise of a new year and a new start. Out of nowhere, light snow began to fall, soft flakes drifting into her hair. "They're beautiful."

"What was it Ivy said to you?"

"She said you have to believe, or the magic won't happen."

She reached up to kiss him and then regarded the snow, which was beginning to come down harder.

"I believe, Theo. So let the magic begin."

EPILOGUE

THEO HAD HIS purple stethoscope and Hope had her new picture frame. It seemed that Maddy had secretly purchased the frame the day they'd shopped for wedding apparel for Marco and Alice's ceremony. Most of the other items from his daughter's wish list had been bought in a mad dash after the carol service yesterday afternoon. Those had been opened in Ivy's hospital room early this morning. All except for two special items, one of which was waiting at home with Judy and the other was hidden in a very special place.

Nestled close to him, as the hospital pulled out all the stops for Christmas Day, was Maddy. He could barely believe she'd agreed to stay in England and work through things with him. He was the luckiest guy on the planet. At least he hoped he would be, very soon.

He squeezed her hand as Father Christmas made his way to the center of a circle of young patients and opened his red sack. Reaching in, he fished out the first of the presents. Ivy was in that crowd of kids, her eyes bright with wonder.

"Ho-ho-ho!" The red-suited character set his bag on the floor with a thump. "I think we have something here for Grant Williamson." He handed the wrapped parcel to Evie, whose fingers lingered over his for a second longer than necessary.

"Wait," Maddy whispered in Theo's ear, her breath warm and silky. "Is that…?"

"Ryan? Yes, but don't tell." He pressed his cheek to hers, uncaring that some of the staff members were looking at them in open speculation.

It didn't matter. All around them were couples, new and old, who were celebrating the day: Ryan and Evie, Finn and Naomi, and across the room from them were Alice and Marco—not here in person, since they'd already arrived in Italy, but they were watching the festivities live via computer. A magic swirled in the air that had nothing to do with Christmas presents or the snow-covered landscape that glimmered just outside the window.

It was love.

Theo could barely believe he'd found Maddy at that carol service. To go from the depths of despair to a joy greater than anything he could imagine boggled his mind and made his heart sing.

Gifts continued to be passed around the room and opened with much laughter and delight. It was wonderful to see their patients—some of whom were quite ill—smile. Ryan would visit those who couldn't leave their rooms and hopefully spread a little happiness to them as well. It was amazing how love could heal.

It had healed him. And Ivy.

"Do you think you could put Hope's picture somewhere other than your office?"

"Sorry?" He glanced down at Maddy as Santa fished for another present.

"It should be where Ivy can see it and grow up knowing how much her mother loved her."

A strange pressure formed behind his eyes. Maddy hadn't known that kind of love. But if she would let him, he would spend the rest of his life showing her what it meant to be loved as an adult. "I'll find a good place for it. Thank you."

She leaned against him, and any lingering tension seemed to drain from her body.

"Ivy Hawkwood, it's your turn."

The sound of his daughter's name made him put his arm around Maddy. "Here we go."

Evie knelt in front of his daughter, who was a few feet away from them. She handed the girl a plain white envelope.

He could almost feel Ivy's confusion. Everyone else had received a festively wrapped box. Since he hadn't been sure this would actually happen, there'd been no time to wrap it. Judy had snapped a picture and sent it to his phone. Theo had barely been able to print it and get it to Ryan before his friend had gone off to dress in his costume.

Everything Maddy had promised had come to pass. She'd pinpointed Ivy's problem and had put his daughter on the fast track to a normal life.

Only because they'd made love, she'd insisted. If her legs hadn't fallen asleep, she might not have thought of the fistula. At least not right away.

He had no doubts, however, that she would have figured it out with or without that clue.

"She's going to love it," Maddy said.

"I hope so."

Ivy ripped open the envelope and the photo fluttered to the floor. Picking it up, she stared at it for a second or two. Then she whirled around to face them. "Is this…? Is this…?"

When Theo nodded, her eyes widened and she snatched the picture to her chest. "He looks just like Doodle!"

The therapy dog had made a huge impression on Ivy. He remembered wondering how smart it was to let her get attached to him. But he'd come to realize that sometimes you just had to take a chance and trust fate.

"*She* is the same color, but she's a toy poodle so she won't get quite as big as Doodle." He reached down and tweaked the photo. "But with her curly coat, I thought she'd be a good reminder. She's at home with Judy."

"Oh, Daddy, thank you so much! I can't wait to see her!" She leaped up and hugged them both.

"You're welcome, sweetheart."

"That's brilliant," said Evie as she stood. She paused then raised her brows in question. "But I know something even more brilliant. May I?"

Theo nodded. "I think this is the perfect time." The perfect time to trust fate—at least he hoped it was.

Ryan reached an arm deep into his bag, soon finding what he was looking for.

"I have one item left."

Maddy glanced at the group and Theo knew exactly what she was thinking. Everyone had already received a gift.

"Madison Archer."

Evie carried the tiny present over to them, but instead of handing it directly to Maddy she handed it to him. "I'll let you do the honors."

Maybe he should have waited to do this in private,

where he wouldn't be publicly crushed if she turned him down.

She wouldn't, would she? She'd told him she loved him. He needed to trust that she'd been telling the truth.

Turning the present over in his hands, he found the taped tab and quickly unwrapped it, revealing a small velvet box.

"Oh, Theo…"

There was no room to kneel with the crowd around them, so he settled for snapping the box open to reveal a diamond ring. He had done some scrambling of his own last night and had called in a favor from a friend—the owner of a local jewelry store who'd reopened his shop just for him.

"I want to be with you. Not just today. Not just tomorrow. But always. Will you marry me?"

She wrapped her arms around his neck and buried her face in his chest. For a long tense minute the room was quiet. Then a muffled "Yes" rose to his ears.

"Stupendo!" Marco's exclamation was the first to break the silence, his fist raised in triumph. "Congratulations, you two."

Finn came over, echoing Marco's sentiment. "It couldn't have happened to a better couple," he said, while Naomi caught Maddy up in a tight hug. More and more people filed over to offer their congratulations, the sincerity of their smiles obliterating any hint of awkwardness.

By the time things died down enough for him to actually put the ring on his soon-to-be bride's finger, people were moving to the other side of the room, where tables of refreshments had been laid out. Soon it was only him, Maddy and Ivy in their little corner.

His daughter handed him the notebook that had started it all. "What about my last wish?"

Theo smiled, taking the book from her and opening it to the first page. By now he had it memorized. "Which one? I think they've all been answered."

"There's still one left."

It seemed like an eternity since he'd watched Maddy pocket that notebook and wondered what secrets it contained. Now he knew.

He took a pen from his pocket and checked off the bullet point next to *Puppy*. "How about that?"

"No, not that one." She grinned, but there was a slight quaver of uncertainty in her voice.

"I know which one you mean. And, yes, it's been answered too."

With that, he checked off *Make Daddy love Christmas*. While he was at it, he circled the key word in that phrase, kissing his daughter's head and sending her off after something to eat.

"Finally. I thought I would never get you to myself." He set the notebook down.

"Do you?" Maddy whispered, her fingers going to his face. "Do you really love it?"

"I do. Almost as much as I love you. Now and forever."

"Me too." She tugged him down for another kiss as the lights on the nearby tree winked their approval. "Oh, yes, Theo. Me too."

* * * * *

COMING SOON!

We really hope you enjoyed reading this book. If you're looking for more romance, be sure to head to the shops when new books are available on

Thursday 27th December

To see which titles are coming soon, please visit **millsandboon.co.uk**

MILLS & BOON

Coming next month

TEMPTED BY HER SINGLE DAD BOSS
Annie O'Neil

Their heads touched, lightly. They both looked up and at each other. He could feel her breath on his lips. He wanted to cup her face in his hands and kiss her. And not just any old kiss. An urgent, hungry, satiating kiss. Something that would answer all of the questions he'd had from the moment he'd laid eyes on her. Something that would tell him if all of this was a hallucination or very, very real.

'Ready, Doc?'

He nodded, not entirely sure what he was saying he was ready for.

Maggie sat back in the chair and detached her prosthetic, their eyes still locked on each other's. He was going to kiss her. Resistance seemed…ridiculous. Why wait for something he'd never known he wanted?

So he did.

He didn't hover nervously. Offer tentative butterfly kisses. No. His mouth crashed down on hers as if he'd been waiting for this moment his entire life.

From the moment his mouth touched hers, he knew that lightning could strike twice. That there was more than one woman he'd been meant to kiss. To hold. To cup her face between his hands. To taste as the water poured over the pair of them, erasing time, history, anything and everything that up until this moment would've kept them apart.

It wasn't a one-sided kiss. Not by a long shot. Maggie's entire body was arching up and toward him. She'd woven her fingers through his hair and was sliding her other hand along his stubble as their kisses gained in intensity.

Just as he was about to slip his hands onto her waist and pull her even closer to him, the bathroom door abruptly slammed open.

Alex pulled himself away from Maggie and turned just in time to see his son walk through the door.

Jake. His little boy. A mop of sandy blond hair, just like his. Brown eyes like his mother's. As if he'd ever forget who had brought this child into the world. His serious, intense, loving son who'd gone through all but a single year of his life without his mother.

'Hey, Dad.' Jakes eyebrows tugged together as he took in the scene then noticed that Maggie was holding one of her legs in her hand. His eyes widened further than Alex had ever seen them.

'Oh....' His eyebrows rose up to his hairline. '*Cool....*'

Continue reading
TEMPTED BY HER SINGLE DAD BOSS
Annie O'Neil

Available next month
www.millsandboon.co.uk

LET'S TALK

Romance

For exclusive extracts, competitions
and special offers, find us online:

f facebook.com/millsandboon

🐦 @MillsandBoon

📷 @MillsandBoonUK

Get in touch on 01413 063232

For all the latest titles coming soon, visit
millsandboon.co.uk/nextmonth